GARDENS OF STONE

"A tender, hilarious, heartbreaking story."

—*Publishers Weekly*

"We waited a long time for a book by this talented foreign correspondent. It was worth it."
—Peter Jennings, ABC Evening News

"Proffitt has successfully captured both the *esprit de corps* of the regular grunts and the emotions of the women they love. . . . His characterizations . . . read true. A most creditable novel."

—King Features Syndicate

NICHOLAS PROFFITT

GARDENS OF STONE

TOR

A TOM DOHERTY ASSOCIATES BOOK

GARDENS OF STONE

Copyright © 1983 by Nicholas Proffitt

Reprinted by arrangement with Carroll & Graf Publishers, Inc.

First Tor Printing: August 1984

A TOR Book

Published by Tom Doherty Associates, Inc.
49 West 24 Street
New York, N.Y. 10010

ISBN: 0-812-58727-8
CAN. ED.: 0-812-58728-6

Printed in the United States of America

0 9 8 7 6 5 4 3 2

This book is for

my wife, Martie Proffitt,
and
my father, Sergeant First Class Stanley Proffitt (1915–1963),
lifers both

Acknowledgments

A writer's most valuable friends are those who provide the basic services: a pat on the head or a boot to the bottom. For their unerring accuracy in knowing which end to tend when, I would like to thank Rod Gander, Frances Fitz Gerald, and Philip Caputo. And a very special thank you to Greg Jaynes, who believed even on those dark days when I did not.

Author's Note

There is a Delta Company, First Battalion (Reinf), Third Infantry (the Old Guard). And, of course, an Arlington National Cemetery and a Fort Myer. There is a Fort Huachuca and a Buena High School. There even was once an Americal Division and a Chu Lai before they were unceremoniously dismantled, one by the United States Army, the other by the North Vietnamese Army. I have used the places I know in this book, but all of the characters and events in these pages are wholly fictitious. No exceptions.

Time has had its little joke on my story. Things and places have changed since the period in which this story is set. Old Guard ceremonial procedures have been modified. Buena High has become large and impressive.

But I bear no grudges. For I have had my own little joke. For the purposes of my narrative, I have rearranged the furniture here and there, curving a street one way when it really goes another, now and then putting up a building where none exists. I have moved Camp A. P. Hill a few miles and changed its design, if not its purpose. I have arbitrarily dispatched the First Infantry Division (the Big Red One) to Vietnam several months earlier than it actually arrived.

And without giving them a chance for a well-deserved rest, I have brought Sam Huff and Jim Brown out of retirement for one last football game. I give the victory to Mr. Huff in this particular instance, but anyone who ever saw Jim Brown run with a football knows that it could just as easily have gone the other way.

——NCP
Wallace Creek Canyon, Montana
Carolina Beach, North Carolina
October 1981–March 1983

Prologue

When he was nine years old, Jackie Willow, lieutenant colonel of Infantry, leading a mixed force of Mississippians, Georgians, and Virginians from Longstreet's First Corps, turned Hancock's flank near Barlow's Outpost in the Wilderness and rolled up the Union line, saving General Lee and the Army of Northern Virginia for yet another year of perilous existence. Before that, and after that, Jackie was with Patton in the hedgerow country of France, with the Ninth U.S. Infantry at Tung P'en, with Alexander at Arbella, and with Bonaparte on the bridge at Arcola. Certainly there was the odd defeat here and there—that was to be expected over the course of such a long military career—but never an inglorious whipping, unmarked by heroism, true grit, and a larger meaning in the overall strategic picture. It was not until he was twenty-five years old and a second lieutenant with the 196th Light Infantry Brigade, Twenty-third "Americal" Division, operating northwest of Chu Lai, RVN, that Jack Willow experienced ignominious defeat on a field of battle. Coming as it did on the heel of brilliant victories and heroic last stands, it was little wonder that he took it hard.

ONE

The Plumed Troop

1

Somewhere deep inside the cemetery a bulldozer worked, its drone rising and falling, riding the air like an eagle aboard a thermal. From the brick chapel by the gate, an organ gathered up its hymn, signaling an ending. The soldiers waiting outside in the broad, cobblestoned street field-stripped their cigarettes and fidgeted into straight ranks. In front of them the caisson stood ready to receive its burden, the early morning sun glinting off a new coat of shiny black paint, the six-horse team blowing steam and fresh straw-studded droppings smoking in the cold November air.

Sergeant First Class Clell Hazard could hear the shuffling gait of the casket bearers coming from the chapel doorway behind him. From his place at the end of the front rank, he hissed a warning from the side of his mouth. "Steadeeeee."

In front of the platoon, facing the troops and the church, Lieutenant Webber glanced over the men's heads to the door, then at Hazard, and said, "Right. Here we go, platoon sergeant." He executed a smart about face and brayed, " 'TOON, tench . . . HUT."

The men came to attention with a clatter of heel taps and rifle buttplates. The U.S. Army Band bugler, bored and

killing time until his solo and long inured to playing the
Carnegie Hall of his calling, yawned and tucked his horn
under an arm. The drummer, a mere warmup act in the
bugler's mind, began a low mournful roll on his snare.
The handler from the caisson section, a cowboy from Utah
whose life had changed little since being drafted except
that the pay was better now, slid his hand up the reins of
the lone mount, pulling the horse's head down, trying to
settle the animal. The horse, a massively muscled stallion
a full seventeen hands high and black as night in a rain
forest, was a new acquisition and on its first job. Skittish
hooves made a resonant, echoing sound on the cobblestones.
A pair of highly polished black cavalry boots sat backwards in the stirrups.

His back to the chapel, Hazard could hear but not see
the funeral party come through the door behind the coffin.
There was muffled sobbing and murmurs meant to soothe.
From the back rank of the honor platoon came a low,
anonymous voice, carefully pitched to fade away before it
could reach the ears of the mourners: "Ashes to ashes
. . ." It was picked up by another man farther down the
line: "Dust to dust . . ." The refrain came from a trooper
at the far end of the front rank: "Let's bury this bastard
and get on the bus." "Steady now, goddammit," Sergeant
Hazard growled wearily.

The party was a large one, even for a full bird colonel,
with plenty of majors and other colonels and even a brigadier general—a large, florid-faced man with the red, fractured nose and cheeks of a boozer. They stood in an
uncertain clump, whispering and smoothing uniforms, while
the casket team slid the flag-draped box onto the caisson, a
simple low, open buckboard. The brigadier held the widow's
hand. She was dressed all in black—dress, hat, veil, and
gloves—but her dress was cut just above the knees and she
showed a pair of very white legs. By her side, eyeballing

the general with unveiled hostility, slouched a gangling
teenaged boy, his face a crimson burst of pimples and his
tie and shirt collar biting into his scrawny neck like a
hangman's rope.

Lieutenant Webber saluted the widow and the brigadier
and whispered a few instructions to them in a solicitous
voice, talking more to the single silver star on the general's
shoulder tab than to the man or the woman. The party
began to board the row of black limousines parked behind
the caisson. In a few moments the procession was under
way, passing through the north gate and into the cemetery:
the riderless horse, still wild-eyed and prancing sideways
while the cowboy fought its head; the six-horse wagon
and its load, the silent star of the show; the casket team
marching alongside the caisson, three men on a side; the
drummer, keeping dolorous step on his snare—ta ta ta
tum; the bugler, out of step, an artist and above it all,
unfettered by military Mickey Mouse; the firing party,
crack shots with nothing more treacherous to shoot at than
empty sky; the honor platoon, Lieutenant Webber strutting
at its head, marching in dress blues at right shoulder arms,
chromed bayonets fixed and flashing in the thin sunlight,
the heel-and-toe horseshoe taps on fifty pairs of shoes
drumming a tattoo on the pavement. Behind them came
the parade of limousines, headlights on, gearboxes in low.
At a discreet distance, far behind, crawled two empty olive
drab Army buses.

The moment they passed through the gate they were in a
different, hushed world. Ancient hardwoods in full autumn
raiment lined the road, their branches forming a vermilion
canopy, the sunlight splintered by the surviving leaves and
falling onto the ground, graves, and grievers below like a
tessellated blanket. This was the older part of the cemetery,
with proper, ornate monuments to proper, ornate dead.
General Jonathan Wainwright and Robert Todd Lincoln.

General John J. Pershing and Admiral Richard Byrd. General George Catlett Marshall and William Howard Taft. Major Pierre-Charles L'Enfant and William Jennings Bryan.

They passed by the junction with the road that led off to the Custis-Lee Mansion and the Memorial Amphitheater and marched into the Fields of the Dead, passing row after row of plain white stone markers that coupled simple, strong, American names like Johnson and White and Smith and Lee with outland sounds like Anzio and Bataan and Pyongyang and Kasserine.

The gravesite was on a bald knot at the edge of a row of new markers beyond the grassy boundary. The stones here had an even more alien sound: Pleiku and Ia Drang and A Shau and Kontum. The section had the raw, unfinished look of a new housing development. There were no trees, only a few recent plantings that might someday provide shade for the dead and their visitors. Not far away a bulldozer worked, clearing away brush for a new section of graves, its clangor loud and disrespectful. Lieutenant Webber, pique spread across his face like a mold, dispatched a soldier to tell the driver to shut down. There was an awkward pause in the ceremony until the noise finally wound down, the last of it carried away on a wind that blew in the direction of the District of Columbia and its own exalted memorials.

The casket team gently eased the coffin from the caisson and carried it to the catafalque built over the rude sore in the ground. The honor platoon stood at rigid attention while an Army chaplain read a eulogy from a piece of paper that blew about in his hand. Gusts of wind bore the words away from the platoon and toward a hummock as nude as the clough in which they stood.

When the chaplain was done, Hazard looked for and caught Webber's slight nod. " 'TOON . . . preseeeent . . . HARMS!'' he barked. Fifty rifles came up together.

Sergeant Louder, commander of the firing party, brought his men from parade rest to attention and then to port arms. The final command sequence popped off his tongue like an extra volley—"Right . . . HACE!"—and the team swung halfway round. "READY . . ." The men planted one foot, the right, back a step. "AIM . . ." The rifles were raised and sighted. "FIRE." The volley sounded as one shot, blowing a hole in the hush. "AIM . . . FIRE!" and another synchronized volley. "AIM . . . FIRE!" and the final crash.

The bugler, at last alert and animated, raised his instrument and blew a faultless taps, the final note holding and then falling away wetly like a tear. Hazard recognized him, by ear as much as by eye, as the boy who had played Kennedy's funeral—the best lip on post.

Hazard gave the command for order arms. The casket team held the flag stretched taut over the coffin while a civilian cemetery employee lowered the box slowly into the ground with a hand winch. The casket bearers quickly folded the flag into a compact triangle, the field of blue with its box of white stars coming up on top, and handed it to Webber. He, in turn, presented the package to the widow, stood back, and saluted.

Mourners began getting back into the cars. The widow turned up her veil. She was pretty, with deep blue eyes and an eggshell complexion, and very young to be the wife of a full colonel or the mother of the acne-plagued boy. Watching her, Hazard felt his stomach clench. She looked like his former wife. The general still held her hand. She thanked Lieutenant Webber in a sad, soft contralto and then looked around her as if noticing her surroundings for the first time. "Such a naked, ugly spot."

"Don't you worry, ma'am," said Webber, still talking more to the brigadier's shoulder tab than to her. "They'll be planting grass here real soon, and they'll bring in some full-grown trees. This time next year it will be lovely.''

"This time next year . . ." she murmured; then she shivered and offered Webber a weak smile and a gloved hand and turned away, helped by the general, who had one meaty hand on her elbow and the other around her trim waist. By the time their car was out of sight, two civilian workers were shoveling dirt into the hole. Hazard waved forward the two green buses lurking like carrion crows off to the side of the gravesite and bawled, "Okay, let's go, people. Get on the buses. We got two more before chow.''

The barracks was across the street from the edge of the parade ground; a two-story, red brick colonial building shaped like a block letter U. The left half of the building, as one faced the front, was the home of Bravo Company; the right, Delta Company. An elaborate sign in Olde English script on the lawn outside the Delta entrance read, *"D" Company, First Battalion (Reinf), Third Infantry (the Old Guard)*. The building, like the other colonial brick barracks that lined the tree-shaded street, had once billeted George Washington's troops.

Delta Company's front door opened onto a long hallway, its floor buffed to a high sheen. Just inside the door, against the right wall, stood a glass trophy case housing a single object: a field marshal's baton attached to a shield. It was called the Chapultepec Baton and had been carried by General Winfield Scott, "Old Fuss and Feathers," when he had reviewed the troops, among them a brilliant young captain of engineers named Robert E. Lee, following the American victory over the Mexicans at Chapultepec in 1847. When the Third Infantry, which had borne the brunt of the fighting, marched by the reviewing stand, Scott was supposed to have said, "Gentlemen, remove your hats. The old guard of the Army is passing by." From that day forward the Third Infantry was called "the Old Guard." The troops in its ranks called it the Third Herd.

Across the hall from the baton was the dayroom, with a pool table and a reading lounge. On the right, just past the trophy case, was the orderly room, lair of the first sergeant and the company commander. At the end of the hall were two large offices, each crammed with a handful of desks. One was the officers' ready room, the other the NCO ready room. There the hallway doglegged to the left. There was a flight of stairs going down to the basement level, where kitchen, mess hall, officer and NCO dining rooms, arms room, and supply room were located. Another, shorter flight of steps went up to a huge troop bay, the bunks of First Platoon on the left, Second Platoon on the right. A double row of wall lockers running down the center of the bay separated the two.

On the second floor were the Third and Fourth Platoon bays, an NCO bay partitioned into separate rooms, and a sleeping bay for the headquarters section of cooks, clerks, and supply people. In the attic was a lounge fitted out with Ping-Pong tables and a television set. On both the main floors, open, covered porches ran along the edges of the building at the rear and on the inside of the U, the three-sided area shared by Delta and Bravo. The verandas at the back overlooked the Fort Myer back fence and the highway and Arlington beyond—civilian territory, another planet.

As United States Army barracks went, it was impressive and comfortable.

When the buses dropped Third Platoon back at Delta Company, Clell Hazard went straight to the NCO ready room, hung up his cap and blue blouse, pulled a cloth from his desk and began to shine his shoes with savage swipes of the rag. He punched the intercom button and spoke to the Third Platoon bay on the second floor. "Flanagan, get your ass to the NCO room, chop-chop."

Corporal Flanagan appeared at the ready room door a moment later, out of breath from the run down the stairs. "Er, is it about Wildman, sarge?" he asked sheepishly.

"You goddamn right it's about Wildman. I've just had my ass bit off by Webber, and it was about Wildman. Every night I have nightmares and *they're* about Wildman, too. He was a disgrace again today. His shoes looked like they'd been shined with a hot Hershey bar. His brass had green stuff growing on it. His uniform was so wrinkled it looked like a contour map. He needed a shave *and* a haircut. His chrome looked like he'd been stirring a pot of shit with his bayonet. And his gloves were not white. This outfit wears white gloves with blues, Flanagan, and Wildman's gloves were not white. I don't know exactly what color they were, but they definitely were not white. They looked like a cum stain. Now, I don't know how I could have missed him at formation this morning, but you should have caught it for me—you're his goddamn squad leader. So now you get a lesson in the chain of command, corporal: Lieutenant Webber chews my ass; I chew your ass; I expect you to chew Wildman's ass. Threaten him with death if you have to, but shape that sorry son of a bitch up. Then I want you to go see the first sergeant and tell Top I want Wildman on guard duty tonight, and I want him on KP every day this week. And if he shows up looking like that again, you'll be pulling shit details right alongside him. Now get the hell out of here."

"Right, sarge," Flanagan said casually with the air of a man who's heard it all before. "By the by, sarge, Third Platoon got a new man this morning while we were in the garden."

"What's his name?"

"Willow. Private First Class Willow. Fresh out of AIT at Ord."

"Okay. Send him in to me in five minutes. Then get to work on Wildman."

"Better make it about half an hour for Willow, sarge," said Flanagan. "He's over at battalion S-4 drawing his dress blues, shower shoes, and thin coat of oil—uniform of the day."

"Okay, wise guy. Send him in when he gets back. If I skip chow, I can give him the briefing before we hit the garden again. Now get to work on Wildman."

Willow was a good-looking kid. He had high, prominent cheek bones, a clean, wide mouth, intelligent brown eyes, and neatly trimmed brown hair. He was wide in the neck and broad in the upper chest, with a trim waist and long, muscular legs. A hot-shit high school jock, no doubt, thought Hazard. The boy's fatigues were tailored and freshly starched. His belt buckle was no stranger to the magic of Brasso. And his boots were spit shined to a high gloss. A good-looking kid.

"Sit down, Willow. I'm Sergeant Hazard, your platoon sergeant. You getting squared away okay? Get yourself a bunk and lockers and everything you were supposed to draw from battalion supply?"

"I think I'm okay, sergeant." A good, strong voice. A command voice. Captain of the football team without a doubt, thought Hazard.

"Well, let's just make sure, because S-4 fucks up a lot," said Hazard, pulling a mimeographed list from his desk drawer. "Let's see, ah, field gear, dress blue blouses, blue trousers, dress belt, blue cap, poplin shirts, black tie, black socks, black shoes, white gloves, blue infantry fourragère, Old Guard buff strap, Old Guard cockades. Everything check?" Willow nodded.

"Okey-doke. Now, the buff strap and cockades are distinctive to the Old Guard," Hazard continued. "There are other distinctive features as well. This is the only regular Army outfit that allows enlisted personnel to wear the dress blue uniform. We're also the only line outfit allowed to march with fixed bayonets. And we use a sliding manual of arms instead of the basic manual. Check?'' Willow nodded.

"A couple of tips," said Hazard. "The buff strap is worn on the left shoulder, the fourragère on the right, as usual. If you look at your gloves, you'll see there are pockets on the insides of the palms. We'll give you a couple of skinny steel plates you can slip into those pockets. That way, when you're going through the manual, there'll be a nice loud crack when you slap the rifle stock. You will also notice that your shoes have double soles. At your first opportunity, you should take them over to the post shoe shop and have taps put on all around, including the inside of the heels. That's so you'll click when you walk and when you slap those heels together when coming to attention. All these little noises seem to titillate officers, civilians, and ladies' auxilaries. Welcome to the Old Guard.''

Willow was smiling. "You don't seem to approve of much of this, sergeant."

Hazard snorted. "Willow, you've just joined the silliest goddamn outfit in the United States Army. We're nothing but a bunch of toy soldiers, and I personally think it's a disgrace that this unit is permitted to wear the crossed rifles of the Infantry. Especially at a time when *real* infantrymen are crawling through rice paddies and buffalo shit in Vietnam. That's what I think, anyway, and I guess I've let enough people know how I feel to make myself pretty unpopular around here.''

"But I fully agree with you, sergeant," Willow said eagerly. "I didn't ask for this assignment. I put in for Vietnam duty when I was at advanced infantry training but was sent here instead. I feel the way you do: that an infantryman's place during time of war is up at the front.''

The boy's eyes were bright and earnest. He smiled at Hazard like he expected to be petted.

"There is no front in Vietnam."

Willow flushed. "You know what I mean, sergeant. Corporal Flanagan told me you did a tour of duty in Vietnam. I'd sure like to talk to you about it; find out what it's really like over there."

"Some other time, kid," said Hazard. "For the record, I did two tours: '62 as an advisor and '65 in a regular line outfit. Most of the officers and senior noncoms in this outfit have Nam time. This was our reward. That's the way they look at it. Myer is considered prime duty. The officers can rub shoulders with the Pentagon brass and give their careers a boost. The NCOs like it, too. They can march around in fancy uniforms and bury themselves in that big typing pool that works across the river. It's a definite plus on the record, the Old Guard. This is the Army's elite outfit—la crème de la crème."

"So I was told," said Willow, smiling again and trying his best to match Hazard's sardonic tone. "But I should inform you that I'm going to keep on putting in for Vietnam."

"Well, I should inform *you* that the Old Man, Captain Thomas, will veto any request for transfer. He believes it's a rare privilege to serve in the Old Guard. I know. I've been trying to get transferred to the Infantry School at Benning as an instructor for a year, ever since I got here."

"How come you want Benning when you believe that a soldier's place is up at the sharp end?" Willow asked.

"The sharp end? Jesus, kid, where do you get this shit? Sergeant Rock comic books? Look, Willow, I didn't say I believe that; you did. I belived it in 1945, and I believed it in Korea. I stopped believing it in Vietnam. This one's different. From what I see we're not gonna win it no matter how many people Johnson and McNamara funnel in there. The United States Army is my family, Willow; the only one I got. And I don't like seeing my family get itself into trouble.

"I'll tell you what I *do* believe in, Willow. Damage control. I want the Infantry School because the best I can do for the Army—*my* Army—is to get snot-noses like you ready for the inevitable. The bloodlust is up, Willow. This thing is gonna get a lot bigger. There are promotions to be made, medals to be won. Don't be in such a hurry to get starched, kid. Let somebody . . . somebody like me . . . first teach you what he knows about surviving the shithole you're so anxious to jump into."

"But, sergeant . . ."

"Let's just drop it, Willow, okay?" Hazard said in a weary voice. "I'm really not interested in discussing this with somebody who doesn't know what the fuck he's talking about."

Willow's face stiffened, and his color drained. Hurt and anger filled the boy's eyes, so naked it was painful for Hazard to look at. How vulnerable they are, Hazard thought. How vulnerable and how stupid. And how smart was he to take it all out on a kid like this? "Look, Willow," he said softly, "you caught me on a bad day. Sometime we'll sit down over a beer and talk about it, okay? Right now I'm supposed to give you the nickel briefing on the Old Guard, so let's just get that done today and we'll talk about other things some other time. Okay?"

"Whatever you say, platoon sergeant," Willow said with exaggerated formality, rage and unforgiveness etched on his face like birthmarks.

Hazard sighed heavily. "Right. Okey-doke. The Old Guard, Third Herd, is a reinforced battalion—about fifteen hundred men. That's counting the battalion HQ and a couple of specialty units like the U.S. Army Band, the Fife and Drum Corps, and the caisson section, which looks after the horses. We got four line companies: Alpha, Bravo, Delta, and Honor Guard Company. Honor Guard is a special case, too. They're the *real* toy soldiers. They've got a Tomb Platoon which does nothing but walk the Tomb of the Unknown Soldier. They got a special color guard made up of a bunch of fairies who dress up in little colonial uniforms and powdered wigs, just like the fife and drum boys, and put on flag shows for the tourists out at Mount Vernon. They got the U.S. Army Drill Team, which travels around the country putting on exhibitions or doing television shows like Ed Sullivan and Mitch Miller. And they pull the occasional drop job—funeral—in Arlington National Cemetery. They're a real snazzy group, *la crème de la crème de la crème*. They're supposed to be the best of the companies, but I think we're better.''

Hazard paused. ''Any questions, so far?'' Willow said nothing. Hazard sighed again and went on. ''The other line companies, including Delta, mostly do drop jobs. Oh, we put a noncom and a couple of men on JFK's grave every day, and we mount an honor platoon at Andrews Air Base for the President when he travels, but mostly we just bury people. Once a year we spend two weeks at Camp A. P. Hill, Virginia, doing field exercises. The brass don't like it much because we leave only one company at a time back here to do the burying of three, but it's necessary to keep our infantry rating. It's also the only time this unit does anything real. So there you have it. The Old Guard is also known as 'The President's Own,' and they tell me we should all be proud to be a part of it.''

Willow said nothing. He sat stiffly in his chair and glared at his platoon sergeant. Hazard shrugged and leaned back in his chair. ''By the way, Willow, are you by any chance the son of Master Sergeant Shelby Willow?''

The boy looked startled. ''Do you know my father?''

''If he's Shelby Willow, I do. Your dad and I were in

the Indianheads together—the Second Infantry Division—in France and again in Korea. We were in the same company in Korea. We also did time at Fort Lewis together. He's a fine soldier. How is he? I've kinda lost touch.''

Willow frowned, annoyed at the introduction of this new information, feeling it balloon into curiosity and threaten to take the edge off his righteous anger. ''He's not so good,'' he said gruffly. ''He had a heart attack a few years ago, and they made him transfer from the Infantry to the Signal Corps. Then he had another attack when he was stationed at Huachuca, just after I graduated from high school, and they made him take a medical discharge. He's a little bitter. He had twenty-three years in, and he wanted to make it to thirty. I think he misses the Army a great deal.''

Hazard nodded sympathetically. ''That's too bad. Me and your dad waded onto Omaha Beach together, and we ran the gauntlet from the Chongchon River together. I guess it takes its toll. If I recollect, he's only three years older than me, which would make him about forty-eight. That's young to have had two heart attacks.''

''Yes, it is,'' Willow said coldly. Curiosity had been wrestled to the ground by injury, and the boy's eyes were hostile once again.

''Well, at least it keeps him out of Nam. He and I are both too old for that shit,'' said Hazard. ''You give your father my best when you talk with him next. Now I suggest you diddely-bop down to the arms room and get assigned a rifle and pick up a bayonet. It's an M-14 Army now, and the new 16 is on its way to Nam, but we still use the M-1 because it's easier to parade with. The bayonet is chrome in this outfit and has to be kept polished. Have you checked in with the orderly room yet?''

''I dropped off my orders this morning,'' Willow said. ''The first sergeant and CO weren't in. The clerk told me to come back later, and I was going to right after chow."

"Okey-doke."

Willow stood and set his jaw. "I'd like to say something before I go." Hazard nodded and Willow, his face agitated, plunged on. "I love the Army as much as you. It's my family, too. I've lived on Army posts all my life, and it's the only life I know and the only life I've ever wanted. And I feel that if a man chooses the Army as his life, then his job is to fight when his country needs him. The reason I picked the Infantry is because the Infantry is the essence of what soldiering is all about. The Army does a lot of things, but its primary function is to fight. So I'll do everything I can to get to Vietnam. And another thing: You're wrong about Vietnam, platoon sergeant. The United States Army has never lost a war, and it's not going to lose its first to a bunch of Asian peasants."

Breathing hard, eyes blazing, and chin stuck out like Floyd Patterson's, Willow waited for Hazard to explode. But Hazard said nothing, just looked at him with wide eyes, like a lizard eyeing an insect, an almost imperceptible smile on his lips. Willow thought he could see laughter in the platoon sergeant's eyes. The boy turned on his heel and left.

Hazard sat quietly for a moment after Willow had gone, then reached into his desk drawer and took out the letter. He opened it and read it again:

November 8, 1966

Dear Clell,

How are you, you old war horse? Don't know if you heard or not but I had me a couple of heart attacks a while back and Uncle Sam gave me the old heave-ho, 7 years short of my 30. Old soljers never die, they just come close over and over. I was up to Fort Knox for a hospital visit the other day and ran into Mickey Tulley from our days in the 2nd. He told me where you were. It seems my boy Jackie has been posted to your outfit, your very company if I'm not mistaken, and I thought I'd write. He should be showing up in a couple of weeks, soon as his post-AIT furlough is up. Could I ask you to do an old buddy a favor and keep an eye on him for me? No special treatment or anything like that, just to kinda keep him on the right track. He's a good boy and I think he'll make a good soldier if he has someone like you to show him the way. I didn't want him to make a career of the Army, but he was determined. If that's the way it's gonna be, then I'll feel a lot better knowing he's learning the ropes from the best. I reckon you understand. Your Mackie is what, 20, now? Mickey told me you and Linda split up and I was real sorry to hear it. Army life is tough on the women. It drove my own Angela half crazy, as you know, but her doctors say she's fine now. Well, that's all for now, Clell, and thanks. I hope we can hoist a few and tell each other lies someday soon. Remember that double-jointed gal at the honky-tonk in Seoul? What was her name anyway?

> your friend,
> Shelby Willow
> M/Sgt, USA (Ret)

2

Willow sat on his bunk in the Third Platoon bay thinking he should probably report back to the orderly room but
reluctant to move. His wall locker and footlocker were
squared away, and he had gone over his boots again with a
rag. At the other end of the bay, his squad leader, Corporal Flanagan, was yelling at a man named Wildman. There
was no one else in the bay. Everyone was at chow, but
Willow did not feel like eating. His gut still churned from
his encounter with the platoon sergeant.

He got up and stepped out onto the veranda, leaned
against the railing, and lit a cigarette. In the square below,
a group of recent arrivals to Bravo Company was being led
through the sliding manual of arms by a buck sergeant who
was yelling at them. In a few days, Willow guessed, he
would be down there with the Delta newmeats and
someone—Flanagan or maybe even Hazard himself—would
be yelling at him. In the Army somebody was always
yelling at somebody else. He felt alone and vaguely
melancholy.

It was funny how poorly he had adjusted to certain
aspects of Army life, he thought. Being an Army brat
should have given him a leg up, but the truth was he had
been no more prepared for the Army than any other kid

right out of school. In some ways his familiarity with the
Army had worked against him. In his first few days of
basic training, he had repeatedly walked past officers on
post without saluting just as he had done all his life. And
as the son of an Army sergeant, used to having noncoms
around the house, he had found it difficult, at first, to
regard NCOs as the demigods they were. He remembered
his first night at the reception center in Monterey. After
drawing their bedding, the new recruits had been marched
to a barracks where a veteran sergeant had given them a
five-minute lesson on how to make an Army bunk. Then
they had turned in. Twenty minutes later the sergeant was
back. He flipped on the lights and began to introduce a
new group of arrivals to the wonderful world of hospital
corners. Willow, exhausted from the long day of travel
from his induction center in Phoenix and jolted awake by
the noise, had rolled over grumpily and yelled, "Why
don't you shut up so people can get some sleep around
here?" Fresh crops of recruits had reported in throughout
the night, and Willow, a glaring sergeant monitoring his
every move, was there to teach them all how to make an
Army bed. He had also spent the next four mornings, his
entire stay at the reception center, pulling KP.

Willow grinned to himself. He had learned that lesson,
and others, but there were still things about Army life he
had not yet fully accepted. Like the absolute lack of
privacy. Willow loathed having to live at such close quarters with dozens of other men. The warring radios in the
troop bays, blaring everything from Bach to Buck Owens
. . . the belchings and fartings of fifty or more disparate
souls . . . the creaking bedsprings and masked groans of
the midnight masturbators . . . the nocturnal weeping of
the homesick . . . the senseless babble that pruned the
achievements of God and Man to three narrow topics of
conversation: the Army, the automobile, and the vagina.

They had even found a way to turn man's most serene moment into a nightmare and a humiliation. He'd turned pale when he first spied the latrine at basic: twenty-four commodes glistening white all in a row, no doors, no partitions, barely knee room between them. He'd heard that at Marine boot camp the men were lined up facing the toilets and given the order *Attack the head*, after which they had exactly one minute to do their business before receiving the command *Clear the head*. Army basic wasn't that bad, but he had often gone a week without a crap.

Even so, even so. He had told Hazard the truth when he said he loved the Army. He loved the tactile things, like getting up before dawn and savoring the crystalline quality of the morning air with the smug thought that most civilians were still abed . . . shining boots and brass and the smell of polish . . . the feel of fresh fatigues against the skin, the creases along knees and elbows starched to a razor edge . . . the honest sweat of PT, physical training, feeling the jumping jacks and push-ups fine-tuning a body already brought to respectable standards by sports . . . dismounted drill, executing the commands with a fluid crispness, the rifle on his shoulder heavy and real and smelling of solvents and linseed oil . . . riding in jeeps, full of admiration for the lean utility of that gutty little snub-nosed vehicle, so straightforward and sensible and honest . . . field exercises, feeling gritty and bone tired and close to the purpose of it all, the fluctuating tide of mock battle washing round him like a heavy surf.

That he loved most of all, because it was as close as he had come to "the *real* thing." Put Willow out in those boonies, even on bloodless maneuvers, and his mind ran amok with possibilities. He was in a nameless, formless patch of jungle in Vietnam . . . or the Philippines . . . or Guadalcanal—it didn't matter. Enfilading fire rolled at them, breaking over the heads of his cowering platoon like thunder. The Cong or Huks or Nips, Orientals of one stripe or another, were invisible, shooting from camouflaged tree platforms and spider holes. His men screamed and fired blind into the verdant wall around them, stacking gekkos like cordwood but accomplishing little else. They were on the edge of panic and Willow knew he must act quickly or lose them. He pulled the handset from the PRC-25 strapped to the back of the dead radioman lying beside him and began reading off coordinates to a forward air controller circling lazily above. He could hear the FAC relaying the grid numbers to the jet jockeys; within minutes the planes were streaking in low, coming over at treetop level, putting their ordnance right on the money. They were F-4 Phantoms so it must be Nam. The Prick-25 should have told you that. Pay attention, man! It's the little things that kill you. No, wait! He was on the radio to division arty—yeah, that's it—talking the big HE shells onto the enemy in a cool, level voice while those around him screamed and cried in terror. The division brass huddled anxiously around their radios back in the rear and asked one another in awed voices: Who *is* that platoon leader? No, no, better yet, he was reading off his *own* coordinates, bringing the fire mission in on his *own* position, sacrificing himself and his platoon so he could bag the enemy battalion threatening to overrun him. Wait. Fuck that! Why should *his* people die? A good leader took care of his men. Then how about this? He was pumping his arm up and down and shouting the cry of the Infantry officer . . . FOLLOW ME! Yeah, that's it. He launched himself over a ridgeline and his adoring troops came up as one man behind him, firing from the hip as they ran and yelling Rebel yells. Well, no matter how it happened, the citation always read the same: "Showing a total disregard for his own personal safety, Lieutenant Willow performed in a manner above and beyond the call of duty."

Willow had harbored such fantasies ever since he could remember. Other boys his age had dreamed of becoming star athletes or James Dean or Elvis Presley, something that would bring them fame and money and, most important, girls. But for Jackie Willow it had always been a warrior's dream, a dream of heroism and the respect of fellow soldiers. Inflamed by his reading, he created scenarios of battles and bravery for hours on end, polishing the scenes over and over. His single-minded preoccupation had been a barrier between him and his peers in high school. He seemed so distant. They never knew about the dreams, of course. Willow told no one. But they could tell he was different. Willow's athletic ability and good looks made boys and girls alike want to get closer to him, but there was a kind of moat around him and the drawbridge was always up. Willow had had friends, people he did things with. He had gone to parties and dances like everyone else. But there was always that difference. He was so serious, his friends told one another, always kinda studying a guy, with this laugh in his eye as if he knew something about life, or death, that you didn't know. He seemed older.

In fact, Willow had preferred the company of older people. He got along especially well with teachers and coaches, and when they had a chore or a leadership role to dole out, they invariably gave it to him. He'd particularly enjoyed those evenings at home when his father and mother entertained other noncom couples. Despite Willow's constant probing, his dad had never told him war stories about France or Korea. But when other NCOs came over and the drinking began, Willow knew that if he unobtrusively kept fetching beer and whiskey for them, he'd be tolerated and allowed to eavesdrop. Then he'd listen to the sergeants tell stories, growing more garrulous with each round of drinks

he brought. He remembered everything and peppered his
next fantasy with new tales and jargon.

His parents' friends seemed to like him. He was quiet
and courteous and attentive. The sergeants followed high
school sports closely and would talk about the games with
him. Their wives seemed to like him, too. He remembered
Sergeant Martinez's wife, a heavyset woman with a doll's
round face and heavy breasts, and how she would watch him.
The Martinezes lived two houses down, and Mrs. Martinez
often found some job for him to do, asking his help with
a breathlessness and a flutter of dark lashes. One hot summer
morning he was lifting some heavy boxes for her, his shirt
off and his torso glistening with perspiration; he had looked
up and found her watching him, her housecoat tied so
loosely that it gaped widely in front to show a long,
heavy, dark line of flesh and pubic hair. He had finished
his task quickly and fled, turning down the offer of a Coke.
Every time the Martinezes came over after that, Mrs.
Martinez tried to catch his eye. He avoided looking at her.

Willow also loved the abstracts of Army life: the sense
of order and discipline, the knowledge that he was acquir-
ing skills to make men tremble. He loved the chain of
command and its inexorable correctness, even if he were
the last, lowest link. It eliminated all interminable debate,
all intellectualizing, all pros and cons. It eliminated all
bullshit. It was clean and it was clear and it worked where
it counted the most: on the battlefield.

But most of all Willow loved the implied promise given
in exchange for his heartfelt oath of allegiance—that with
hard work and attention to detail, he would one day earn
the most honored and important of all the fine gifts the
Army could bestow, more valuable even than the gifts of
comradeship and a sense of duty well done: the privilege
of command. That, and the opportunity to exercise that
privilege in the crucible of combat.

"This session of the board is convened as of 1000 hours, this day of November 29, 1969. Please state your name, rank, serial number, unit, and present duties."

"Willow, Jack, N-M-I, second lieutenant, 0-196691, Bravo Company, Second Battalion, 196th Light Infantry Brigade, Twenty-third "American" Division, United States Army. Platoon leader, third platoon Bravo, sir."

Major Pyle sat in a straight-backed wooden chair behind the middle of three card tables set up at one end of the large, carpeted quonset hut. On either side of him sat a captain, selected, like Pyle, from among the division's staff officers. In one corner of the room, in the spectators' seats, sat another group of officers, including the Americal's commanding general and a major from the Judge Advocate's Corps, up from MACV in Saigon. Pyle, who had been appointed chairman of the investigating board, was a dapper, slightly balding man with Army-issue wire-rim spectacles and a sour, pinched face. He, like the two captains, wore the green Class A uniform. Willow wore his usual fatigues, but they were freshly laundered and starched and represented his most presentable pair.

"I would like to remind you, lieutenant, that this is not a court-martial board, merely a board of inquiry," Pyle said. *"Just answer our questions as fully as you are able. We'll try to be as informal as possible, but we do ask that you limit your testimony to what you personally saw and heard on the night in question. Any questions at this time?"*

Yes. Why not a court-martial? Why not a court-martial for Lieutenant Colonel Abner Bean? *"No, sir."*

"Good. Now, perhaps we can begin by hearing your understanding of your unit's position, posture, and mission at the time of the attack."

"Yes, sir. The company, Bravo Company, was left be-

hind on Fire Support Base Daisy Mae in Quang Tin
Province to secure that position while Second Battalion
was in the process of moving to Firebase Li'l Abner,
approximately thirty miles to the southeast. Division
intelligence, G-Two, had somehow come to the remarkable
conclusion that the area around Daisy Mae was clear of
enemy forces and that the new position, Li'l Abner, would
be closer to suspected enemy lines of infiltration and
supply. . . .''

"We are privy to division's conclusions, lieutenant,"
Pyle said dryly. "Kindly restrict yourself to company
operations."

"Yessir. Well, sir, six of the battalion's 155 mm artillery pieces and four mortars were lifted to Li'l Abner
by chopper at dawn, and Alpha, Charlie, and Delta companies had already been transferred over there and were out
on patrol to secure the area around the new firebase. We
had been told by the battalion commander, Lieutenant
Colonel Bean, that Bravo would be joining the rest of the
battalion on Li'l Abner the next day. At Daisy Mae, we
were left with two 155's, four mortars and about two
hundred men: That was Bravo and a few battalion personnel, including Colonel Bean himself. The end result
was a split command and a resourceful enemy who not
only knew that it was split but who also had a detailed
working knowledge of the compound and our dispositions
within it."

"Wait just a minute, lieutenant," Major Pyle interjected
sharply. "Just what makes you think the North Vietnamese
knew all this?"

"For one thing, sir," said Willow, "it is now obvious
the enemy was getting information about the base and
what was going on there from the South Vietnamese working at Daisy Mae. For another, the Vietnamese working in
our compound seemed to know that an attack was coming.

We were hit at 0230 hours. That day . . . or rather the day before . . . none of the Viets who usually reported at daybreak showed up, and we didn't see them at all during the day. Obviously they had been told to stay away by the North Vietnamese or their Viet Cong leaders.''

"Excuse me, Lieutenant Willow,'' said one of the captains flanking Pyle, "but just who were these Vietnamese working at the base? Where did they come from and what exactly did they do?''

"Well, sir, the nearest established Vietnamese village was about ten miles away,'' said Willow. "When we first set up Daisy Mae three months ago, many of the people in the ville and from others in the area of operations set up a makeshift camp near the bottom of our hill. You know how they always congregate around American troops. Colonel Bean called the place Dogpatch. Some of the old men and children would help dig bunkers and fill sandbags, that sort of thing, in exchange for a few piasters or cigarettes and C-rations. There didn't seem to be any young men around. We figured they were all in the ARVN or, more likely, out in the boonies with the VC. There were also several young women. They did some housekeeping chores, sweeping hootches and washing clothes, that kind of stuff, and . . . uh, . . . they also served as . . . uh . . . prostitutes. These girls also sold drugs to some of the men. We gave them a cursory body search at the gate each morning, but some of the men told me that the girls would smuggle it in by poking it up their . . . uh, vaginas. I told Colonel Bean about it myself and suggested that we either search them down there, too, or keep them off the base altogether. He got angry and said that officers and gentlemen did not humiliate allied nationals in such a manner.''

One of the division officers in the spectator section behind Willow began to cough wildly. Major Pyle was looking coldly at the captain, a man named Hanks from

G-4, supply, who looked sorry he had asked the question and who said hurriedly, "Yes, uh, I see, thank you, lieutenant. Please go on with your report . . . the previous line of testimony."

"Yes, sir," said Willow, suppressing a grin. "Well, sir, as I said, none of our dinks . . . er, Vietnamese . . . showed up that morning. In all the confusion of moving the other three companies and the guns over to Li'l Abner, we didn't even notice their absence for a while. Once we did, Bravo's platoon leaders—myself and lieutenants Harmon, Dell, and Earp—went to the company commander, Captain Crowder, and told him about it. We thought it might mean something. About four days before that, one of our patrols, our last patrol in fact, had found a cache of rice belts and ammunition in the bush not far from Dogpatch. The two things together made us think something might be going on. Captain Crowder agreed to talk to Colonel Bean about it. And he did, but when he got back he said the battalion commander had not seemed worried. Colonel Bean told the captain that it was probably some Vietnamese or Buddhist holiday and that was why nobody had shown up. The colonel told him that G-2 had no evidence of any enemy force in the area. The colonel was very busy on the radio checking to see how our people on Li'l Abner were setting up, and he more or less shooed Captain Crowder away."

Major Pyle was leaning back in his chair, twirling a pencil between the thumbs and forefingers of both hands and looking over the tops of his glasses at Willow with arctic eyes. Willow took a deep breath and plunged on.

"We then asked the captain if either me or Lieutenant Harmon could take our platoon on a recon patrol that evening, or at least go out and sit on the trails, maybe set up some claymores. He took the proposal to Colonel Bean, who said no. The colonel said Bravo was scheduled to

relieve one of the companies on patrol around Li'l Abner when we moved over there the next day and that he wanted us rested. Captain Crowder then proposed that we at least put a little H and I fire from the remaining 155's on the trail intersections that night, but Colonel Bean said no to that, too, saying it would be a waste of ammo and that he wanted all the shells packed on pallets and ready to move at first light. Captain Crowder then offered to put the entire company on the perimeter that night, but the colonel said no again, repeating that he wanted Bravo rested for the next day. As a result we had no patrols out, no claymores set up, no harassment and interdiction fire on the trails, and only one platoon on line when . . ."

"This is a lot of hearsay and nothing else, lieutenant," Pyle interrupted brusquely. "It will be some time before we know what was said between Captain Crowder and Colonel Bean. Captain Crowder is dead and Colonel Bean is seriously wounded. Now then, you said earlier that the enemy had a detailed knowledge of the base and our dispositions. What brings you to this remarkable conclusion?"

"The remarkable fact that they knew right where everything was," flared Willow, smarting from Pyle's admonition.

"At ease, Lieutenant Willow, before you find yourself in contempt of this board," snapped Pyle.

Willow reined himself in, took a deep breath and said, "Yessir. Sorry, sir. Shall I continue, sir?" Pyle nodded.

"It was a company of sappers. We know that from the bodies we found after the assault. They were dressed in loincloths and were covered all over with grease. They carried AK-47s, B-40 grenade launchers, satchel charges and even had two recoilless rifles. They cut through all but the last string of our wire undetected; there was a fog that night and that helped them. Then they started a mortar bombardment. They put the rounds right in among our perimeter troops, then cut the last line of wire and came in *under their own mortar fire. Our men must have put their faces in the dirt when the incoming started, because the sappers came right past them without slowing down. Once inside they didn't waste any steps at all. Some of them headed straight for the arty and mortar emplacements and got them all with B-40s and satchel charges.*

"*Captain Crowder was in the TOC, the command bunker, when it started. I guess this is hearsay, too, but I heard it from our company clerk who was in the TOC with Captain Crowder and Colonel Bean . . . but when the first rounds hit, Captain Crowder tried to switch on the camp alarm only to find the lines out. He then tried to call the mortar crews and found the field phone wires cut. The NVA went straight to the TOC and began throwing satchel charges down the entrance. They knew where everything was—the TOC, the wires, the guns, everything. They came by the gun pits and the TOC in single file, each of them firing or throwing a satchel as they went by, then running right on through the compound toward a prearranged escape route at the north end. It was all over so fast. We got only five of them. It was all over in thirty minutes and we only got five of them.*"

There was a stillness in the quonset hut while everyone waited to see if Willow was going to continue. When it became apparent that he was not, Major Pyle cleared his throat loudly and asked, "And where were you, Lieutenant Willow, while all this activity was taking place?"

Both the first sergeant and the company commander were still out when Willow returned to the Delta Company orderly room. Even though it was well past noon, the company clerk, Specialist Fourth Class DeVeber, was still working on the morning report. The clerk gave Willow a friendly smile and informed him the topkick and CO were expected back any time. Willow decided to wait.

"You've got a real experience ahead of you," DeVeber said with a Boston accent. "Meeting Slasher Boudin for the first time is one of those things people tell their grandchildren about."

"Slasher? Is that the first sergeant?" Willow asked.

DeVeber smiled a tickled smile and nodded.

"Why do they call him Slasher?" Willow asked.

"He was heavyweight champion of the Army," DeVeber said. "He got in the ring with Joe Louis once, one of those exhibition fights for the boys in France or something, and after the fight the Brown Bomber is supposed to have said, 'That guy is some slasher.' "

"What's his real name?"

"Louis. But the last person who called the Slasher Louie and lived was probably his mama."

"Anything special I should know about him before I meet him?"

"Yeah," DeVeber said. "But where to start? He's big, he's mean, and he's crazy. I don't know how he got crazy, but I think he was born mean. He's one of those Cajuns from Louisiana, and people from that part of the country tell me a person doesn't have to know any more than that. He was also some kind of war hero in Korea. He's got four Purple Hearts and a couple of Silver Stars, and when he put on blues with full medals, he can barely walk upright. He's got more of that garbage than Sergeant Hazard. And every officer in the company is scared shitless of him except for the Old Man. Captain Thomas is the only one who can handle the Slasher. They served together in Korea. The Slasher will only call two officers in the whole battalion *sir*. One's Thomas and the other is the battalion exec, Colonel Johnson, who wears the Congressional Medal of Honor."

"He can't be all that bad," Willow said skeptically.

"Oh no? You just wait," DeVeber chuckled. "The

Slasher is a real piece of work. Just being in the same office with him every day is about to send me round the bend. The only reason I stick it out is it keeps me off shit details and outta the fuckin' garden."

"The garden?"

"The garden . . . the cemetery . . . Arlington National Cemetery."

"Oh. What's so bad about the . . . uh, the garden?" Willow asked.

"Oh, nuthin much," the clerk laughed. "Just shining shoes and brass till your fingers fall off. And polishing chrome and patent leather. And shaving twice a day and gettin' a haircut every other day. All that Mickey Mouse shit. Then there's the work load. When I came to the Third Herd two years ago, Delta would pull four, maybe five drop jobs a day." DeVeber fingered through the papers on his desk and pulled out a sheaf of stapled papers. "Today it was fourteen. Yesterday it was fifteen. Let's see . . . um . . . um . . . tomorrow it's fifteen again. That's just our company. Directing traffic at the chapel is like working the tower at Logan. That fuckin' Vietnam has made burying folks a real growth industry. They're running outta space over there. They got bulldozers working damn near around the clock to clear out more parking places for all the poor dumb bastards comin' home in boxes. They're so hard up for available ground they've ruled that no more dependents can be buried at Arlington. They're even talking about tearing down part of South Post so they can expand the garden. They'll be planting them in the Pentagon lawn next. I hear that one of our outfits in Vietnam has these calling cards that say 'Killing is our business and business is good.' Well, burying is our business and our business is better."

Willow was trying to formulate a response to the clerk's cynicism when a giant walked into the orderly room, dropped a bundle of manila folders on the first sergeant's desk, and plopped down in his chair with a crash that shook the orderly-room floor. Even sitting down, the creature was nearly five feet tall. He had a massive chest, a lifer's beer gut, and no neck. None whatsoever. Deltoid muscle began directly under each earlobe and found its angle of repose at the tip of each shoulder. He had a fishhook for a mouth, an ugly gash with one corner turned down and in; a large nose that looked as if it had been badly broken and just as badly reset; small, puckered, boxer's ears; and a gray crewcut. His eyes were gray, too. They swung slowly up and across the room, moving with his whole head like a gun barrel tracking a target, and settled on Willow.

"WHO THE FUCK ARE YOU AND WHAT THE FUCK DO YOU WANT?" boomed Slasher Boudin.

Willow opened his mouth to speak but nothing came out. DeVeber jumped in and said, "He's PFC Willow, Top. His orders are on your desk there. He just reported in today."

The first sergeant's head swiveled like a tank turret, and the cold gray eyes fixed on the clerk. "Who the fuck asked you, numbnuts?" Boudin stared at DeVeber until the flustered clerk mumbled, "Nobody, Top," and then the gray eyes picked up their primary target once again.

Willow had found his voice somewhere. "Private First Class Willow, first sergeant, reporting as ordered. I was told to see you first thing."

"Okay, you seen me. Now get the fuck outta here."

"Uh, Sergeant Hazard said I should see the company commander as well."

"Fuck Sergeant Hazard. Get outta here."

"Yes, sir," Willow said, moving toward the door.

Boudin's eyes snapped wide. "SIR?" he roared. "SIR?" The giant stood, filling the space between floor and ceiling.

"You don't sir noncommissioned officers, Dildo, or whatever your fuckin' name is. And nobody *ever* sirs me. You
got that, Dildo?"

"Y-y-yes . . . first sergeant," Willow stammered. He
was petrified. He stood braced like a West Point plebe told
to assume the position. His eyes rattled round the room,
searching for succor, sliding in disgust over DeVeber, the
only possible source of help, when he saw the clerk with
his shoulders hunched, his head buried in a book of Army
regulations.

Without warning, Boudin's eyes grew crafty and he
tried to smile reassuringly, the bend of the fishhook manag-
ing only to come up to a straight line. "Tell me, Dildo,
how do you feel about officers?" he asked with a quiet-
ness that was somehow more sinister than the screaming.
It was the overly friendly tone a man would use to call a
dog he fully intended to kick shit out of. "You know,
officers as a class?"

"Officers?" Willow asked warily. "Okay, I guess, first
sergeant. They are entitled to the respect their rank
demands." Willow relaxed a little and added brightly, "In
fact, Top, I plan on putting in for Officers Candidate
School and becoming one myself."

"YOU DO, DO YOU?" Boudin screamed, the gro-
tesque caricature of a smile gone. Out of the corner of his
eye Willow saw DeVeber shake his head with ineffable
sadness, the gesture of a man powerless to save the
condemned. "Well, let me tell you, Dildo, there ain't an
officer in this man's Army worth the shit God made him
outta, except for Captain Thomas. They're all a bunch of
fuckin' cowards." The first sergeant pulled a ring of keys
from his fatigues pocket and opened the top drawer of an
olive drab steel filing cabinet. He pulled out a small red
notebook and waved it at Willow. "It's all in here, Dildo:
places, dates, witnesses. A record of officer cowardice

under fire in Korea. Every time I saw an officer in combat over there, I saw chicken shit. One of these days I'm gonna use this book and put all those yellow pussies up against a wall. You wanna be an officer, huh? You ain't goin' to no OCS, Dildo. The only place you goin' is on my shit list. NOW GET THE FUCK OUTTA HERE.''

The man was crazy! Willow was about to bolt from the room when the company commander walked through the door. Willow slammed back against the wall and saluted. Captain Thomas stopped, looked at him carefully. ''You a new man?''

''Yes . . . sir.''

''Outstanding. Come into my office and we'll have a little chat.''

''Yessir.'' Willow followed close behind the officer, sidling past a glaring Slasher Boudin.

The CO sat behind his desk and motioned for Willow to take the chair opposite. On the desk was a nameplate with the twin silver tracks of a captain's bars, the crossed rifles of the Infantry, and ''Captain Charles Thomas.'' There was an ashtray made from the bottom section of a 105-mm shell casing and a paperweight that looked like a live fragmentation grenade. In the corner behind the desk was an American flag and the Delta Company guidon. On the wall were framed pictures of Thomas and certificates from various Army schools. Willow saw a diploma from jump school and another from Ranger school. On one corner of the desk, side by side, were pictures of an attractive blonde woman and the ugliest kid Willow had ever seen.

Thomas pushed a button on his intercom. ''Top, you got this man's two-oh-one file?''

''Yo. I'll bring it in,'' Boudin's voice came back, sounding tinny and almost civilized. A moment later the first sergeant dropped the folder on the company commander's

desk. "See me when you're through here, Dildo," he said
to Willow, then left, closing the door behind him.

"Well, then," Thomas said with a smile. "Welcome to
Delta Company, PFC Dildo."

"It's Willow, sir. PFC Willow."

The captain looked puzzled and leaned forward to scan
Willow's nametag. "So it is, so it is." Thomas opened
Willow's file and began skimming through it, mumbling to
himself as he read. "Hmm, home of record Fort Huachuca.
You an Army brat, Dil . . . Willow?"

"Yessir. My father is, or he was, a master sergeant.
He's retired now."

"Outstanding." Thomas dropped his head and continued to read. "Lettered in four sports in high school, I see.
Outstanding. You'll have to go out for the company basketball team, Willow. They've already begun practice but
there's always room for one more good player, especially
a good white boy—we've got too few of those. Hmm,
some college, I see, and outstanding test scores, simply
outstanding. And you seem to have done well in AIT. A
fine record here, son. Work hard and keep your nose clean
and you should be an NCO yourself in no time. Chip off
the old block, eh?" The CO was giving Willow the big
smile again.

"Actually, sir, I was thinking of shooting a little higher
than that. I'm interested in applying for OCS. And while
we're on the subject, I'd also like to apply for a transfer to
a line outfit in Vietnam."

Thomas's smile vanished, leaving little void. "I see,"
he said curtly. "A transfer anywhere at this time is out of
the question, Willow. You just got here. I don't think you
fully realize what a privilege it is to serve in the Old
Guard. We are the President's Own. This is the most
STRAC outfit in the United States Army." Thomas's

frown slid into a look of suspicion. "Have you been talking to Sergeant Hazard? Did he suggest this?"

"I have talked with Sergeant Hazard, sir, but when I mentioned my interest in Vietnam, he tried to dissuade me. He said I shouldn't be in such a hurry to get killed."

"For once Sergeant Hazard is absolutely right," said Thomas, leaning back in his chair and looking stern. "Hazard is a good man. He and First Sergeant Boudin are the finest combat NCOs I've ever seen. I had the Top with me in Korea when I was a very green young second john, and Sergeant Hazard was one of my platoon sergeants when I was a CO in Vietnam, just over a year ago. I specifically asked for both of them when I got this command. When it comes to soldiering, Willow, you listen to your platoon sergeant. But when it comes to matters of, uh, philosophy, you should take what he has to say with a grain of salt. Sergeant Hazard is going through a . . . uh, an attitude crisis at the moment and has been heard to expound some rather dubious ideas of late. But in your case, he's right." Thomas shook his head and smiled kindly. His tone took on a patina of fatherly concern. "Look, son, there will be plenty of time for Vietnam. Even if we finish it off quickly, and we probably will, the Communists will be up to mischief in some other part of the world soon enough, and you'll get your chance to earn your spurs. You do your tour of duty here. It will look damn fine on your record. As for OCS, you do a good job for me here . . . show me you are good officer material . . . and I'll personally see that you get a shot at it. This Army can always use another bright young shavetail. Whadaya say? Okay?"

"Yes, sir." Willow stood, backed off two steps, and saluted. The CO returned the salute with a casual flip of the wrist and picked up a paper and began to read, Willow completely gone from his mind.

As he closed the door to Thomas's office, Willow was relieved to see that Slasher Boudin was not in the orderly room. DeVeber looked up from his desk and grinned widely. "There's one more thing you should know about the first sergeant. He hates officers." The clerk laughed and shook his head. "Jeez, Willow. I've never seen anyone get on the Slasher's shit list as fast as you. You can't blame me for not warning you. How was I supposed to know you were gonna tell him you wanted to be an officer? Hoo wee! You couldn't have pissed him off any more if you had peed on his spit shine. Top had to go out, but he left you a message. You got guard duty tonight."

"Great," sighed Willow. First his platoon sergeant. Then the first sergeant. Now the commanding officer. After only a few hours with the Old Guard, Vietnam was sounding better by the minute. Maybe the VC would be friendlier.

3

Hazard stopped at the package store across the highway from the rear gate and picked up a couple of six packs before trudging toward his apartment building. He had lasted two weeks in the company NCO room before looking for off-post housing, his prerogative as a noncommissioned officer. The rude and empty gab, the joyless poker games, and the desperate boozing of the other unmarried NCOs had driven him out. On the lip of forty-five, he found he no longer had the necessary resilience to live so close to so many.

He had found a large one-bedroom apartment in a building less than ten minutes from the company. His old friend Thurgood Nelson, the battalion sergeant-major, had an apartment on the third floor, and had tipped Hazard to a vacancy on the fifth. It was expensive for a man on service pay, but it was worth every penny. It had enabled Hazard to take back the household goods he had rather foolishly put into storage when Linda left him, just before he had gone back overseas. She hadn't wanted any of it. He could still hear her voice, heavy with scorn, saying that the last thing she needed were reminders of more than twenty years of living hell.

Hazard turned his mind to a more pleasant association,

his friend and neighbor. He often wondered how he would have survived the Old Guard if he had not found Goody Nelson at Myer when he arrived. They saw each other often, going out for a quick supper a couple of times a week or cooking at home, each of them competent bachelor chefs. Hazard had been divorced for nearly three years, Nelson for thirteen years. Nelson lost his wife while he was in Korea, lost her to a man who stayed home. Hazard lost his when he re-upped for the second Vietnam tour.

The two men had first met during the Korean War when they were both E-6s, platoon sergeants in the same company. It had taken them a while to become friends. Both were quiet men who did not mix well with the other noncoms in the company. They got to know each other because of a book. Two books, really.

There had not been much room in his combat pack for nonessentials, but Hazard had shoehorned in a couple of paperbacks anyway. Books were essentials, as far as he was concerned, far more nourishing than the K-rations he jettisoned to make room for them. He had read those two books over and over again until they had become worn and filthy. And while they were two of his favorites, even they began to lose the power to take him out of Korea for an hour or two at a time. He had become desperate for something new. Anything. As long as it was different. And then one day he walked past Thurgood Nelson's hole and saw the huge, bald NCO, looking like a white Nubian, lying there reading a book as tattered as his own. Probably some western or detective story, Hazard had thought, but he was in no position to be choosy. He remembered the way the conversation had gone.

Hazard: Hey there, Sergeant Nelson. You wouldn't care to swap books with me when you finish that, would you?

Nelson: You bet your ass I would. Let's do it now. I've read this fucker a hundred times. Whatcha got?

Hazard, fishing in his pack: You probably won't like it much, but at least it'll be a change.

They had made the eager exchange and then had begun to laugh. It was the same book: Caesar's account of his campaigns in Gaul.

"Hold on, I got another one here," Hazard had said. Nelson said, "Me, too," and dug into his pack. And they pulled out the same book once again, Napoleon's *Maxims* this time. They howled with laughter. More important, Hazard sat down and they began to talk. They discovered the obvious. Both men shared a passion for military history. They also enjoyed reading the less obtuse philosophers, like Marcus Aurelius. Neither man had much formal education; both had turned to reading as an antidote to barracks life, much like the way men serving prison terms sometimes turn to books. Neither went in for contemporary literature, but Nelson adored Shakespeare and persuaded Hazard to make it a *ménage à trois*. Hazard had read Shakespeare in high school, of course, but it wasn't until Nelson led him through *Julius Caesar* and *Othello*, wisely picking two soldiers as an introduction, that he began to like Shakespeare.

After Korea they had kept in touch through the occasional letter, and then they had pitched up in the same advisory group in the Mekong Delta. And here they were in the same outfit once again. That was one of the good, enduring things about the Army. It *was* like a family, just as he had told Willow, with paths crossing and recrossing if a man stayed in long enough.

Seeing that kid Willow today brought it all back. Willow wouldn't remember it, but he and Mackie Hazard had played together at Fort Lewis when they were kids. It was like being from a small but mobile civilian town. People changed, they stayed the same. So, in a way, did the place. The place was always changing in the Army, but all

Army posts looked alike and a man could close his eyes
and feel he had a real home town. Hardly a day went by
that Hazard did not hear news of some long-ago friend or
acquaintance. And just as in civilian life, there were those
precious friendships that could be picked up just where
they had been so precipitously cut off by transfer years
before. As with Thurgood Nelson. Or Shelby Willow.

The woman who lived across the hall from him was
waiting for the elevator when Hazard entered the lobby of
his building. She had a large bag of groceries in her arms.
Without chewing it over in his mind, Hazard amazed
himself. "Hi. Here, let me take that up for you." He
smiled cordially, shifted his beer under one arm, and took
the bag from her.

The woman looked startled but let him take it, then
smiled tentatively and said, "Hello. And thank you. It *is*
heavy."

According to the nameplate on the row of mailboxes in
the lobby, her name was S. Huff. She had been in the
apartment across from his ever since he had moved in. She
seemed to live alone—he had never seen a man, any man,
coming or going. That was difficult to understand. She
was no girl, maybe forty or a year or two either way, but
she was a very handsome woman: short auburn hair, blue
gray eyes, a fine oval face, and a full, generous mouth.
The body was generous in places, the proper places, as
well. She wore expensive clothes, conservatively cut to
divert attention from those places, but there was no disguis-
ing a surprisingly ample bosom for so small-boned a woman,
nor the trim waist, taut bottom, and well-turned pair of
legs. Hazard had often noticed her and had even paid a
visit in his mind—the usual sexual fantasies—but he had
never said more than a passing hello in the hallway and
had never received more than an echoing hello in return.
He had never analyzed his reluctance to try the next step

with this attractive woman. Perhaps it was the disdainful look she had given his uniform the first time they had passed in the corridor. Hazard was well aware that enlisted military men did not exactly rank at the top of the social ladder with most civilians.

The elevator, normally a lumbering beast, shot through the first couple of floors like a missile, leaving a wake in the thick and awkward silence. Say something, asshole, Hazard told himself. You've come this far. Gambits swirled round his head; a doughy knot began to form somewhere between stomach and sternum. He had never been good at this sort of thing. "Susan? Shirley? Sarah?" he blurted.

S. Huff jumped like she'd been shot. "W-What?"

"Uh, your name. On the mailbox. I just, uh, wondered what the S stands for."

"Oh. Samantha."

Hazard barked a short laugh. "And everyone calls you Sam, right?" he said, grinning hugely.

"Why yes, they do," the woman said archly, looking at him as if he had lost his mind. "Do you find that amusing?"

"Oh, well no . . . uh . . . well yes kind of . . . uh . . . you know, Sam Huff, the linebacker."

"The what?"

He saw her eyes ricochet with alarm around the confined space of the small box in which she was trapped with this madman. They finally came to rest on the bag in his arms as if she were calculating the odds against getting out alive if she paused to snatch her property before bolting when the doors opened; or should she play it safe and save herself and to hell with the groceries? Jesus, he was making a mess of it.

"The linebacker. Sam Huff is the name of a famous football player. He played middle linebacker for the Giants. Now he's here, right here with the Redskins. He's the best in the game."

"I'm afraid I don't know anything about football," the woman said curtly.

"Oh, well, I just thought it was kind of . . . I mean he's so tall and wide and mean, and you're so . . . I, uh . . . just thought it was kind of funny," Hazard ended lamely.

Samantha Huff stared straight ahead at the elevator door and said nothing. Praying for deliverance, no doubt, thought Hazard. Christ, I'm forty-four years old. I've been married and divorced. I've seen the world, and I have a tattoo on my right arm that says *Airborne* and proves I'm a big tough man. And when it comes to chatting up the girls, I might as well still be a sophomore in high school with a face full of zits. He sighed deeply and said aloud, "I'm sorry, ma'am. I'm not very good at making small talk with the ladies. I think it comes from having spent most of my life in an all-male environment."

The woman turned to him with a brief, surprised look, then her face softened slightly and she smiled. "That's quite all right. Actually, a lot of people have laughed when I told them my name and I never knew why. Now I do. Thank you."

The elevator stopped at the fifth floor and the two of them walked toward their apartments. At her door the woman fished in her purse for her keys and Hazard, having come this astounding distance over treacherous terrain to reach the objective, steeled himself for a frontal assault. "Uh, Miss Huff, I'm . . . uh . . . fixing supper tonight for Sergeant-Major Nelson and his lady friend . . . uh, he lives down on the third floor, and . . . uh, perhaps you would care to join us. It would be just the four of us and very informal. I'm a pretty good cook . . ." He faltered and stopped.

It was her turn to be flustered. The invitation caught her unprepared. Usually whenever a strange man struck up a seemingly casual conversation, she'd take a few seconds in her mind to quickly and efficiently prepare a defense against possible encroachment. With this clumsy soldier she had not thought such precautions necessary.

"Oh, I, I don't know," she said, her mind working frantically. "I'm, um, expecting an important phone call this evening, and I don't know what time it might come through." Not bad, she thought. Not great, but not bad.

Hazard knew the woman was stalling and suddenly his uncertainty disappeared. Nothing like a little resistance to clear the head of an infantryman. "I'll tell you what," he said smoothly. "I'll go ahead and prepare enough for four. We plan to rendezvous around 1930 . . . I mean seven-thirty. If your call hasn't come by then, we'll just leave our doors open. You'll be able to hear the telephone across the hall."

Samantha Huff's flank had been turned and rolled, and she reluctantly capitulated. "Oh, I . . . uh, all right."

Hazard smiled and surrendered the captive sack of groceries. "My name is Hazard. Clell Hazard. Now *you* can laugh." He made a sloppy about face and turned the key in his door.

Hazard had lied through his teeth. He stashed the beer in the refrigerator and ran for the phone. He dialed Thurgood Nelson's apartment, got no answer, and redialed, trying battalion headquarters. A reedy, whining voice told him Sergeant-Major Nelson was extremely busy and could not possibly come to the telephone, to try again tomorrow during normal office hours. Hazard insisted roughly, without saying who he was or what he wanted, and finally the petulant clerk went away to fetch his master. Then Nelson came on the line, his voice raspy and nasty, the perfect noncom's instrument. "This better be important, asshole. Right up there with the Second fucking Coming."

The Chairman of the Joint Chiefs could have been on

the line, and Thurgood Nelson would not have altered his
salutation. In a legion that had taken scatology to the outer
limits, Nelson was renowned as a connoisseur, keeper of
the foulest tongue in the ranks. Nelson stories were coin of
the realm in the Old Guard. During the Kennedy funeral,
for example, the sergeant-major had been in charge of VIP
seating and had been overheard telling the French liaison
officer, "You go tell that tall cocksucker over there to
stand where I told him to stand, or I'll kick his Frog ass
back to the swamp you two cunt-licking snail-eaters come
from." Then Nelson had paused in his tirade to wonder,
". . . or is it snail-licking cunt-eaters?" The blood had
drained from the Frenchman's face, but he had scuttled
over to put DeGaulle in his proper spot. But Hazard's
favorite was one he had personally witnessed: General
Douglas MacArthur was being shown around a night defensive position on the Yalu River by a group of Second
Division officers and noncoms, including Nelson and
Hazard. Dugout Doug was in a philosophical frame of
mind that evening and had thrown out the rhetorical question "Do any of you gentlemen know why Rome was not
built in a day?" He was about to supply his own answer
when Nelson piped up from the rear of the entourage.
"Yessir. Because I wasn't in charge of that fuckin' detail."

Only those who had known Nelson for a long time ever
suspected that behind the terrifying tongue and manner
was a gentle, intelligent man who adored opera, collected
Oriental carpets, and was fond of quoting long passages of
poetry from memory. But none of the few who knew this
side of Thurgood Nelson were ever so foolish as to get
caught spreading the word. Nelson would have pulled the
culprit's heart out through his nose and eaten it.

"Goody, it's Clell. Listen, you gotta help me. You and
Betty Lou *must* come to dinner at my place tonight. I've
asked the woman who lives across the hall, and I told her

you two would be there. I didn't think she'd come otherwise, and I know she won't stay if you aren't there."

Nelson laughed. "You mean that little bitty gal with Sophia Loren's tits and Twiggy's ass? Nice going, pal. But no can do. I figure to be right here until at least 2200 hours. I got paperwork up the wazoo."

"Goddammit, Goody," Hazard shouted into the phone. "I wasn't ever going to mention this, but you force me. Did I or did I not, on a certain day in August of the year of our Lord 1962, in or about a certain provincial capital in the Mekong Delta of the Republic of Vietnam, save your sorry hairy ass at extreme risk to my own?"

"Wasn't ever gonna mention it, my ass," snorted Nelson. "You prick. You been waitin' for years for this. Listen, turkey turd, I wouldn't have been in that fuckin' mess in the first place if it wasn't for you. And I sure as shit could've gotten out of it without your help, thank you. You got a lot of nerve, Clell, seeing as how I was coming to help you. Here you are today able to leap tall buildings in a single fuckin' bound while I'm still so full of frags I can't lie down on a beach without attracting assholes with metal detectors."

"Correct me if I'm mistaken," Hazard replied sarcastically, "but I distinctly remember that the same round that got you got me. I also recall that you were out of the hospital a full month before me. So cut the goddamn crap and quit evading the issue. You owe me, Goody, and I'm calling in my marker."

"If I do this, do I have your solemn oath that I will never hear about that ancient history horseshit ever again?"

"You do."

"Okay. What time?"

"Nineteen-thirty hours."

"Okay. I'll call Betty Lou."

"Thanks, Goody. And Goody, please, please watch

your mouth tonight. This seems like a real nice lady, and I don't want you scaring her off with that garbage can you call a mouth before I can even get a goodnight kiss.''

Nelson laughed. "Oh, yeah? Before you entertain any thoughts about kissing this fragile flower of yours good-night—not that a wimp like you is going to get even that far—keep in mind Goody's definition of kissing: It's sucking on one end of a thirty-foot long tube, the last five feet of which is packed with shit.'' Nelson roared at his own wit and hung up.

Hazard wanted desperately to make a good impression on Samantha Huff. He did not stop to consider why it was important to him, only conceded that it was. It would be his first date, such as it was, in months.

He ran his best dress inspection eye over the apartment. God knew what she would expect an Army sergeant's place to look like, he thought—probably a camp cot and an open fire in the middle of the floor. Maybe she would be pleasantly surprised. The living room was informal and comfortable. There was a sectional sofa, a worn second-hand leather armchair, a butcher-block coffee table, and two leather poufs from Lebanon, souvenirs from 1958 when Hazard had been part of Ike's Marine-Army task force sent in to quell the political squabbling in Beirut. The one expensive piece was an antique pine dining table that had once been the centerpiece of an English farm kitchen. Along one wall were built-in bookshelves, full. On the other walls were colorful framed batiks from Thailand and Bali and a couple of mounted black-and-white rubbings from the temples at Angkor Wat. On the floor were scattered the inexpensive but respectable carpets Thurgood Nelson had so expertly and painstakingly helped him find and buy: a large and frayed Shiraz, two Bokharas, an antique kalim from Kurdistan and a small Isfahan, its blue the color of the waters off the Cypriot coast. In the corners were three wooden Buddhas painted in gold flake, and a garish ceramic elephant he had picked up cheap on rue Catinat in Saigon. Hazard was secretly very proud of what he had done with the place, even though he liked to joke that he had decorated the apartment in Early Puerto Rican Taxicab.

The apartment was clean.

Food and drink were his immediate concern. He was a good cook. He could thank Linda for that, although as far as she knew he could barely boil an egg.

Cooking was a skill he had picked up in reaction to Linda's leaving. Hurt and angry, he had convinced himself that he could live without a woman. All they were good for was cooking and fucking anyway, and he could pick up the slack in those two departments with no sweat whatsoever. And he had set out to prove his point.

He went to the post library and checked out every book on the subject of cooking. He spent a small fortune in civilian bookstores and supermarkets, buying up cookbooks and fancy cuts of meat. He experimented freely on himself and on the succession of brainless bodies he picked up in the town bars and cocktail lounges, hapless women he used as guinea pigs, both in the kitchen and the bedroom. He never saw the same woman twice, and that was usually dandy with them. Hazard brought little joy to his work in either part of the house.

After a while Hazard had calmed down, disgusted with himself. He stopped the empty sex cold. But the cooking skills stuck. He discovered that he enjoyed it. He brought the same dogged determination and concentration to it that he did to his job and, as he became more accomplished, he found it gave him the same kind of pride in return.

He wanted this evening's meal to be memorable. But given the amount of drinking that went on when Goody

and Betty Lou were around, it also had to be light. And he
had less than two hours to fix it.

He scribbled out a quick shopping list, rushed down to
the lot and lashed his battered 1956 Pontiac Chieftain in the
direction of a specialty shop he knew in Alexandria, taking
side streets to avoid the worst of the rush-hour traffic. He
was back in his kitchen in forty minutes . . . broke. He
might have to eat beans for the rest of the month, but he
had no second thoughts. He was splurging and he damn
well knew why. Sitting in his stomach like a yeasty ball
of dough were rising excitement and anticipation about
Samantha Huff.

For a starter he chose a tomato and aubergine casserole.
For dessert, baked pears in white wine. Both took forty-
five minutes in the oven at 375 degrees, and he decided to
put them in together to save time.

For the main course he had decided on saltimbocca—
wine-glazed rolls of veal and Parma ham—accompanied
by a chilled Italian bean salad, nothing more than steamed
green beans flavored with a French dressing and a little
finely chopped garlic and fresh parsley. He fixed the salad
and prepared the saltimbocca, even though he would not
begin cooking it until it was almost time to eat. All he had
to do was heat it over high flame for a moment when the
time came, then cover the pan and simmer until tender. He
would serve a 1957 Pouilly-Fuissé with the main meal,
even if he had to use every one of the five bottles he had
bought, and a strong kirsch with the pears.

It was going to be excellent. If it was not, he knew,
Thurgood Nelson would bitch mightily with every bite.

The doorbell rang at 1930 sharp. She wore a white
blouse with ruffles at the neck, a tartan kilt fixed with a
foot-long silver safety pin . . . and an unconvincing smile.

Her eyes searched the room for the others. "Oh, I'm early. I'm sorry," she said.

"Nope. You're right on time. Goody and Betty Lou are habitually tardy." Hazard was wearing civvies: slacks, a muted non-Day-Glo western shirt, and his best boots, the Luccheses he had had ever since Fort Sam Houston. "Did you get your call?"

"My what? Oh, yes. Yes, I did," she lied.

"Good, then we can close the door." He ushered her into the room, sat her down on the sofa, and took her drink order.

She asked for a glass of white wine, mentally slapped herself for her faux pas, faltered, and amended her impossible request with ". . . or anything, anything at all." Hazard smiled, went to the refrigerator, and returned with a chilled wine glass and a bottle of the Pouilly wrapped in a cold towel, the label hidden. He poured her a glass, then returned to the kitchen to fix himself a Wild Turkey and water.

Samantha took a sip, gulping it down, stared at the glass, and took another, this time letting the wine sit in her mouth a moment. "This is wonderful," she called out, unsuccessful at keeping the surprise out of her voice. "What is it?"

In the kitchen, Hazard grinned with malefic pleasure and called back, "A Pouilly-Fuissé, 1957. It was a truly great year for the white burgundies, don't you think?" That'll fix the snooty bitch, he thought. He was weary of having to perform social back flips for condescending females, trying to prove that military men—at least some military men—had come a considerable distance from the primordial slime. The prejudice of civilians, the unquestioned assumption that all career military types were cretins, was tiresome—all too often accurate, but tiresome nonetheless.

It was one of the reasons he had been celibate during most of his time at Myer. The women who had come from the rural villages of America to pound typewriters in the Federal Triangle were, for the most part, too young and too silly for him, but at least they did not look down their noses at servicemen. Soldiering was still an honorable profession back home in West Virginia and, what's more, the Army was a steady job. But the better dressed, better educated, "better class" of women was virtually inaccessible to men like Hazard. They were difficult to meet and even more difficult to bed. There was nothing in it for them, nothing at all. Hazard and Nelson had often discussed the problem, but Nelson had found his solution in Betty Lou Farmer, the daughter of a wealthy North Carolina tobacco planter. Betty Lou had a master's degree in political science from Chapel Hill and a good job on Capitol Hill as an administrative assistant to Senator Sam Ervin. She was an earthy and unpretentious woman who sported a mouth almost as foul as Goody's. Hazard despaired of ever finding as compatible a match and was growing ever less inclined to make the effort. He was getting too old for silly mating dances. Trying to persuade some dubious female that he was better than his chosen profession offended his sense of dignity and the real pride he took in his work. But what the hell, he thought, this one looked like she might be worth the trouble—one last time into the breach, lads.

Hazard sat, raised his glass, and said, "Welcome. I'm glad you're here." Samantha Huff tentatively lifted her glass in acknowledgement.

"You have some lovely things here," she said quickly, making a vague sweeping motion with her arm. "It's all so . . . exotic."

Hazard shrugged. "Just knick-knacks. The debris of foreign travel, the kind of stuff you pick up along with the dysentery and the worms." By Christ she was good-looking. Hazard stared openly at her and saw the color rise out of her neck and settle high on her cheeks like mercury in a thermometer thrust suddenly into direct sunlight. Imagine that, he thought, a full-grown woman who blushes. The swooping sensation was back in his midsection. With a slight shake he rose and walked to the phonograph to put on some music. "What is it that you do for a living, Miss Huff?"

"I'm a reporter for the *Washington Post*. On the metro staff. I cover northern Virginia."

"That must be interesting work. Been with it long?"

"About three years with the *Post*," she said. "I came up here from the *Charlotte Observer*, in North Carolina."

Hazard's ears perked up. "Are you from North Carolina?" he asked, full of hope.

"Yes, I'm a native Tar Heel. Born and raised in Wilmington, over on the southeastern coast."

Hallelujah. Hazard felt like bursting into song. "You didn't happen to go to the University of North Carolina at Chapel Hill, did you?"

"Yes, I did. Class of 19 . . ."—she hesitated, then plunged on—". . . 47. Why?"

"Sergeant-Major Nelson's lady friend, Betty Lou, went to school there. She's from North Carolina, too. Raleigh, I think. She works for Senator Ervin up on the Hill."

"What was her name?" Samantha asked.

"Betty Lou Farmer. Dayady's in ta-baccer, doncha know."

Samantha laughed at his attempt at a Tar Heel accent. There was little trace of the south in her own. "Actually, the name is familiar to me," she said. "I don't think I know her, but it is possible we were at Chapel Hill at the same time." She was talking easily now. Thank Christ for Betty Lou Farmer.

"Where are you from . . . Clell?"

"Helena, Montana. Home of Gary Cooper. Me and the Coop were like that." Hazard grinned and crossed his fingers. "He was just about to get me a starring role in a movie when he died."

She smiled and said, "By the way, I think Clell is a nice name. It's different. Furthermore, you look a bit like Gary Cooper, don't you think?"

"Yup."

Samantha laughed outright this time. "Sound like him, too."

"It's one of my most successful impressions," said Hazard. "Want to hear the whole thing?" She nodded, and he squinted against a merciless high plains sun and intoned without facial expression, "Yup . . . Nope . . . Mebbe."

They were both laughing when the doorbell rang. Hazard hugged Betty Lou and shook hands formally with Goody, hissing into the sergeant-major's ear as he took their coats, "Be good, you sonofabitch, or I'll have your guts for garters."

"My, my, we are a bit anxious this evening, aren't we?" Nelson whispered back, grinning evilly. "Don't sweat it, shit-for-brains. I will comport myself with my usual charm and dignity." Hazard groaned.

He made the introductions. Nelson took Samantha's tiny hand in his own massive mitt and raised it to his lips. "I'm delighted to meet you, my dear." Hazard groaned again and turned to Betty Lou. "I've discovered that Samantha is a Tar Foot, or whatever it is you people call yourselves, and that she went to Chapel Hill."

"No! Really? That's marvelous!" exclaimed Betty Lou, her Carolina accent as fresh as the day she left the Piedmont ten years before. "When were you there? Who do you know? C'mon, sit down and talk to Betty Lou." The women were already comparing dates, places, and names when Hazard pulled Nelson into the kitchen to help fetch drinks.

From the living room Betty Lou squealed, "Clell, Goody, we were at Chapel Hill at the same time! We have mutual friends. Samantha is from Wilmington, which is right next to Wrightsville Beach, which is where my family has a cottage and where we've summered for years and years."

"That's real nice, Betty Lou," Hazard yelled back. "Y'all just go ahead and talk about why you lost the war and make your plans for fighting the next one, and Goody and I will go over them with you later to see if we can help y'all win it this time around." He pronounced it *wo-wah*.

Nelson gave Hazard a sly, appraising look. "Clell ol' buddy, I must say you never cease to amaze me. Your sudden attack of good taste is surprising, to say nothing of your newfound nerve. That is some fine-looking woman. A real live honest-to-shit high class lady. Why I do believe I'd drag my balls over ten miles of ground glass just to hear her pee in a tin cup over the phone."

"Keep your voice down. Goddammit, Goody, you promised me."

"I surely did. And I'll honor that promise, Clell. Trust me. Now let's get back in there so's I can oogle them titties some more." Hazard gave Nelson a look that promised a slow and painful death, picked up the tray of drinks, and led the way back to the ladies.

The evening was beginning well. Samantha and Betty Lou chatted easily on the couch like long-lost sisters, still talking of familiar places and people, Samantha's native accent creeping softly back into her voice the longer she was exposed to Betty Lou's unexpurgated drawl, a drawl that disguised a quick and informed mind. And Goody was behaving himself, coming into the conversation now and then with an observation or aside that managed to be both entertaining and clean. Everybody knew that the sergeant-major could be entertaining, but only a few suspected that he could be clean. Hazard felt a mixture of pride, relief, and affection for this bear of a man.

He caught Samantha sneaking surreptitious looks at Nelson, saw her take in the unlikely size of him; the craggy face tracked with deep arroyos, barrancas that led nowhere; the hooked Syrian nose, pitted on the end as if someone had pummeled it with an icepick; the deep-set twinkling eyes, full of mischief and on the prowl for victims; and the whole amazing edifice topped by a shocking dome of a head, shaved clean as an ostrich egg. Then she would look back at Betty Lou's deceptively sweet valentine of a face and Junior League uniform—white turtleneck, Carolina-blue blazer, sweptback frosted hair. There was something akin to wonder on Samantha's face.

Hazard smiled inwardly and got up to open another bottle of wine and put out some cheese and crackers. It was plain Wisconsin cheddar and saltines, pedestrian fare alongside the Pouilly, but all he'd been able to afford on top of his other purchases. He went to the window and pulled wide the drapes to unveil a crisp, clear night, the lights of D.C. strung along the horizon like lanterns on a Hong Kong junk. "No more Tar Foot talk," he called. "Goody and me are Union men through and through."

"It's Tar *Heel*, idjit," Betty Lou said, while Hazard and Nelson, as if responding to some invisible conductor's baton, began to sing on cue, "Union forever, hurrah, boys, hurrah. . . ."

"We surrender," Samantha laughed. "We'll stop the Tar Foot talk if you'll explain to me what it is you gentlemen do on that Army post over there."

"You mean you don't know?" boomed Goody. "I am aghast, madame, simply aghast. Why, we are the Old Guard. The President's Own. The renowned Third Herd.

We are the nation's toy soldiers. We march with rifles that cannot shoot. We fix bayonets that cannot stick. And we preside over rituals that do not matter, at least not to the principal character. We are the Kabuki theater of the profession of arms; the jesters at the court of Mars, god of war. Doo-dah, doo-dah.''

"Now you just hush, Goody Nelson," Betty Lou said in a scolding, schoolmarm voice. "You've been hanging around Clell so long you're beginning to sound just like him, bitter and cynical and irreverent, and I, for one, do not find it becoming." She turned to Samantha and said earnestly, "They are the Army's ceremonial unit, and it's a right nice one indeed. They add ever so much to the color of life in Washington. You have to be among the Army's top people to get in, and it's a right nice honor and compliment for both Goody and Clell to have been asked to join."

"We weren't asked, we were ordered," Nelson cut in, all playfulness gone. "Both Clell and I asked for cadre positions at the Infantry School. We thought our skill and experience—and they are considerable I might add—might prove useful to the children they're shipping to that garden of the Orient called Vietnam. We thought we could help a few of them come back standing up instead of stretched out in one of the cute little boxes we plant in the ground every day. All we really do on that Army post over there, Samantha my dear, is serve as pallbearers. We strut to the fife and drum and add 'ever so much to the color of life in Washington.' We are the plumed troop, Samantha.''

"The what?" Samantha asked.

"The plumed troop," Goody repeated. He began to recite:

> Farewell the plumed troop and the big wars that
> make ambition virtue! O, farewell!

> Farewell the neighing steed and the shrill trump,
>   the spirit stirring drum, and the ear piercing
>   fife, the royal banner, and all quality, pride,
>   pomp and circumstances of glorious war!
>
> And, O you mortal engines, whose rude throats
>   the immortal Jove's dread clamors counterfeit,
>   farewell!
>
> Othello's occupation's gone!

There was a thick silence and then Goody laughed bitterly and said, "I am startin' to sound like Clell, ain't I? Well, that's okay by me. He's one of the few people in that flock of strutting peacocks, our 'right nice' Old Guard, who can see where this damn war of theirs is headed, that we're in the wrong place at the wrong time. This is 1966, not 1956, and if we gotta wage war, hot or cold, against somebody, it should be the Russians, not a bunch of slant-eyed rice farmers who didn't like the Rooskies any more'n we did until we pushed them into the Commies' arms. Most of the higher ranking people at Myer have been over there already, just like me'n Clell, and they should know better. They're so caught up in the stampede for merit badges, medals, and promotions, they can't see down the road a bit to the time when we're gonna be up to our elbows in blood. Then, when it's too late, they'll be the ones quotin' the bard, not me. They'll be doin the scene from *Macbeth*—'out, out damned spot'—and all the perfumes of Araby ain't gonna get the stink off their hands."

"Okay, honey, okay," Betty Lou said softly. "I didn't mean to get you all het up." She turned to Hazard. "Now aren't you sorry you put a stop to all that Tar Foot talk?"

Hazard smiled and walked over to put an arm around Nelson's wide shoulders. "C'mon, Black Moor. Come help me in the kitchen so we can get supper on the table. The girls must be starving." As they left the room, Hazard saw that Samantha was gaping at Goody, her eyes wide as tiddlywinks.

"How did you and Goody ever come to meet?" Samantha asked Betty Lou.

"Oh that," Betty Lou said with a laugh. "Well, one day a constituent from home walked into Senator Ervin's office—a big car dealer from Charlotte. You know the type . . . a big bore but an even bigger campaign contributor. Now Sam knows that the southern male loves anything having to do with the military, so to get rid of this man he turns to me and says, sweet as pie, 'Betty Lou, why don't you take Mr. Chevrolet here over to Fort Myer to see our fine boys in the Old Guard.' And I said, just as sweet, 'Why of course, Senator, I think Mr. Ford would like that.' I didn't even know what the Old Guard was or exactly where Fort Myer was. But I called over there and told them that guests of Senator Ervin were on their way, and they assigned Sergeant-Major Nelson himself to show us around.

"Well, Goody was just charming. He was quoting poetry all over the place—that's one of his little parlor tricks, you know—and I was understandably swept right off my feet.

"Then toward the end of the afternoon we walked past a drill field and stopped to watch the boys practice their marching. Well, Goody apparently saw something he didn't like, because he turned from Dr. Jekyll into Mr. Hyde right before my eyes. He came out with a stream of the most imaginative and physically impossible—to the best of my limited knowledge—obscenities I have ever heard, and I grew up on a farm. He went on for a full five minutes and never once repeated himself It was a virtuoso performance. I, of course, fell in love on the spot. Any well-bred, genteel, southern girl would have.''

Samantha was clapping her hands and giggling with delight.

Hazard cut into the laughter. "Okay, y'all, chow time. Would you well-bred, genteel, southern girls like to come and get it 'fore I slop it to the hogs?''

He put the first course on the table, dimmed the room lights and lit the candles, the amber teardrops reflecting softly off the damask tablecloth he had picked out in the huge covered souk in Damascus. He poured the wine and proposed a toast: "To friendships, old . . . and new.'' His eyes met Samantha's and they all drank. Then Goody Nelson raised his glass and said, "Here's to us and those like us.'' They laughed and drank. "Damn few,'' Goody added, and they laughed and drank again. "And most of them are dead,'' he finished, and they laughed and drank yet again, but Hazard and Nelson looked at each other over the lips of their raised glasses and neither man's eyes were smiling.

Everyone, even Goody, praised the aubergines. Everyone, even Goody, praised the salad. And everyone, even Goody, praised the saltimbocca.

All went well until dessert. The sergeant-major was having such a good time that he relaxed . . . and forgot himself. The conversation had swung round to films and someone mentioned the name of Hollywood's newest sex goddess "Yeah,'' Goody announced in a pleasant, conversational tone, "they say she's a real, honest-to-shit nympho. Can't get enough. She does squat-jumps over fire hydrants. I guess the only way to satisfy her would be to stick your head up her twat and vomit.''

There was a gasp from Samantha, and a shattering hush

fell over the table. Hazard closed his eyes, his worst fears
realized. He heard Samantha say, slowly and somberly,
"That is the most disgusting thing I ever heard." Hazard's
eyes stayed closed . . . until he heard a choking giggle
from Samantha's place at the table. The giggle pedaled
itself into a laugh, and the laugh geared up to a roar.
Hazard peeked and saw Samantha sitting helpless in her
chair, her head thrown back, her jaw loose, braying at the
ceiling like a donkey.

He looked at the others in amazement, and they all
began to howl with her. At her. Each time they tried to
stop, the sound of Samantha's wild honk, an atrocious
sound from so petite and proper a lady, kept them going.
After a while the laughter subsided to a hoarse medley of
whimperings and mewlings, and Hazard stood weakly to
start clearing the table. Only then did Samantha Huff begin
to blush.

They had coffee and cognac in the living room, chatting
languidly and smiling for no apparent reason at Samantha.
Every once in a while one or another would start to
chuckle, then cut it off quickly before it could climb on the
roller coaster. Finally, a little after midnight, Nelson rose
and said, "Othello's occupation may be gone, but ol'
Goody's ain't. I gotta kick the rooster out of bed in the
morning." Hazard got their coats. Goody kissed Samantha
on the cheek, just like a sophisticated civilian, and the two
women swapped promises to telephone soon. After Goody
and Betty Lou had gone, Hazard asked Samantha, "Nightcap?" and she nodded. He brought her another cognac and
cup of coffee. She sat on the couch with her shoes off and
her feet propped on a pouf.

"Are all Army sergeants like you two?" she asked.

"No," said Hazard.

"That's a shame." She looked down at the glass in her
hand, swirling the cognac gently. "I had a nice time

tonight, Clell. It was the best evening I've had in a long, long time. Thank you for asking me."

"Aw shucks, ma'am, t'warnt nuthin," Hazard said in his best Gary Cooper voice, staring at her and feeling the snakes crawl back into his belly.

Samantha flushed under the scrutiny and finished her drink with a gulp. She got to her feet, slipped on her shoes, and said, "I'd better go. I've got a busy day tomorrow, too."

Hazard walked her to the door, then blurted, "Are you busy Sunday afternoon?"

She looked at him levelly. "No, I'm not busy."

"Good. I'd like to take you to see someone who is very special to me."

"Who?"

"Sam Huff," he said with a grin. "The real Sam Huff. A southern girl who doesn't know anything about football can't go home again. It's high time this serious gap in your education was filled."

She laughed. "All right. I'm willing to learn."

"Great. I'll call you Sunday morning, not too early, and give you the plan of attack." He awkwardly stuck out a hand. She shook it and crossed the corridor to her own door, turned back to say a soft "Good-night," and was gone.

4

There were no seats on the bus. Willow looked around in confusion. There were only handrails under the windows on both sides, running the length of the vehicle. A man behind him explained with a peeved grin, "They don't let us sit down. They're afraid it might put wrinkles in the uniform."

The ride to the chapel took less than two minutes. They piled out and formed into ranks. Lieutenant Webber looked at his watch and exhorted them to hurry. Sergeant Hazard peered down the lines like a man sighting a rifle and called, "C'mon, people, straighten it up. Number Five, come up half a step. Number Eight, back a step. That's too goddamn far, Five; back off a half step. Too far back again, Five. Goddammit, Wildman, get your shit together, boy. Okay, that's good; hold it there." Hazard took his place at the end of the front rank and saluted the platoon leader. "Platoon ready, sir."

And not a moment too soon. The chapel doors swung open and the men were called to attention. The drummer started his sad cadence: ta ta ta *tum*. Willow felt a thrill go through him, the sound of the snare touching something deep and primitive inside, some elementary place. When he saw the flag-draped coffin placed onto the caisson, emotion filled his throat and he felt tears well in his eyes. It was his first drop job.

According to the day's detail sheet, inside the box was a young Infantry lieutenant killed less than five days ago in the Ia Drang Valley. Standing with the widow and an older couple, obviously the dead man's parents, was another lieutenant from the same company, who had accompanied the body of his fallen comrade home. The officer wore the shoulder patch of the First Cavalry (Air Mobile) Division, the black bar cutting diagonally through the large bright yellow field, the black horse head in the upper cantle. The Third Brigade of the First Cav, Willow knew, was the direct descendant of the famed Seventh Cavalry, Custer's doomed regiment. Willow blinked damp eyes and pondered historical ironies.

It was a raw, gray day; the sky threatened to weep for slain warriors. It had rained hard earlier in the morning. Wet leaves clogged the gutters and a thin sheet of water covered the road. The platoon splashed behind the slow-moving caisson, and spit shines that had taken hours to build slowly eroded away with each step. Halfway to the gravesite, the sky opened and it began to pour again. Water sluiced off patent leather cap visors and ran down the rifled bores of the M-1s. The procession marched on, the tenor of the snare joined occasionally by the deep bass of a thunderclap.

They marched through the Fields of the Dead, its precise rows of plain stones laid out in the pattern adopted for all United States cemeteries in 1872. Willow had been to the post library and had boned up on the cemetery. He looked for landmarks as he marched.

Arlington National Cemetery, he knew, was roughly semicircular in shape and covered more than five hundred acres. To the right of where they marched was the Memorial Amphitheater, built by the Grand Army of the Republic and dedicated in 1920 as a place to hold Memorial Day services. It was an imposing structure of white marble modeled after both the Theater of Dionysus at Athens and the Roman theater at Orange in France. The Tomb of the Unknown Soldier sat in front, and in the bowels of the building was the basement ready room, where troops from Honor Guard Company's tomb platoon took their two-hour breaks between hour-long walking tours, spending the "off" time shining shoes, brass, and leather and refreshing uniforms on the large, floor-mounted steam press. On nice summer days, Willow had been told, crowds of five thousand people or more would gather to watch the changing of the guard at the Tomb.

Not far from the Amphitheater, on a hilltop just above JFK's grave, was the centerpiece of the cemetery: the Custis-Lee Mansion. The mansion had been built in 1802 on the estate of George Washington Parke Custis, the adopted son of the first President. The home was copied from the Temple of Theseus in Athens, and the portico, with its eight Doric columns of white marble, could be seen from across the Potomac.

Robert E. Lee had married Mary Anne Randolph Custis in the house in 1831, and it was Lee's home until 1861, when he left Arlington to join the Confederacy. Willow could imagine Lee pacing the rooms of the great house or strolling the spacious grounds as he wrestled with the terrible decision. Should he turn against the Union he had so faithfully and well served as a career Army officer; against the flag he honored and the West Point classmates he cherished? Or turn against his family and his region and his state, the sustaining and nurturing Commonwealth of Virginia he so dearly loved? It was in those rooms and on those grounds that Lee chose to fight for his land and his people rather than his ideas.

When Lee left, the Union Army had turned the mansion

into an HQ and the grounds into a camp. In 1864 the
Secretary of War ordered that the estate become a military
cemetery, just to spite Lee, some said, and the first soldier
was buried there on May 13, 1864—a Confederate prisoner who had died in hospital. Now the mansion served as
administrative offices for the cemetery.

The gravesite was a quagmire. It had been cleared only
days before, and there were still deep bulldozer tracks in
the mud. The machine itself was still working nearby,
clearing the next section, but the gusty wind carried its
sound away. The troops could see the Cat moving, white
tufts of smoke popping from its exhaust, its operator in a
yellow rain slicker under a makeshift awning. The driver
waved merrily to the funeral party.

It was a mere twenty yards from the curb to the hole,
but not short enough to be traversed without mishap. First
a member of the platoon slipped in the mud. It was
Wildman. With a quick reflex action that surprised everyone who knew him, the pudgy Wildman whipped the rifle
off his shoulder in a forward arc and plunged the bayonet
into the soft ground, making a crutch that saved him from
going all the way down. Wildman quickly straightened and
put the weapon back to right shoulder arms, but the shiny
line of bayonets was rent beyond repair, sullied by the
maverick dripping ooze, a solitary jarring break in the
symmetry of chrome.

Then a pallbearer fell, halfway between caisson and
grave. It was an end man, and his lurching sprawl threw
the others off balance so that two more went down. The
metal box hit the ground with a wet plop. The members of
the funeral party looked away, unsure of how to react—all
except the widow, who gasped and stared bug-eyed while
the soldiers scrambled to their feet and rehoisted their
load, the bottom of the casket spotted with clumps of goo.

Lieutenant Webber's lips were tight with rage. He was

already anxious about the next job, and the sight of his troopers' uniforms caked with mud to the knees, together with these new disasters, threatened to nudge him over the edge of sanity. He stood rigid, fixing in mind names and faces for retribution while the casket team grappled the coffin to the grave, taking careful, mincing steps the rest of the way.

The mourners reluctantly turned their attention back to the main show, gathering under large, black umbrellas. Willow could not hear what was being said. All he could hear was a man behind him mutter, "Ashes to ashes . . ." Then someone else down his rank: "Dust to dust . . ." And finally another man, behind him and to the left: "Let's plant this prick and get on the bus."

Willow could not believe his ears. Was nothing sacred to these people? Couldn't they see the poignancy of this ceremony? Jesus Christ, one of *them* . . . an *infantryman*. . . . was dead, killed in action while they pulled cushy garrison duty stateside. Willow was filled with disgust.

The firing party shot off its three volleys of blank rounds, and the bugler stepped up to blow taps, the rain dripping off his instrument.

> Day is done
> Gone the sun
> From the lake
> From the hill
> From the sky
> Rest in peace
> Soldier brave
> God is nigh

Willow had heard it nearly every night of his life, the spare, haunting notes floating dreamily over Fort Benning or Fort Lewis or Fort Huachuca or Maginot Caserne in

France and into his bedroom where he lay waiting for it. Some nights he could not get to sleep until he'd heard it. It was his lullaby. And not once since those boyhood days had it failed to summon up images of glorious fights and proud warriors, of battles long ago and far away. How did that Wordsworth poem go? "Will no one tell me what she sings? Perhaps the plaintive numbers flow, For old, un-happy far-off things, And battles long ago."

The noise. If it would just stop for one minute, for half a minute, he could think. Flashes of light and the concussion from the explosions made it impossible for him to focus, to get a fix. Brilliant illumination one moment, inky black-ness the next. Then incandescence again, but this time light-ing a new, unfamiliar scene as men ran and fell in confusion.

The noise was awful, an assault on the senses that left him stunned. Each new explosion, each new burst of auto-matic weapons fire, each new scream in the dark caused him to swing his head wildly in that direction and think, There! No, there! No, there is where I should go. And so he went nowhere. He stood transfixed, his body jerking around like the needle on a compass gone haywire.

His sense of dislocation was not helped by the fact that he had been yanked out of a deep sleep by the first salvo of mortar rounds impacting in the center of the compound, bracketing the tactical operations center, the TOC.

He had been dreaming jumbled dreams. He was trout fishing with Sergeant Hazard . . . or maybe it was his father; he couldn't be sure. But it was a peaceful place of trees and mountains and swift water, and the narrow loops of the fly lines arced lazily behind them, tracing delicate arabesques in the air. Then he was lying on a blanket with Rachel Field in a brown canyon watching a desert rain flash across the mountain wall, and he could smell the wet sage and could almost see the country turn from brown to

green as he watched. They were naked, and as the first
large drops began to pelt their bodies, Rachel laughed and
arched her back and shot wide dark nipples to the heavens.
Then he was standing tall, resplendent in dress blues,
facing the reviewing stand at Myer while the band finished
up a martial air and General Field placed the Medal of
Honor around his neck: a wreathed, five-pointed star topped
by a bar reading Valor and an eagle and all strung on a
shiny blue ribbon with thirteen white stars.

Then he was jolted awake and it was 1969 again and he
was back at Daisy Mae, the place his troops called "Fort
Doom." He had grabbed a steel pot and his M-16 and had
bolted from the bunker in his skivvies, out into a world
that seemed far less real than those of his dreams.

So he stood paralyzed, trying to get his bearings. Then
the light from a raw, shockingly close blast brought Sergeant Robinson's lean black face out of the gloom. His
platoon sergeant was lurching oddly. The man must be as
confused as he was, Willow thought. He grabbed Robinson's
arm and yelled into his ears, "Robbie, get our people and
whoever else you can round up and get 'em on line,
chop-chop."

Robinson began to giggle insanely. "Ain't no muthafuckin'
line, Loo-tenant. Them slopeheads is inside the wire. They
come through Loo-tenant Harmon's people like they wasn't
even there." Sergeant Robinson was laughing now, his
mouth twisted and twitching in his face as if it were being
worked by a demented puppeteer. Then he buckled, going
down in a series of sharp bends—at the knees, waist, and
neck—as though whoever was working the strings had let
go. Robinson began to weep in huge, racking sobs, and
then Willow saw that his platoon sergeant had been shot,
high up in the thigh, through the femoral. It was a small,
rather neat hole that pumped blood with every heartbeat.
"Ahh, Jesus . . . Ahh, Jesus, Robbie. MEDIC!"

*   *   *

"We're waiting, Lieutenant Willow," said Major Pyle, impatiently tapping his pencil against his palm and staring over the top of the wire-rim spectacles.

"Uh, yessir. Sorry, sir. When the attack began, I was asleep in my bunker about fifty yards from the TOC. I started to get my men to the perimeter to help Lieutenant Harmon's second platoon—they were on line that night— but I was informed by my platoon sergeant that the wire had already been breached and that the sappers were inside the firebase. I then ran toward the TOC thinking that Captain Crowder and Colonel Bean would be there and that they could tell me where I was needed most. Halfway there I came upon Doc, ah, Specialist Four Ramiriz, one of our medics, working on Captain Crowder. Apparently when Captain Crowder discovered that the line to the mortar pits had been cut, he decided to go over there himself and see what was wrong—why there was no fire support. He . . . He didn't get very far."

5

On this Saturday, Delta Company was up at 0500 hours. Breakfast was at 0530. The latrines had to be cleared by 0600. The pace was frenzied. Everyone shaved twice. Those deemed by their squad leaders to need haircuts were herded down to the basement, where PFC Samson, the company barber, had set up shop in a corner of the supply room. Work parties, grim-faced commandos armed with a lethal assortment of mops, sponges, brushes, brooms, and spirits of ammonia, formed up to attack and subdue the day room, the attic lounge, and the latrines. Even chemical warfare was authorized for a command inspection.

The inspection team from battalion headquarters was scheduled to arrive at 1000 hours.

In the arms room, Specialist Four Ronald Birmingham, the armorer, inspected rifles and bayonets for cleanliness and checked to see that each M-1 was in its assigned numbered slot in the wooden rifle racks. Owners of weapons judged unworthy were summoned downstairs by intercom and made to clean them again. The air in the room was clogged with the smell of solvents and linseed oil, and soiled bore patches littered the floor.

In the supply room, Supply Sergeant Gillespie Beech and his assistants counted and stacked blankets and mat-

tress covers, then recounted and restacked them. They
tidied up bins of assorted gear, from canteen covers to
entrenching tools. Extra items, those over and above the
count listed on the TO and E sheet—the Table of Organization and Equipment—were hauled out and hidden away in
private automobiles. These extras, accumulated by Beech
through astute trading and outright theft, were to be sold
on the side to men who had lost gear for which they were
accountable.

In the mess hall and kitchen, Mess Sergeant Eucher T.
July hectored his cooks and the kitchen police detail,
which had been doubled in size for this special day. The
wreckage from breakfast had to be repaired, the milk
machines swabbed out, salt and pepper shakers and ketchup
bottles refilled, trays cleaned and stacked, floors shined,
and grill and ovens Brilloed back to base metal. Great
slabs of meat and five-gallon drums of ice cream, extra
food that appeared on no battalion larder lists, had to be
taken out and stashed in a large refrigerated trunk rented
for the day. Like the supply sergeant, the mess sergeant
moonlighted, selling prime government beef—obtained
through trades, favors, and fancy pencil work—to nearby
civilian eateries. The line of KPs hauling the contraband
from the cold lockers to the truck, some of them with
whole sides of beef on their shoulders, looked like ants at
a picnic. On this chaotic morning, the smiling, cherubic
black face that Sergeant July always wore for the brass,
was gone. So, too, were the fawning *yassuhs* and *nawsuhs*
and *lawdy-lawdys* with which July invariably greeted any
commissioned officer who wandered by Delta's mess, as
many did because of the mess sergeant's reputation for
setting a fine table in the officers' dining room. Somewhere along the line, early in his career, Sergeant July had
decided to play the faithful plantation slave for officers,
always good for a toothy smile and happy talk and a gratis

carton of ice cream or thick T-bone to take home to the
little woman. The cooks and KPs knew him to be a savage
despot: five-foot-two, shaped like a Shmoo, and rapacious
as a piranha. He was considered by many officers to be the
best mess sergeant in the Old Guard, if not the entire U.S.
Army. The enlisted men knew that he often sold or traded
away their foodstuffs for the delicacies that earned him his
reputation among the brass.

In the orderly room the company clerk, Specialist Four
Peter DeVeber, worked under the malevolent eye of First
Sergeant Boudin. Boudin prowled the office like a caged
bear, worry stamped on his face like a skin disease. Inspections always brought out the worst in the first sergeant. He
was hopeless at paperwork and had to rely totally on clever
clerks, whom he mistrusted as he mistrusted everyone,
perhaps more. DeVeber checked his file of morning reports to see that all the carbons were in order and smudge
free. He combed the file cabinets, seeing that all ARs and
additions, deletions, and amendments were in place, jerking all extraneous material. Most important, he checked
over the first sergeant's duty rosters—the official duty
rosters. Boudin kept two sets of duty rosters. The set that
the inspector would see this morning was as neatly drawn
as a defense contract and virtually reeked of justice. The
guard duty and kitchen police lists went through the company roster with a meticulous regard for fair play, working
through the names in strict rotation, every man below the
rank of noncommissioned officer coming up for his turn
when the snake of the alphabet flicked its forked tongue.
The other set of duty rosters, the actual working set, was
squirreled away from prying eyes—a hideously deformed
child locked away in the attic while company was in the
parlor. On that list, the same names appeared over and
over again: troublemakers, malingerers, hapless victims of
Slasher Boudin's instant and irreversible prejudices, guilt-

less men who had done nothing more heinous than walk past the orderly room door just when the first sergeant was looking up, trying to think of someone to nail for KP the next day. Company veterans always used the back doors when leaving the building during duty hours and only got their fingers caught in the slamming door of Cajun justice when the Slasher crossed them up by working late. Each new stack of papers finished by the feverish DeVeber was laboriously signed by Boudin, even this simple act of administration painful for him. His beady eyes squinted with concentration, the pencil stub moving slowly and awkwardly in his hamlike left hand, his thick tongue pushed out through the end of the fishhook.

In the troop bays the men put finishing touches on boots, shoes, and patent leather, and twirled their brass on woolen blankets, the discs stuck onto the end of the tent poles and spun between the palms like Boy Scouts trying to start a fire with sticks. Field packs, rigged horseshoe style, were set atop wall lockers. Beds were made and remade, the blankets and dust covers stretched tight as the skin of ancient, tucked actresses. Fresh fatigues, inspection uniform of the day, were laid out with a gentleness rarely accorded the utility uniform. Dress blue blouses and Class A's, brass attached, were hung neatly in the wall lockers, shoulders two carefully calibrated inches apart, left patches facing out. Poplin shirts, white gloves, and skivvies were set in the bottom of the footlockers at the end of the bunks. The top trays, lined with white towels, were arranged as carefully as Japanese floral displays: the rolled socks, shoe brushes, combs, double-edged razors and tooth brushes, none of them ever used, set in the prescribed places, the prescribed distances apart. All personal items were stuffed into duffel bags and stacked near the bay doors for pickup by yet another work party, which would hide them in Bravo Company next door, a favor that would be returned when it was Bravo's turn to face the inspectors.

Throughout the building, floor buffers whirred, their droning hum as natural a background noise to the men as the sound of cicadas to a farmer. And over the intercom came a steady stream of orders and advice from the NCO ready room, where noncoms racked their brains for small details they might have forgotten and pored over scouting reports on the officers and NCOs in the inspection team, looking for idiosyncrasies that could mean the difference between winning the day's game and losing it.

Listening to the squawk box in the Third Platoon bay, the flow of announcements coming like that at a busy international airport, Willow marveled again at the odd language spoken by Army NCOs, the easy mixture of hundred-dollar words and grammatical barbarisms that made up the noncom patois. It was a language he had heard all his life, his father's native tongue. He could understand it, even speak a few words, but after all these years he was still not fluent. It was a skill, he thought, that must come automatically when they sew on the stripes.

". . . Okay, listen up, you personnel. I don't wanna see nuthin but stocking feet until oh-nine-five-eight hours. Put on boots last thing, when you are in penultimate inspection position adjacent to your bunk. Scuff marks will not be condoned. Anyone what fucks up the floors is gonna have his health record fucked up by me in reciprocation."

". . . Use Q-tips to clean the inside of your belt buckles. Brasso gets in there and dries to an opaque, milky white color that looks like shit. They's an E-6 on the inspection team who makes that his specialty. You been warned, and a word to the wise should keep my boot outta your ass."

". . . Listen up, people. Colonel Godwin likes to stop and chat with the troops. It's a nice, homey touch. Shit like 'Where you from, soldier' and 'How d'ya like the

Army?' He's fairly harmless if you watch your mouth and avoid stepping on your dick. We want you people to just answer 'Asshole, Arkansas,' or wherever, and 'I love the Army, sir.' "

". . . Here's a follow-up on that last announcement, people. The one you gotta be real careful of is Sergeant-Major Nelson. The battalion sergeant-major likes to ask questions, too, but here you people gotta watch yourselfs. He always picks on the same people the colonel talks to, but he don't ask you no proper shit like where you from. Uh-uh. He asks weird shit like 'Does you mamma have big tits.' Sergeant Hazard, who knows the sergeant-major well, advises that you try to be clever or funny. His theory is that Nelson does this for a coupla reasons. One is to poke some fun at the colonel's well-meaning misguided attempts to talk to 'the little people.' The other reason he does it is to see how well a man thinks on his feet, how sharp you are. So even though he ain't smiling when he asks his dipshit questions, he's real disappointed when you play it straight. We'll give you an example. Last year Nelson asks this guy in Honor Guard Company when was the last time he beat his meat. This guy keeps a straight face. He just looks down at his watch and asks Nelson, 'What time is it?' The sergeant-major cracks up and takes his team right on to the next platoon without inspecting nothing. They didn't get a single gig just because this guy made Nelson laugh. So use your heads, people, and try your best to amuse His Highness."

". . . One last thing, people. Keep in mind what's at stake here. Top company in this here circle jerk gets free beer in the mess hall every Sunday for a month. Bottom company gets every shit detail HQ can think up till some other outfit gets on their shit list. This is serious stuff, troopers. . . ."

At five minutes to ten everything was as ready as it

would ever be. At precisely 1000 hours, Delta's front
doors swung open and the inspection team, in full dress
blues, entered the building according to rank. First Colonel
Godwin, slender, erect, with a patrician's face, hollow-
cheeked and the correct amount of gray at the temples. He
carried an ebony swagger stick topped with German silver
and inscribed with the regimental crest of the Royal Ben-
gal Fusiliers, a gift from a British officer he had met while
assigned to NATO. Then came the battalion executive
officer, Lieutenant Colonel John Johnson, a burly man
who looked as coarse as Godwin was sleek, but distinguished nonetheless by the blue ribbon and five-pointed
star around his neck. It was the only one of his many
decorations that the XO wore, but it was more than enough.
It required even the Chairman of the Joint Chiefs to salute
him first. Blackjack Pershing had once commented that he
would gladly trade all five of his stars for that one—the
Congressional Medal of Honor. With the battalion's top
two officers came a galaxy of lesser lights, majors and
captains and lieutenants. Some were specialists. The battalion supply officer would inspect the supply room, the
personnel officer would inspect the orderly room, and the
officer in charge of mess would look at the kitchen. The
rest were clipboard holders.

Right behind the brass came Sergeant-Major Thurgood
Nelson and his retinue of noncommissioned officers.
Nelson's team would do the actual troop inspections, and
it was he who would make or break the company.

Even Delta's hoariest veterans were nervous. A command inspection had that effect, no matter how many of
them a man had been through. In fact, the veterans were
especially stricken, more than even the newest draftee
who, after all, knew that the ultimate responsibility rested
on loftier shoulders than his. Captain Thomas, waiting in
the hallway in front of the Chapultepec Baton, a sickly

smile on his face, looked as if he wanted to vomit. Instead, he snapped a crisp salute and boomed, "Sir, Delta Company, First Battalion, Third Infantry, the Old Guard, Captain Charles Thomas commanding, is ready for inspection."

Colonel Godwin casually returned the salute by touching the swagger stick to his hat brim, smiled coolly and answered, "We'll see, Tommy, we'll see. We did Honor Guard yesterday, and they are going to be very hard to beat."

The specialists broke away immediately, each heading in the direction of his own narrow interest. Little trouble was expected from them. Young DeVeber was a superior company clerk, and his files were always meticulous. Besides, the battalion personnel expert, a chief warrant officer, was deathly afraid of Slasher Boudin. The officer responsible for company messes was particularly fond of the obsequious Sergeant July. Choice free meats from Delta's cold locker graced his dinner table at home two or three nights a week. And the battalion S-4, an Army shooting champion despite his nonmartial specialty, would never forget that Sergeant Beech had somewhere found and given him an Ithaca Grade Seven single-barreled shotgun, built in 1916, designed by Emil Flues and engraved by Bill McGuire, legendary craftsmen both. Carefully nurtured relationships were about to pay off yet again.

No, it was in the troop bays that Delta's fate lay. Procedure was well established. The battalion commander and the XO would walk through the bays on the lookout for general appearance. Only glaring errors would cause them to comment. But behind them would come Sergeant-Major Nelson and his team. It was their job to rip the place apart. There was no way to influence the sergeant-major, a man immune to fear or favors. He could not be bought for less than excellence. Clell Hazard was especially worried about Nelson. The sergeant-major went out of his way not to favor friends at times like this.

The inspectors moved in a phalanx up the short flight of steps and into the First Platoon bay. The commander of the First, Second Lieutenant Hiram Waters, saluted, gulped, and squeaked, "First Platoon ready for inspection, sir." The look on SFC Jimmy Louder's face as he stood at attention behind his lieutenant suggested he was not so sure. On the other side of the double row of wall lockers, Second Platoon's commander and platoon sergeant, Second Lieutenant Samuel Grove and Sergeant First Class Billy Cook, conferred in whispers and cast anxious eyes up and down the row of men standing at the foot of their bunks. The two men put their ears to the lockers and tried to overhear what was being said on the other side, listening desperately for last-second clues to emphasis and eccentricity. They could hear colonels Godwin and Johnson and their retinue pass slowly through First Platoon, Godwin stopping to ask this man and that where he was from and how he liked the Army. So far it was SOP, standard operating procedure. The eavesdropping leaders of Second Platoon winced when they heard Nelson or one of his henchmen turn over a footlocker and dump its contents on the floor. Still SOP.

Up on the second floor, Second Lieutenant Ronald Webber and Sergeant First Class Clell Hazard of Third Platoon and Second Lieutenant Ronald Shimkin and Sergeant First Class Alec Moreau of Fourth Platoon stood in a knot and waited. A man had been posted on the landing as an early warning system.

"I wish we could see what was going on down there," Webber said, straightening his gig line. ". . . some idea of what they're concentrating on."

Hazard smiled and shook his head. "It's too late now, lieutenant. We live or die on what's already done."

Lieutenant Shimkin snapped at his platoon sergeant, "Quit pacing around, Moreau, you're scuffing the god-damned floor." Moreau froze and looked over at Hazard. "I wish to fuck you and Nelson weren't such big buddies, Clell," he whined. "You know how he is. He's gonna make a special effort to fuck you over, and it's gonna carry over to our side of the bay."

Hazard laughed. "Yeah. Well, if you lie down with pigs, you're going to get covered with shit."

The picket came running into the bay shouting, "They're coming." Lieutenant Shimkin screamed at him, "Your boots, man, you're fucking up the floor," then grabbed Sergeant Moreau by the lapel and hauled him around the lockers to the temporary safety of the Fourth Platoon side, ignoring Moreau's hysteric protest, "My blouse, lieutenant, you're fuckin' up my blouse."

"Third Platoon ready for inspection, sir."

"At ease, Lieutenant Webber," Godwin said with a paternal air. "Care to show me through?"

"Yes, sir, I'd be delighted, sir," Webber said, as if he had a choice.

As Webber and the battalion officers started slowly down the line, Hazard hung back and greeted Goody Nelson at the entryway. The sergeant-major grinned. "How you doin', Clell? Your boys ready for me?"

"They're ready, sergeant-major," Hazard said formally, but smiling warily.

Nelson was still grinning. "Even Wildman?"

Hazard's smile died a quick, brutal death. How the hell did Nelson do it? How could he know so much about the workings of a single fire team in a single squad in a single platoon in a single company? The man's intelligence system was awesome. But Hazard regained his composure quickly and smiled again. "Even Wildman, Goody. Even Wildman."

I've outfoxed you this time you oversized tub of guts, Hazard thought with glee. For the past four days he and Corporal Flanagan had worked on Wildman. Flanagan had done Wildman's brass and chrome. Hazard himself had spit shined Wildman's boots, shoes, and patent leather. Together they had arranged his field pack and lockers. They had let Wildman make his own bunk—it was the one thing the worthless bastard was any good at—and they had let him shave himself this morning, but both of them had watched him do it and had made him go over his face until it was red and raw.

"We'll see about that," said Nelson. "By the way, which one is this boy Willow you told me about? Shelby's kid."

"Seventh bunk from the end. Three ahead of Wildman."

"Okay, Clell. You better catch up with the Old Man. Me and my boys won't start until he's all the way through."

When Hazard caught up with the parade he saw that his platoon leader looked more at ease. Colonel Godwin's lone comment through the halfway mark had been "A good-looking bunch, Webber." Godwin had stopped to talk to only one man so far, Specialist Four Shallote. Now he stopped again, in front of Willow. He started with Willow's boots, polished to a dazzling brilliance, then let his eyes slowly inch their way up, along the knife-edge crease in the bloused fatigue trousers, over the lustrous belt buckle, up the precise gig line, to the snow-white triangle of t-shirt at the throat. Finally they rested on Willow's stony face.

"Excellent, excellent," Godwin murmured. "What's your name, son?"

"PFC Willow, sir."

"Where are you from, Willow?"

"Arizona, sir."

"Indian country, eh?"

"Yessir."

"How do you like the Army, Willow?"

"I like it fine, sir."

"Good, good. Ah, what is your first general order, son?"

"Sir, I will guard everything within the limits of my post and quit my post only when properly relieved," Willow said promptly, fighting the almost uncontrollable urge to sing the more familiar ditty: To walk my post from flank to flank and salute all bastards above my rank.

"Excellent, excellent," said Godwin.

The colonel and his tick birds walked quickly to the end of the row, turned, and walked straight back to the head of the platoon. Godwin returned Webber's parting salute with another flick of the swagger stick. "Good show, Webber."

Sergeant-Major Nelson turned to Hazard, "Now it's *my* turn," and he actually rubbed his hands in anticipation.

Nelson's team ran white-gloved fingers over window sills and along the inner edge of bed frames. They tore apart footlockers and wall lockers. They stripped field packs. They checked for dust in the crack under the locking screw on entrenching tools. They looked for moisture inside canteen lips. They checked over each man carefully, even peering inside ears, looking for excessive wax buildup. One sergeant, an E-6, made each man take off his belt and squinted into the buckle casing for opaque traces of dried Brasso.

Nelson had made note of the two Third Platoon men to whom the battalion commander had spoken, and he stopped in front of Specialist Fourth Class Shallote.

"Where you from, soldier?" Nelson asked mockingly.

"Columbus, Ohio, sergeant-major."

"How do you like the Army?" Nelson leered.

"I love the Army, sergeant-major."

"Tell me, son, do you have any sisters back home in Columbus, Ohio?"

"Yes, sergeant-major. One."

"Did you ever fuck her?"

Shallote looked stunned. "N-n-no, of course not, sergeant major. She's my *sister*. She's only thirteen."

Nelson looked disappointed. "That's too bad. Never underestimate the value of early training and proper breaking in, trooper."

The demolition crew worked its way down the rank. Nelson was growing surly. He had been unable to find anything major to get his teeth into. His team's clipboards were empty except for a couple of minor, marginal calls. Hazard was having trouble suppressing a smile at Nelson's discomfort.

The sergeant-major stopped in front of Willow. He looked Willow over carefully, even making the lad tilt his head back so he could look up his nostrils, hoping to find excess hair. The kid was clean. Better than clean. The kid was perfect. Nelson peered intently at Willow's nametag, leaning close, then he snapped his head up sharply, hoping to catch the lad glancing down. Willow was staring straight ahead.

"What's your name, soldier?" Nelson snapped, thinking he might throw the kid off balance. After all, Willow had just seen Nelson stare at his nametag for a full minute.

"PFC Willow, sergeant-major," Willow shot back with no trace of hesitation or the slightest tremor in his voice.

"Where are you from, Willow?"

"Arizona, sergeant-major."

"Isn't that where queers live?"

"Sometimes they do, sergeant-major."

"How do you like the Army?"

"I like it very much, sergeant-major."

"Uh-huh. Willow, I'd like to get your opinion on a matter that's been bothering me for a long time. It's a centuries-old question, Willow, one that has puzzled phi-

losophers since the time of Thales of Miletus. A question
that has confounded monists, dualists, and pluralists alike.
The question is this, Willow: Should Man eat pussy?''

Willow blinked once. ''Yes, sergeant-major, I think he
should.''

''I see. Do *you* eat pussy, Willow?''

''Yes, sergeant-major, I do.''

''I see. And how do you feel about that, Willow?''

''Well, sergeant-major, it's a dark and lonely job''—
Willow paused, then continued—''but *somebody's* got to
do it.''

Nelson stared expressionless at Willow for a moment,
then his craggy face wrinkled up like a prune and he threw
his head back and roared. The entire inspection team was
laughing. Hazard grinned at Willow with pride. Willow
remained stone-faced.

Finally Nelson wiped his eyes with one hand and ran the
other over his glistening skull. Still chuckling, he repeated,
''But *somebody's* got to do it,'' and turned toward the bay
entrance, motioning the rest of his men to follow.

He was halfway out of the bay when he suddenly stopped.
''Wildman.'' He turned around and walked swiftly toward
the end of the row of bunks.

Sergeant-Major Nelson stood in front of Wildman. ''Let's
just see what we got here,'' he said. He looked Wildman
up and down. He ordered Wildman to step out into the
center aisle and walked slowly around him like a suspicious buyer circling a used car. Wildman, short and dumpy
and with the lugubrious face and doleful eyes of a basset
hound, would never look good in a uniform, but there was
no penalty box for body shape on Nelson's clipboard. How
Wildman had ever been accepted into the Old Guard was a
mystery that even the Army's fabled assignment policies
failed to explain. And yet . . . and yet . . . Wildman's
boots sparkled. His brass was polished. His fatigues were

fresh and wrinkle free. His hair was cut. His chin was smooth. His fingernails were pared. The sergeant-major was extremely agitated. He could find nothing wrong.

Nelson personally ransacked Wildman's footlocker, taking out a small custom-made measuring tool to gauge the distance between razor and toothbrush. He then moved to Wildman's wall locker and used the tool again to measure the spaces between hanging uniforms. He savagely threw Wildman's field pack onto the floor and began rummaging through it wildly, checking the E-tool handle for flecks of peeling paint and sniffing the canteen cover for evidence of mildew. Nothing.

With frustration and rage palpable on his pitted face, the sergeant-major bounced a coin off Wildman's bunk. It hit the dust cover with a *poiiing,* arced high into the air, and bounced a few extra times, like a child on a trampoline, before coming to rest. Nelson did not even have the heart left to retrieve it. Then, in a vicious but absentminded gesture, Nelson flipped Wildman's mattress to the floor.

There . . . on top of the springs . . . was the magazine.

Hazard's eyes widened with shock. He could barely focus on the grainy black-and-white picture on the cover: a nude, vacant-faced, washed-out blonde woman with both hands wrapped around the base of an enormous blood-engorged penis that stared her full in the face. The tip of her tongue was but a millimeter away from the clear drop of semen that hung in the monster's eye like a Lucite tear.

Hazard raised a stricken face to Sergeant-Major Thurgood Nelson. Goody was beaming at him in triumph.

6

"Oh Jesus, Clell, you shoulda seen your face when I turned over that bunk. I'd give up two *rockers* before I'da missed that. It was beautiful, bee-yoo-tee-ful."

"I'm so pleased we could find something to amuse the sergeant-major," Hazard said sourly. The two men passed through the post's rear gate and waited for a break in the traffic rushing along the highway. Their destination was a small saloon just on the other side.

"You can tell me now, Clell ol' pal. Did you do his shoes and brass and lockers and all?"

"We did *everything* for that fucker," Hazard spat. "Everything but make his goddamn bunk. It's the only thing he knows how to do, and he muffs it."

"Well, if it's any consolation to you, you had me going right up 'til then. I was teetering on the edge of panic, I don't mind admitting. You damn near did it."

"Gee, thanks, Goody. That sure means a lot, coming from a grizzled old veteran like you."

"Now, now. No call for bitterness, Clell ol' buddy. Some days you eat the bear, some days the bear eats you." Nelson was practically giggling.

They crossed the road, walked across the parking lot of a small shopping center—unconsciously in step—and pushed into the narrow, dark tavern. The proprietor, a retired E-8, yelled a greeting from behind the bar and automatically turned to draw a couple of draft beers. Hazard and Nelson picked up the beers at the bar, then walked back to their usual booth, the last in the single line against the wall, and plopped down on the torn Naughahyde. Both men were tired.

"Did you remember to ask that kid Willow to join us?" asked Nelson.

"Yup. He's coming as soon as he finishes putting his gear away. He's probably shitting his pants and wondering how long he's going to have to serve at Leavenworth."

"I hope you don't mind, Clell. I just wanted to meet the kid, proper like. Christ, I met his old man in W-W Two at Saint Lo. It's hard to believe. Besides, he was pretty damn good in there today." Goody laughed and said, " 'But *somebody's* got to do it.' "

"Nah, I don't mind," laughed Hazard. "I promised the kid I'd treat him to a beer anyhow. We got off to kind of a bad start. He wants me to tell him all about Vietnam."

"Oooo shit. Ah, you can't blame him, Clell. Think back to when you were his age and on your way to France and bugging all the oldtimers to tell you what combat was like. You remember, back when Christ was a corporal."

"Yeah, I guess so. But what can you tell them, Goody? How do you describe those times when everything in the world is reduced to two kinds of things, and two only: things that provide cover and things that don't?"

Nelson shrugged and nodded and hollered to the bartender: "HEY, ZEKE, two more over here, chop-chop. QUICK-TIME, HARCH!" Zeke brought the beers, chatted for a moment about the next day's game between the Redskins and Browns, and scuttled back to the bar when another group of soldiers came in.

"Okay, Goody, stalling time is over," said Hazard. "How'd we do?"

"Why, Clell," Nelson said in a shocked voice. "You know that's confidential information. Besides, the final tallys aren't finished yet."

"But you know, Goody. You always know. Tell me, and I buy the beer."

"All of it?"

"All of it."

"For the rest of the evening?"

"For the rest of the evening."

"For as long as that might be?"

"Yes, goddammit. Tell me."

"Weeell, I did make a few inquiries and did a little quick figuring, and my preliminary findings would suggest that Delta will squeak past Honor Guard by a few points. We do Bravo on Monday, but they're so fucked up over there they could have a year to get ready and still couldn't beat you. It'll be between them and Alpha for last place."

"So Wildman didn't sink us," Hazard said with wonder.

"Nah. Even with Wildman, your platoon came out tops in the company. Unfortunately there's only so many points I could take off for unauthorized items in the bunk. Lucky for you there's no grading system for types of unauthorized items. Did you see that goddamn fist book? When we got it back to HQ, we had quite a look. There was a picture in there of a woman with a *pig,* for chrissakes. Actually, it was kinda funny. The woman and this pig are layin' there in the bed, and the pig's got this weird-looking corkscrew pecker and somebody had put a cigarette in the pig's mouth. That Wildman is one sick boy."

"That Wildman's gonna be on Monday morning's list of drop jobs," growled Hazard. "Shit, to be honest, there isn't a hell of a lot I can do to him. He's already pulling every shit detail we got. Maybe I should turn him over to the Slasher for a little of Boudin's unique brand of company punishment.''

''I've heard me some talk about Boudin's unique brand of company punishment,'' said Nelson. ''Does he really take guys out into the square and beat shit out of them?''

''Yup.''

''If I catch him at it, his ass is grass.''

''If anyone can turn the Slasher's ass into grass, it's probably you, Goody,'' Hazard said, ''but to tell the truth it's not such a bad system. Top gives the offender a choice: the usual company-level punishment, an Article 15, or three minutes of bare fists with him. You'd be surprised how many guys go for the bare fists. First of all, it keeps a man's record clean. I'm sure you've noticed that Delta has fewer Article 15s than any other company in the battalion. Then there's the fact that it's all over quickly, hardly ever lasting more than one or two punches, while an Article 15 means the poor bastard is mopping floors and pulling KP and restricted to barracks for weeks. This way, the poor fuck wakes up five minutes later and it's all over. He's been asleep most of the time. The Slasher don't hold no grudges. His left hook wipes the slate clean. And last of all, every guy who goes out there with him has this thought that maybe, just maybe, he can get in a lucky punch and put out the Slasher's lights. It's never happened, but who knows. . . .''

''Well, it's still against regs.''

Hazard laughed. ''Right, and we know what a champion of Army regulations the sergeant-major is.''

Nelson grinned back. ''Well, I guess it is Oooold Army to handle it that way. And we all know the Oooooold Army was the best Army.''

The front door opened and Willow walked into the saloon, searching for them in the gloom. Hazard leaned partway out of the back booth and waved. The boy approached stiffly. "Evening, sergeant-major. Evening, platoon sergeant," he said uncertainly. "Uh, you wanted to see me?"

"Hell, Willow, we don't want to see you," Hazard said with a smile, "we want to buy you a beer. Sit down and relax." Hazard slid over on the seat and Willow took off his fatigue cap and sat. The boy jumped when Nelson boomed, "HEY, ZEKE, DRAW THREE."

Hazard formally introduced Nelson and Willow, then added, "The sergeant-major also knows your father, from World War Two days." Willow took Nelson's offered hand as if he expected to find a practical joker's buzzer in it.

"You looked real good today, Willow," said Nelson. "You were the sharpest looking trooper I've seen all week, and that includes those prima donna geeks in Honor Guard Company. Congratulations."

"Thank you, sergeant-major."

"A simple sarge will do," Nelson said with a grin. "We don't want your tongue to get tired. Gotta save it for more important things, don't we? 'Because *somebody's* got to do it.' " Willow laughed and started to relax.

Hazard said to Nelson, "Willow's been so sharp he's driving Boudin crazy. For some reason the first sergeant has a hard-on for Willow. He's stuck him with guard duty three times in the last week, but the kid here hasn't had to pull the duty once. He takes point every time."

"I've been meaning to ask you about that, sarge," said Willow. "Is that something unique to the Old Guard? Excusing the most presentable man on guard mount, the point, from duty?"

"Nope. It's done most places. The idea is to mount one more man than necessary and use the point-man system to inspire everybody to look as good as possible. Works pretty good, too."

"I've just been lucky so far," Willow said.

"Sure . . . if you think it's lucky to piss off the top sergeant. If you find yourself getting too many shit details, tell me about it and I'll have a little chat with Top. Tell me, what did you do to get him on your back?"

"Told him I wanted to go to OCS and become an officer."

Hazard and Nelson laughed. "That'll do it," said Nelson. "The Slasher has let it be known he ain't too fond of officers."

"Slap me down if I'm out of line," said Willow, "but is the first sergeant completely sane?" Hazard and Nelson laughed again. "You're not supposed to be completely sane if you're a first sergeant," Hazard said. "And by the time you get to be a sergeant-major like Goody here, it's actually against regs to be even slightly sane." The two noncoms laughed heartily at this. Willow restricted himself to an uncertain smile, unsure of how to react to the bantering. He felt the way he did whenever he heard one black man call another *nigger*. They might laugh and joke that way, but he knew that if he tried to join in, he'd end up getting cut three ways: long, deep, and often.

"I was an officer once," mused Nelson. "I got a battlefield commission in '44, but soon as the war ended, I was bumped back to the ranks. It came as a great relief to be back among a better class of people."

Willow said, "I realize that the Army could get along much better without its officer corps than its NCOs, but I'd still like to take it as far as I can."

"Why not?" Nelson agreed. "You got any college?"

"Two years."

"Hell, with two years of higher learning and Clell here for a platoon sergeant, you can't miss. Sergeant Hazard is the second best noncom in the United States Army. Modesty prevents me from telling you who's number one."

"Actually, the sergeant-major wanted to go to West Point as a young man," Hazard told Willow with mock earnestness. "But they've got some strict entrance requirements. You can't have a horse, a moustache, or a wife. He was okay there. Height, weight, and brains were no problem either, at least not then. But they also have this rule against extreme ugliness. Disqualified him on the spot."

Willow knew there actually was such a rule at the Military Academy. He also knew Sergeant-Major Nelson could not have passed it. He couldn't help it. He laughed. Lightning did not strike him dead.

This easy, joking Hazard was a far different man than the one he had met on his first day in the company, Willow thought. He wondered if he could bring up the subject of Vietnam again without having his head taken off.

As if his platoon sergeant had read his mind, Willow heard Hazard say, "Willow wants to go to Vietnam, Goody. He feels that an infantryman's place in time of war is up at the front."

"There ain't no front in Vietnam."

"That's what Sergeant Hazard said," Willow said with a sheepish grin.

Nelson ran a hand over his bald dome. "It's a funny little war, kid," he said. "Clell and I saw it together in the early stages, and he was over there again just about a year ago. A lot has happened lately, and I'm sure things have changed some, but we both saw enough to make us think twice about this one."

"Like what?" Willow asked.

"Lots of things, some little, some not so little," said Hazard. "To begin with, I'm not so sure we're supporting the right side. You can't believe how fucked up the South Slopes are. The corruption in the government is mind boggling, but you expect that. What you don't expect is the same kind of shit in the army, the Arvin. The troops ain't all that bad, but the majority of their officers are shit. They get assignments and promotions through family connections, not ability. And when you ask an officer what he does for a living, he don't say soldiering, he says he's a businessman. He's not lying, either. When an Arvin officer reaches the rank of major, he's half soldier, half entrepeneur. By the time he's a colonel, he's *all* entrepreneur. We give them artillery shells and he sells them on the black market, knowing full well they'll get resold or given to the VC and will be killing his own men a month later. He sells his men's medical supplies, his weapons, and even the poor fuckers' food. He fails to report his casualties because it makes him look better to his superiors in Saigon and because it allows him to continue to draw the dead's pay and put it in his pocket. The result of that is that we sit there with an Arvin battalion supposedly covering our flank and it's only got two hundred men instead of the eight hundred it says it has on paper.''

"Then there's the other side," said Nelson. "Jesus, Willow, you never seen such infantry. They're slicker'n snot on a door knob. They are disciplined, they are tough, and they know their trade. They can march thirty miles a day every day for a week through jungle you wouldn't believe, mount an attack, and march back again. Our gooks need a fuckin' jeep to get them from tent flap to piss tube. Ol' Chuck had that war won until we stepped in.''

"They may still win it; it's just gonna take them longer now," said Hazard.

"You can't really believe that," Willow said with an arched eyebrow. "They don't have a chance against our firepower and technology. I saw a picture in a magazine a few months ago showing one of our choppers coming back from a mission with arrows stuck in it. How can you beat helicopter gunships with bows and arrows?''

"How can you beat an enemy who will fight a helicopter gunship with a bow and arrow?" countered Hazard.

"The Rooshians and the Chinese are pouring stuff into North Vietnam, and it ain't bows and arrows," said Nelson.

"Besides," said Hazard, "technology don't mean shit in a guerrilla war. Only a few years ago, when Kennedy was president and the Special Forces was being built up, everybody at the Infantry School and the War College was running around quoting Mao and Che and Ho Chi Minh. They seem to have forgotten everything they read."

"I've read them," Willow said. "But none of them ever had to wage war against a country with the kind of resources this one has."

"It's not a matter of resources, but how you use them," said Hazard. "That was a nice speech you gave the other day about the role of the infantryman, but you don't really seem to believe it. You're right about the Infantry, Willow, she *is* the Queen of Battle. You win wars with men on the ground rooting the bastards out. But that's not the way we're fighting this one. We're relying too heavily on that technology you're so proud of. Our infantry tactics seem to consist of making contact with the enemy, then backing off and calling in ordnance—tac air and arty. We're not going in and rooting them out."

"Why not expend ordnance instead of lives?" Willow demanded.

"Because it's not working," Hazard said softly. "We spend a million bucks worth of ordnance to blow some hilltop to smithereens, then can't find a single body to show for it."

"It's a concession to politics," interjected Nelson. "We want to keep casualties down because sentiment against this war is growing."

"That sentiment would be stopped dead in its tracks if we won it quickly," said Willow.

"But we ain't gonna win it quickly," countered Hazard. "The NVA and the VC aren't quitters; they're fighters. They didn't quit against the Chinese or the Japs or the French, all of whom were blessed with superior technology, and they ain't gonna quit against us. Every time I hear some intellectual use the phrase 'the peace-loving people of Vietnam' I want to puke. I've never seen a more bellicose race. They've been fighting somebody for a thousand years, and they like it. The reason they're so damn good is because of all the practice they've had."

"Okay, what would you do if you were Westmoreland?" Willow asked Hazard with a smirk.

"I'd recommend we get the fuck out, because we got nothing to gain and everything to lose. That probably wouldn't work, because LBJ would just get himself another boy, so I'd change strategy and tactics. I'd withhold aid until the Arvin was revamped. Officers and NCOs would be assigned and promoted strictly on merit, like the bad guys do it. The South Slopes could do great things if properly trained and led—after all, they're the same stock the other side draws its people from. Then I'd end this reliance on air and arty. Use it when you should, but not to dig five dinks out of a clump of bushes. You do that with infantry. On the American side, I'd put an immediate screeching halt to this policy of one-year tours."

Goody Nelson banged his fist on the table. "Yeah. Fuckin' -A."

"Why?" asked Willow, a condescending smile still on his face.

"Me and your father hit Omaha Beach on June 6, 1944, and we didn't come off the line until we occupied Berlin," said Hazard. "We landed at Inchon on September 5, 1950, and didn't come home until autumn of '53. Dammit, Willow, you fight until you win the thing or lose it or come home in a plastic bag. The minute you tell a man that all he's got to serve is three hundred sixty-five days, he forgets all about busting his nut to finish the thing off so he can go home. He *knows* when he's going home. He's got only one thing on his mind—survive three hundred sixty-five days—and he don't give a shit about anything else. And you can't really blame him. That policy sets up a false objective.''

"Fuckin'-A,'' boomed Nelson, who was getting drunk while Hazard did all the talking.

"That's what it will take, then, to keep South Vietnam from going Communist?'' Willow asked.

"That's what it will take for us not to lose this goddamn war,'' snapped Hazard. "I don't give a rat's ass whether South Vietnam goes Communist or not. Ho was probably right in thinking that his brand of communism was what the country needed. Who cares? We're fighting a 1960s war for 1950s reasons. Let the dinks drive the Russkies crazy for a while instead of us. I don't give a dab of wombat shit about what's good for Vietnam. To be totally honest, I don't even really care about what's good for the U. S. of A.''

"Do you care about anything?'' Willow asked hotly.

"Yeah,'' Hazard said quietly. "I care a lot about what's good for the United States Army. It's important for the *Army* that we not lose. If we do, the gulf between the Army and civilian America, already much too wide, is gonna get wider. We'll stop attracting the brighter, better motivated kids—kids like you. Then the hunt for scapegoats will begin, and factions within the services will start fighting among themselves, trying to assess the blame for losing the first war this country ever lost. What's worse, they'll start tinkering with the institution in their search for a quick fix. We're already starting to see signs of it with the speeding up of the cycles at the NCO Academy, OCS, and the Infantry School. They're becoming assembly lines to produce cogs for the machine, and quality control is goin' down the tube. Shit, kids are now makin' buck sergeant in two years when it took me nine. Shake-'n-bake noncoms and officers may fill the holes in the line in Nam, but it's fuckin' up the Army, *my* Army.''

Nelson cut in. ''The Pentagon sees Nam as a new kind of war for the Army, Willow, and every time those bastards get their teeth into a new idea, they worry it like a dog does a bone and start makin' dumbshit changes. After W-W Two those assholes decided the next war would be nuclear, so they adopted the Pentomic organization plan and did away with the old regimental system. Instead of havin' three regiments of three battalions of five companies each in a division, they went to five battle groups of four companies each. That move damn near killed us oldtimers. Goddammit, a regiment meant something! A man took pride in his regiment, was loyal to it, and spent his whole career in one unit. Who in the fuck can get excited about belonging to a 'battle group'? You take pride out of a service career and you suck the marrow right out of its bones. Why else does a man stay in? It ain't the money or the prestige. And having a nuclear arsenal didn't change shit in the way we fight. What good is it doing us in Nam, where the politicians won't let us obliterate the North?''

''There are no new ideas in war,'' said Hazard. ''Spilled guts look and smell the same whether they were spilled by a smart bomb or a broad axe. And kids your age are always going to have to do it on the ground, as infantry. You just have to adjust your small-unit tactics to meet the situation. That's all a guerrilla war requires. We found that out in 1776 when we put musketeers behind stone walls and up trees, Indian style, while the Brits were still doing that front-rank-kneel shit.''

No one spoke for a moment and then Willow said to

Hazard, "We haven't lost yet, sarge. Aren't you overstating the case a little?"

"Maybe so, Willow. I hope so. But I'm worried. Because if we don't win this war, especially after that tie game we played in Korea, there's gonna be hell to pay throughout the ranks."

Goody Nelson intoned solemnly: ". . . should we leave our weary bones to bleach on the tracts of the desert in vain, then beware the anger of the Legions."

Willow grinned and said, "Marcus Flavinius, Centurion of the Second, Cohort of the Augusta Legion, S-P-Q-R."

Nelson spewed a mouthful of beer over the table and stared slack-jawed at Willow. "You know that?" He turned to Hazard in amazement. "I'll be goddamned. There may be hope for us all yet."

"I've read a little," Willow said with a shrug.

"Von Clauswitz, of course," said Nelson.

"Of course," Willow replied with the haughty air of a professor lecturing a classroom of numbskulls. "But one must be extremely careful. A hasty reading of Von Clauswitz can lead to misinterpretation. Such superficial study doomed the French high command during World War One. Today, the Communist bloc countries are prone to the same mistake." It was the classic West Point textbook response, and Willow grinned inwardly.

"Henri Jomini?" Nelson asked with suspicion.

Willow casually studied his fingernails and said, "We must give Jomini credit for being the first to try to determine the underlying principles which govern warfare." Willow was in his element. He knew this stuff like some boys his age knew baseball trivia.

Nelson, secure in the knowledge that Willow had invaded their turf, his and Hazard's, turned to Hazard and asked, "What do you think, Clell? Shall we see if this punk is bluffing?"

"Let's," snapped Hazard. He turned to Willow. "What's the best account of small-unit tactics and leadership?"

"Well, it depends on your personal tastes," Willow began, faking a hedge and noting the grin grow on Hazard's face, "but you're probably thinking of one or two books. It would be either *The Attack and Defense of Little Round Top* by Norton, or *Infantry Attacks* by Rommel."

"Rommel," Hazard muttered darkly.

"The best book on the Spanish-American War?" demanded Nelson.

"Sargent's *The Campaign of Santiago de Cuba*."

"The best book on a single campaign of the Civil War?" fired Hazard.

"*The Campaign of Chancellorsville*. I think it was Bellow . . . or Bigelow."

"Bigelow," grumbled Hazard.

"According to the British historian JFC Fuller, what was it that made Lee a better general than Grant?" Nelson asked with a sly smile.

"According to Fuller," said Willow, smiling back sweetly, "Grant was far superior to Lee."

"Who wrote *The Art of War*?"

"Sun Tzu."

"*Military Institutions?*"

"Vegetius."

"*Reveries on the Art of War?*"

"Saxe."

"He'll never get this one," cackled Hazard. "I'm thinking of something written before . . . ah, let's say 1700. Very influential on early American military theory. And you can't repeat any author or book already mentioned."

"It's all highly subjective, of course," mused Willow, "but I'd bet you're thinking of *The Instructions of Frederick the Great for His Generals*."

Hazard said nothing, just stared into his beer glass with disgust.

"Okay, kid, last question," said Nelson. "Who was the most brilliant military thinker of the nineteenth century . . ."

"Nap—"

". . . after Napoleon."

"Easy. Moltke. The uncle, not the nephew."

"One more, one more," said Nelson. "Who is the most brilliant military thinker today?"

"Easy again. Sergeant–Major Thurgood Nelson."

"The kid's a fuckin' genius," shrugged Nelson. "HEY, ZEKE, DRAW THREE."

7

Hazard awoke feeling terrible and wonderful. The source of the terrible was easy enough to find. He and Nelson and Willow had sat in Zeke's until well past midnight, talking and drinking and even, he shuddered at the memory, singing.

There had been a near fist fight when they had been approached by a drunk and angry NCO from Honor Guard Company who had used his sources at battalion HQ to learn that Delta had indeed edged Honor Guard in the command inspection. Goody Nelson had put an end to the brewing fracas simply by standing up and reminding the man that the top of his head was on an even plane with the sergeant-major's solar plexus. They had ended up buying the man a beer and singing, joined by the other Old Guardsmen in the place, the unit's own macabre version of ''As the Caissons Go Rolling Along,'' a song full of graves and ghosts. That had led to a medley of such popular paratrooper tunes as ''Blood upon the Risers,'' which, in turn, led to an attempt to teach young Willow how to do a proper PLF, a parachute landing fall. On his first try, Willow had shown the aptitude of a born natural. On the second attempt, Willow had passed out while standing on the table, apparently unable to handle the rarified air up there. Instead of landing with feet together, breaking at the ankles and knees and rolling onto his hip, he had landed square on his head, breaking at the neck and rolling onto his back. Fortunately, he had been far too loose to kill himself. Goody Nelson had deposited the boy's limp body on his bunk at Delta Company, carrying Willow effortlessly over his shoulder like a duffel bag while Hazard directed traffic with a flourish on the four-lane highway separating post and pub.

The years of discipline and physical conditioning paid off, and Hazard was able to get his feet onto the floor and shuffle like an old man into the bathroom for a shower and a shave with trembling hands. He could neither pinpoint nor account for the incongruous feeling of euphoria that shadowed his pain. When he had toweled himself off, he went into the kitchen to mix himself a bloody mary to settle his jangled nerves. He was just sitting down with the drink, looking at the glass with the same wariness he would a stray cat, wondering if he would get a purr or a claw across the nose for his trouble, when suddenly he remembered: Today was the day he was taking Samantha Huff to the football game.

Hazard knocked back the drink in a single gulp and reached for the telephone. The sound of her hello, full of the huskiness that envelopes the first word of the day, was like a soothing hand on his brow. His headache vanished.

"Good morning. It's Clell. Can you be ready to go by noon?"

"Good morning. Are you sure you're feeling up to it?"

"Certainly. Why do you ask?"

"I was just sure you would call to cancel."

"Why would I want to do that?" Hazard asked with exasperation.

"Well, after last night, you must be feeling awful."

A cold hand grabbed Hazard's heart. "Last night? What do you mean?"

"I heard you come in around two A.M. The whole building heard you come in. You were *careening* down the hall."

"I wasn't," Hazard said without conviction.

"You were. Not only that, you sang for us."

"I didn't," Hazard said with dread.

"You did. Want proof?" She began to sing to the tune of "The Battle Hymn of the Republic."

> There was blood upon the risers,
> There was blood upon the chute;
> Intestines were a-danglin'
> From his paratrooper's boot. . . .

"No, no," gurgled Hazard.

"But there's more," said Samantha, starting to sing again.

> Gory, Gory, what a helluva way to die,
> Gory, Gory, what a helluva way to die. . . .

"Please," Hazard begged.

"You don't like that song anymore? How about this one?"

> I wanna be an Airborne Ranger
> I wanna live a life of danger. . . .

"Sam—"

"And then I wrote—"

"Sam, please!"

"And then I wrote . . ."

> The girl that I marry will have to be
> Airborne, Ranger, and U.D.T. . . . .

"I surrender."

Samantha relented. "What in the world is a riser?" she laughed. "Or U.D.T.? Don't answer. Go back to bed and get some sleep. I'll be ready at noon. By the way, if you happen to meet Mr. or Mrs. Slocum in the corridor, try to be especially nice to them."

"What for?"

"Well, they were coming home from a party or something when you came home last night. Apparently Mr. Slocum said hello and you yelled *'What?'* at the top of your lungs. He said hello again, loudly enough for me to hear it through the walls. And you screamed back—and I'll quote you directly—DAMMIT, MAN, SPEAK UP! SOUND OFF LIKE YOU GOT A PAIR."

"Argghh."

"A pair of what, Clell?"

"Arrrggghhh."

"Bye," Samantha said sweetly. As she hung up, Hazard could hear her singing, "There was blood upon the risers, there was blood upon the chute. . . ."

The seats were the best he could get—at the edge of the end zone, but down close to the field. It was a sparkling day, sunny and clear and cold enough for a man to blow steam each time he opened his mouth.

"Which one is me?" Samantha was excited. Her cheeks were flushed, and she held tightly to Hazard's arm, running her eyes up, down, and around the stadium. She had never been to a football game in her life.

"Number seventy," Hazard said, pointing. "There he is over there, doing calisthenics with the Redskin defense."

She raised her binoculars and played with the dials.

"Ooo, he's big. But you're right, he doesn't look at all like me."

"Samantha, do you know anything at all about how this game is played?"

"Actually, yes, quite a bit. I lied. I once dated a man who watched two games a week on television, from August through January. He talked about nothing but football. He was more interested in football than he was me. I've just never been to a game in person before."

"Well, if you have any questions, just ask."

"I know what a *red dog* is," she announced proudly.

"Terrific."

"I know what a *buttonhook* is."

"Great."

"I know what a *safety blitz* is."

"Wonderful. Uh, look, Sam, why don't you just tell me what you don't know."

She ignored him and looked around some more. "It's all so . . . so much better in person than on TV," she said. "The size of it all, and the noise and the colors. I think I'm going to like this. Oooh, Clell, one is supposed to drink beer at a football game. Out of a paper cup. I want a beer, Clell. A beer in a paper cup. Please, Clell."

"Jesus," Hazard groaned with false irritation as he got up.

He returned with two beers in paper cups and two hot dogs. "You forgot hot dogs. One is supposed to eat hot dogs at a football game, too."

She laughed and took one, bit into it, and exclaimed, "These are wonderful! Why are these wonderful, Clell? I don't even like hot dogs."

Hazard smiled and shook his head. "All food tastes better outdoors. Now be quiet. You're driving me crazy."

They stood for the national anthem and Samantha, hand over her heart like a good citizen, whispered, " 'The Star

Spangled Banner' sounds better outdoors, too.'' She giggled when she said it.

As the teams lined up for the kickoff, Hazard told
Samantha, ''You are about to witness a classic confrontation.
Keep your eye on Number Thirty-two for Cleveland. That's
Jimmy Brown, the greatest running back in the history of
the game. It's Huff's job to stop him. He's going to be
keying on Brown on every play, whether Brown's got the
ball or not. Wherever Brown lines up, Huff will line up
opposite. Those two have been doing this for several
seasons now. It's one of the great feuds in football. Nobody can stop Brown altogether, but Huff does as good a
job as anyone.'' Samantha nodded eagerly, signaling that
she understood.

When Washington's kicker hit the ball to start the game,
Samantha jumped up and down and yelled, ''YEAAAAA.''
Hazard did not see the runback which, judging from the
crowd noise, was thoroughly spectacular. He was watching Samantha and the pure joy she was taking from the
scene. She was grinning and biting on her lower lip with
teeth as perfect as pearls. She threw him a quick glance
with eyes that cracked like those of a gypsy flamenco
dancer. Hazard fell in love. Right then and there.

Clell Hazard was a hardbitten man in many ways, a man
with few illusions. But he was also a man of the 1940s, of
a generation that truly and wholeheartedly believed in
love—every smarmy bit of it. He was not sanguine about
being in love with Samantha Huff. He doubted that very
much could come of it, given a woman like her and a man
like him and the vast chasms of social grace, education,
and class that would have to be jumped. But in love he
was, and he could no more stop it from happening to him
than that psychic stomach of his could digest nails.

By half-time Hazard had a sore right arm and a sore
right ear. Every time Sam Huff made a tackle—and he

made a great many in the course of the afternoon—Samantha Huff screamed into Hazard's ear and punched him excitedly on the shoulder. "Jesus, Sam," he cried after Huff made a particularly bone-jarring tackle on Brown at the eleven-yard line, stopping a Cleveland drive. "If the hitting down there is half as hard as the hitting up here, somebody's going to get killed."

By the end of the game Samantha was as hoarse as a drill instructor, and Hazard was half deaf and crippled.

The Washington Redskins won the game by a single point. Jimmy Brown and Clell Hazard fought valiantly, but both, in the end, were simply overwhelmed by Sam Huff.

Hazard had chosen a small rustic restaurant in rural Maryland for supper. It was hidden away down a dusty lane outside Claggettsville near the Patuxent River and had a local reputation for good, honest food. He had never eaten there, but he had once sold the cook a string of skillet-sized trout taken from the river in the park and had marked it in his mind as a place to try. Hazard had briefly entertained the notion of impressing Samantha with a fancy French restaurant in Washington but had discarded the idea for a couple of reasons: He could not afford it, and he was not fond of Washington, a city that represented to him manipulation and deceit.

The walls of the restaurant were chinked logs, and they were hung with glassy-eyed deer heads and mounted trout. A bearskin had been nailed up behind the cash register near the entrance. The place reminded him of every restaurant he had ever seen in Montana, and that, more than anything else, had lured him back. The tables, no more than a handful, were scattered around a large, open flagstone fireplace, and a wood fire burned merrily. Only one other pair of diners was in evidence.

He and Samantha took a table next to a large picture window that overlooked a long expanse of lawn and the boundary of the state park. A waiter was with them instantly and they ordered drinks: Wild Turkey and water for Hazard; a dry martini with a twist for Samantha. They ordered mirror meals: smoked trout—Hazard's recommendation—tossed salad, baked potatoes, and T-bones, hers medium rare, his *bleu*.

When the waiter had gone, Hazard said, "Sam, I hope you don't mind coming all the way out here, but I don't much like going into Washington unless I have to. It's a pretty enough town to look at, but I always feel out of place. It's full of people preoccupied with a subject that doesn't interest me in the slightest."

"Politics?" Samantha asked, somewhat surprised. "You may find it boring, Clell, but you have to admit it's pretty important."

"Very important," Hazard conceded. "I guess I didn't express myself very well. What I mean is that the subject gets me riled. I cannot abide politicians. They are people in a profession making decisions that end up, often as not, in getting people in my profession killed. They make those decisions based on considerations of money or power or getting a cheap vote, and the last thing on their list, if it's on there at all, is the eighteen-year-old Iowa farm boy who's gonna get greased in some damn country he couldn't find on a map when he was seventeen."

"I don't mind coming here at all," Samantha said hastily, nudging the conversation back toward safer ground. "It was a nice drive and this place is, um, unusual. Really, I don't much like Washington either. It's supposed to be a southern city, at least that's what everyone says, but it doesn't strike me that way at all. The south is a place that appeals to the senses, and Washington is the most unsensuous place I've ever seen. It's all done with the mind there."

Hazard smiled. "You mean the mouth. Why did you come up here, then?"

Samantha shrugged. "The *Post* is a good paper. It was quite a coup for my career to land a job with them. It's like being called up to the majors from a minor league farm club."

Hazard laughed. "You little sneak. You know a lot about sports, don't you?"

She smiled. "Every woman knows more about sports than she lets on. The way to a man's heart is not through his stomach; it's through the box scores."

"So you wanted to play in the big leagues, eh?"

"That was part of it. The other part was to get away from . . . um . . . a sticky personal situation."

"What was that?"

"The breakup of my marriage."

"Oh." He had not known that she had been married, but the news did not really surprise him. "Want to talk about it?" he asked after a moment.

"No."

"Okey-doke."

The drinks came. Hazard lifted his and said, "Here's to us and those like us."

Samantha smiled, touched glasses, and said, "Damn few."

It was still early, just after six o'clock, but outside, darkness dropped with surprising suddenness. The waiter came back to light the candle on their table.

"Betty Lou called me yesterday," Samantha said. "We had lunch. I really like her."

"Good," said Hazard.

"I put Betty Lou through the third degree about you. I

did everything but shine a light in her face and pull her fingernails one by one.''

''Did she break?''

''Yes. She had no choice. She still has family living in my country, behind the grits curtain.''

Hazard smiled. ''We give them cyanide capsules for times like that, but I guess you can't really expect anyone to take one. So, what secrets did she spill?''

''That you were married and that you were divorced about three years ago.''

''That's true.''

''That you have a son in college.''

''That's true.''

''That you've been, uh, lonely since your divorce.''

''That's true.''

''That there is no woman in your life at the present time.''

''That's not true. Not anymore.''

There it was again—that blush, visible even in the dim candlelight. Samantha opened her mouth to say something, then closed it, opened it again, and closed it again. She looked like a feeding guppy. The waiter, bringing the smoked trout, saved her. Hazard helped him. He ordered a half bottle of chablis to go with the fish and asked that a bottle of claret be opened, decanted, and held until the steaks arrived. Then the chef joined the rescue party. Coming out to confer with the waiter, he recognized Hazard and came over. ''When you goin' ta bring me some more of them trout?'' he asked Hazard. ''Them there on your plates are the last I got.''

''I haven't been fishing since the last time I was up here,'' Hazard replied. ''Reckon it's all over until next spring.''

The cook was a lanky country man with bad teeth and large, clean hands. ''You leave me your name and phone number, and I'll give ya a call when they do the first stocking. You only fish flies, if I recollect right?'' Hazard nodded and the man went on. ''They'll be hittin Hare's Ear nymphs fished deep and maybe a size eighteen Adams or Light Cahill on top during them early hatches. You should be able to do some good. Course, I fish worms myself.''

''The calling card of the Philistine,'' Hazard said with a grin. ''I'm not sure I want you touching our steaks.''

''Them steaks for you two? I'll jist get on back and make sure they're extra big and extra good. They ain't just the way you like 'em, you send 'em on back to me. Nice talkin to ya. Evenin', lady.'' He left through a swinging door.

''This is delicious,'' Samantha said, sampling the fish. ''Did you catch these, Clell?''

''Not those exactly. I was up here a few months ago and brought the cook some like them.''

''Is fishing your hobby?''

''Trout fishing is. The thing about trout is their impeccable taste. I don't just mean on the tongue, I mean they have class. Trout won't live in ugly places. They've got to have clear, bright, moving waters and you only find that in nice country, country with mountains and trees in it. Besides, the only way a man can stand in the middle of a river without cutting the fool is to have a fishing rod in his hands. Most of all, nothing takes your mind away like fishing. Some Spaniard named Ortega called the blood sports 'a vacation from the human condition.' ''

Samantha smiled. ''Oh he did, did he?''

Hazard smiled back. ''Lord Byron called fishing 'a solitary vice.' ''

''Lord Byron yet,'' Samantha said with a laugh. ''Who are these guys? Fishing buddies of yours?''

''Okay, okay. What I'm trying to say is that when you

are on the stream all your problems, in work or at home or whatever, are wiped away and replaced by a whole new set of problems, more enjoyable problems of natural science. Like reading the water for the holding pockets and determining which insects are on the water and which one of them the fish are feeding on that day and how best to match the hatch and present the artificial. It's totally absorbing.''

"Do you have all that many problems to get away from?'' Samantha asked with a smile.

"No more than anyone else, I reckon. Why?''

"Just wondering if you were trying to change the subject.''

"What subject?''

"The one we were about to discuss when we got off onto fishing, your marriage. Do you want to talk about it?''

Hazard shrugged. "There ain't a lot to talk about. It's the old, classic story: Boy meets girl. Boy gets girl. Boy joins Army. Boy loses girl.''

"I don't know that story. Tell me.''

Hazard shrugged again. "It's not very interesting.''

"Tell me anyway.''

He sighed. "Alright. Linda and I started going together in high school. Everybody figured we'd get married. Even I thought so, I guess. When you went with a girl for more than a year in the thirties, you damn near had to get married. The summer we graduated I spent working for one of the local outfitters, guiding his fishing clients on the Missouri River. It didn't hardly pay anything at all, certainly not enough to start married life on, but I sure did love the life. I'd take the party out every morning in the boat, and we'd fish til the light was gone. The Missouri was so big you had to float-fish it, and—''

"You just hold it right there, Clell Hazard,'' Samantha

broke in, her smile now accented by a squint of suspicion. "You wouldn't by any chance be trying to change the subject back to fishing again, would you?"

Hazard laughed. "No ma'am, I wouldn't dream of it. So where was I? Oh, yes. Well, it didn't pay anything, but there weren't any other jobs to be had in those days. What Linda wanted was to get married and to get out of Montana; I ain't sure in which order. She wanted to travel and see a bit of the world. Talked about it constantly. Montana is still pretty far back in the woods, but you can't imagine how isolated it seemed back at the tail end of the Great Depression. Anyway, she kept picking at me and picking at me until I finally came up with a way to grant both her heart's desires. As it turned out, I don't think it was exactly what she had in mind."

"The Army?"

"The Army."

"She didn't like it?" Samantha asked.

"Nope. She hated it right off the bat. And just about as much as I grew to like it. I guess you couldn't blame her. It was rugged right from the start. A hell of a way to start a marriage. She followed me to training camp, but I wasn't allowed off base until it was over. For weeks she lived in a tar paper shack in a whole cluster of tar paper shacks just outside the gate. She was all by herself and in some pretty rough company. All kinds of losers were joining up in those days to get away from the hard times, and the kind of women they dragged around with them were not the wholesome, outdoorsy types Linda was used to."

Samantha made a grimace of sympathy. "Go on," she prodded.

"Well, our first post was another camp just like that one. We were together, but that was about all you could say for it. We lived in a real dump. We were both homesick as hell, but Linda more than me. I was discovering that I liked soldiering and that I was good at it. Linda didn't have anything like that to hold on to. She missed Montana, she missed her old friends, she missed her old life. Then all of a sudden we were at war and the inevitable happened. I got shipped overseas. That got Linda back to Montana, because she waited it out with her folks in Helena, but I was gone three long years, and that sure didn't help the marriage any. We started growing apart right from the beginning.''

"How was it when you got back?'' Samantha asked.

Hazard shrugged. "More of the same. We had Mackie and were just really starting to settle down—or what passes for settling down in the Army, moving every couple of years from one dump to another—when the Korean thing came along. I was gone for nearly another three years. Her folks and my folks were gone by then, and Linda decided to wait it out right where she was, which was Columbus, Georgia, just outside Fort Benning. She had no other place to go, really.''

Samantha made a clucking sound and Hazard nodded in agreement.

"Yeah. It was rough. She had to raise Mack all by herself. It wasn't a good time for her. Most of our friends at Benning left. The menfolk went to Korea, just like me, and the wives Linda knew all went home to their parents to wait. Me coming back didn't solve the problem either. The old cycle started up again, one post after another. Linda was after me to quit, but I wouldn't do it. I loved it. And by this time I had a lot of years invested. We fought a lot about it. And then came Vietnam. I was one of the early advisors. I volunteered—probably to get away from the fights at home, although I didn't see it that way at the time. When I got back from that first tour is when it all hit the fan. The whole business of Vietnam troubled me, even

back then, but by God when I was there, I was soldiering.
The adrenaline was flowing and I was practicing my trade.
When I got back, I was bored to death with garrison duty.
I had other problems, too. I got assigned to a company
where I didn't get along with my platoon leader. And
things were still bad on the home front. So I solved all *my*
problems. I volunteered for another tour in Nam."

"Oh, Clell, how could you! That poor woman!"

"That was her reaction, too," Hazard said. "The day I
came home and told her was the day she left me. We went
to the NCO club that night and she got drunk. First she
cried, then she screamed. It all came up that night, like
some kind of poisoned meat she'd eaten; twenty years of
bitterness and frustration. We were sitting there with three
other couples and she told me and them that she hated the
Army and she hated me for making her live with it. She
told us all that she'd had affairs when I was overseas—a
lot of 'em. Then she gave us the details: names, places,
the full nomenclature."

"What did you do?" Samantha asked, wide-eyed.

Hazard shrugged. "What could I do? I just sat there and
listened. Then she left. She went home and got Mackie,
and they got on a bus. I haven't seen either one of them
since."

Samantha was quiet for a moment, then asked, "Do you
still love her? Did you *ever* love her?"

"No, I guess I didn't, or else I wouldn't have done the
things I did. Mostly I feel sorry for having made her life a
hell on earth. I'm just surprised she took it for so long,
feeling the way she did."

"What about your son?" Samantha asked.

Hazard looked uncomfortable. "We don't have a
relationship. I hardly know the boy. He seemed to do all
his growing up in spurts, during those times I wasn't there.

Every time I came home from overseas there was this new kid in the house, one I didn't recognize.''

"What about now?"

"There's not much opportunity to get to know him now," said Hazard. "Linda moved him to California. She's remarried, a respectable civilian. She put Mack into college out there. She makes darn sure there's no contact between us. She's scared to death I'm gonna get my hooks into him and talk him into enlisting in the Army."

"Would you try to get him into the Army?"

Hazard shook his head. "Nope. It's been a decent enough life for me, but kids should do better for themselves than the generation before. Besides, I don't much like the way things are going in the Army these days. There's not enough pride in it anymore."

Samantha did not want to talk about the Army. "Do you write to him?" she asked.

Hazard shook his head again. "No. His mother won't tell me what college he's in."

"Can't you take her to court and force her to give you visiting rights?"

"I guess so, but maybe it's better this way. It wouldn't do me much good with him clear across the country, and she knows it. Anyway, he doesn't like me much more than his mother does. When I wasn't there for her, I wasn't there for him, either."

"Clell, you could try," Samantha said.

"The truth is, Sam, he and I wouldn't have much in common. He's a stranger to me and I'm a stranger to him. I'm reluctant to force a relationship where none really exists. It would be founded on little more than an accident of birth, a freak genetic collision."

"You could still try," Samantha insisted, refusing to give ground.

Hazard gave her a quizzical look. "How come you're so interested in all this?" he asked.

"I don't know," she mumbled, looking away.

"Sam, do you have children?" he asked softly, the notion just coming to him.

She looked straight at him with the saddest eyes he'd ever seen. "No. I'm . . . I'm not able to have children."

He nodded and put a hand over one of hers. "I'm sorry." Just then the waiter arrived. The steaks were as good as the cook had promised. They ate slowly and without much conversation, each of them busy with private thoughts.

Samantha could tell that the subject of his son bothered Hazard more than he let on, so she did not pursue it. She watched him cut his meat with strong, sure strokes, the steak knife like a weapon in his hands. He had long, supple fingers; corded veins in the backs of his hands tunneled along thick wrists and into powerful forearms. His hands moved with the sure, easy grace evident in all his movements.

His face was a little too long and hawkish, the hollows in his cheeks a bit too pronounced. He looked vaguely dangerous, but was nonetheless physically the sexiest man Samantha had ever met. There was nothing contrived about his masculinity, no false bravado, none of the pouter-pigeon strutting so common among southern men. Just a quiet, understated, steely quality. He was like . . . well . . . like Gary Cooper.

She had noticed many of these things earlier in the day when she had trailed behind him as he pushed a hole for her through the crowd in the stadium. It had been warm in the crush. When he had struggled out of his jacket, she could not keep her eyes from tracing the lines of his back, tapering from wide shoulder to slim hips and bunched buttocks. He had a loose-hipped walk that suggested fluid, coiled power, the result of hundreds of hours on the parade ground.

On its own, without calculation and seemingly unprovoked by will, her brain tried to picture him without clothes. While certain vital features refused to materialize for her—even running rampant her mind drew the line— she saw enough. A slight dampness began to well between her legs, a reaction that horrified her and sent blood coursing to her head. Samantha was no prude, but she had never experienced such a purely physical reaction to a man before. She willed herself to stop thinking about such things and bent to her dinner.

Samantha's sudden agitation escaped Hazard. He was coping with his own tremors. He was thinking, I can talk to this woman. I've never been able to talk to women, but I can talk to this one. She had that instinct, rare enough in men and almost unheard of in the women of his acquaintance, for knowing when to talk and when to be still. Each new side of Samantha Huff, each new face she presented as he turned her slowly in his mind like a man examining the beveled cuts on a diamond, ratcheted his infatuation up another notch, stretching tighter in his already-strained cables. Steadeeeee, he admonished himself, as if talking to some dipshit recruit. He was leaving himself far too wide open to this woman. If he had been on the bayonet course, he would have been marked dead by now.

Little was said on the long drive back. A light snow had begun to fall and Hazard drove with exaggerated care, like a trucker with precious cargo. It took a long while to get through the portion of D.C. they had to cross to reach the bridge to Arlington. Washington's drivers, as always, had panicked with the first snowflake, and minor fenderbenders and spun-out cars made the streets an obstacle course.

From the time they crossed the Potomac until the time

they reached their apartment doors, not a word was exchanged. A tension had developed in the car as it rolled through Arlington, a tension that was transferred to the parking lot, then to the elevator, and then to the corridor. It was unlike the atmosphere in the elevator the first time Hazard had been closed up with Samantha Huff. That had been a nervous electricity, so charged that it had sparked a slow man to action. This was different: a heavy, smothering air like the muggy and oppressive dank before a Key West squall, an air that slowed things down and left Hazard feeling drowsy. It seemed a mile from the elevator to the door.

To all outward appearances, Hazard's mind was hardly working. His mouth hung slightly open, and his eyelids slumped to half mast. But behind this mask, Hazard's brain was jumping around like a Mexican shortstop. What to do now? Should he invite her in? Was it too soon to try and touch her? He wanted to. He had not wanted to touch a female so badly since he was eighteen, a time of life when he'd walked around in a daze for weeks at a stretch, his whole body a pulsating prick seeking a home. Several times during the long day, Hazard had suppressed the urge to stroke her . . . to just reach out and run a hand on her skin, any piece of skin—her face, forehead, fingers. But he was terrified of frightening her.

Once when he had been fishing the Yellowstone River, he had felt a bump on his waders and had looked down in surprise to find a large cutthroat trout using his legs as a breakwater. He had kept perfectly still, watching the fish until his feet had grown numb. The longer he'd watched the more enchanted he'd become. And after a while he had fallen in love with the fish—with that particular fish. He did not want to catch it. He just wanted to touch it. Very slowly, barely moving, he'd inched his hand down, down into the water. Finally his fingers brushed the trout's back.

The fish shot away like a goosed nun. Against all reason, all knowledge, all experience, Hazard had been stunned at the trout's fleeing his touch.

No. This woman was too valuable to spook. He was about to say good-night with another handshake when Samantha turned a mottled face to him, took a deep breath, and said in an unsteady voice, "Could we please use my apartment? It's been a long time for me, and I'm a little frightened. I know it's silly, but I need to have my own things around me for this."

8

Samantha Huff had known fewer than a handful of men in her life, including her husband. None had been casual affairs, yet for one reason or another—unrealistic expectations on her part, most likely—none had turned out very well. Even so, she thought she knew what there was to know about sex. She had always looked upon copulation sensibly. It was a short, not unpleasant activity that needed doing from time to time—like shopping for shoes. In her experience, no one episode ever lasted more than an hour from start to finish, and the sweaty, heaving, slightly distasteful part of it was always over far quicker than that.

It was not that Samantha didn't like sex. It could be nice. But it was not vital. It was something a woman did with a man to enable their relationship to get on with more important things, a way station on the road to friendship.

She had trouble with her apartment door The key stubbornly balked at the lock until Clell gently took it away from her and had the door open in an instant. She refused to turn on a light, unwilling—or unable—to look at his face or have him see hers. Why am I doing this if it upsets me? she asked herself rhetorically. She briefly considered abandoning the whole thing, then discarded the thought, reluctant to shoulder the humiliation and, quite frankly, reluctant to turn her back on an undeniable desire.

There was a floating, discombobulated journey across her living room in the dark, the once familiar terrain suddenly uncharted territory with nothing quite where she remembered putting it. "Ouch! Damn!" She painfully bashed her hip on the sharp corner of a highboy, noisily rattling the dishes inside. That was when he touched her for the first time, laying one strong hand on the back of her neck to brace her and the other on her bruised hip, rubbing the spot softly and crooning into her ear like a wrangler gentling a spooked horse, "Steady, Sam . . . steady now." And from that moment on he was the driver, she a mere passenger, on a wild ride through foreign alleys in a city she thought she knew but where now she could not recognize a single landmark.

Clell, one hand still on her nape and the other still on her hip, guided her unerringly into her bedroom as if it were his apartment, not hers, and a path that he had trod a thousand times before. He snapped on a bedside lamp. When she reached over to turn it off, he kindly but firmly caught her arm and pinned it to her side. "Not a chance," he said with a tight smile and a shake of his head.

Then he undressed her slowly and deliberately, while she stood there with eyes pressed shut, weaving slightly, neither helping nor hindering. When he was done she felt him move away. Her eyes still closed, she could hear him removing his own clothes, the soft rubbing of cloth on cloth set against the menacing rasp of a zipper.

There followed a short silence, broken when she heard him breathe out, "Oh my." She opened her eyes then and saw him staring at her, taking her all in with wide, moist eyes.

It was a look of homage, one that made her feel simultaneously all-powerful and completely helpless. She felt her whole body flush and cast her eyes to the floor in consternation. Then she set her resolve and raised her head. She intended to look him straight in the eye, to accept the compliment. She honestly meant to. But instead her gaze locked at the halfway point, at the very spot she had meant to avoid for as long as she could. There was no alternative. His penis demanded acknowledgement. She gaped and blurted an echoing "Oh my," and they both began to laugh.

Their laugh served to break the gathering tension, and he came toward her, his phallus soaring out of his groin and swaying like a cobra. It seemed to reach her long before the rest of him did, poking its head into her belly and slithering up her midriff as he stepped closer, the tip of it bulbous and looking as big around as a ram's heart. As he bent to kiss her, it lay there between them, pulsing in rhythm with his heartbeat.

It was a long, deep, probing, yet tender kiss, one that buckled her knees. Once, twice, and again. Then he slid his tongue to her eyes, her ears, her neck, her breasts, her stomach. He shimmied slowly down her body to bury his face between her legs, then started to lap at her like a starving cat at a milk bowl. She gasped and took a backward step. "Wh-What are you doing?" No man had ever put his mouth on her like that before. He looked surprised, then said softly, "Steady now. It's alright. Really." Then he laid her back on the bed and began again. His tongue seemed a separate living thing, scion of the great cobra. After an exploratory tour it wrapped itself around the hooded core of her, forming in her mind a caduceus that symbolized her helplessness.

Her limbs trembled uncontrollably in response to his unmannered expertise. He did not assault her with stilted and memorized technique, like some expedition attacking a route up one of Everest's rocky faces. There was no rushing through the positions, no predictable trek from point A to point B, as if she were the Via Dolorosa and he a pilgrim retracing the stations of the cross. He simply took his pleasure with huge and obvious enjoyment, and so gave pleasure in kind. She had not suspected that such sensations were there to be had, or that they could go on and on, flow without ebb.

She thought it would be one of the shorter sessions of her experience. They were both so excited, so wrought up by the long preliminaries that it was over for both of them only a few minutes after he mounted her. As wonderful as those few minutes were, she was vaguely disappointed. It didn't occur to her that it might not be finished. He was not immediately ready to go again, of course—he was no boy of eighteen, full of sap and regenerative as crabgrass. He spent the interim using his hands and mouth on her.

She lay spent and slick with sweat, and he licked her dry, from top to bottom, stem to stern. He turned her over and kissed her wetly all over her back, running his tongue down her spine and into the furrow at its base, then plunging it deep into the dark burrow itself. She could bear it only a moment or two before she pulled away to straddle him, riding him slow and deep and forever, her great breasts swinging across his face. He looked at her with the eyes of a dying saint. It was easier than the first time. Wet and ready as she had been then, the passage was difficult at first. She could still feel the knotted veins that ran the whole remarkable length of him like dark highways; still feel the knobby junctures where intersecting roads banded him. He had pushed through to vernal territories and she had felt at times as if he were trying to pierce through to her very heart.

They lay in the clotted sheets, he asleep, she up on an elbow hunting for scars. She'd felt them during the night but then had had neither the time nor the presence of mind to explore them further.

Now, in the diffused light of the lamp, they jumped out at her, great rifts in an otherwise perfect landscape. There were two, side by side, two inches above his right nipple—small puckered circles the size of nickles, the edges ragged with starbursts. A similar mark lay on the side of his right bicep, just below a tattoo of a parachute with wings and the word *Airborne*. His chest was clear. So was his stomach which, even when he was supine, was furrowed with lines of muscle and looked like a rutted country road. But down his right side, low along the waist, was a massive tear four inches wide and white and puckered up like skin left too long in water. It ran on down his hip and across his right buttock and disappeared beneath him. Two more of the starred holes dotted his right thigh, and another long rent ran down the side of his right calf, the patch hairless and irate-looking.

Samantha traced the scar on his side with a sharp finger-nail but failed to rouse him. Then she cupped his testicles, the stones heavy in her hand like two Grade A eggs. When that elicited no response, she reached over and picked up his penis, lying in repose across his thigh. She glanced up to make sure he was still sleeping, then touched it gingerly with her tongue. She checked his face again, saw nothing, then put the head of it in her mouth. She had never done that to a man before.

A single eye popped open. "Enough, woman," he said. "I sure hope you don't have anything of a strenuous nature in mind, because you're trying to start an overworked engine with a dead battery."

She dropped his penis like she'd been caught shoplifting. "I-I'm just trying to get your attention," she said in embarrassment. "Clell, tell me about these horrible marks on you."

"Aha. You already want somebody with a prettier body."

"No, your body is pretty enough for me, thank you very much. I just want you to tell me how you got these."

"It's just the flesh breaking up on me," he said, smiling ruefully. "It's a common affliction among old people. Like liver spots. You'll find out when you get to be my age."

"I *am* your age, silly. Now are you going to give me a straight answer or not?" She picked up his penis again, gave it a gentle pull, and said in a Teutonic accent, "Ve haf vays to make you talk."

"Yeoww. Okay, okay," he laughed. "They are the result of mistakes."

"What kind of mistakes?" she asked dubiously. "Even a pacifist like me knows that some of these are bullet holes."

"The kind of mistakes that end up as bullet holes," he said. "I zigged when I should have zagged. I was standing up when I should have been sitting down. I stayed still when I should have been making tracks. I keep these scars around to remind me of all the errors of judgment over the years. I find it's handier than tying a string around my finger."

Samantha ignored that. "Did they all happen at the same time?" she asked with a slight shudder.

"Nope. I got to demonstrate how dumb I could be on a couple of separate occasions. Those neat little holes you so astutely diagnosed as bullet holes I got in Korea. The not-so-neat scars came from Veet Nam, the garden of the Orient."

"I suppose you think it's terribly romantic to have war wounds," she said with disapproval.

"I most certainly do not," he said seriously. "Getting wounded means you screwed up in most cases. You didn't do your job right. A man who's been hit isn't much good to anyone else."

She was not listening. She was preoccupied with a new

observation. "Why always on the right side of your body?" she asked.

He laughed. "You know, I've often wondered about that myself. There must be something about my right side that pisses folks off. From now on I'm only going to show my left profile—like an actor with a wart. I'll walk down the street sideways like a big ol' crab—"

"Would you please be serious?" She gave another exasperated pull on his penis. "Answer me this, then: Why do you stay in the Army?"

"I gotta finish my hitch or they'll toss me in Leavenworth for desertion," he laughed.

"You know what I mean." She tugged firmly for emphasis.

"Yeowww. Alright, alright." He pretended to give the question some thought, knitting his brows and scratching his chin. Then he said, "I stay in because I'm afraid I couldn't make it on the outside. I'm too nervous to steal and too proud to run for Congress."

"Damn you, Clell Hazard." Another tug. "You'll still be a relatively young man when your whatchamacallit— your hitch—is up. What do you plan to do then?"

"I'm gonna retire to some quiet place where the sun sets between me and town."

Another pull. "But why can't you—"

"Godalmighty, woman, hush! Who? What? When? Where? Why? Is this what I get for taking up with a newspaper woman? And quit pulling on that thing. It's just hanging by a thread as it is." He was laughing. She laughed back and tightened her grip. "That thing" began to grow in her hand like some magical beanstalk. Clell Hazard reconsidered. "On the other hand, as long as we're all *three* awake . . ." he said with a theatrical leer. And reached for her.

Samantha managed only three hours of fitful sleep. When she awoke she found herself suffering what could only be a sexual hangover.

She was sore, inside and out, and buffeted by feelings ranging from exhilaration to mortification. Her face burned when she thought about the things they—she—had done; things new and unsettling to a proper middle-aged southern gentlewoman who had come to puberty in the early 1940s. It was not so much a moral squeamishness—she had long since shunted off the bulk of her Baptist upbringing. What she could not quite cope with was the picture of herself as she had been the night before. She had been as pathetically coquettish as some poor white trash slut, as shamelessly demanding as Queen Ranavalona of Madagascar, as whimperingly submissive as Scarlett O'Hara on the night Rhett Butler decided to get rough. She had been completely out of control. She had no idea what Clell Hazard thought of her. She had no idea what she thought of herself.

Samantha was confused and frightened. Clell had pried open doors to forbidden rooms and forced her to look inside. She was not sure she liked what she'd seen. Again, it was not so much the physical acts themselves. While it was true that she had never taken a man into her mouth before or let a man use his mouth on her like that, she suspected it was all tame enough by the standards of the day. What's more, she had liked it, more than liked it. What scared her was the power he seemed to have over her, the ease with which he had come through the wall of reserve guarding the core of her, as if it were no more than a flimsy bead curtain. He had bored straight into that core, and she knew a woman without secrets was as vulnerable as a newborn fawn.

She felt an overwhelming need to get away from him, to get off somewhere where she could examine what had happened to her without his disturbing physical presence there to confuse her further.

Hazard awoke abruptly and without the slightest disorientation. He knew where he was and how he was: as happy, as content, as suffused with well-being as he had ever felt in his life. The soaring sensation was checked somewhat, however, when he turned his head on the pillow and saw Samantha hurriedly dressing, her back modestly to him as she stepped into her clothes. "Good morning," he said. He saw her flinch at the sound of his voice. She neither turned nor answered. She merely quickened her pace.

"Ahem, good morning," he said again. Samantha wriggled into her blouse and did not answer.

Hazard sat up in the bed and asked, "Is anything wrong, Sam?"

"I've g-got to get to work," she mumbled, her back still to him.

He glanced at the clock on the bedside table and raised an eyebrow. "Sam, it's only six-thirty."

She finally turned and faced him, a distance in her eyes. "Alright then," she said defiantly, "I want to go home and think about some things."

Hazard smiled. "You are home. You live here, remember? If you want to be by yourself, I'd better do the leaving." He threw back the bedcovers, and she spun around and gave him her back again. With a puzzled face, he began to dress. "What kind of things are you gonna be thinking about?" he asked.

"Just things."

He nodded at her stiff back. "Well, as long as you're at it, you might as well put one more thing on your list. I love you, Sam."

9

"Ashes to ashes . . ."

"Dust to dust . . ."

"Let's dump this dick and get on the bus."

Sergeant Hazard's sigh was audible clear to the end of the rank. "Steadeeeee."

This one looked promising. The widow was drunk.

Willow watched the ceremony from the corner of his eye. It was the last job of the day, and he was exhausted—they all were—but every man was alert to the possibilities.

She had fallen down the steps coming out of the chapel. Their backs to the door, the troopers of the honor platoon had not seen it, but they had heard it. They heard people trying to help her up, and they heard her brush them off with a slurred "Lemmelone."

The dead captain must not have been popular. The funeral party was small, no more than half a dozen people. But he'd obviously had connections. The gravesite was only a short distance from the gate, in the older, verdant part of the cemetery. It was the first drop job Willow could remember where bulldozers had not played a dirge. The distance to the grave was so short that it had been a walking procession, the small clot of mourners tramping slowly behind the casket and platoon.

Again it had happened. Behind them and out of eyeshot, they had heard her stumble off the road and vomit copiously behind a tree. Lieutenant Webber had glanced to the rear at the noise, and they had all watched his shocked face with amusement as he rummaged through his mind for an appropriate response, then ordered the platoon to march at half step until she could catch up.

Now, at the gravesite itself, Willow and the others sneaked glances at the woman and clamped down on twitching mouths as she winced with each volley from the firing party and swayed through taps, two embarrassed officers beside her, ready to catch her if she took a notion to hit the dirt again.

The box was cranked into the ground. The casket team did its handjive with the flag, folding it neatly into the SOP triangle and handing it to Lieutenant Webber. Webber turned and handed it to the widow, stood back, and saluted. The woman ignored him and walked unsteadily to the lip of the hole, the flag held loosely in one hand, unraveling and trailing on the ground behind her. She peered intently into the grave, teetering on the edge. Then she lifted her veil, exposing a puffy, sullen face, hawked loudly, and spat a ball of phlegm at the lowered casket. "At least now I know where you're spending your nights, you sonofabitch!"

There was a moment of stunned silence, and Sergeant Hazard used the opportunity to whisper fiercely, punctuating each word with a menacing pause, "I . . . will . . . court . . . martial . . . the . . . first . . . man . . . who . . . makes . . . a . . . sound." Anything else he might have said disappeared in the explosion of laughter.

They marched through the late December cold, eyes alert for ice on the road. Down through the Fields of the

Dead they went, the rows of graves ticking past like the mile markers on a turnpike. Ta ta ta *tum*. They marched with that odd Old Guard stride, moving only from the waist down, hips rolling like ball bearings packed in grease. Ta ta ta *tum*.

Tata tata tata *tumtum*. At first Willow thought it was an echo, the pecking of the snare thrown back to them by the wind. Tata tata tata *tumtum*. Then the other funeral party hove into view, topping the rise of a steep dip in the road ahead. Marines! A shudder rippled through the platoon. The Navy, Air Force, even the Coast Guard, all had honor guard units posted in the D.C. area, but only the marines from Marine Barracks at Fort McNair, were considered serious rivals by the Old Guard. The leathernecks were good, very good. The two funerals slithered toward each other like dragons joining in combat.

They passed on the right. As the two platoons glided by each other, only a few inches apart in the congested road, the men studied their opposite numbers out of the corners of their eyes. The jarheads with their white caps, blue blouses with choke collars and crimson rank stripes, blue trousers with red stripes. The doggies with blue caps, blue blouses with yellow rockers, poplin shirts and black windsor-knotted ties, blue pants with yellow stripes. The marines, Willow noted, did their shoes the same way, with double soles, taps all around, and obsidian spit shines. The men in both platoons straightened imperceptibly as they passed, bringing shoulders to an even truer temper, strutting for each other like dressage horses.

Moving only the side of his mouth closest to the marines, a Delta Company man hissed the Marines' unofficial battle cry: "Eat the apple . . . and fuck the Corps." A passing marine countered with the Third Herd's own: "The Old Guaaaaard . . . sucks!" From his guide spot in the front rank, Sergeant Hazard rolled his eyes and called, "Steadeeeeee."

The two coffins passed without acknowledgments, despite everything the men inside had in common.

"Ashes to ashes . . ."
"Dust to dust . . ."
"Let's cover this cunt and get on the bus."
"Christ," wailed Hazard. "Steadeeeeeee."

Like old friends, the bulldozers were waiting for them. Two of them this time, working in tandem to pull the stump and roots of an old, gnarled oak that had been marked for sacrifice to the war effort. The drivers waved and shut down. They climbed down off the tracks, lit cigarettes, and watched, welcoming the break.

Willow's eyes teared. Not from emotion, but from the mid-January cold. After more than a hundred burials, he was immune to pageantry. Even with the gloves his fingers were numb; he could not feel the rifle stock. The morning paper had predicted sub-teen temperatures for the day. It had also reported that the U.S. troop level in Vietnam had hit the 400,000 mark. Make that 399,999, thought Willow. The second lieutenant in the box was from the First Infantry Division: The Big Red One. Willow had heard someone say he was only six months out of West Point.

Willow was curious about him. They had been at the chapel early for this job, and before the service, another lieutenant, a firstie, had approached Sergeant Hazard off to the side and the two men had embraced. This officer also wore the Big Red One patch. Willow could not hear what he and Hazard were saying, but seeing the two together, it registered that Sergeant Hazard's right shoulder patch, the one designating prior overseas service unit, was also that of the First Infantry. The NCO and the officer had wrapped their arms around each other and rocked back and forth a while before disengaging and starting to talk animatedly. Willow saw his platoon sergeant nod toward the coffin as it was carted from the funeral home hearse into the chapel and saw the lieutenant shake his head—negative. Willow would have to ask Hazard about it.

It was also curious that no family was present at the gravesite. There was the lieutenant in his dress blues. There was a civilian somberly dressed in black suit and black overcoat who seemed to be a representative from the funeral parlor. And there was a captain, apparently representing the Pentagon, since he sported the MDW—Military District of Washington—patch on his left, active unit, shoulder, the Washington Monument with a sword running it through. The men of the Old Guard wore the same patch on their left shoulders. Their right shoulders, except for the lifers among them, were bare.

Willow thought it odd that he had not really noticed Hazard's overseas patch before. He usually noticed things like that right away. He had, however, carefully studied the phalanx of medals his platoon sergeant wore with dress blues. He had recognized the yellow ribbon with the thin red stripes, patterned after the flag of South Vietnam, marking the Nam tours. He had recognized the distinctive Purple Hearts, two of them. There was a slew of campaign medals Willow did not know, Korea and Second World War stuff. There were two that impressed him mightily: A Silver Star, awarded only for bravery under fire; a Bronze Star, with V for valor and two oak leaf clusters, which showed that Hazard had been awarded the medal on three different occasions. Just below the mass of medals pinned over the left breast pocket were the wings and chute of the paratrooper. At the top of them all was the one most valued by veteran infantrymen, and, Willow had noticed, the only one besides the jump wings that Hazard wore on other uniforms: the long blue enamel rectangle with the silver Kentucky rifle and wreath—the Combat Infantryman's Badge.

On the other side, over the right breast pocket, was a single ribbon, blue with a cluster, the same one Willow's father wore: the Presidential Unit Citation. It occurred to Willow that his father and his platoon sergeant had received the citation at the same time: for service with the Second Infantry Division.

Hazard had five rows of medals in all. His whole professional biography was pinned on his chest for the initiated to read. It was very impressive, thought Willow, but he would match that accomplishment before he was done—match it and go beyond. Not for the sake of medals alone, but for what they represented: the sacrifices, the correct calls of judgment, the top-notch soldiering. Medals were a diary of the special moments in a soldier's life, entries which at a glance summoned up hot jungles and iced-over potato fields, joys and terrors, moments of exhilaration and moments of despair . . . and the faces of lost friends.

The Old Man was dead. Willow could tell just by looking, but Doc was working on him anyway. Half of Crowder's face had been torn away, and the exposed molars and pieces of jawbone glinted luminiferously in the weak moonlight. There was another wound just below the captain's rib cage and it was on this less significant tear that Ramiriz worked furiously, refusing to look at or acknowledge the ruined face.

Willow grabbed at Ramiriz's arm. "Doc, he's dead. He's dead, Doc. Go help Rawlins with Sergeant Robinson. Robbie's hurt bad, Doc. He's losing blood fast. He needs you, Doc. Doc, GODDAMNIT." Ramiriz shook off Willow's hand and continued to tape a sulfa dressing to the com-

*pany commander's side, still careful not to let his gaze
wander toward Crowder's head. Willow tried again and
Ramiriz slapped his hand away viciously and turned his
head to hiss through clenched teeth, "I will kill you for
this. I will kill you." The medic's eyes were wide and
wild. Dried blood clotted his moustache.*

*Willow backed off and stumbled on toward the command
bunker to find Colonel Bean. He flinched with every new
explosion, and his heart hammered in his chest. He was
afraid. Not of getting hurt—he had not even thought about
that. He was afraid of fucking up. So far he had not done
a single thing to effectively cope with what was happening
around him. He had issued two orders: one to Robinson to
get his men on line and one to Ramiriz to help Robinson.
The first had proved uninformed, irrelevant, and impossible.
The second had been ignored. As he made his way toward
the TOC, he stuck his head into each hooch he passed.
They were all empty. How could he lead his men when he
couldn't even find them? Helmeted figures ran past him in
the dark, toward what or away from what, Willow could
not see. He hollered at them, but no one stopped or
answered.*

*He heard another voice yelling in the pitch, somehow
recognized it over the noise, and ran toward it. "Otis,
GODDAMN! Otis, I can't find any of my men."*

*Harmon was feeding a stubby, egg-nosed shell into an
M-79 grenade launcher. He snapped the fat-barreled blooker
shut and hollered back, "Me neither. I think half my boys
are K-I-A. The other half started chasin' gooks once they
got past us on the wire. This is like a fuckin' pig scramble
at the rodeo."*

*Out of the darkness came a flash followed instantane-
ously by an explosion twenty feet away. Both men hit the
ground. Harmon rolled over and fired the blooker at the*

spot where they had seen the flash. There was a scream from the darkness, and Harmon whooped, "GET SOME, MOTHERFUCKER!" He grinned a manic grin at Willow, his teeth showing whitely in his sooty face and patted the M-79. "I picked this baby off'n a dead dink. These cocksuckers are killing us with our own shit."

Willow scrambled to his feet. "I gotta DO something," he shouted, starting to run again toward the command bunker. As he neared the TOC, he could see shadowy forms racing past the bunker, running hunched over, something strapped to their backs. Willow stopped and raised his rifle and squeezed. Nothing happened. He pulled again, jerking the trigger hard, as he had been taught not to do, as if he could force out the round. Nothing. He stood bewildered, the M-16 still at his shoulder, thinking, The fucker's jammed. Oh, God, not now, NOT NOW! Those lousy fuckers, those lousy cocksucking motherfucking fuckers were supposed to have fixed that. He lowered the weapon and stared at it stupidly, feeling vulnerable and afraid for the first time. Then he realized that he had not taken off the safety. Oh Jesus! He glanced around furtively, half expecting to see an OCS cadre standing there, glaring at him with contempt, pencil poised above clipboard. Willow flipped the tang to full automatic and raised the rifle again. There was nothing to shoot at. The shadows were gone. Cursing wildly, he sprinted toward the command bunker.

The bus swayed around a curve and men grabbed handrails with one hand and held tight to their weapons with the other. Willow inched his way up to Sergeant Hazard, careful to keep off other people's spit shines.

"Was that lieutenant a friend of yours, sarge? You seemed to know him."

"He was my platoon leader in Nam."

150   *Nicholas Proffitt*

"Did you know the . . . ah . . . the deceased, too?"

"No. He was a new meat, greased on his first day in the bush."

"What hap—"

"Put a cork in it, Willow."

"Right, sarge. Sorry, sarge."

10

A blast of Sergeant Jones' whistle brought them up short, their sneakers squealing on the polished floor. "Let's do it again, gentlemen," said Jones. "Willow, you gotta get closer to the pick when you make your cut, boy. I want you and his jocks to get tangled when you go by, hear? You swing way out like you just done and the defense can slide off the pick and pick you up. Got it?"

Willow nodded. Jones flipped the ball to him so he could try it again. Willow saw DeVeber come into the gym and motion to Jones. He wondered idly what the clerk was doing there at that time of night. He saw Jones go over, listen while DeVeber whispered something, then heard him call out, "Hey, Willow, c'mere a minute." As he jogged over, Willow thought Jones's black face seemed even darker than usual.

"You want me, coach?"

"Uh, yeah. DeVeber here says you wanted back in the orderly room, quick time."

"What's it all about?"

Jones fiddled with the whistle around his neck and stared out at the court, where the team stood in the three lines and watched them. "Uh, don't know. All we know is

151

the Ol' Man wants to see you. You best not bother with no shower or nuthin.''

Willow shrugged. He picked up his equipment bag and left with the clerk. On the walk back to the company, he tried to get DeVeber to talk. The clerk, normally a gushing fountain of wisecracks and gossip, was strangely mute.

"What's the Old Man want, Pete?"

"I don't know.''

"C'mon, Pete, you gotta have some idea.''

"Well, I don't,'' the clerk said testily.

"Okay, okay. I just thought that if I fucked up somehow, if I knew what it was, I could prepare a defense or something, you know?'' DeVeber said nothing.

Willow tried to think of something he had done wrong. He couldn't. "Maybe the Old Man has finally decided to give me my transfer to Nam, eh? Yeah, that's probably it,'' he said, not believing it but trying to cover his growing anxiety. "Maybe he doesn't want to wait to give me the good news.''

"Maybe,'' said DeVeber, not looking at him.

"At the TOC everything was a shambles. You could hardly see through the smoke. All the radio equipment was damaged and all the tables and chairs and cots and map boards and everything had been smashed. The sappers had thrown more than a dozen satchel charges through the doorway. Everybody inside was dead or wounded. I saw four or five KIAs lying in the wreckage. The battalion radio operator—I don't know his name—was one of them. He had his headphones on, but . . . but he didn't have any head. His head was on the floor. The headphones were still on it. It . . . It looked like he was still talking, you know, still trying to call for some help. He . . .'' Willow stopped and passed a hand over his face. Someone in the room coughed. Major Pyle said nothing; he just watched

Willow over the tops of his Army-issue glasses, waiting for him to go on.

"Colonel Bean was badly wounded. He was propped up in a corner, and a couple of men were tending to him. At first I thought he was dead, he looked so bad. Lifer, that's Specialist Four Leiferman, our company clerk, was there, only slightly wounded, and he told me that the NVA tried to get into the bunker and that the colonel had kept them out. He said the sappers would throw in a satchel charge, then rush the entrance, and that Colonel Bean stopped them every time they tried. The colonel would pick it up and throw it back through the door. When he couldn't get to it in time, he'd get blown across the TOC, but then he'd get up and start firing at the entryway when they tried to come through. He got up off the floor three times and stopped them. The fourth time he went down for good. Fortunately, the sappers had had enough and didn't rush the door after that one."

At the testimony to the battalion commander's performance, Major Pyle nodded approvingly at Willow. His voice was gentle, almost fatherly, when he asked, "And then what did you do, lieutenant?"

"The firing had died down considerably by then. Most of what there was was coming from the north end of the base, where the sappers were dee-deeing through their escape hatch. I thought maybe our mortars could get them as they went down the trails, before they got into the deep bush. Then I realized that during the whole thing I hadn't heard our tubes fire a single round. There was nothing I could do to help at the TOC, so I took off for the mortar pits to see what the problem was—you know, why nobody was firing. When I got there I found out why. Our tubes were all torn up and the crews were dead—all of 'em. Among the bodies was the Marshal, uh, Lieutenant Earp, our weapons platoon leader."

Sergeant Hazard, First Sergeant Boudin, and Sergeant-Major Nelson, all in civilian clothes, were waiting for him in the orderly room. DeVeber, his errand complete, left in a hurry. The Slasher was looking at Willow without his usual hostility. Hazard's long, wolfish face was drawn even tighter than usual, and Willow felt a premonition of trouble. No one said anything. Nelson just pointed to the Old Man's office and Willow went in, followed by the three noncoms.

Captain Thomas was sitting behind his desk. He, too, was in civvies. He motioned for Willow to sit. He was not smiling.

"Willow, I . . . Uh, Willow, I . . . Uh, Sergeant Hazard, why don't you tell him."

Willow turned to Hazard. "Tell me what, sarge?"

"Jackie . . ." Hazard began, and Willow wondered what it could be that would merit the use of his given name for the first time. His stomach clutched. "Jackie, your dad is dead. His heart." Hazard stopped. They all watched Willow carefully for his reaction. The silence grew as Willow just watched them back.

When it became evident that the boy was not going to speak, the sergeant-major said, "I've already cut papers for an emergency leave. There's a late plane to Lexington tonight, if you want it, or you can go first thing in the morning."

"Tonight," Willow said calmly. His face still betrayed nothing.

"I didn't have time to check on the best way to get from there down to Harlan County," Nelson said. "I'm . . . I'm sorry, son. I just didn't have time."

"No sweat," said Willow. "I can get a bus down from Lex."

"I'm sorry, Willow," said Captain Thomas.

"Yeah. Me too," rumbled Slasher Boudin.

"Yes. Thank you," said Willow.

Hazard and Nelson walked him up to the Third Platoon bay and packed him a suitcase while he showered and got into fresh Class A's.

"I'll drive you to the airport," said Hazard.

"Thanks."

"How you fixed for money?"

Willow did not answer. Hazard fished two hundred-dollar bills out of his shirt pocket, where they had obviously been waiting, and pressed them into Willow's hand. "Here. No, don't argue. We'll work it out later. You can pay me back over a few paydays."

"Thanks."

Nelson handed Willow another hundred. "Use this to get some flowers from me and Clell." When Willow opened his mouth to protest, Nelson said gruffly, "And don't gimme no shit. We knew your daddy a lot longer than you did."

"I guess you did at that," Willow said. "Thanks."

"There's a coupla things to think about," said Nelson. "First, uh . . . we can bury him here if you want. Full honors. I can fix it so Delta does it. He's entitled to it."

Willow shook his head. "Thank you, sergeant-major, but no. There's a family plot in Harlan."

"Whatever you think is best. Second, gimme the word and I'll get on the horn to Fort Knox or Campbell and have a color guard come down there with flag, firing party, the whole ball of wax."

Willow shook his head again. "I don't think so."

Nelson started to say something but caught a look from Hazard and stopped. Then he said, "Okay. Look, Jack, I'll piss off. You . . . uh, you say goodbye to your daddy for me. He was a damn fine soldier. You tell him Goody Nelson said so."

"I'll do that, sergeant-major."

Hazard and Willow were quiet on the drive to National Airport. Hazard sneaked side glances at the boy; Willow stared straight ahead. When Hazard turned into the airport parking lot, Willow said, "You don't have to park. Just drop me at the door." Hazard ignored him, parked the Pontiac, got Willow's suitcase out of the back seat, and carried it into the terminal. After Willow had checked in, the two of them walked to the departure lounge and sat. They smoked without talking until Willow's flight was called. They stood and Hazard reached into his coat pocket. "Jack, I'd like you to put these in the box with him, if it's all right." He handed Willow a shoulder patch—a black shield with a white star and the head of an Indian chief—the patch of the Second Infantry Division. Then he gave Willow two combat infantryman badges. "One's mine and one's Goody's. Is it okay?"

"Yes, it's okay," said Willow, his eyes starting to tear. He stuck out a hand. Hazard ignored it and hugged the boy, his own eyes red.

Across the lounge an elderly couple watched them. "Hiram, look at that," said the woman, digging an elbow into her husband's ribs. "That boy in uniform is about Donnie's age. He's saying goodbye to his father. Ain't it sad?"

The old man snorted. "Fucking war."

Hazard walked into the gloom of the Old Guard NCO Lounge at the back of the battalion headquarters building and found Goody Nelson sipping a beer at the bar.

"He get off okay?"

"Yup."

"Is he okay?"

"Yup."

Nelson signaled for two more beers. When they came,

he lifted his and said, "Here's to us and those like us."

"Damn few," said Hazard.

"And most of them are dead."

TWO

A Good Inheritance

11

They rolled into Tucson in the middle of the night and crawled along a neon strip, searching for a cheap motel. They had come straight through from Joplin, taking Route 66 most of the way, and they stumbled from the car to the room without noticing a thing. His mother and father took the lone bed while he and his brothers curled up on the floor like family dogs.

A harbinger of disaster came when the boy awoke and walked out into a 9 A.M. sunlight so intense that it felt like his epidermis was being peeled away. They barely made it to the air-conditioned sanctuary of the car.

The depth of their error was fully realized only when they had cleared the outskirts of the city and were heading south, toward Mexico, on the last leg of the long journey. The boy could not believe his eyes. It was a moonscape. Great brown boulders and faraway, mud-colored mountains. Small clumps of sagebrush and an occasional saguaro, its arms spread wide like a boogeyman's. Shimmering waves of heat came off the highway in front of them, and dust devils blew up here and there between them and the horizon. They went mile after mile without seeing a single sign of human habitation. That did not surprise the boy at all. Who could live in such country? Every now and then they would see a tarantula cross the road, black and big around as a baby's head, or snakes squished flat by trucks. The road was covered with grasshoppers the size of a big man's thumb and they went *pop*, *pop*, *pop* under the tires.

The boy gave voice to his rising panic. "We left Paris, France, for *this*?"

"It *is* different," chuckled his father, apparently too dim to comprehend their predicament. His mother sat in stunned silence, looking as if a total stranger had just walked up to her on a crowded street and slapped her face.

The boy refused to let it drop. "I'm not living here," he announced. "This Fort Hootchie Kootchie is at the end of the world, and I'm not going to live there. I'm running away from home first chance I get. I swear I will."

His father grinned at him in the rearview mirror. "I figger you'd get about ten miles in this here country before the buzzards have you. And the name of your new home is Fort Huachuca, Wa-Choo-Ka, not Hootchie Kootchie."

The boy slumped wordlessly into his corner of the back seat. His two younger brothers stared at him bug-eyed. His father continued to smile. The fool. The boy was not kidding. He'd leave. He'd work his way back to Paris on a tramp steamer or something and return to the American high school. He'd stay in the dorm. He closed his eyes and tried to think of his friends. What would they be doing now? What time was it over there, anyhow? Was it five hours difference, or six? No, that was to the east coast. What time zone was this stupid place? The Twilight Zone. He tried to figure it out while the grasshoppers went *pop*, *pop*, *pop*.

"Sir, we're about to serve your meal now. Would you please put down your tray table."

"I don't care for anything, thank you," said Willow.

"Nothing at all?" asked the stewardess, smiling brightly even at that ungodly hour.

"No, thank you."

"Are you sure?"

"I'm sure."

West Apache was bad, as bad as any Suds Row the boy could remember. The houses were small two-bedroom duplexes built of asbestos shingles, with rickety wooden front stoops. They must have been of prewar vintage. His mother took one look, made sure that the bed was the first thing off the truck, and took to it with the vapors. She spent the entire afternoon *"resting"* with a damp cloth on her forehead while his father, accustomed to her spells of sudden ennui, supervised the movers. The boy was no help at all. He roamed the neighborhood, confirming his initial impression of unrelieved squalor and plotting his escape.

The town and the high school were just as bad. The boy sat alone on the school bus, hunched in the corner of the long rear seat as they crawled around the post; then through the dusty town of Sierra Vista, sitting like an unlanced boil just outside the main gate; and finally into the even dustier parking lot of Buena High School.

The bus route was like an ascent up through the circles of Dante's hell. Fort Huachuca spread like warm oleo across a plateau overlooking a wide valley and ringed with brown mountains. At the bottom, with no view at all, were the Apaches, East and West. These were housing areas for the lower-ranking NCOs and the higher-ranking noncoms, like Shelby Willow, who had recently arrived and were on the bottom of the list for the move up to better housing. Better housing meant Huachuca Villages, Number One and Number Two. The Villages were on the lowest part of the plateau, but they had a view of the valley floor to the

north. They were twisting streets of cheek-by-jowl duplexes made of pastel-painted concrete and shaped like an
L. The waiting list was long, and the boy had heard his
father tell his mother that it would be at least a year before
they could get out of West Apache.

On the next level of groundswell were more modern,
larger, flat-roofed houses with sliding glass doors opening
onto small concrete patios surrounded by high wood-slat
fences. This style home was of two grades really, the
lesser model reserved for chief warrant officers and married lieutenants while the up-scale model, with slightly
more floor space, went to captains and majors. Then, at
the top, just before the mountains climbed away, was a
long, curving, tree-shaded street dotted with fine two-story
homes. The boy heard it called Colonels' Row.

All the school buses took a similar route, and the boy's
bus was no exception. It started at the bottom and worked
its way up through the ranks, the children of the brass
getting to sleep a good hour longer than those of the
enlisted ranks. Once the bus completed its military duties,
it passed through the fort's main gate and began its circu-
itous climb up through the circles of the Inferno once
again, this time on the civilian side. It stopped first at
crumbling Mexican shacks with tin roofs, worked up to
single-width trailer homes, then double-wides, and finally
stopped for passengers in front of pleasant brick ranchstyle
houses.

The boy was stared at and whispered about the whole
way. The girls giggled and cupped their hands to one
another's ears and then looked back at him and laughed
tinkling laughs. The boys put on their best tough-guy looks
and openly sized him up. Most of them wore pegged,
button-fly Levis with cut-off belt loops, motorcycle boots
or snapjacks, white t-shirts or white t-shirts under Buena
High letter jackets, and duck's-ass or rain-drain haircuts.

The boy sighed heavily. He had been through this scene
what? . . . eight times now? The next few weeks would be
the worst of his life. The only consoling thought was that
maybe he was old enough now—after all, he *was* a junior—
not to have to fight a dozen guys to find his proper spot in
the pecking order. But from the glares he was getting from
the young pachucos on the bus, he wasn't very hopeful.
He'd just have to kick ass and take names, then.

One curious observation on the way to school did manage to poke through the boy's crust of misery and self-
pity. The kids who got on the bus in the Apaches and the
Villages, even in the junior officer developments, had
been a mixed lot. But on Colonels' Row it was different.
The girls were better dressed, certainly, with fine cash-
mere sweaters and gleaming Bass Weejun loafers. That
was to be expected. The thing was, they were almost *all*
girls. Only one boy boarded at the stops along Colonels'
Row. Maybe colonels only had females in their loins.
When it came to the brass, anything was possible.

One of the girls who got on there was a black-haired
beauty with Mediterranean looks. She had begun watching
him almost immediately. She sat several rows in front of
him and turned halfway round in her seat to stare. Her
eyes were deep brown, bold and unwavering. She had a
slight smile on her lips. When her seatmate started to
giggle and whisper something in her ear, she had pushed
the other girl away in annoyance and continued to look at
him. The boy tried to stare her down, but in the end,
turned his face to the window, completely routed.

When the bus finally pulled into the school grounds, the
boy was once again heartsick. The school yard was rock-
strewn ground so layered with dust that every footstep
kicked up swirling clouds. The school itself, two ram-
shackle structures built of stucco and painted in garish
pastels.

When the boy stepped off the bus, the black-haired girl was waiting for him, her books clutched to her blossoming, cashmere-covered chest. So was a circle of boys, standing hip-shot with thumbs hooked in their jeans, flexing biceps and trying their best to look like killers.

"Hello there," said the girl. "My name is Rachel Field."

How could she do this to him with those punks looking on and leering? One of them laughed and mimicked in a falsetto, "Hellllo there. My name is Rachel Field."

"Uh, hello," he said to the girl. "Uh, mine's Jack Willow."

"Welcome to our fair high school," she smiled, sticking out a hand. A boy with a greasy DA held out a limp-wristed hand and parroted in a high, sing-song whine, "Yes, welcome to our fair high school."

The boy looked at her hand for a moment, then took it. "Uh, yeah, thanks."

"Willow, get your goddamn hand off that girl," a voice behind him thundered. The boy spun around, jerking the girl, still attached, half off her feet. He shook her paw loose and stood with an incredulous grin on his face. "McCauley! Charlie McCauley! I'll be damned!"

"Hiya, dork."

"What are you doing here? You're Air Force. When you left Paris you were going to Wright-Patterson."

"Our orders were changed," said McCauley with a grin and a shrug. He was a tall, handsome boy, dressed like the others. "My dad's been seconded to the grubby Army, working on drones or some hush-hush shit."

"Jesus, Charlie, I'm glad to see you."

"I just bet you are," McCauley said with a smile. He turned to the circle of toughs, still there and openly listening, and said, "Why don't you homos fuck off? This guy is an old pal of mine. Furthermore, he was the king of Paris American, a *real* school, and he can kick any ass in this rinky-dink hole without working up a sweat. Go on. I'll introduce him around later.'' There was a murmur of hey-man-how-ya-doin's and hey-man-see-ya-laters directed toward them as the group reluctantly drifted off to class.

"Well, Jackie me boy, I see you still go straight for the expensive whiskey, even though you were born to rotgut.''

"What's that supposed to mean?''

"The girl.''

Jackie looked around. He had forgotten all about the girl. She was gone.

"Who is she?'' he asked.

"Rachel Field. We call her the Snow Queen. Every guy in this school has tried to get into her knickers, including old loverboy McCauley himself. Nobody's even got close. You got good taste, Jackie, but that one is nothing but a terminal case of blue balls.''

Jackie shrugged. "So who's interested? She said hello to me first; I didn't start it.''

"Just warning you. Don't want you to get all worked up over nothing.''

"Why do you say she's expensive whiskey?''

"Her daddy is deputy commander of this here U.S. Army Electronics Proving Ground. He's some hotshit scientist and the ranking colonel on post.''

"Oh.''

"Oh, indeed,'' said McCauley. "Colonel Herschel Field. He's also a Jew. One of the highest ranking Jews in the Army, I hear. Course, there ain't that many in the Army. You should also know that there's only one thing in the whole wide world Colonel Field hates more than Hitler.''

"What's that?''

"Army brats.''

"Army brats?''

"Army brats.''

"How can he hate Army brats? His daughter is an Army brat."

McCauley grinned. "I'll be more specific. He hates little boy Army brats who come sniffing around his princess. And there's only one thing in the whole wide world he hates more than little boy Army brats: little boy Army brats whose fathers are, yech, enlisted men."

"How the hell do you know all this?"

"From some of his comments. I take Rachel out once in a while. I'm an Air Force major's son, one of the elite. And Colonel Field hates me."

"That's not hard to understand. You're an elite asshole, Charlie. Besides, as I said, who's interested?"

"Sir, please put your seat back up. We're about to land in Lexington."

"Yes. Thank you."

12

Colonels' Row sat on the post's highest point, in the foothills of the Huachuca Mountains. The big, wooden houses with their screened porches were tucked beneath transplanted elms and oaks, huge, broad-leafed trees that threw dappled light on the coaxed-up lawns. Fronting the Row was the post parade ground. Sere, sage-pocked hills rose up behind.

Across the parade ground from Colonels' Row was a string of large wooden buildings: the post headquarters and other administrative offices. The Row itself went on and up until it petered out in the arroyos and lizard lairs of the climbing mountains, passing the Officers Swimming Pool on the way. The lower end of the Row came past the bottom of the parade ground, then curved sharply away and ran for a few hundred yards before dipping down into the world of non-field-grade officers, the slight drop in elevation as much a demarcation line for the officers as West Apache and the Villages were for the noncoms.

Even on the Row, rank was everything. The house of the post commander, a brigadier general, was no different in size or style from any of the others. The only distinction was that it sat directly across the street from the flagpole that neatly bisected the parade field. On either side of the general's house were the houses of the colonels, going away in both directions at a pace commensurate with rank and seniority. At the nether reaches of the Row were a few favored majors and the leaf colonels. Then came the bird colonels, creeping toward the center of the Row and the commander's house in order of their time in grade. An officer could measure his precise position in the post's social structure by the number of steps it took him to reach the general's front porch from his own. Each time a senior officer was transferred or retired, unless his replacement was identical in rank and seniority, the whole Row moved house. The only thing that kept life at the top from bogging down in a never-ending game of musical chairs was the fact that the nature of the work done at Fort Huachuca did not necessitate the constant transfers that plagued the arms branches of the service.

Huachuca was a very specialized place. It had once been a Negro cavalry post, home to a troop of Buffalo Soldiers. Their mission had been to chase, catch, and hang any Chiricahua Apaches and Mexican bandits inconsiderate enough to annoy the white ranchers in the area. And although that mission changed over the years, Fort Huachuca did not change in one respect: It remained a burial pit for Army careers. A posting to the ugly fort on the ragged edge of the Arizona desert, only thirty miles or so from the wastelands of Sonora, told a man that his services were no longer considered vital to the national defense. Only when the Army, for reasons of elbow room and security, decided to turn the desolate place into an electronics proving ground under the direction of the Signal Corps, did all that change. It was still a way station on the road to undistinguished retirement for many of the administrative officers, but for the officer/scientist it was a garden spot. These officers, using state-of-the-art equipment and drawing from a seemingly inexhaustible budget, worked on the frontiers of electronics technology, developing sophisticated killer drones and guidance systems for that new celestial toy, the satellite.

The Field home was next to the post commander's, to its right as it faced the parade ground. From without, it looked like all the others. Jackie did not get to see the inside right off. Rachel Field, so curious and bold that first day, did not approach him again. They did share several classes, however, and now and then Jackie would catch her looking at him the way she had that first time. Encouraged by these tantalizing glances, one day he cornered her in the hallway between classes and asked her for a date.

That was several weeks into the school year. Jackie had already made the football team's starting eleven and had already proved to be a standout, playing left guard on offense and middle linebacker on defense, where his vicious tackling made him popular among the boys. He also was a hit with the girls. The consensus among them was that he was "cute." The boy exploited his popularity with a vengeance, dating every pretty girl not already committed to someone else. He had shunned Rachel Field, however, because of McCauley's words of warning . . . until those classroom glances, reeking of smoldering desire, to Jackie's way of thinking, changed his mind.

It was typical that while many of the "townies" had been slow to grant him acceptance, the majority of the students, the Army brats, had not. Military kids, used to changing schools at a moment's notice, did not fool around. With them, all social mores, from drinking to dry fucking, were accelerated to the point of spin-out. They knew they did not have time to slowly build friendships or feuds. Their judgments were quick and lasting. They either wanted to fight you or fuck you, Jackie thought. At Buena High School he had come up a winner, thanks largely to Charlie McCauley's early endorsement. He was, in McCauley's sardonic phrase, "a social comet whose light has lit up the dark universe of Buena High."

Jackie did not become cocky over his success. He had been through enough of these transitions to know it could easily have gone the other way. Even so, it still came as something of a shock when Rachel Field turned him down flat. He had taken what seemed an hour to burble his request that she accompany him to a pregame victory dance set for the night before the Buena Colts would demolish Benson. She had taken what seemed a second to say "Don't be silly" and walk away. Jackie had stood there glassy-eyed for a moment, until noticing that others, including the eagle-eyed McCauley, were starting to look at him. Then he had hooked his thumbs into his low-riding Levis and swaggered off to his next class, whistling jauntily through dry lips.

"Excuse me, when is the next bus to Harlan?"
"Not till six A.M., soldier."
"I'd like a ticket, please."
"One way or round trip?"
"Round trip."
"That'll be twenty-six dollars American."

It was no time at all before Jackie solved the mystery of Colonels' Row. It wasn't that colonels had only girls in their loins; it was that their sons were away at military school or expensive prep schools in the east. Buena High was good enough for the daughters of the Row, but not the sons. The girls would not need an expensive education to marry the promising junior officers they would marry, but a piece of paper from a sorry place like Buena was not going to get a boy into West Point or a good engineering school like MIT. For that they needed a place like NMMI, the New Mexico Military Institute. Besides, even colonels were hard pressed to send *two* children to private school at

The

hters in their group. With one exception:
ver any parties at the Field house. Rachel
ome to the parties, but she never played
nd the boy never heard anyone suggest she
still smarting from her cut in the corridor,
er to dance at these affairs, but he often
ing him one of those maddening looks of
o idea what they meant anymore, now that
out romantic interest. Perhaps he had some
nity only she could see. Whatever it was,
im.

as always an inexplicable relief for him to
at a party. Or to see that she never came
with any one boy. Or to see that she never
o one of the empty rooms with any of her
vay he did with his, first making certain that
ot miss noticing. Her date was usually one
who had cracked the tight Army-brat circle,
or Beau Lewis, the only boy living on the
ad been booted out of three eastern prep
MMI for unruly behavior, leaving Buena to
othered Jackie to see Rachel arrive with
d a reputation as a cocksman. He watched
lly for telltale signs of intimacy and told
d find none.

END OF THE LINE. HARLAN!'' The
even though the sole remaining passenger,
, was already at the door.

the same time. The one problem with such custom, and it was one much discussed at the officers club, was that it left the girls of Colonels' Row with no alternative but to socialize with the boys of Suds Row.

The colonels' dilemma was Jackie's boon. He dated colonels' daughters almost exclusively, not so much because he liked them better than sergeants' daughters, but because they provided him a passport to the Row itself. The Row was so quiet. There were no Filipino noncom children yapping away in their native Tagalog. No frustrated A. J. Foyts working on superchargers and shattering the golden desert air with the sound of 450 cubic inches. No smells of sour diapers and frying fats. No, Colonels' Row was a dreamy world that whispered, never shouted, and it whispered of power and wealth and *class*. Inside the houses of the girls he took out were exotic items harvested from overseas postings. Not crudely carved lazy susans topped with wooden peasants riding wooden water buffaloes. Not beer mugs from Bavaria that played "Lili Marlene" when you lifted the lid. Not any of the vulgar curios so prevalent in NCO houses that at times it seemed the same cut-rate decorator had done them all. No. The Row had dining tables made of solid oak, not formica. The Row had delicate jade sculptures, not cheap cuckoo clocks that never worked. The Row had hand-knotted Persian carpets on the floor, not yellowing linoleum. The Row had Filipino or Mexican servants in white coats . . . paneled rooms just for books . . . end-tables with damask inlay as complicated as a kaleidoscope . . . Morris chairs of rich leather and padded wet bars adorned with regimental crests. The Row had mothers who were pretty and soft-spoken instead of dowdy and shrill, fathers who gave a boy knowing winks and avuncular pats on the back instead of threats of violence and drunken war stories.

Jackie was never quite sure what the fathers of these

girls did in their jobs. "Officer" things, he guessed. They must have been administrators or scientists. There were no Infantry line commands at Huachuca. Jackie always felt vague feelings of inferiority and shame when he entered any of the houses on the Row, and he could only protect his pride and sense of worth by nurturing secret contempt for officers without troop commands. All the boy knew was that the colonels were unfailingly and coolly polite to him. At first meeting they would be friendly and jovial and man-to-man in a burst of inappropriate interest, the way adults often are with adolescents they don't know. Once he told them where he lived and what his father was, they were still polite and still friendly, but polite above all, with everything else suddenly mechanical and forced.

Nor, at first, did he know where such people went in the evenings, only that they went out almost every night. Later he learned that it was invariably to parties or, more often, to the officers club. When he picked up one of the girls for a date, her parents, too, would be preparing to go out. The colonels would be wearing full dress uniforms or expensive civilian suits or sports jackets. The colonels' wives would be in formal gowns or cocktail dresses and sometimes a fur coat, if there was a chill in the desert night air. "We'll be at The Club, dear," the mothers would say to their daughters, and the boy would think that The Club must be a wonderful place. His own parents would go out maybe once a month at most and then only to a 25-cent movie at one of the post theaters or, if a celebration were in order, to the NCO Club for the $1.99 fried shrimp dinner.

Jackie and his buddies had their own haunts. They could take their girls to a movie at the Apache Drive-In or grab a foot-long hot dog at Sue 'n' Herb's. And they had their *boondocker*, taking their keg of beer, their old blankets, and their dates to some dry desert river bed, where they

would build a fire, tun⌐
work on getting drunk ⌐

The important thing ⌐
wives off to The Club⌐
when Jackie brought he⌐
ately and ineptly on th⌐
with only one ear det⌐
lay on a rug in front of⌐
own house had nothing ⌐
Those carpets were a⌐
symbol of luxury, and ⌐
him up onto a sofa, co⌐
floor gave them rug bu⌐

The nicest thing abo⌐
that they were large ⌐
could slow dance to Jo⌐
bumping into one anot⌐
each with large scree⌐
with rooms where a c⌐
fumbling, molten kiss⌐
not be disturbed. The⌐
with the parents off to⌐
they left, saying "Goo⌐
teenagers and then dra⌐
unsmiling moments o⌐
colonels, all wonderfu⌐
at the boys and say sor⌐
foot on the floor at all⌐
to the liquor cabinet, ⌐
fellows, heh heh heh.⌐
the door, the juvenile ⌐
make a beeline for th⌐
house laughed nervou⌐

Their parties rota⌐
Colonels' Row, that ⌐

colonels' da⌐
There were ⌐
Field would ⌐
hostess to on⌐
do so. Jacki⌐
never asked ⌐
caught her g⌐
hers. He had⌐
he had to ru⌐
amusing defe⌐
she infuriate⌐

And yet it⌐
see her arriv⌐
twice in a ro⌐
disappeared i⌐
dates . . . the⌐
Rachel could ⌐
of the townie⌐
or McCauley.⌐
Row. Lewis ⌐
schools *and* ⌐
mop up. It ⌐
Lewis, who h⌐
the pair care⌐
himself he co⌐

"HARLAN⌐
driver shouted⌐
a young soldi⌐

13

It took Jackie some time to realize he was hopelessly in love with Rachel Field. There was no blinding revelation, no turning point, nothing he could put his finger on. First she filled his night thoughts, then his daydreams, then every crack and crevice of his life. He began to pine for her. He stopped dating. He stopped going to the parties on Colonels' Row. He stayed home—once only a place to eat and sleep, a forced exile from the glamorous life of the Row—and played the same records over and over in his room, torch songs by Elvis, like "Don't" and "Love Me."

Solicitous friends asked whether anything was wrong. He brushed them off with James Dean mumbles. His father, who had scornfully mocked Jackie's nocturnal forays to Colonels' Row and called his friends "that hoity-toity crowd," noticed and asked sarcastically, "You get tired of brown-nosing the brass, or did that hoity-toity crowd decide you weren't good enough for them after all and throw you out?" Then he saw the undiluted misery in the boy's face and said, "Sorry I said that, boy. You got a problem I can help you with?" Jackie just shook his head and locked himself in his room for yet another evening of elegies and Elvis.

In class he would stare at the back of Rachel's head, wondering why his inflamed eyes did not set her lustrous black hair afire, trying to will her into turning and giving him one of those old, now longed-for looks. But she had stopped watching him. He could no longer catch her eye.

His grades began to slip. Then it affected his football. Coach Winslow bawled him out for loafing and not paying attention at practice, then benched him altogether when he failed to pull from his left guard position and lead the blocking on a crucial third-and-three in the final game against Douglas. He had simply forgotten the assignment between the huddle and the three-point stance, searching instead for Rachel Field among the pom-pom girls on the sideline. He was seventeen years old and in love. His improvident heart ruled every facet of his life.

One afternoon, after three weeks of such behavior, Charlie McCauley grabbed him by the shirt collar and threw him bodily into his Ford Fairlane. They drove off in the direction of Naco, a tiny Mexican border town across the line from Bisbee, populated by twenty-five bartenders, fifty whores, seventy-five three-legged yellow dogs, and a dozen cantinas with names like The White Rat and The Blue Moon.

"It's gotta stop, Jackie," McCauley said. "You're coming apart at the goddamn seams. The only sure cure is to go to Naco and have Lupe sit on your face for an hour or so."

"Turn the car around, Charlie," Jackie said in a listless voice. "I can't. Not today."

"Then ask the goddamn bitch out and quit fartin' around."

"What bitch?"

"Rachel Field, of course. You think everybody in the goddamn school don't know? You've been mooning after her for weeks. It's disgusting. Everybody's laughing at you."

"They are?"

"Of course. Look, just ask her out. She likes you, for chrissakes."

"She does?"

"Of course. Every time I take her to one of those damn parties all she does is pump me for information about you and our days at Paris American together. What you were like. Who you went out with. Blah blah blah."

"She does?"

"How many times do I have to say it? Everybody's sick to death of listening to her talk about you."

"They are?"

McCauley rolled his eyes. He pulled the car to the shoulder of the the road and stopped. "Anybody ever tell you you're a hell of a conversationalist? 'They are? She does? She does? They are?' Christ, what a basket case." He pulled the car around and headed slowly back toward Sierra Vista. "Look, Jackie, do something, huh? Either ask her out or kill yourself, but stop all this goddamn suffering! It's enough to make a person barf."

"It is?"

His uncle was waiting for him at the depot in Harlan. Zeke Willow was wearing dirty overalls, but so were half the men in sight. If Jack Willow had not been in uniform, they might have missed each other. It had been seven years since he had been in Harlan County, and it occurred to him that he did not really know these people, his father's people. There had been the odd two- or three-day visit over the years, always when they were en route from one post to another. Willow had always had trouble putting the right name to the right face. And they always got him mixed up with his brothers, calling him by their names and them by his.

His uncle did not offer to shake hands. He did not even

say hello. He just said, "We laid him out over to Taggart's. I reckon you'll be wantin' to see him right off," then picked up the young soldier's suitcase and led the way to a decrepit pickup truck.

"How's my mother?" Willow asked.

Uncle Zeke's eyes narrowed, and he spit an amber string of tobacco juice. "She's restin' . . ." he said, using the family euphemism, ". . . up at the house." The Willow clan had never understood why Shelby had up and married such a "peak-ed" woman, frail as a baby bird and of a mind to put on airs. From up north somewhere, which explained a lot. There were stories about some trouble with her head.

They drove in silence to the funeral parlor. Willow shivered in the unheated cab, not so much from the air, which was cold, but from the passing scene. It was a gray, blustery day, and dirty slush left over from the last snow packed the gutters and stacked up in the town's corners. The buildings of the business district looked heartbroken, and a century's worth of coal dust seemed ineradicably ingrained in their sagging faces. The surrounding hills were equally depressing. The few trees on them had been stripped nude by winter, and the scars from years of strip mining completed the look of violation. The town wore its history over its shoulders like a filthy blanket.

What Willow knew of these other Willows was sketchy at best, picked up over the years in a remark here, a story there. Willow knew that until the late 1930s they had worked the coal, generation following generation into the mine shafts. He knew there had been bad trouble during the effort to unionize and that the Willows had been in the thick of it. He knew they had barricaded themselves in Uncle Zeke's house and that when the company's Pinkertons marched on the house, shots were fired and two deputies had fallen dead.

When the law—the law being the company—failed to pinpoint which Willow had fired the shots, every male occupant of the house had been arrested and charged with murder. Zeke had served seven years in prison, and Uncle Lonzo had done three. The presiding judge, another good company man, had taken pity on young Shelby Willow, who was only sixteen and had already worked two years in the mines. He ordered Shelby into the CCC, the Civilian Conservation Corps, until the age of eighteen, when he would be allowed to choose between jail and the Army.

Willow knew his father had found a refuge and a home in the Army: three hots and a cot and a way to live above ground. The rest of the Willows, exiled from coal, had managed to scratch out a meager living working tobacco several miles outside Harlan, in narrow Cumberland range valleys not suited for it.

"Jimmy Taggart's done a right fine job on 'im," his uncle volunteered as they pulled into the funeral home parking lot. "Looks like he could sit right up and talk to you."

They parked, went inside, and found Taggart in his office, sitting with his feet propped on his desk and using a small penknife to cut a plug off a twisted rope of black tobacco. The undertaker was a tall, gaunt man. Just like Uncle Zeke. In fact, just like all the Willows and, it often seemed, just like everyone else in southeastern Kentucky. Taggart rose and shook the soldier's hand and said, "We're all real grieved about your pappy, son. I was just now sittin' here thinkin' about how us Taggarts have been burying you Willows ever since Dan'l Boone brought both our families through the Gap from Carolina. It's funny—funny strange—when you think on it."

The casket was on a bed of flowers on a raised platform in the chapel adjoining the office and laboratory. The hinged viewing lid was raised, showing his father from the waist up. Taggart stood easily with his hands clasped behind his back, looking solemn and watching for a discreet opportunity to spit into a small paper cup he carried. Willow's taciturn uncle suddenly turned garrulous. "We was out in the field tryin' to see just how deep that last frost went and worryin' on next season when he just grabbed his chest and pitched over. I wasn't but ten foot away when it happened, and he was gone before I could get to 'im, so I don't reckon he suffered none. I cain't think of any Willow what died so young. Not from natural causes no-how. I reckon it was them wars he was in what wore him out like that."

Willow only half heard his uncle. He stood looking at his father and wondering what it was that did not seem right. Taggart had done a fine job on him. He did look like he could sit right up and talk to you. His color was good. His face was calm. The new blue suit he wore was clean and looked expensive. That was it. His father was not wearing a uniform. Willow could not fully recognize his father in civilian clothes.

Jackie was shaken to the core. For three days he mulled over what Charlie McCauley had said, worrying it, examining it, believing it, not believing it. On the fourth day he ambushed Rachel Field in the middle of the Dust Bowl, the school lot halfway between the two pastel-colored buildings.

"Rachel, wait up a minute."

She stopped and waited without smiling.

"Uh, willyagotathedanzfridayniwime?"

"What did you say?"

The boy breathed deeply and repeated himself, this time forming the words slowly and carefully as if addressing a deaf-mute. "Will . . . you . . . go . . . to . . . the . . . dance . . . Friday . . . night . . . with . . . me?"

"Yes . . . I . . . would . . . love . . . to," she said.

"You . . . would? I mean, you would?"

"Yes."

"I'll pick you up at seven."

"I live—"

"I know where you live."

His aunts hugged him, and he shook hands with a dozen men he did not know. His cousins gawked at his uniform. He was set down in an overstuffed chair covered in chintz, and someone shoved a glass of cold lemonade at him while someone else brought him a cup of hot coffee and still another told him that they had waited dinner on him. That was the noon meal in these parts, he remembered.

"Have you seen your daddy yet?" asked Aunt Martha, Lonzo's wife. Without waiting for his reply, she rattled on. "Don't he look so natural? Don't he look like he could just sit right up and talk to you?" Willow said that he did.

He was led to the table. "It ain't proper dinner," his Aunt Thelma, Zeke's wife, explained. "It's more of a late breakfast. What do some folks call it? Brunch?" Willow said that they did.

There were biscuits and gravy and three kinds of eggs. There were griddlecakes and grits and store-bought bread. There was ham and bacon and link sausage and patty sausage. There was fried chicken and chicken-fried steak. There were hash-brown potatoes and hard-boiled eggs. There was coffee and milk and lemonade and iced tea. The womenfolk apologized for the sparseness of the meal but said they had not even known he was coming until a nice man from the Army, name of Sarjenmager Nelson, called early this morning. Willow said it would do nicely.

The talk around the table flowed smoothly, just as if Willow knew who everybody was and had lived among them all his life.

"Your mama is still restin' and the boys are with her. I thought about gettin' them up, but she needs her sleep at a time like this. She knows you're comin', though."

"Them brothers of yours have fit in right nice down here. The bigun's on the high school football team, and the littleun's bound to make it next year if'n he grows some . . . and if'n your mama decides to stay in these parts."

"The service is this evenin', if that's right by you . . . over to Taggart's. Reverend Slade will do the preachin'."

"Shelby didn't take to bein' home near as well as those two boys of his. Been away too long, I s'pose. He jest fretted about the Army and talked about his Army buddies."

"Shelby was up to Fort Knox ever' other week to see them Army doctors. He was always hopin' they could give him a clean bill of health so the Army would see he was recovered and would take him back."

"He wasn't no tabacca man, that's fer sure. Not that he didn't work hard. Your daddy could work harder'n a fresh-whipped mule. It was jest that when his body was in the field, his mind was off soldiering."

"You gonna make the Army your life, boy? Like your daddy did?"

"Don't you let 'em send you to Veet Nam, now, y'hear? Harlan County's already lost itself three boys. There was that Jessup boy and the Hicks boy and the Williams boy. And Billy Fink's boy done got both his legs blowed off. You stay outta that Veet Nam lest it wear you down and kill you before your time, like your daddy."

"If'n it don't kill him right off instead of waitin'."

"Which one of them Williams boys was it what got killed over there, Lonzo? Was it that red-headed Billy Williams or that mean-as-a-snake Dickie Williams, what was always in trouble with the law?"

"More chicken, boy?"

"You ever think about farming, boy? They's worse ways a man can make a livin'."

"Hell, Zeke—excuse me for cussin', ever'body—but you call what we do makin' a livin'? We made more in the mines in nineteen and thirty-seven than we do now, thirty years later. Boy's better off in the Army. Hell, Shelby knowed that."

Willow listened politely, following one, then another with his eyes, nodding or shaking his head when a question came his way, using packed cheeks as an excuse for not joining in. He was ravenous. He should have eaten on the plane instead of gorging himself at a time like this. But the women beamed down on his gluttony and kept passing plates in his direction.

After the meal, the men went into the sitting room while the women cleared the table. Willow wandered around the parlor, then froze when he saw a picture of his father on the mantle: a color polaroid of his father lying in his coffin. It already had a cheap cardboard frame. "Looks real natural, don't he?" said Aunt Polly, his father's sister, coming up behind him. "Looks like he could sit right up and talk to you."

14

Jackie was disappointed. The inside of the Field home looked the same as the inside of every other home he had seen on Colonels' Row: the same fine rugs; the same expensive, sturdy furniture; the same objects d'art. The only difference was a grand piano and a funny-looking candelabra sitting on a low table in a corner of the living room.

He was not disappointed in Colonel and Mrs. Field. Colonel Field was trim, gray-haired, and distinguished, even in civilian clothes. Mrs. Field was gorgeous. Jackie openly ogled her the first time he met her.

He was greeted at the door by a white-jacketed Filipino and ushered in to Mrs. Field in the living room. She was dressed to go out. Rachel was nowhere in sight.

The mother was, Jackie hoped fervently, a premonition of what the daughter would look like in maturity. She had the same anthracite black hair, the same oval face, the same olive complexion, the same sloe eyes. The difference was in the body. Mrs. Field had a full, lush woman's body that was only just beginning to broaden at the hips, the ripe body of a *Jewess*. The word itself dripped with musk in his mind. A Jewess right out of *Look Homeward Angel*. How had Wolfe described his Jewess? Melon-breasted,

that was it. Mrs. Field was melon-breasted. Jackie almost
drooled on his best shirt. Mrs. Field smiled. "How do you
do?" she said in a throaty voice. She was fully aware of
the effect she was having on him. He croaked a socially
acceptable response, and then he was marched into the
library, where Colonel Field was waiting. The colonel was
also dressed to go out. There was still no sign of Rachel.

"Jack is it?" the colonel asked after the introductions.

"Yessir."

"Short for John, I suppose."

"Uh, nossir. Just Jack."

"I see. Do you attend Buena . . . Jack?"

"Yessir."

"I see."

Jackie would have traded his soul for a proper first
name, something with a little dignity. Or for the ability to
say breezily, No, sir, I don't go to Buena. I'm just down
from NMMI visiting my father. You must know my father,
Major General Willow? Or down from Harvard. Or Tim-
buktu U. Anyplace but Buena.

"Do you live here on post, Jack?"

"Yessir." Volunteer nothing. Maybe he won't ask.

Colonel Field looked him over carefully, a faint smile
on his lip. "One of the Villages, perhaps?"

Shit, he knows I'm Suds Row. "Uh, nossir. West
Apache."

"I see."

"We would be in one of the Villages but we haven't
been here long." Jackie said hastily. "My father is a
master sergeant."

"Sergeants are the backbone of the Army," said the
colonel, making the cliche sound even more trite than it
was.

He knows I'm ashamed, Jackie thought, and that made
him even more ashamed—and a little angry. "Yessir, they

are. And until he developed medical problems he was in
the Infantry, not the Signal Corps.''

"That's too bad. But I guess the Infantry has to have
men, too, and I suppose it is inevitable that the Army must
have its infantry,'' said the colonel, misunderstanding the
boy completely.

"But, sir. The Infantry is the Army!''

"Only a small part of it, Jack, a very small part. Of all
the many and varied fields the Army embraces, the Infantry is the least demanding.'' Colonel Field smiled coolly
and shook the boy's hand. "It was a pleasure to meet you,
Jack.'' And he left the room.

Jackie waited alone in the library until Rachel was ready.

Supper that evening was even more sumptuous than
dinner had been. Willow thought he had never seen people
eat so much. It had been decided that everyone should eat
before the funeral service because, as Aunt Martha said,
"It's not something a body wants to go through on an
empty stomach.''

Two more distant relatives had arrived during the
afternoon, each fresh from Taggart's and bearing a small
gift: more snapshots of his dead father in cardboard frames.
They were given prominent display in the living room.

Willow's brothers had grown considerably in the months
since he had seen them last, and they were shy and distant
with him. His mother seemed unchanged by events.

"Take off that uniform'' was the first thing she said. "I
despise the sight of it.''

"Now, mother. Why do you say that?''

"That uniform put the knife in your father's chest. And
these . . . these *hillbillies* twisted it once it was in.''

"Now, mother. These are good people. They're a little
different, but they're good people. They helped you and
dad a lot.''

"They helped kill him. He was so embarrassed by their charity that he worked himself to death for them."

"Now, mother. You can't blame them or the Army. The Army was what dad lived for."

"It's what he died for. It will kill you, too, if you don't give up this nonsense and find yourself a decent occupation. You should go back to college."

"Now, mother."

His mother announced that she would attend neither the funeral service nor the burial. She wandered around the house pressing a damp cloth to her forehead at regular intervals. The Kentucky relatives were not dismayed. They were solicitous, fetching whatever her whim required, offering her this chair or that spot on the couch, pressing food and drink on her. It was partly the respect due a fresh widow, partly the indulgence hill people have always accorded to the "tetched." They seemed to know instinctively that she *was* tetched. They did not know all the details: that she had suffered a complete nervous breakdown when Shelby was in Korea; that her spells of depression came and went unpredictably; that months of electric shock treatments in Army hospitals had not made a whit of difference. They never came right out and said anything. They only told each other what Shelby himself had told them years before—that she was "awfully high strung."

Willow asked his mother what her plans were.

"I'm leaving this horrid place tomorrow," she said. "I loved your father, but he dragged me to some horrid places because of that stupid Army of his. First it was that horrid place in the desert, and then it was this horrid place. I'm going back to Buffalo and *my* family. The men in *my* family are real gentlemen. The men in *my* family do not have disgusting habits. The men in *my* family do not spit tobacco juice."

They drove to Taggart's in a convoy, without his mother.

Willow sat in the cab of the pickup, sandwiched between Uncle Zeke and Aunt Thelma. His brothers rode in the back.

In the foyer of the funeral parlor a quartet of local men were singing "Peace in the Valley," his father's favorite. One by one, Willows and friends of the family trooped past the open casket for a last look. Willow paused only long enough to put the patch and badges from Sergeant Hazard into the box.

He had just sat down in the front pew when a commotion at the coffin made him look up. His youngest brother had not wanted to look at the body of his dead father. Uncle Lonzo had picked the crying boy off his feet and had carried him to the casket. "Now you jest hush up that caterwauling and kiss your daddy goodbye."

Willow jumped up and ran to the boy's rescue, imploring his uncle, "Please. Don't make him do that. He doesn't want to. Please don't." Uncle Lonzo let go of the boy, but it was clear he considered the whole thing disgraceful.

The mourners took their seats, Willow and his brothers in the front row with his father's brothers and sisters; friends of the family behind. While they waited for the service to begin, his uncles talked tobacco prices, and his aunts and cousins gossipped merrily across the pews. When the minister finally emerged from the side door and took the podium, all chattering ceased and, as if someone had thrown a switch, was replaced by shrill weeping and keening. "O Lordy, Lordy, *take him*, Lord," wailed his Aunt Thelma. "O Jesus, oh we loved him *so*, dear Jesus," cried his Aunt Polly. "O Lordy, take him to your bosom and *rock* him, Lord," shouted his Aunt Martha. Each lament was punctuated by *Amens* from the others.

With a wave of his gnarled hand, the preacher stopped the noise dead, and everyone sat back with expectant

smiles, all outward signs of grief gone as quickly as they
had risen. The preacher was an ancient man with a thin,
heavily wrinkled face and long, whispy white hair. He was
dressed in black broadcloth, and he held a Bible in each
hand. He waited for the coughing and shuffling and squirming to die away, glaring out at the congregation, and then
began:

"Friends, ol' John Willow was a good man. You all
know that's so. He sired fine sons and sturdy, God-fearin'
daughters who gave him fine grandchildren. Oh, surely he
had sins. Yes, friends, he had him some sins. We all
knowed he ran a little moon to make ends meet, and I once
seed' him whip a fine young setter bitch half to death with
a switch. But them was little sins, friends. Why, that fool
dog—" The preacher had caught a distressed signal from
Uncle Zeke. He stopped and said with considerable
annoyance, "What in tarnation do you want, Zeke? You
done broke my rhythm."

Zeke left his seat in the front row, whispered something
to the reverend, and sat back down with an apologetic
smile. The preacher coughed loudly and began again:

"Friends, I just been tole that this man we're sendin' off
to the glorious Kingdom of Jesus today ain't ol' John
Willow. It's his boy Shelby. His youngest. I guess I
shoulda knowed that since I myself buried ol' John Willow
some twenty-five years ago. Well, friends, I caint' rightly
say I knowed ol' John's boy Shelby all that well. He went
off to the Army at a tender age, right after the troubles.
But I can tell you this, friends: if'n he was a Willow, he
was a fine man. Amen."

A chorus of *Amens* rocketed around the chapel. Everyone rose and headed for the door so they could get a good
place in the motorcade to the cemetery. Uncle Zeke led the
wobbly preacher over to Willow, looking sheepish. The
reverend said, "I'm right sorry, son. For some dang rea-

son I had it in my old addled head that it was ol' John Willow, your grandaddy, I was saying words over. I reckon I'm gettin' old. I sure hope you've taken no offense.'' Willow mumbled something reassuring to the old minister and drew Uncle Zeke aside, signaling for Taggart to join them.

"Uncle Zeke, Mr. Taggart . . . uh, look, I don't mean to offend you in any way. It was a fine service. Don't worry about the mixup—it didn't matter. Uh, you've all been wonderful to me and to my mother and by brothers . . . and you were wonderful to my father before he died. I can't thank you enough for making a place here for them. And I'm glad the service was held here in Harlan County, really I am. But I've changed my mind. I've decided not to bury my father here after all. I'm going to bury him at Arlington National Cemetery. Please forgive me and please don't be sore.''

His uncle looked dumbfounded. "But the family ground is here, boy.''

"*Your* family ground is here, Uncle Zeke, not his. Can't you see. *His* family ground is there. He was a soldier. He . . . He doesn't belong here. He belongs there. With other soldiers.''

The two men were silent a moment. Then Zeke said, "I reckon I best tell the others.'' And Taggart said, "I'll get him ready to go.''

"Thank you. Thank you both,'' Willow said with relief. He turned to his uncle. "Did my father keep any uniforms at the house?'' His uncle nodded, and Willow said to Taggart, "Put him in uniform. Full decorations.''

15

The boy nuzzled the girl's bare breast like a newborn infant. One hand was tucked around her waist, the other was under her skirt. She held her thighs pressed together to trap it far short of its goal.

"Jackie, please," she moaned.

"Rachel, please," he moaned back.

"Not down there. Do what you want up here, but not down there."

The boy sighed a heartbreaking sigh and sat up, knocking the speaker off the car window and cutting Sal Mineo off just as he was about to give James Dean the real lowdown on the game of chicken. It didn't matter anyway. They couldn't see the screen because the windshield was fogged.

"I love you, Rachel."

"I know. I love you, too. But we can't go all the way until we're married. We agreed."

"I know. It's just that I'm going crazy. You've got the softest skin in the world. It's like a spider web."

"Ugh."

Jackie laughed and reached a hand down to grope among the pedals, searching for the speaker.

"Oh, leave it off," Rachel said. "We've seen this

movie a million times already. Let's talk. It will take your mind— and your hands—off things.''

He laughed again. "Okay. What'll we talk about?"

"I don't know. Wait, yes I do. Let's ask each other questions about each other. Things we always secretly wanted to know. The other person has to be completely honest or else . . . or else no making out for a week.''

"A week? How 'bout twenty-four hours?"

"A week."

"Okay. You can start."

"Alright. Ummmmm, I got one. Why do you call the NCO housing *Suds Row*? I've never understood where the term came from."

"That's easy enough. In frontier days, the wives of the enlisted men, the few who lived on the forts, did all the post's laundry. They usually lived in a row of adobe shacks out behind the stables, and they would scrub the clothes on washboards in big tubs just outside the front doors. So everyone called it Suds Row.''

"See how educational this is? Okay, your turn."

Jackie thought awhile, then asked, "Remember the first time I asked you for a date? That time in the hallway? Why did you say no? Didn't you like me then?"

Rachel giggled. "I *loved* you then. I fell in love with you the first time I set eyes on you, on the bus. Something just popped inside me, and I knew you were the boy for me. But I was furious that you didn't see that I was the girl for you right away. You were running around and dating every girl in school. You were soooo dumb. So I decided to punish you until you came to your senses. If only you hadn't been so dense. Think of all the time we wasted."

"Yeah. I was dumb. Well, that answers my question. Your turn."

"Okay. Why do you want to join the Army after you

graduate? I would think you'd have had enough of it as a dependent.''

Jackie shrugged. "I don't know."

"Completely honest, remember? A week without fooling around, remember?"

He shrugged again. "I've wanted to be a soldier all my life. I don't really remember when it started. My father has always been my hero, I guess. At Fort Lewis we had a house with an attic where my dad used to keep his things. That was the nicest house we ever lived in. Anyway, I used to go up in the attic and play with his medals and look at all his scrapbooks. They were full of newspaper stories about the Second Division in World War Two. There were a lot of photographs in there, too. He had these pictures of him and his Army buddies after the liberation of Paris. They had their arms around each other, and they had bottles of wine in their hands and flowers stuck in their helmets. My father always looked so . . . so *happy* in those pictures. Much happier than when he was home. Maybe it was because he was away from my mother and her problems. I've told you all about that. She didn't get real sick until he was in Korea, but I think she was, uh, high strung, right from the beginning.

"Anyway, I started reading all the books on military history I could handle. I've read every book on the military in the post library here. What I learned was that soldiers, much more than politicians, even presidents, can change the whole destiny of nations. Think about that, Rache. A soldier in the right place at the right time can change the world. I love my father and I admire him, but I don't want to spend the rest of my life on Suds Row. I'm going to be an officer. And I'm going into one of the arms branches—Infantry or Armor or Artillery—and I don't care what your father says. No supply officer or signal officer ever changed the world. Julius Caesar, Napoleon,

Stilwell, Patton, Rommel—they're the ones who made history. Do you understand what I'm trying to say?''

"I guess so," Rachel said without enthusiasm. "But I'm not exactly thrilled with the idea of being an Army wife. It hasn't been a bed of roses for my mother. Or for your mother."

"I know," the boy agreed. "My mom's crazy as a loon and your mom drinks like a goldfish." The moment the words were out of his mouth he shut his eyes and prayed that lightning would strike him dead.

He felt the girl stiffen beside him. "What makes you say that?" she asked in a tight voice.

Jackie opened his eyes and backpedaled. "Nothing, Rache. I'm sorry. I didn't mean anything."

"You answer me, Jackie Willow. Right now. What do you know about that? Who's been telling you stories?"

"Nobody. Honest."

"You got that idea from somewhere, and I want . . . no, I demand to know where."

"Rachel, I've got two good eyes," he said softly. "I spend too much time at your house not to notice something like that. Every time I pick you up, your mother is already in her cups, even before they go out. A couple of times I saw your folks coming home from the club as I was leaving and your father had to carry her up the steps. Aw look, hon, it's no big deal. All families have problems. It's got nothing to do with you, with who you are or what you are. What you are is wonderful."

Rachel was crying. Jackie gently pulled her face to his chest and stroked her long black hair. He murmured something brilliant like "There, there, now. Don't cry. There, there." He thought about the last time he had seen her mother come home drunk from the club. He had dropped Rachel off and was sitting in his father's car smoking a cigarette and watching her bedroom window, waiting for the light to go off, when the Fields had pulled up and got out. They could not see him parked in the shadows, did not know he had overheard their conversation:

"Don't you tell me, you slut! His hand was on your ass."

"But, darling, when a brigadier general asks one to dance, one dances. Isn't that what you taught me, oh so many years gone by?"

"Don't you tell me, you slut! His hand was on your ass!"

"You've already said that. Besides, it wasn't exactly the first time a man has put his hand on my ass while we were dancing. And isn't it strange that it didn't seem to bother you this much when you were bucking for captain . . . or major . . . or colonel?"

"Slut! Not only was his hand on your ass, but anyone could see the bastard had a hard-on and that you were rubbing against it. There I sit with the bastard's wife, and you and him are humping each other on the dance floor. Goddamn slut!"

"At least the old coot is still able to *get* a hard-on, Herschel my love. Do you suppose that once you finally get your precious star, *you* might be able to get it up again, too?"

There had followed a slap that sounded like a pistol shot. Jackie had sat there mortified, wanting desperately to flee but unable to move without revealing his presence. He heard Mrs. Field's ragged sobbing as the two of them clumped up the porch steps and into the house. He prayed that Rachel had not overheard them. He sat there in the car for a long time, until long after all the lights in the big house had gone out, and then he had driven slowly back to West Apache, happy for the first time to be heading away from Colonels' Row rather than toward it.

Rachel, too, was thinking of her parents. She thought

about how, just a few days before, she had come into her mother's bedroom and found her there, sitting at her dressing table, weeping over an album of discolored photographs. It was not the first time Rachel had walked in upon this scene. She knew what was in that album: pictures of her mother as a young woman. In a tutu. In tights and leg warmers. On stage. At the exercise bar. Relaxing between work sessions. Laughing with friends. Leaping among placid pigeons in Central Park, arms and legs akimbo in a parody of Nijinsky.

Her mother had been a dancer, a skilled enough dancer to have performed with a small troupe in New York. With that amazon's chest of hers, she would never have been a principal in a big company, but she had been good enough to dance secondary roles. But more than that, Rachel knew, her mother had loved the life, the people, the *idea* of the dance. She had even loved the work and the pain of it. Rachel knew something about that herself. She had taken lessons since the age of four. She wasn't good enough to think of making a career of it, but her mother had quietly encouraged her to consider a career of some sort, something beyond that of a housewife. "Find something you love to do and then carry it as far as you can," she would say. "Don't give it up so easily . . . like I did."

Rachel knew her mother had tried to go on dancing for a while after marrying Lieutenant Herschel Field. She had tried to put together amateur dance groups at this duty station or that. Finally she had given up in despair at the constant uprootings, the moving from one hick post to another, all of them so painfully provincial that the officers and their henna-haired wives all thought Balanchine was a brand of ale.

Rachel had watched her mother grow more withdrawn over the years, an intelligent woman surrounded by women who were merely wily. She had seen her mother forced to smile and flatter the poison-tongued wives of higher-ranking officers, watched her feign interest in their constant jabber of who was sleeping with whom, whose husband had made the latest promotion list and whose husband had been passed over. She had seen her mother manhandled on the dance floor at the club, those long dancer's legs and billowing breasts sending false signals to drunken, would-be Lotharios. And she had seen her father pretend not to notice if the man happened to outrank him.

Rachel hated her father. He was a cold calculating man who never displayed any visible sign of affection for either her or her mother unless he had an appreciative audience. All he cared about was his career. How often had she heard her father berate her mother over her mother's drinking? Not because he cared for her, or feared for her health, but because he worried about how it made him look to the others at The Club, how it might affect his career. An officer who could not control his wife could not be expected to control an important scientific project. Colonel Field was not a teetotaler himself—men who did not drink at all were suspect in the Army—but Rachel had often seen him artfully nurse a single highball for an entire evening. It was too easy to say the wrong thing, do the wrong thing, if you were looped.

She could guess why her father had married her mother. A beautiful wife could do a lot for an officer's career. What Rachel would never understand was why her mother had married him.

Rachel loved Jackie Willow. She truly did. He was smart and handsome and gentle and loving. He was everything her father was not. She wanted to marry him. But whatever she decided to do with her own life, dancing or something else, she wanted to do it as more than just an

Army officer's wife. She loved Jackie's contagious enthusiasm, and she could listen to him talk and dream out loud for hours on end, but the object of his passion disturbed her. Why someone with his resources would choose to channel his energy into an Army career bewildered her. It was such a sterile, demeaning way of life. But if that was what he wanted, she would stick by him. He would be different from her father. And she from her mother.

The phone rang only once before someone picked it up and Willow heard a voice with a Boston accent say, "Delta Company, First Battalion, Third Infantry, the Old Guard, sir. Specialist Four DeVeber speaking."

"You do that real well, Pete."

"Who the hell is this?"

"Willow."

"Oh, hi, Jack. You still in Kentucky?"

"Affirmative. Listen, Pete, is Sergeant Hazard around? I waited to call until I thought he'd be back from the garden."

"He's at chow. Want me to get him?"

"Please, Pete." Willow heard the clerk page Hazard on the intercom and tell him who was calling. After a few moments his platoon sergeant came on the line. "How'd it go, Jack? Anything wrong?"

"No, sarge, nothing wrong. Uh, look, sarge, is it too late to change plans and get my father into Arlington?"

There was a slight pause before Hazard said, "Of course not. You know Goody. He can fix anything. You want Delta to do the job?"

"Yes."

"Okey-doke. Jack . . . uh . . . you do realize that because your dad's not an officer there can't be a full honor platoon? Even Goody can't override sacred Old

Guard scripture. There'll just be the casket team, firing party, bugler, and caisson.''

"I know. That's fine.''

"Okey-doke. I'll get on the horn to Goody, and we'll get it done. When do you want it?''

"How about day after tomorrow? I'll be flying back tomorrow and the . . . he'll be coming on the same plane . . . in the cargo hold.''

"Day after tomorrow is fine. Anything else?''

"Uh, yeah. I want you to say the words.''

There was another pause, a long one. Then, "I'd be honored, Jack. You have anything special in mind? A favorite poem or something from the Bible?''

"No. You pick something.''

"Alright. By the way, how's Angela holding up? She coming with you?''

"Mom's okay. No, she won't be there. She's going back to her family in Buffalo. There'll just be me and you and Sergeant-Major Nelson.''

"Okey-doke.''

16

They left the car on the side of the highway and clambered across the red rocks, scuttling like arachnids, Jackie slowed by the huge picnic basket Rachel had packed. They climbed and climbed, up and down the stony gullies, keeping a watchful eye out for scorpions and rattlers. Rachel led the way. Each time Jackie suggested a spot to light, she vetoed the place and pushed on. She seemed to have a particular destination in mind, or at least a certain kind of spot. He just cursed and followed, sighting in on her valentine ass switching back and forth under the slacks, lured like a foolish ship onto a siren's shoals.

After a while Jackie began to get excited. They were far off the beaten track. There would be no tourists, no rock hunters. They would be alone, really *alone*. The possibilities were tantalizing. He began to make lusty plans and a pressure formed against the buttons of his Levis.

Finally Rachel stopped, looked around carefully, nodded to herself, and said, "Here." They were in a brown canyon, close to the mountain wall, the rise dotted with gigantic boulders. Rachel spread out the Army blanket she had been carrying and flopped down. Jackie caught up and set down his burden. His arms felt like dumbbells.

She set out the food, and they ate silently and hurriedly,

ravenous after the long hike. When they were done, Rachel gathered up the debris and, always the tidy one, carefully packed it back in the basket.

Then she took off her shirt and brassiere and lay back.

His mouth fell open. He had seen her undressed to the waist before, but it had always been he who took off her clothes and then only after desperate entreaties. Her boldness unnerved him. The horny plans hatched on the long climb vanished into the rising breeze.

He pretended he did not notice the perfectly round breasts with their rich brown aureoles, even as his mind screamed, TITS! MY GOD, LOOK AT THOSE TITS!

With flushed face and thudding heart, he ostentatiously studied the terrain and said, "No wonder it took so long for the Army to subdue the Apache. Look at this country. We never really did whip Cochise and Geronimo, and you can see why. I see a hundred perfect ambush sites from here. Our horse soldiers never had a chance." He casually peeked over at Rachel and saw her looking back with a mixture of amusement and disgust on her face.

He quickly looked away and droned on. "The Chiricahua Apache used this land like it was an extra army. I'll bet anything Chato and his band came right through here, this very spot, on their raid of March 1883. Chato and twenty-five warriors came out of Mexico over near Fort Huachuca and went through these mountains into New Mexico, then dipped back down into Sonora again. They killed at least eleven white people. The Army mounted a chase expedition at Huachuca but never did lay eyes on the Apaches."

Jackie glanced out of the corner of his eye again, just in time to see Rachel stand, unzip her pants, and slide them off, taking bright yellow panties with them. He was thunderstruck. "R-Rachel, what are you d-doing?" he blurted, mesmerized. She was the most beautiful thing he had ever seen. His eyes riveted on her surprisingly thick bush. It was as jet black as the hair on her head and had the same luster. He imagined he could see sparks of light like angel dust in it.

Rachel did not answer him. She had a strange half-smile on her face. She knelt beside him and began to unbutton his shirt.

"G-Gee, Rache," the boy stammered. "You better watch out. You know w-what this could lead to. Ha, ha. You know how I am. You b-better put your clothes back on, or you'll have to take the consequences, ha, ha." The false bravado did not even convince him. She pulled his shirt off and, still smiling the half-smile, dropped her hand to his fly.

Jackie was panicked. "But, Rache, I thought you wanted to wait until we got married?" he said desperately.

"I've changed my mind," she said matter-of-factly. "Now, would you please shut up and start doing whatever it is you're supposed to be doing."

Her brassy declaration left him no option. He shed his jeans like they were on fire and laid her down on the scratchy woolen blanket, falling on top of her with a force that made her grunt. "I'm sorry, hon," he mumbled. He covered her face with kisses, then kissed her on the mouth, probing deep with his tongue, grateful to be back on familiar ground. He tried not to think of the treasure waiting below.

Jackie had been with the whores of the Blue Moon and the White Rat in Naco, but this was entirely different. This was Rachel! He almost swooned with the idea, and his penis ballooned with blood. Still stalling, he moved his mouth to her breasts, licking and nibbling, content to stay there forever. Rachel moved her hand down between their heaving bodies and grabbed him with what felt like fingers of fire. She began to jerk awkwardly. "No, don't do that," he had to plead, afraid that in his condition it would be all over in seconds. He was about to burst just thinking about it.

He sensed Rachel's growing impatience. She kept hunching around, trying to maneuver him on top of her like a jockey trying to get a recalcitrant horse into the starting gate. He tried to buy some time by cupping her mound and easing a finger gently into the thicket and the wet cavern it protected. God, she was tight. The thought of *that* once again nearly made him come.

Finally she put voice to it. "Jackie, please, please, put it in me," she groaned. He could delay no longer. He straightened out between her legs, balancing on one quivering arm and fumbling around with his free hand. And got exactly nowhere.

His face burned. "Rache, you'll have to help me," he said in a small voice. He held himself up with both arms now while she reached down with both hands. She used one to spread herself and the other to guide him to her. She managed to establish a beachhead and the boy pushed in an inch. She moaned and he stopped. She pushed her pelvis forward, and he went on to the halfway mark. She cried out in pain and he stopped again. Then he went in to the hilt. She yelped and he stopped. He reeled with the sensation. It was as if he had dipped it into a hot puddle of melted gold. He moved once, twice, froze, exploded . . . and collapsed, as empty as a shed snake skin.

He was mortified. "I'm sorry, Rache. Oh, God, I'm sorry."

She began to cry softly. From unquenched desire, Jackie imagined, wanting to die. He felt himself shrivel inside her.

"It wasn't long enough," Rachel whimpered.

"I-I know. I'm sorry," he whimpered back, burning with shame.

"It wasn't long enough for a baby."

Jackie was confused. "A *baby*?" He rolled off and stared at her.

"We didn't do it long enough to make a baby, did we?" she asked with a quivering mouth. She made it sound like an accusation.

"We didn't do it long enough to enjoy it, but we sure as hell did it long enough for a baby," he said with anguish. "I'm sorry, honey. I didn't bring anything, uh, safe, because I never dreamed . . . I-I shoulda pulled out before anything happened, but I . . . it happened so quick. I'm sorry, Rache, I just didn't think. But don't worry; the chances are very slim you got pregnant."

"I *want* a baby, you idiot," she snuffled.

"WHAT? You *want* a baby? Christ, Rache, *why*?"

She would not look at him. "To make sure," she said in a small voice.

"Make sure of *what*?"

"That you marry me."

"Aw, honey. Of course I'm gonna marry you. Soon as we graduate and I get OCS, just like we planned. You didn't have to do this. It'll only be a few more months. Less than a year if everything works out."

She was sitting up on the blanket now and looking at him, her lips swollen, her eyes puffy. She shook her head. "Everything's not going to work out. Something's going to go wrong. I can feel it," she said with conviction.

"Aw, Rache. Nothing's gonna go wrong. I love you so much. What could possibly go wrong?"

"My father."

"Your father?" Jackie said, laughing. "What does your father have to do with anything?"

"Everything," she said, looking ready to cry again. "He's going to find a way to stop us. I know he will. He hates you, Jack."

He smiled indulgently and pulled her to him and stroked

her hair. "He doesn't hate me, Rache. Why should he hate me? Even if he did, he can't do anything to stop me from marrying you. You're getting all upset over nothing. Believe me, hon."

Rachel was silent, content to let herself be petted and reassured. Then she asked in a tremulous voice, "Jackie, can . . . can we do it again? Longer?" For emphasis, she reached down between his legs and began to fondle him.

Jackie tried to calculate the odds, the thought of babies now planted in his mind. Then his penis began to respond to her ministrations. He kissed her and lay back down beside her, and they started over, without the frenzy this time. When he entered her again, it was like stepping into a furnace. He thought he would be consumed, by love as much as by lust this time. He kept a slow, steady stroke, and it seemed to last forever. Rachel rolled and bucked under him, mewing, and they both forgot all about babies.

Afterward they lay content and happy, wrapped in each other's arms. The desert air dried their sweat and cooled their bodies. Rachel dozed, and after a while Jackie sat up and watched her sleep, hypnotized by her loveliness and filled with an aching love for her. He studied every inch of her and mapped the delicious contours in his mind. He could hardly believe his good fortune. If a day like this could happen, then everything was possible—OCS, general officer rank, big battles that would alter the course of history, everything. The wonder of this day would have to last him until they were married, however. They couldn't take any more chances. A baby now would interfere, would sidetrack his grand plans. But now that he had had this taste of her, there was no harm in savoring the thought of feasts to come. He smiled tenderly and leaned over her and stuck his tongue into her deeply recessed belly button. Her eyes fluttered open and she giggled and sat up and put an arm around him.

Way above them dark clouds had gathered, and the breeze stiffened. A line of rain, a sudden desert squall, flashed across the mountain wall, moving slowly their way, and they could smell the wet sage and could almost see the country turn from brown to green as they watched. As the first large drops began to pelt their bodies, Rachel laughed an abandoned laugh, arched her back, and shot wide dark nipples to the heavens.

"Ladies and gentlemen, we are now beginning our descent into National Airport. Please fasten your seat belts, extinguish all smoking material, and put your seat backs in the original upright position."

The young soldier in seat 22-C stopped a passing stewardess and asked, "Excuse me, miss, but do you know how cold it gets in the cargo hold? Is it terribly . . . uncomfortable?"

The young man was handsome, but the attendant had landing chores and it was a weird question. "Don't worry, sir, it's not too bad," she said with a false smile. "Do you have a pet aboard, sir?"

"No. No, I just wondered."

Colonel Field took him into the library and offered him a chair. He poured himself a cognac and asked Jackie if he wanted one. When Jackie shook his head, Colonel Field sat down and said, "Rachel and her mother are out shopping. I asked you over because there are some things I think we should talk about, Jack."

"Yessir."

The colonel pursed his lips. "You and Rachel have been, ah, going together for more than a year now, isn't that right?"

"Yessir."

"And you'll be graduating from Buena in a couple of months?"

"Yessir."

"Do you still plan to go into the Army right away?"

"Yessir."

"Rachel tells me you two want to get married before you go in."

"Yessir."

"Do you think that's a very good idea?"

"Yessir."

"I don't."

Jackie squirmed in his seat. "Sir, may I ask why you don't like me?"

Colonel Field arched his eyebrows. "Whatever gave you the idea that I don't like you, Jack? I think you're a fine boy. You're a good student, a superior athlete, and a born leader. By the way, I never properly congratulated you on getting senior class president this year. Congratulations."

"Thank you, sir. But why don't you think I'm good enough for Rachel?"

"It's nothing like that at all, Jack. I just don't think the two of you are ready for a step like this. And, to be frank, I'm not sure that Rachel is ready to be the wife of an Army private. Are you?"

"I'm certain I can get into OCS and get my commission, colonel. She wouldn't be a private's wife for very long."

"I'm sure she wouldn't, Jack. But what if something goes wrong? What if you don't make OCS? Or flunk out once you're in? You know the Army well enough to know that nothing ever works the way it's supposed to. Are you prepared for that?"

"No, sir, I'm not." Jackie leaned forward earnestly, his elbows on his knees, his hands clasped under his chin. "Sir, are you about to suggest that we hold off for a few months, until I'm accepted for OCS or even through it? If you are, I might agree to it. But Rachel does not want to wait.''

"So she says. She's very young, Jack. Only eighteen. I'm not sure she knows what is best for herself . . . or for you.''

The boy said nothing. Colonel Field got up and went to the bar to refill his snifter from a silver decanter. He sat back down and said, "Look, Jack, here's the situation. I want Rachel to go to college. I have already enrolled her in a good English-speaking school in Gstaad, in Switzerland. She says she won't go, that she is going to marry you with or without my blessing. She has pointed out that a girl can get married at eighteen without parental permission. She is adamant about this. So I thought I would appeal to your good sense.''

Jackie stood his ground. "I'm afraid, sir, that if Rachel is adamant, then so am I.''

Colonel Field smiled. "I thought you might be. So I've come up with an alternative idea, Jack. It is one in which I'm sure you will see wisdom. And from our little talks over the past year about your ambitions and goals, I think it is one you will like.''

"What's that, sir?''

"First, let me ask you this: I believe Rachel told me that you have taken the College Board exams, even though you have no plans to attend a college?''

"That's right, I did.''

"What were your scores, if I may ask?''

"I got a seven-ten on the English part and a six-fifty on the math.''

"Excellent. Now then. I was in Phoenix a couple of weeks ago. I had lunch with Senator Goldwater, who is, as you might know, a general in the Air Force Reserve, and, as you may not know, a good friend of a good friend of mine." Colonel Field stopped and smiled again, and the boy, somewhat puzzled, said, "Yessir?"

"On the condition that your test scores were adequate—and I'm delighted to learn that they are more than adequate—I arranged with the senator to secure for you his appointment to the United States Military Academy at West Point."

Jackie was speechless, then overcome. He sat ramrod straight in his chair and tears filled his eyes. Colonel Field, still smiling, stood and gave the boy a fatherly pat on the shoulder. "I take it, then, that you will accept?" he asked.

"It's . . . it's all my dreams come true."

"Yes it is," said the colonel. "Congratulations, Jack."

Jackie stopped blubbering long enough to ask, "But what about Rachel? Cadets are not permitted to marry."

Colonel Field waved the question away. "She'll understand. It's good for everyone, believe me. Rachel can get her degree. You'll get your degree and a commission, and you will have the so-called West Point Protective Association behind you for the rest of your career. In four years, when you graduate, you can get married beneath crossed swords at the West Point chapel. I'll throw you a wedding reception at the Waldorf in New York and treat you to a world cruise for a wedding and graduation present. How's that?"

"That's . . . that's wonderful, sir!"

"Yes it is. It is wonderful," said Colonel Field. "You will have a brilliant and important career, Jack. I'm sure of it. And a wonderful marriage. You've made me very proud and very happy . . . son."

Sergeant Hazard met his plane. He stood off to the side, in uniform, as Willow came through the gate.

"Welcome back, Jack. Goody's around here somewhere arranging to get the casket off and have it shipped over to

Myer. You don't have to do a thing. Everything's set for tomorrow morning at 0900.''

"Thanks, sarge. It's good to be . . . home.''

Jackie had never seen her like this. She screamed at him, her voice shrill, tears running down her cheeks. Her voice was growing hoarse. She had been screaming at him for over an hour. His mother and father had scooped up his bug-eyed brothers and taken them for a walk, both to provide the quarreling couple some privacy and to get out of harm's way.

"How could you agree to such a thing, Jack? How could you?"

"We've been over it time and again. Rachel, listen to me. Please listen. This is the opportunity of a lifetime. Can't you see? Think about it. West Point, for chrissakes. With that kind of training anything is possible. I could be a philosopher-warrior, a perfect fusion of the man of action and the man of intellect.''

"You could be a perfect asshole. Can't you see he hates you? Can't you see what he's trying to do? He's trying to separate us, to split us up. And it's working. He's dangled this . . . this bauble in front of your face, and you're falling for it.''

"He doesn't hate me. He likes me. He told me. Look, sweetie, this way we, you, can have his blessing. He said he would personally arrange our wedding as soon as I graduate. He said he was happy.''

"Fuck his blessing," she said bitterly, spitting out the words. "And why shouldn't he be happy. The new promotion lists have just been posted. He gets rid of you and gets his star all in the same week. You bet your ass he's happy.''

Jackie had never heard her swear before. "Rachel, please—''

"NO! I want to marry you. Right now. You can join your fucking Army. You can get your precious commission once you're in. I don't care. I don't care if you spend the rest of your life as a sergeant. What's wrong with that? Your father is a sergeant and a wonderful man. My father is an officer and a shitheel."

"Rachel—"

"NO! You've got to choose, Jack. West Point or me. Either we get married now or we're finished. I will never see you or speak to you again."

"Rachel, you don't mean that."

"Oh yes I do," she hissed at him. "West Point or me, Jack. Which will it be?"

"Rachel, you can't make me choose like that. I want both and there's no reason—"

"You can't have both. Choose one, Jack."

"Then I choose West Point. Now, honey, aren't you being silly about this? And unfair? Can't you . . ." He was talking to himself. Rachel, a stricken look on her beautiful face, had gotten up and walked out of the house.

School was finished. In three days it would be commencement. He had thought she would cool off and come to her senses. She did not call and he did not see her. On the day of commencement he suffered a flutter of panic and called her house. He was informed by Mrs. Field that Rachel had left for a summer holiday in Europe and that come fall she would be attending school in Switzerland.

"Did she leave any message for me?"

"No, Jack, she didn't," said Mrs. Field, her voice filled with pity for him.

A week after that Colonel Field called Jackie to request another meeting. They sat in the same chairs in the library, and Colonel Field poured himself a cognac from the same silver decanter. There had been a terrible mix-up, the colonel told him. Senator Goldwater had appointed someone else, a boy from Scottsdale, to the Academy in his place. He would be first alternate, of course, so if anything happened to the principal appointee . . . at any rate, there was a good chance for next year. The colonel was so sorry.

From Mrs. Field Jackie got Rachel's address—general delivery, U.S. Embassy, Bern—and wrote long, passionate letters, beseeching her to return to the States. They would get married. There was no response.

In the fall, he entered the University of Arizona at Tucson, cobbling together a mixture of small scholarships and his father's life savings to pay the fees. He wrote Rachel at her school in Gstaad, explaining that he was enrolled in college and that he had given up on the military as a career, that he loved her and wanted to marry her, now. There was no response. He wrote to her at least once a week. He tried to call her, but each time he was told that Miss Field could not come to the telephone.

It was two years before his financial string ran out. The day he left school, he packed a knapsack, hitch-hiked to Phoenix, and enlisted in the Regular Army.

They gathered at the Fort Myer chapel. Not for a service— Willow had ruled that out—but for a place to start. Willow, Hazard, and Nelson were there in dress blues, and there was a firing party and a casket team from Delta Company, a bugler from the Army Band and a six-horse caisson. There was no chaplain, again at Willow's request. And there was no riderless horse. Noncommissioned officers did not rate one.

Sergeant Hazard brought a woman over to Willow. "Jack, this is Samantha Huff, a friend of mine. Would you mind if she came along?"

"No, of course not. How do you do, ma'am?"

"Hello, Jack," she said in a husky voice, holding out a

gloved hand. "I've heard so much about you and your
father from Clell that I feel I know you. Thank you for
letting me attend." She was a lovely woman. She wore a
black hat and a black dress, and she held tight to Sergeant
Hazard's hand.

Sergeant-Major Nelson joined them. "I got us a pretty
good spot, Jack," he said. "It's not close enough to walk
to, but it's got grass and trees."

"That's good. There won't be any bulldozers. Thank
you, sergeant-major . . . for everything you've done."

"*De nada*, son, *de nada*."

They rode to the gravesite in one car, Hazard's battered
Pontiac. The machine labored at a slow crawl behind the
caisson. On the way, there was only one short exchange.

Hazard said, "Jack, I didn't feel up to the task of
writing anything myself, so we picked something from
Ecclesiasticus. Goody helped me find it. It's Ecclesiasticus
forty-four, whatever that is."

"I'm sure it will be fine, sarge," said Willow.

"I want you to understand. Ecclesiasticus is not from
the Bible. If you'd like something from the Bible, I got a
backup or two."

"No sweat, sarge. Whatever you picked will be fine."

"Okey-doke."

Goody Nelson had worked magic. The gravesite was
perfect. It was at the end of a row that, through some
bureaucratic oversight or other, had not been filled. It was
near the road and, as Nelson had said, had full grass.
There was even an oak close enough to throw a shadow
over the waiting hole.

They parked, disembarked, and waited beside the grave
while the casket team gently slid Shelby Willow off the
caisson and carried him to the scaffolding. The pallbearers
picked the flag off the coffin and held it taut. Hazard
watched Willow for a signal to begin. When he got it, he

took a sheet of paper from his blouse jacket pocket and began to read:

"And some there be which have no memorial
 and who are perished as though they had never been
 and who are become as though they had never been born
 and their children after them.
But these were merciful men
 whose righteousness hath not been forgotten.
With their seed shall continually remain
 a good inheritance,
 and their children are within the covenant."

Even before the firing party completed its volleys, and before the first lean note of taps had sounded, Private First Class Jack Willow finally cried for his father.

THREE

Battles Long Ago

17

Their affair marched through the Washington spring like Tamerlane through Anatolia, sweeping all before it and leaving a sacked city in its wake. They went to look at the cherry blossoms and ended up smooching on the grass beside the Reflecting Pool. They parked at Hains Point to watch the planes take off and land at the airport across the river and ended up petting like horny teenagers. They went to the National Gallery to see the paintings and ended up holding hands in front of all the naked statues.

Into the long, hot summer they went. There were riots in Newark and Detroit that summer. It was an ugly, angry time. The lovers took no notice. She took him on a tour of the *Washington Post* building on L Street, taking care to pick a time when the city room was full and frantic with an approaching deadline. He took her on a tour of Delta Company, taking care to pick a time when most of the troops were in the cemetery. They took long weekends in the sand of Virginia Beach or in cool mountain air of the Blue Ridge. She taught him how to body surf. He taught her how to fly fish. They ate out in cozy restaurants. They ate in bed. They spent their evenings with Goody Nelson and Betty Lou Farmer. They spent their evenings in bed.

He cajoled a three-day pass out of Slasher Boudin and

she took him off to North Carolina to meet her parents, both of them still alive and high-stepping as they approached the age of seventy, both openly delighted that their daughter had found a new man, a polite, soft-spoken gentleman who had exquisite table manners and insisted on calling Mr. Huff *sir*. Mrs. Huff, with little success, quizzed Samantha about the couple's plans. Mr. Huff, with more success, took his little girl's new fella fishing for bass on the Northeast Cape Fear River.

They slept in separate bedrooms . . . and thought they would die from want.

Then Samantha took Clell to a party in Georgetown—a party where, Samantha assured him, there would be "just a few newspaper people."

The few turned out to be more than fifty, most of them *Post* staffers and other journalists, with a sprinkling of minor government functionaries. There was even a Navy captain in uniform, equivalent in rank to an Army colonel. They were all crammed into a small row house on N Street, the overflow backing into a tiny garden patio at the rear of the house. The garden patio was a walled-in slab of concrete, and the only patch of green to be found anywhere was Hazard's face. He felt as out of place as a turd in a punch bowl. He was the only man there with a thin tie, the only man there in a suit that cost less than $200, and the only man there with short hair. Even the Navy captain, a Pentagon spokesman, had long hair. Hazard quickly found the bar, secured a sturdy drink, and found a corner to put his back to. He felt like Wild Bill Hickok.

Samantha stuck close by his side until he shooed her away, telling her to circulate and have fun.

"Come and meet some people," she said.

"Not now, honey. Maybe later," he said.

"Will you be alright by yourself?"

"Of course."

Hazard watched her careless grace as she joined one group, then another, laughing and chatting easily. He watched her with mixed feelings of pride, envy, and resentment. It bothered him that she could have such a good time without him within touching range. He knew it was petty, but he did not want to share her company with anyone. He also could not help noticing that whenever she joined a group, the eyes of the men flew immediately to her breasts. So did the eyes of more than one woman.

"You must be Sam's sergeant. The word is around that she has one." The man had come up on Hazard's right flank. He had hair to his shoulders, granny glasses, and a Zapata moustache.

"How could you tell?" asked Hazard.

"The hair and the shoes, or rather boots in your case. They're spit shined." The man was grinning. "I saw you come in with Sam, but even if I hadn't, I still would have known. You always step off on your left foot first."

"You must have been in the service," said Hazard.

"Me? Heavens no. I'm a reporter. I cover the Pentagon. I noticed because I'm forced to spend most of my time around military types."

"It must be a very draining job." Hazard could feel a nerve jumping along the line of his jaw.

"Yes, it is," the man went on, oblivious to Hazard's sarcasm. "I have an adversarial relationship with the majority of my sources, I'm afraid. It's a constant battle. They're so defensive over there these days. But I guess that's to be expected when an administration is waging an increasingly unpopular war."

"Yes, I guess it is."

"But then you must have some pretty strong feelings yourself. After all, you're in a position where you might find yourself fighting over there one of these days."

"Yes, there is always that possibility."

"So tell me, then, are you a hawk or a dove?"

"I haven't really thought about it in those terms," said Hazard. "I guess you would have to say I'm a turkey."

"A turkey?"

"Yes. That's a bird that is sacrificed, stuffed, and served up to the masses on momentous patriotic occasions."

The man was not listening. He was motioning across the patio to someone and saying loudly, "Hey, Larry. Come over here. I've found us a real live military type who's going to defend the war for us."

The man thus summoned came over, drink in hand and smile on lips. "Really? That should be interesting . . . and impossible." Larry was a large man with a body obviously once heavily muscled but now beginning to go slack. He looked like a retired athlete. His hair was cut in Prince Valiant bangs, and he wore a fancy Nehru jacket and an 18-carat gold peace medallion. He stuck out a beefy hand. "Hi, I'm Larry Brubaker," he said with the air of someone who expects his name to trigger instant recognition. Hazard shook the man's hand and found himself locked into one of those puerile hand-vise games. Larry smiled and squeezed.

"I'm Clell Hazard," Hazard said evenly. He did not squeeze back.

"*Sergeant* Clell Hazard of the United States Army," chimed the first man. "Defender of the faith."

"That's a hard faith to defend, don't you think?" said Brubaker, still smiling pleasantly. A few other people, men and women, began closing in. Over their shoulders, Hazard saw Samantha look over from across the patio with alarm on her face.

Hazard smiled back at Brubaker and shrugged.

"How 'bout it, Hazard?" the big man pressed. "Are we winning in Vietnam like Westy says?"

Hazard shrugged again. "The kill ratio is running about ten to one. That's not too bad."

"Is that what it's all about? Kill ratios?" asked Brubaker with a mocking smile. "I thought it was a fight for hearts and minds. Are we winning their hearts and minds, Sergeant?"

"As the man says, if you get 'em by the balls, their hearts and minds are sure to follow."

Several people tittered. The group around them had grown. At its fringe Hazard could see the Navy captain from the Pentagon and Samantha, a look of worry still on her face. Brubaker stopped smiling. "That's a rather Neanderthal attitude, isn't it? Is getting them by the balls the official policy of our military leaders these days?"

"Look," said Hazard. "I don't know what the official policy of our military leaders is. Why don't you ask the good captain back there? He works for the people who set military policy. I just work for the people who implement it. I'm a grunt, not a strategist."

"Spoken like a true storm trooper. That's what the SS people said at Nuremburg. I'm asking *you*. Why are we fighting in Vietnam?"

"*We* aren't fighting in Vietnam, Mr. Brubaker. I don't see any combat troops in the room." Behind Brubaker, Hazard could see the Navy man scowl.

"That was a cheap shot, Hazard, but I'll let it pass because I really want to hear your answer. I'll rephrase the question. Why are *you* people fighting in Vietnam?"

"To stop monolithic communism on the beaches of Danang so we won't have to stop it on the beaches of Santa Monica," Hazard droned.

"You can't be serious," hooted Brubaker, looking around to make sure everyone realized he had scored a major point.

The first man, the one with the Zapata moustache, jumped in. "Larry is chairman of Attorneys Against the War. That's why he's so interested."

"Attorneys Against the War?" asked Hazard. "Aaw, that's too bad." A few people got the joke, and another titter went around the circle.

"In my opinion, we have no business in Vietnam," announced Brubaker.

"Opinions are like assholes," said Hazard. "Everybody's got one."

Samantha pushed her way through the laughing ring of people and linked arms with Hazard. There was a forced smile on her face. "Come on, Clell," she said hurriedly. "Come get me a drink. I'm dying of thirst." Hazard gave Brubaker a slight bow and let himself be led toward the bar.

As they made their way, Samantha whispered harshly, "What are you doing, Clell? You don't really believe one bit of what you told that man. Why are you pretending that you do? It makes you look foolish."

"*I* looked foolish?" Hazard asked petulantly. "Look, that creep doesn't have the right to talk about Vietnam! None of these damn draft dodgers have any right. I don't see any of *them*, or any of *their* kids over there winning hearts and minds. Who the hell do they think they are?"

"They're Americans, just like you. They pay taxes. Of course they have the right to talk about Vietnam. Some of them, like Attorneys Against the War, are even doing something about their beliefs. Unlike you, who say you disagree with what the Army is doing but continue to wear the uniform. Or maybe you *did* mean those things you said. It wouldn't surprise me. Most Army people think like that."

"Aw, Sam, come on. Try to understand. I may disagree with what the Army is doing in Vietnam, but I'm still proud of the uniform and I don't want jerks throwing mud at it. I've been getting a lot of this kind of garbage lately, and I'm getting fed up . . . ." Someone tapped him on the shoulder. When he turned around, there was Brubaker, his face flushed. Zapata and a few others were with him, up on tip-toes and peering over and around him like a golf gallery on the eighteenth green.

"I want to get something straight, Hazard," Brubaker said menacingly. "Did you just call me an asshole back there?"

Hazard sighed. He didn't want any trouble. He wasn't even really angry at the oaf. He was upset with Samantha for not seeing his side of things and withholding blind allegiance. All he wanted was this gorilla out of his face so he could patch things up with Sam. With weary annoyance, he said, "Oh Christ, Brubaker. If the shoe fits, wear it, huh? Now, why don't you just fuck off?"

A gasp went up from the gallery. Samantha looked at him in horror. Brubaker said coldly, "I think it's about time we took this little discussion outside, don't you?"

Zapata butted in once again. "I'd stay right here if I were you, sergeant. Larry was an All-American lineman at Minnesota. He played two years with the Green Bay Packers before his right knee went blooey." The little man reminded Hazard of a cartoon chihuahua dancing around his bulldog hero, shadow-boxing and yammering, "Get 'im, Spike, get 'im."

"I'd be more impressed if he had played with the Green Berets," Hazard said to him.

"Let's go outside, Hazard," said Brubaker, unbuttoning the Nehru jacket.

"Clell, don't you dare leave this house," said Samantha.

Hazard laughed. The absurdity of the situation had hit him in full. He smiled what he hoped was a placating smile. "You can't mean *fisticuffs*?" he said. "I haven't been in a fist fight since grade school. Why don't we have a drink together instead, and you can tell me all about how you won the big game against Michigan? We're both alleged grown-ups. We should have known better than to talk politics when we're supposed to be having a good time.''

"Outside, Hazard."

"C'mon now. This isn't necessary."

"I said *outside*."

Hazard felt like a fox harried by hounds. First a feeling of being put upon, of being badgered beyond endurance, came over him. Then a white rage began to build in him. Fuck this clown. Hazard started toward the front door. Samantha trailed behind him yelling, "Clell, don't you dare!"

The two men faced off on the cobblestone sidewalk. The Navy captain announced, "I don't want to witness this. I'm leaving." As he started walking off, he turned to Hazard and said, "Whip his ass, soldier." The rest of the party-goers jostled for good seats on the front stoop, drinking and laughing and yelling their support for Brubaker. Hazard could hear someone asking for bets, giving odds.

Hazard blotted everything out of his mind. What had that little shit-stirring guy with the moustache said? Right knee? Brubaker opened his mouth to say something and Hazard kicked him in the right knee, aiming the kick soccer style so that his cowboy boot heel struck just under the kneecap. Without a sound the big man started down. As he dropped, Hazard gave him two savage chops to the side of the neck with the flat edge of his hand, his arm moving so quickly that it was a blur to the onlookers. Brubaker lay paralyzed on the sidewalk, flat on his back, eyes popping out like a frog's. Hazard grabbed him by the Prince Valiant hair, flipped him over and pried open his jaw. He set Brubaker's yawning mouth over the angle of the curb. Then he stomped hard on the back of his head. There was a loud splintering sound as the jawbone split up both sides and blood sluiced into the gutter in a frothy, dark pink spate studded with little white bits of tooth enamel. All the laughing and yelling had stopped. There was utter silence from the stoop except for the muffled sobbing of a woman. Then a man's awed voice said, "Holy shit. Somebody call an ambulance."

Hazard had spent the brief flash of violence in a kind of trance. It took a few seconds for his brain to clear, and his eyes to focus. When they did he saw a sea of shocked faces staring at him. He looked down at the mess at his feet, then back up, looking for Samantha. "I tried to . . . I didn't mean . . . I'm sorry." He passed a hand over his face and tried again, this time in a calm, even, but dead-sounding voice. "Somebody please try to remember what I'm about to say. My name is Hazard. Sergeant First Class Clell Hazard. I'm at Delta Company, Third Infantry, Fort Myer. Send any . . . medical bills to me. If . . . if Brubaker wants to press criminal charges, he can find me there. I . . . I'm sorry. So sorry."

He found Samantha, who was staring at him with a stunned look on her face. He took a step toward her and held out his hand. "C'mon, Sam. Let's get out of here."

She backed away from him. She was crying softly. "Don't touch me . . .!"

Hazard turned and walked to his car. It took him a minute to get the key in the ignition. His hands were trembling. Finally he started the engine and drove off in the direction of Key Bridge and Arlington. Before he reached the bridge, he passed an ambulance, siren screaming and lights flashing, coming fast the other way.

18

Willow lay on his bunk in the fading light, trying to concentrate on Mahan's *Advanced-Guard, Out-Post and Detachment Service of Troops*. The Third Platoon bay was busy with men preparing to sally out in search of an evening's diversion. They whooped and hollered and snapped towels at bare asses. Locker doors rattled and slammed as uniforms came off and went in and civvies came out and went on. Men with towels around their waists and soap dishes in their hands padded to and from the latrine, their shower shoes slap-slap-slapping along the center aisle. Throughout the bay, radios dueled for air supremacy. Black soldiers scat-sang the complicated riffs of John Coltrane. Southern white boys warbled the simpler tunes of Hank Williams, using nasal membranes the way clarinets use reeds. Somewhere in the middle, other men, tuned to a popular rock 'n' roll station, sang along with a song that advised those going to San Francisco to wear some flowers in their hair. All mixed together, thought Willow as he read the same paragraph for the third time, it sounded like . . . like ducks fucking. That's how he had once heard Sergeant Hazard describe the Vietnamese language.

"Whatcha readin, Jack?" Wildman was standing alongside Willow's bunk, his head canted crazily on the fat stem of his neck as he tried to read the book's cover. Willow turned the book so Wildman could see the title and was rewarded with "Whassat?"

"*That* is the first serious American book to deal with things military," said Willow. "It was published in 1847 and was used as a primer by both sides in the Civil War."

"No shit?"

"No shit."

"Well, gee, if you're busy, maybe I shouldn't bother you."

"You've already bothered me," Willow sighed, marking his place and closing the book. "Who can read with all the noise around here, anyway? What can I do for you?"

"You ain't goin' out tonight? No hot-to-trot date or nuthin'?" Wildman asked.

"No. What do you need?"

"Uh, well, I've noticed that your shoes are always STRAC, ya know? And I'm always gettin' in trouble on account of mine, ya know? So I was thinkin' maybe you could gimme a lesson on spit shining. Ya know?"

"How long have you been in the Old Guard, Wildman?"

"Bout a year."

"And you still don't know how to spit shine a shoe?"

"Guess not. At least they never seem good enough for Hazard."

Willow sighed again. "Okay. Bring me the following: a shoe, some cotton balls, a can of black polish. Take the top off the polish can, go to the latrine and fill the lid with cold water. Think you can handle all that?"

"Sure thing, Jack. Be right back."

As Wildman trotted off on his mission, another man, wearing Class A's, approached Willow's area and said, "Hey, Jack. I got guard tonight. Take a look, willya?" The man did a slow pirouette. "I'm a cinch to take point, right?"

"Wrong. You've got a couple of loose threads on the back of your blouse," said Willow.

"Shit. Pull 'em out for me, willya?"

"No. All that does is unravel the material even more, and you'll have strings again in twenty minutes. Do it this way." Willow flicked his cigarette lighter and touched the ends of the offending threads. They flared like thin fuses and when they had burned down to the body of the jacket, Willow snuffed them out with a thumb.

"Hey, cat's ass. Thanks, Jack." The man went away whistling.

Wildman was returning, walking down the aisle with prissy steps, his eyes crossed in concentration on the lid full of water. In his other hand he held polish and a box of cotton balls, and his shoes were tucked under an arm. He made it to Willow, then stumbled and spilled half the water on Willow's blanket.

"Jesus Christ, Wildman," snapped Willow. "You couldn't pour piss out of a boot if directions were written on the heel. Just set it down on the footlocker. Okay, come here. Now, how have you been doing it?"

"I put the polish on with a rag, then spit on it. Ain't that why they call it a spit shine? Then I buff it with a shoe brush."

"That explains everything," moaned Willow. "Look, it doesn't work that way at all. You can't do it with real spit because you always run out long before you get a shine. And the brush just smears it. Now watch." He dipped a cotton ball into the can of water and then into the can of polish. He put the polish on the toe of the shoe, applying it in tight, counterclockwise circles. "That's all there is to it. First you have to build up a good base. That takes a while but once you have it the shine comes up easily. Then you just make sure you keep it touched up all the time. Don't use a brush at all. You can use a rag for quick touch-ups, but use the cotton for a few minutes every couple of days. All it takes to start with is some time and some elbow grease."

Wildman gawked as if Willow had just unlocked the secret of DNA molecules. "Ahhhaaa."

"I cannot believe that nobody has shown you how to do this before," said Willow. "You'd think Flanagan would have done it just to keep Sergeant Hazard off his ass."

"Flanagan never showed me nuthin," pouted Wildman. "He enjoyed screaming at me too much. At least I won't have to put up with any more of his shit."

"Oh yeah? What did you do? Promise to turn over your pay packet every month?"

"Ain't you heard?" Wildman smiled the first smile Willow could remember. "Flanagan got busted this afternoon. He's now PFC Flanagan."

"What! What happened?"

"He got drunk and tore up the Rocket Room last night," Wildman said with glee. "Threw a bottle at the band or something and started a riot. The D.C. cops arrested him and turned him over to the MPs on the main gate. They kept him in the guardhouse overnight and turned him over to the Slasher this morning. The Old Man busted him down a stripe, and it looks like they'll be docking his pay for a year to cover damages. He was lucky he didn't get the stockade. That's one prick who won't be yelling at me no more. Well, I think I got the hang of this now. Thanks, Jack." Wildman gathered up his things and made his way gingerly toward his own area a mere three bunks away, spilling more water on the floor as he went.

Willow lay back on his bunk and thought about what Wildman had told him. Flanagan would be no great loss. He had never done the things a good squad leader is supposed to do. Little things like showing a man how to spit shine a shoe, or how to get rid of threads, or how to

pin weights inside uniforms in the locker to make them
hang straight and true as a plumb line. He had picked up
such tricks by watching his father. Of late, more and more
men in the squad were coming to him for such things,
impressed with the fact that he took point every time the
Slasher stuck him with guard and that Hazard always
singled out his lockers as models of Old Guard SOP. He
might complain and sigh and roll his eyes when the others
badgered him with their requests for help, but secretly he
relished the role. If he was going to be an officer—*and he
was*—it was important to be a leader, to help care for the
men. A good leader was a teacher, a teacher through
example. An effective leader was someone who could be a
friend to his men. Someone they could turn to whenever
anything was bothering them. Willow lay there and made a
solemn vow that he would always take care of his friends.

*The Marshal lay at the edge of the pit, crumpled up like
a doll that had lost some of its stuffing. A piece of a
mortar baseplate had been blown through his middle body,
and he had died with both hands fused to the terrible spot,
as if he could hold the halves of himself together.*

*Other men lay around the pit in all the varied and
exaggerated attitudes of violent death. Willow counted
eight in all. Some he could even recognize. There was
Grampa and Beer Belly . . . and the one they called
Peaches. Peaches was curled up in the fetal position with
his hands over his eyes. They had shot him just like that.
There was a single hole just above his ear.*

*The tubes were all dented, splintered, or cracked. Satchel
charges and RPGs, rocket-propelled grenades, had done a
job on the Bravo mortars. Even if they had been functional,
it was too late to put them to use. All the firing had died
away, abating in stages, going from a sustained crescendo
to staccato bursts of automatic fire to isolated nervous*

tics of single fire to stone silence. The sappers were gone.

Willow sat down beside the Marshal's body. Lieutenant Richard Earp had only been with Bravo little more than a month, but he had quickly become a favorite with the other officers and, surprisingly, with the men. As soon as he had announced his name, people began calling him Wyatt and then the Marshal. A drooping gunfighter's moustache fixed the nickname fast. It had been the Marshal who had taken one look at the exposed position of Fire Support Base Daisy Mae, atop its bald knob rising out of the Quang Tin jungle like an inflamed carbuncle, and had dubbed the place Fort Doom. It was a name everyone much preferred to Lieutenant Colonel Abner Bean's cute, cartoon-strip Dogpatch nonsense. And the Marshal had stunned the grunts when, on his first hump through the boonies as leader of the weapons platoon, he had insisted on taking a turn as pigman and humped the M-60, a job usually reserved for the rawest newmeat. He would often watch carefully for signs of exhaustion among men carrying tubes or tripods or ammo or baseplates and spell a man. He had been the only officer that the men had truly liked.

The guileless friendliness of the man had been infectious. Earp was a quick-to-laugh Nebraskan who reminded Willow of Jimmy Stewart in Destry Rides Again. Like Stewart's Destry, little in life ever happened to Earp personally, but he always had a story about a friend or acquaintance to illustrate any point. All the Marshal would have to say was, "I once knew a fella . . . ," and everyone within earshot would stop what they were doing and start to grin in anticipation. Just the day before a couple of the men were talking about losing girl friends when the Marshal had sauntered up, listened for a moment, and said, "I once knew a fella who had the best piece of ass he'd ever known get up and walk away from him . . ." Earp had *paused for effect, then continued, ". . . so he picked up a rock and knocked her damn horn off."*

More important, the Marshal had been good at his job. He never needed more than one marking round to zero his mortars on target. And a mosquito could not have found a safe flight path across a position where the Marshal had set up interlocking fields of fire. When it was Willow's turn to run night ambush, he would often talk the Marshal into coming along just to help position the claymores and the riflemen for the U-shaped or V-shaped or L-shaped ambushes. The Marshal was a master of lethal angles.

Willow looked at the corpse for a long time, then leaned over and whispered into its ear, "I once knew a fella . . ."

Willow heard his name on the bay squawk box: "Willow. Get your ass to the NCO room. Chop-chop." It was Sergeant Hazard's voice and it sounded pissed off. Taking the stairs four at a time, Willow went back over the day's drop jobs in his mind, trying to remember where he had screwed up.

The NCO room was full. The usual tenants, the platoon sergeants, were all in residence: Louder, Cook, Moreau, and Hazard. More unusual, the supply and mess sergeants, Beech and July, were there. The first sergeant, Slasher Boudin, was there, too, his disfigured scowl firmly in place, his blank gray eyes as cold as a metal crucifix. And a distinguished guest, Sergeant-Major Nelson, was there, filling a whole corner of the room, as big as Boudin. Willow's heart began to hammer. He planted himself at attention in front of Hazard and stifled the twin urges to salute and to drop to his knees and beg for clemency, even though he could not identify his crime. The room was deathly quiet and no one was smiling. A line of poetry flashed through Willow's brain: *as noiseless as fear in a wide wilderness.*

Hazard, sitting behind his desk with his feet up, studied Willow critically for a moment and then snapped, "You're out of uniform, soljer."

Willow dipped his head in astonishment and looked himself up and down. All seemed okay to him. "I am?" he asked in a tremulous voice.

"That's what I say, fuckhead," snarled his platoon sergeant. "And you will be until these are on." Hazard casually flipped something onto the desk: two cardboard squares covered in black felt. A pair of chevrons, two yellow stripes each, was pinned to each square. Willow just stared, incomprehension clouding his face. Then he looked up at Hazard and grinned. Hazard was grinning back. "Congratulations, corporal," Hazard said. "You are now a squad leader."

Willow could not wipe the silly grin off his face. Flabbergasted as he was, the significance of the promotion did not escape him. Every other squad leader in the company was a buck sergeant, an E-5. Flanagan had been the only corporal. All other E-4s were specialists fourth class. The difference between a spec four and a corporal, though both drew the same pay, was immense. A spec four was not an NCO. A corporal was. The lowliest of all NCOs, it was true, but an NCO nonetheless. It was a *pure* Infantry rating. It meant that he commanded troops. Only a squad, of course, but real flesh-and-blood troops. Willow's mouth quivered. "Th-thanks, Sergeant," he said with genuine emotion.

"Don't thank me," shrugged Hazard. "You should be thanking a certain Mr. and Mrs. Flanagan for raising one stupid shit of a son."

The other noncoms gathered around to shake Willow's hand. Even the Slasher shook his hand, although he added a quiet postscript to his congratulations. "I'll be keeping a close eye on you, Dildo."

Hazard was back on the intercom, ordering all men still in the Third Platoon bay to report to the ready room and line up in single file outside the door. Then he turned to Willow and said, "There are a couple of archaic rituals that go along with these stripes." He produced a razor blade from his desk drawer and ceremoniously cut off Willow's PFC stripes. Then he found a couple of safety pins and pinned the new chevrons on the sleeves of the boy's fatigue blouse. While this was going on, the other NCOs began to form a line behind Hazard. Hazard explained to Willow with a smile, "This promotion is not official until these stripes have been tagged."

"Tagged?" the new corporal asked, smiling back uncertainly.

"Yup. Tagged." Hazard hauled off and punched Willow hard on the shoulder. The boy, caught by surprise, almost went down. Then he smiled with understanding and braced himself, determined to take it like a man—like an NCO. Hazard hit him twice on each arm, once for each stripe. Then one by one the other noncoms tagged Willow's new chevrons. Goody Nelson, beaming affectionately at him, had the good grace to pull his punches. Slasher Boudin did not. The first sergeant's first punch sent the boy sprawling over a chair and dumped him on his butt in the middle of the floor. Willow smiled through clenched teeth and resumed his position. The Slasher's second punch, a mere six-inch shot, had the same result. Willow stayed on his feet for the third and fourth and even managed to say politely at the end, "Gee, thanks, Top."

When the noncoms were finished, Hazard invited in the Third Platoon troopers one at a time. They took their turns pounding on Willow and, with the understanding that amnesty was in effect, added their sincere condolences: ". . . another good man turned into an insufferable prick by the mere stroke of a pen." "Corporals, you understand, are lower than shark shit." "Try not to forget us little people now that you've reached the heights." "Can we still call you Jack, or are you going to be Corporal Jack Off now?" "Hey, corporal, my girl's got this friend with monster tits, and anytime you feel like double-dating you just let me know, huh, old buddy, old pal?" "Just don't forget who taught you all you know, numbnuts. . . ."

When everyone had had their fun, Hazard announced, "Okey-doke, listen up, people. There will be two, count 'em, two celebrations to mark this momentous occasion. First, we *real* noncoms will take Corporal Willow for his first drink at the Old Guard NCO club. It hurts me to say that protocol demands that we *real* noncoms each buy him a round. But after that we will retreat . . . no, let me rephrase that, since Old Guardsmen never retreat. We will advance in a backward direction and for strategic purposes only, to Zeke's across the road, and you peasants can get in on the action. It pleases me to say that on *that* occasion protocol demands that Corporal Willow buy the drinks." A raucus cheer went up. Willow just stood there, smiling inanely, his dead arms hanging useless, as limp as overcooked pasta.

Seven hours later Sergeant Hazard was once again standing in the middle of U.S. Highway 50 directing traffic. And once again Goody Nelson carried Willow's lax body over his shoulder. Both Hazard and Nelson wore their fatigue caps backwards on their heads, and their blouses were out of their pants, which was just as well, since their trousers were unzipped. The MPs on the rear gate recognized the battalion sergeant-major instantly and smiled indulgently after checking to see if Nelson's cargo was alive, first peeling back one of Willow's eyelids, then checking for a pulse when the eye check proved inconclusive. The difference on this return from Zeke's was that Willow's limp body was not unceremoniously dumped onto his old bunk in the Third Platoon bay. That space was now the property of Private First Class William Flanagan. PFC Flanagan's first specific order on his first day back in the lower enlisted ranks had been to switch locker contents with Willow. This time, Willow was tucked gently away in his new partitioned, private cubicle in the Delta Company NCO quarters.

Hazard and Nelson, experienced veterans both, sensibly agreed that they were both too drunk to make it home. They curled up on the floor beside Willow's bunk and fell instantly asleep. Their snores kept the rest of Delta's resident noncoms awake most of the night. Singly, sometimes in pairs, they stomped irately into Willow's room, determined to teach the company's freshest NCO the outward boundary of his new powers. Singly, and sometimes in pairs, they slunk quietly away when they spied the bulk of the battalion sergeant-major stretched out on the floor like a beached whale.

19

Samantha found Betty Lou Farmer already at a table, a table tucked back in a quiet corner of the restaurant. Every other time they had lunched together, Betty Lou had always been the last to arrive, often as much as a half an hour late. The fact that Betty Lou had arranged this lunch, had gotten there early, and had picked a spot where conversation was possible, told Samantha that she was in for a lecture.

"Hi, Sam honey," Betty Lou chirped brightly. "I've gone ahead and ordered you a martini. Just the way you like it, with a twist. It should be along any minute now."

"Hello and thank you," Samantha said. She sat down and asked, "Well, do we get right to the woman-to-woman, heart-to-heart talk, or do we wait until the booze gets here?"

"Why, darlin', whatever are you talking about?" Betty Lou asked, her immaculately shaped eyebrows squinched together quizzically, her puzzled smile a lazy hammock between chipmunk cheeks.

Samantha laughed with appreciation. "Please don't pull that innocent southern belle crapola with me, Betty Lou Farmer. You're very good, but I went to the same finishing school, remember? Now, I only have an hour for lunch, and I don't have time for your full act. So, the question is: Did Clell send you or are you here all on your own?''

Betty Lou gave it up with a grin and a shrug that said she had tried. "All by my lonesome, hon. Goody and I are worried about y'all. We couldn't help but notice something is just not right. We haven't seen you in days, and Clell is walking around with his chin dragging on the ground. So we cornered Clell. He absolutely forbade me to discuss this . . . ah, this little lover's quarrel, with you. So, naturally, here I am.''

"It is not a little lover's quarrel, Betty Lou. It is a fundamental disagreement over the use of violence to settle a difference of opinion, whether the argument is between nations or individuals.''

"Well la di da,'' said Betty Lou. "We're going to have to get your halo cleaned and blocked, honey. You can't possibly go to Stockholm to pick up your Nobel Peace Prize looking like that.''

"Please don't be flip, Betty Lou. This is serious. You didn't see what Clell did to that poor man.''

"No, no I didn't,'' Betty Lou agreed. "But Clell told us about it. In detail. And he was not easy on himself in the telling. Sam, he's heartsick about the whole thing. He really is. He said something just snapped inside of him, that he didn't know where he was for a minute. He thought he was fighting for survival.''

Samantha harrumphed.

"The day after it happened he went to the hospital to apologize in person and to arrange to pay all that man's medical expenses,'' Betty Lou said. "He also told Mr. . . . Brubaker, is it? . . . that he would not contest an assault charge if Mr. Brubaker decides to take him to court. Brubaker told Clell that he would accept Clell's apology and think about not pressing charges. His medical insurance will pay the hospital.''

"And just how did he manage to say all this?'' Samantha asked sarcastically. "From what people at the paper tell me, his jaw is wired shut.''

"He communicated by note,'' Betty Lou said impatiently. "The point is, he practically admitted he was the one who insisted on fighting, and that Clell had tried his best to avoid it. Now, if this Brubaker can forgive and forget, why can't you? God's sake, you're supposed to be in love with the man.''

"I was . . . I am . . . I don't know,'' Samantha said with honest anguish. "Oh, Betty Lou, the man who beat up Brubaker is not the man I thought I knew. I have never seen such viciousness in my life. It was frightening. I never suspected that Clell had that kind of savagery in him.''

"Oh bullshit,'' said Betty Lou. "What did you expect? Clell is in a savage line of work. It wasn't his talent for civilized debate that got him safely across France and half of Germany, or up and down the Korean peninsula. You don't deal with bullies, whether they are named Hitler or Brubaker, with repartee. That is not Clell Hazard's style, and you should thank God for it.''

"Betty Lou, you cannot equate Brubaker with Adolf Hitler, not even for the sake of argument.''

"Maybe not, but I *can* lump him with anyone who insists on violence and then gets what he asked for. You should be proud of Clell for not allowing himself to be pushed around.''

Samantha shook her head. "I just can't get that picture out of my mind . . . or that awful sound. Oh, Betty Lou, it was so scary. Clell was like a wild animal. His eyes went all funny, and he was snarling like a rabid dog. He was not the Clell Hazard I know. The Clell Hazard I know is so loving and so tender and so gentle.''

"You make him sound like Young Werther,'' snorted Betty Lou. "Listen, Clell Hazard is a man, probably the first real man you've ever had. I would wager that you fell in love with Clell for many of the same reasons I fell in love with Goody: because he's strong and, yes, a bit dangerous. But if they were just those things we wouldn't feel the way we do. They *are* loving and tender and gentle. It's the mixture that makes them so special. But you can't act shocked when you see the hard side.''

"I don't know, Betty Lou," Samantha said in a lost voice. "I'm so confused.''

"Look, hon," Betty Lou said softly, putting a hand over one of Samantha's. "Don't you worry none about Clell Hazard's heart. He's a good man, and you and I both know it. Believe me, if Goody dropped dead in the street tomorrow, I'd fight you for Clell Hazard myself. There are only three men of integrity in this whole goddamn town, and Clell Hazard is one of them.''

"Who are the other two?" Samantha asked with a shaky smile, the first evidence that she was feeling any better.

Betty Lou grinned mischievously, a grin that made her look, just for a second, exactly like Thurgood Nelson. "I'll give you a hint: One I work for and the other I fuck.''

"Betty Lou!''

"Oh, pshaw. If a girl can do it, she can say it.''

A waiter arrived with their drinks, and they gave him their lunch orders. When he had gone, Samantha turned to Betty Lou and asked, "Do you ever wish that Goody was not in the Army? That he had a civilian job instead?''

Betty Lou shrugged. "I guess I did at first. And I probably will again when he comes up for transfer and we have to face some tough decisions. But no, not really. The way I look at it is this: I like what Goody Nelson is, and the Army made Goody Nelson what he is. So how can I not like the Army?''

"Well *I* don't like the Army," Samantha said emphatically. "I don't like what it's done to Clell. And I'm going to do everything I can to get Clell to leave it."

"Does that mean you're going to patch things up?"

"I'll think about that and about what you've said," said Samantha. "But in exchange I want a favor from you. Can you ply your feminine wiles and find out from Goody when Clell's enlistment expires?"

"Why, Samantha, that's downright devious and underhanded," said Betty Lou, feigning shock.

"Yes, I know. But it's a poor reporter who doesn't know her deadline. Will you do it for me?"

"I guess I'll have to," Betty Lou said with resignation. "After all, we did go to the same finishing school, remember?"

Clell Hazard sat at his desk in the NCO ready room with a cup of coffee and the morning paper. "SON OF A BITCH!"

Sergeant Moreau, who was at his desk and shining a pair of shoes, and Slasher Boudin, who was busy raiding the platoon sergeants' coffee machine, looked over. "What's the matter now?" Boudin asked without real interest.

"The VC hit the airbase at Danang last night," said Hazard. "Twelve Americans killed, forty-five wounded, and twenty-five aircraft destroyed."

"I bet it was some fuckin' officer's fault," grumbled the first sergeant, helping himself to a couple of the platoon sergeants' doughnuts. Moreau said nothing and went back to his shoes.

The morning newspaper had become a cathartic for Hazard over the past few months. It had all started when he had begun to search out Samantha's articles. Each day he would be the first to get to the *Post* that was delivered to the NCO room—one of four copies that came to Delta Company. Another was laid on the company commander's desk, a third in the officers' ready room, and a fourth was put in the company day room for the troops to read. After Hazard found or didn't find something by Sam, he would read the war news in the front section. And as far as the other NCOs were concerned, that's when the trouble began.

Delta's noncoms got used to strolling into the ready room each morning to find Hazard sitting behind his newspaper and talking to himself in a sputtering soliloquy. They would tiptoe to the coffee machine, hoping to get a cup and get out before Clell could notice and trap them with a harangue. Many of them had begun to go to the mess hall for their first cup of coffee, preferring even Sergeant July's slimy good cheer to Hazard's honest, but unrelentingly sour puss. They couldn't see what the shouting was about. Westy and administration officials spoke with unfettered optimism. From what they read, the war was going fine. American forces were piling up staggering numbers of enemy dead. The Commies were clearly on the ropes.

Hazard was buying none of it. He would quickly read over the official pronouncements of success and search the stories for clues to the contrary, ammo for his instincts. He paid special attention to stories about the First Infantry Division, the Big Red One. That was his unit in Vietnam. He knew its strengths and its weaknesses intimately, and he knew its AO, its area of operations.

In January he read about Operation Cedar Falls in the Iron Triangle. The Big Red One had attacked and destroyed Ben Suc and nearby villages, then used the Rome plows, the oversized bulldozers with the wide and deep cutting blades, to clear the surrounding jungle into a flat and open killing ground for any VC or NVA dumb enough to expose themselves upon it. At long last, the Iron Triangle was secure.

Bullshit. Hazard had spent his entire second tour in the Triangle. While it sure as hell didn't break his heart to hear that Ben Suc, that viper's nest, had been razed, he didn't believe a word of it. The Iron Triangle would *never* be secure. Only a few days ago he had met a new platoon sergeant from Alpha Company who had just been transferred to the Old Guard from the First Infantry. The man had told Hazard an all too familiar tale of ambushes, booby traps, and mazes of enemy bunker complexes so well camouflaged that you couldn't see them until you were standing in them. The sergeant had also told Hazard a story that shook him to his very core. The troopers of the First Infantry had taken up the habit of disfiguring enemy dead. They would cut off the dead man's nose and, in the new flat spot on his face, they would place the Big Red One shoulder patch.

In the spring, he had read about the hill fights near Khe Sanh . . . Hill 881 North, Hill 881 South, and Hill 861. The Marines had fought off savage North Vietnamese assaults. Marine casualties had been heavy, but NVA casualties far heavier, and Eye Corps commanders had called the drawn-out series of bitter fights a triumph of American arms. What impressed Hazard most, however, was the disturbing news that most of the Marine dead were found with their rifles broken down beside them or their cleaning rods joined together and stuck in the barrels, trying to dislodge jammed cartridges. The new M-16 rifles were pieces of shit. They had been recalled and revamped since then and were now on their way back to Nam, but Hazard wondered aloud why the Pentagon didn't just build an American version of the AK-47, an equally accurate and far more reliable weapon.

Then in July, just last month, he had read of a Big Red One battalion getting chopped up in a brief but ferocious fight in the elephant grass on the fringe of the newly "pacified" Iron Triangle. There had been sixty-one dead and fifty-eight wounded. Among the dead was the battalion commander, Lieutenant Colonel Terry Allen, Jr., the son of the legendary General Terry Allen, the Big Red One's commander during World War Two. Also killed when he rushed up to take over command had been the battalion exec, Major Don Holleder, the former football All-American at West Point. Those were experienced officers, Hazard told the Delta Company NCO ready room, and if they could get caught in such a shit storm, then the enemy strength in the Triangle had not been reduced one iota. They could Rome plow all of Vietnam, and it would not mean a fucking thing.

On this particular morning, Hazard threw the paper on the floor and fumed at Slasher Boudin, "If that goddamn central casting general, Westfuckingmoreland, had half a brain, he'd be a halfwit. You set up big sprawling bases like that, and there's no way you can secure them. You ain't been to Nam, Slasher. You haven't seen the damn metropolises those sorry REMF's, the rear echelon motherfuckers, have set up. That airbase at Danang is about three times the size of Kennedy, and the jungle starts up about a foot beyond the runways. You could hide a division in there within mortaring distance of the tower. And they've got so many gooks coming and going through the gates that the VC know the base better than its commander. If they've got to have the goddamn thing there instead of running their sorties off the carriers, they should at least clear a thousand yards or so around it and set up adequate observation posts and a real defensive perimeter."

"It was some fuckin' officer," Boudin mumbled with certainty, his face full of doughnut.

"Ahhhh," Hazard said in disgust. "It's typical of the geniuses running this war. They set up these huge operational and logistical bases back in the rear—as if there *is* any goddamn rear—and then they sprinkle the boonies with fire support bases, all set up on convenient hilltops. The gooks never have to hunt for *us*. They know just where to find us anytime they feel strong enough to kick our ass. Every goddamn one of those combat bases is a fuckin' Alamo just asking to get blown away. But can we find them? Fuck no. They can hear the helicopters coming five miles out, and all they have to do is count them to figure the exact number of troops on the combat assault. If they outnumber us, they zero in on the LZ and waste us on our CA. If we outnumber them, they just dee-dee. The only people halfway fighting this war the way they should are the green beanies, the Special Forces. And even those crazy bastards are doing more and more of this fortified base camp shit. The only person really fighting the war the way it should be fought is Mister Charles, and if we ever—" Hazard sensed a change in the atmosphere in the room and looked up to see Boudin and Moreau staring at the doorway. Captain Thomas was standing there. "Can we help you, sir?" Hazard asked politely.

"I was looking for the first sergeant," Thomas said primly, "but I think I'd like to see you instead, Sergeant Hazard. Now. In my office." The company commander turned and walked toward the orderly room. Hazard sighed heavily, picked up and folded the paper neatly, and followed.

When he was at attention in front of the CO's desk he asked innocently, "You wanted to see me, captain?"

"Yes. Please sit down," Thomas said calmly. When Hazard was seated, Thomas exploded. "Goddammit, Clell. What the fuck is the matter with you? Why can't you keep your half-assed opinions to yourself? Just once. When they start appointing sergeants first class to the Joint Chiefs perhaps we'll let you tell us all how to fight the war, but until then I would suggest that you keep your fucking mouth shut.''

"I was not aware that it was against regs to voice an opinion . . . sir,'' Hazard said with a blank face.

"Don't be a fool and don't be a smart-ass,'' snapped Thomas. "You know damn well that it has *always* been against regulations to voice an opinion in the United States Army. The United States Army is not interested in opinions. The United States Army does not need platoon sergeants determining its strategy. Am I making myself perfectly clear?''

"Yessir.''

Thomas sighed melodramatically and said in a softer, kinder tone, "Goddammit, Clell, what am I going to do with you? You are one of the best noncoms I've ever had the honor of serving with. No, really, I mean that. If I live to be a hundred, I will never, ever, forget that day at Ben Suc. You saved your platoon that day and maybe my whole company as well. You should have gotten another Silver Star for that instead of just a Bronze. Hell, if I'd had my way you'd have been put up for a Congressional. You were outstanding. That was one of the reasons I wanted you here with me. But to be frank, I may have made a mistake. You have been nothing but a pain in the ass since the day you got here, Clell . . . and an embarrassment to me. Your asinine views on the war have not only reached the ears of the other company commanders, but they have become a joke at battalion as well. It does not reflect well on *me*, the man who brought you to the Old Guard. My friends keep asking me how's *my* peacenik platoon sergeant.''

"I'm no peacenik, sir. I'm just not in favor of this particular war. And I think that if we are going to fight it, we should at least do it properly.''

"Don't *think*, Clell," said Thomas. "That's what I'm trying to get through to you. It's not up to you to think about how the war should be fought. And it's certainly not your place to mouth off about it. Actually, you can think anything you want. Just keep it to yourself."

"Perhaps it was a mistake for you to have asked for me here, captain. You can rectify it by approving my transfer request."

"No! You are *not* going to Fort Benning, Sergeant Hazard. You're not going anywhere. You're going to stay right here and make me proud of you. Okay?"

"Yessir," Hazard said after a pause.

"Okay," Thomas said, giving Hazard a look of concerned affection. "By the way, your recommendation of Willow to take Flanagan's place looks like a good one. As you well know, because of his relatively short time with us, I was somewhat reluctant to make the promotion despite his fine record. But I saw Private Wildman on my way in this morning, and I'm damned if he didn't half look like an Old Guardsman. I take it that that's Willow's doing?"

"Yessir. He's been working with Wildman ever since he got his stripes."

"Well, if he can make a soldier out of that gob of dog vomit, he deserves a Congressional, too." The company commander gave Hazard a long look and a wan smile. "Well, go get your gardening clothes on, Clell, and send Top in to see me. This seems to be my morning for kicking ass. The Slasher has Padelli from Second Platoon listed for KP four times this week. Sergeant Cook is complaining about it, and it does seem that Top has gone a bit overboard—again. You have any idea why Padelli is on the Slasher's shit list?"

"No, sir," said Hazard. "With the Slasher there doesn't always have to be a reason."

Thomas issued another melodramatic sigh, one that suggested that command was indeed a lonely job. "Yes, I know. But he does run a tight ship for me. Well, get out of here, Clell. Go and sin no more."

Samantha found the right room after a few false starts and then by stopping for directions at the nurses' duty station on the floor. She tapped twice on the door and entered when she thought she heard an answering grunt.

Brubaker was reading, his bed cranked up to a sitting position. Flowers, fruit baskets, and paperback books covered the bedside tables. His jaw was trussed in a Rube Goldberg sling that fitted over the top of the Prince Valiant hair. He stared at Samantha with puzzled but interested eyes. "Ummmm?" was all he could say.

"Mr. Brubaker, my name is Samantha Huff." There was still no sign of recognition in Brubaker's eyes, and Samantha took a deep breath and added: "I'm the one who brought Clell Hazard to the party."

Brubaker nodded this time. "Mmmmmmmmm."

Samantha sat down in the visitor's chair and said, "I've come here for two reasons. The first is to apologize. I brought Clell Hazard to that party and I shouldn't have. The other thing was that I wanted to ask you, to plead with you, not to bring criminal charges against Clell. I'm not saying that he doesn't deserve it. It's just that with him being in the Army and all, it would ruin his record and severely damage his career. Don't get me wrong. I don't give a hoot for his Army career. I don't approve of it at all. But I do want him to leave the Army of his own accord and with his record and reputation intact, not get thrown out. He couldn't take that. He's a very proud man and he . . ." Samantha realized that she was babbling and she stopped.

Brubaker was watching her with amused eyes and the

locked mouth almost managed a grin. He rummaged through the debris on the medicine table and came up with a notepad and a gold-plated pen. He scribbled something and tore off the sheet and handed it to Samantha. It read, "I will not press charges against your precious sergeant on one condition—that you let me take you to dinner when I get out of here, and when I can manage to eat again."

"That's blackmail, isn't it?" Samantha responded.

Brubaker nodded merrily.

Samantha hesitated a moment, then said, "Okay, it's a deal." She took the pen from him and scrawled on the back of his note. "There's my phone number," she said. "Call me when you're ready."

Hazard rapped at the open door of Goody Nelson's office at battalion headquarters. "You busy?"

Nelson looked up. "E-9s are always busy, numbnuts. Don't you know that E-9s run the Army?" Nelson had charts and maps strewn across his desk. A high-intensity lamp shone down on the mess, even though it was midday and there was ample natural light in the office. Goody wore a green eyeshade and the smooth crown of his head poked up through it like the sun rising out of a jade sea.

"Umm-hmm," Hazard agreed genially. "You're damn near as important as platoon sergeants. What are you up to?"

"I am making a schedule for November's field exercises."

"What a wonderful coincidence. That's just what I wanted to talk to you about."

"Talk how?" Nelson asked warily.

"When is Delta scheduled to go?"

"NO, goddammit. Not this time. I can't tell you that, and you know it. Part of the object of this exercise is to see how long you assholes take to saddle up and move 'em out after you get the word."

Hazard spread his arms wide and crooned like an encyclopedia salesman, "Heeeeey, Gooooody. It's me."

"Oh yeah? Fuck you. The answer is no. Listen, you already know the general time frame. Any time in November after Veterans Day. You just make sure everybody's back in the barracks after dark and you'll be okay. I will tell you that the call is gonna come sometime between 2100 hours and reveille. And that's all I'm gonna tell you, so fuck off."

"That's more than I thought I'd get," Hazard grinned. "But that's not what I wanted to talk to you about."

Nelson put down his pencil and asked suspiciously, "No? Whadaya want, then?"

"I want you to assign my platoon to be the aggressor team."

"Whaaat?" Nelson choked. "Are you crazy? You know that's the shittiest job in the field on these things. You and your boys would be lucky to get eight hours' sleep during the whole two weeks."

"Yup," Hazard smiled.

"Whadaya mean *yup*, you ignorant cowboy? Fuck *yup*. Why?"

"Because while most of the officers and noncoms in this Mickey Mouse outfit have combat experience, none of the troops have, and they're the ones who are gonna need it. Their training at basic and AIT gave them a *tee-tee* idea of how to be riflemen in W-W Two or even Korea, but not in Veet Nam. These silly exercises represent the only opportunity these kids are going to get to learn anything about fighting gooks until they find themselves in the middle of on-the-job training. C'mon, Goody, what do you say? If the bastards won't give us cadre duty at Benning, let's do it right here under their noses. If my platoon can be the enemy, I can show them how an NVA or VC platoon manuevers in the bush. And we can give the rest of them a taste of what they'll be up against when they ship over. C'mon, Goody. This is the only chance to play soldier we get in this goofy outfit. Let's not blow it. Whadaya say?''

"I say no. N-O," said Nelson, but Hazard could see he was weakening. "The brass have already talked about using first platoon Alpha as aggressors. Battalion wants to punish Alpha for finishing last in the last three parades.''

"Can't you tell them I volunteered for it?'' asked Hazard.

"Sure I can," snorted Nelson. "They already think you should be up for a Section Eight because of the mouthing off you been doing. This should convince them beyond a shadow of a doubt that you're looney tunes.''

"If the brass has a hard-on for me, why don't you suggest that they can punish me by making me aggressors. They can fuck with Alpha anytime.''

"Nah. Wouldn't work. They may not like you much, but they know you're a damn good soldier.''

"You can think of something, Goody. Please.''

"What about Thomas? He'll go batshit if he hears that one of his platoons has been picked to get the dirty digit.''

"Thomas is so worried about his next efficiency rating he'd slice off his dick with a dull dime if battalion HQ told him to.''

Nelson ran his fingers through imaginary hair. "Maybe I could make a case that we should have a good outfit playing bad guys this time around—to give the battalion a real test and all that shit, given the times we live in and all.''

"Yeah," grinned Hazard. "See, I told you you'd think of something.''

"Look, I ain't sure anything is gonna work. But if it means this much to you, I'll give it a shot.''

"Thanks, Goody. By the way, where are you getting the umpires?''

"MDW."

"You know anything about them?"

"I got a list of names and a little poop on 'em."

"Who's picking the umpire who'll be assigned to the aggressors?"

"Colonel Godwin, of course," Nelson said cuttingly, pointing to the clutter on his desk. "Who do you think is doing the planning for this cluster-fuck?"

"Good," said Hazard. "Can you get me a Nam veteran for an ump? Somebody who doesn't always go by the book? And I need an officer who is physically fit. I plan to run his ass off."

"I'll see, I'll see," Nelson said irritably. "Is there anything else I can do for you?"

"Yup. You can tell me which three companies are going out first."

"You know something, Hazard? You're getting to be a monumental pain in the ass."

Hazard laughed. "That's funny, that's just what my CO told me this morning. You better watch yourself, Goody. You're starting to think like an officer."

"Okay, okay. Alpha, Bravo, and Delta for the first week. Honor Guard is first to stay back here and play in the garden."

Hazard shook his head. "They're going to be working harder than we are."

"Just remember, your turn to do it all by yourself is coming, too."

"I know. But Christ, Goody, we're doing fifteen or sixteen a day now. It's getting to be a bitch. It seems like I spend three-fourths of my life in that fuckin' cemetery."

"It's going to get worse, amigo," said Nelson. "I just got some very interesting stats from a buddy of mine over at the Pentagon. Just a sec." Nelson rustled among the rubble on his desk and came up with a piece of paper.

"Okay, listen to this. In 1965—you should remember 1965, Clell; that's the year you took your sabbatical for foreign travel—the monthly average number of American dead in Vietnam was 114. In 1966, it was 417 U.S. dead a month. This year it's running at an average of nearly 800 a month. Whadaya think of them apples?"

"I think it's a damn good thing we're 'winning'," said Hazard.

20

Willow placed the small bouquet of goldenrod, the Kentucky state flower, against the headstone and sat down on grass still damp with dew. He lit a cigarette and listened to the soft, warm wind rattle the leaves in the nearby oak. Far away, on the edge of the cemetery, he could hear the faint sound of a bulldozer.

He was ghosting. Sergeant Hazard thought he was at battalion headquarters straightening out a glitch in his pay records. It would have been no sweat if he had told Hazard he was coming here, he knew, but he did not want anyone, not even Hazard, to know. Know what? That he had feelings?

When he finished smoking, he field-stripped the cigarette and scattered the remaining bits of tobacco to the breeze. He rolled the inch or so of paper into a tiny ball and put it in his pocket. It was funny how so many lifers smoked filterless cigarettes because they were so much easier to dispose of. Let a man pick up a few thousand of the fucking things and he became aware of such things. He smoked Camels, same as his father. He did not know whether it was because he had cut his teeth on cigarettes stolen from his father's bedroom dresser drawer or whether it was an unconscious emulation of the man. What did it matter now?

Willow sat and stared at the simple white marker, an exact copy of the hundreds of other stones spread out around him. "I made corporal," he said conversationally. "Yeah, I know, I know; it took you six years to make corporal in the Ollllld Army. You and Sergeant Hazard sound just alike. You'd probably agree with him that the Army is going to hell in a handbasket. I wonder if you'd agree with him on other things as well? You know, it's strange; I never once heard you say anything about Vietnam— anything at all. You never mentioned it. It might as well not have been happening. Why was that?" There was no answer from the sun-splashed stone, but Willow had not expected one.

"I really like it, Pop. Even more than I thought I would. I don't know why you tried to talk me out of it, especially knowing the way you loved it. Was it because of Mom? What it did to her? Or Rachel? You really liked her, didn't you? So did I, Pop. So did I. I still think about her all the time. Guess that's pretty dumb, huh?"

Willow lit another cigarette and adjusted the goldenrod, which had fallen over on its long stems. "I'm really sorry you didn't get to see these stripes," he said wistfully. "We could have had a drink together at the NCO club. Wouldn't that have been something?" he laughed. "You won't see me get my commission, either. I was going to make sure that you would be the one to give me my first salute. See what you get for dying on me? You pissed away an easy dollar."

Willow got up and policed the area, picking up leaves and twigs and pebbles. He could hear his father telling him and his brothers to police the yard at Huachuca, to pick up everything that wasn't nailed down and, if it was nailed down, to paint it OD. He stuffed all the garbage into his trouser pockets and sat back down. "I was looking forward to a good, long talk when I got back from Vietnam," he said. "Not father to son, but soldier to soldier. Combat is the great dividing line among soldiers, isn't it, Pop? I always noticed that all your close friends, all your cut-buddies, wore the CIB. Those were the only people you'd talk to about Korea or W-W Two. Remember how I used to pester you for war stories and how you'd always change the subject, even after I grew up? When I got back from Nam, you could have talked to me about it. We would have had so much to talk about then. So much in common. Wouldn't we, Pop?"

"The sappers got out and disappeared into the jungle. They even managed to take their wounded out with them. We found only their five dead and no wounded at all. We had thirty-eight dead—thirty-six from Bravo Company and two from battalion—and seventy-seven wounded. It was a disaster, a disaster that wouldn't have happened if we had had some patrols out or some claymores set up. It wouldn't have happened if G-2 hadn't been so complacent and—"

"That's quite enough Monday morning quarterbacking, Lieutenant Willow," said Major Pyle.

"I just wish our intelligence had been as good as theirs," said Willow, his voice rising in anger. "And I wish our leadership had been as good as theirs."

"That's enough, I said," Major Pyle said coldly. "While you seemed to be running hither and yon and accomplishing nothing, Colonel Bean was keeping enemy soldiers out of the command bunker. For your information, lieutenant, the colonel has been recommended for the Silver Star. It will be his second in a long and distinguished combat career."

"That's not my point, sir," said Willow. "I do not deny that Colonel Bean performed bravely once the fight began. I'm only saying—"

"That will be all, lieutenant," said Pyle, shuffling the

sheaf of papers on the table before him. "If we need to hear from you again, you will be notified. This board is adjourned until 1400 hours."

The three officers stood and began to collect their things. Willow, his face flushed, snapped off a salute that was not returned and wheeled and headed for the door. The division brass had also risen from their seats in the observers' section and were standing in a clot, some of the officers glaring at Willow. Major Burns, the battalion executive officer who had been in charge on Li'l Abner on the night of the attack and so had missed the Daisy Mae fight, broke out of the bunch and intercepted Willow at the door.

"Hey, Jack. Hey listen, Jack," he said with a disingenuous smile. "You've been through a lot, kid. Hey, we understand that. Something like this hits everybody real hard. Hey, I tell you what. It's going to be some time before we get our replacements in and start putting the company back together, so why don't you take a leave? Hey? Don't worry about whether you got the time coming or not. It's on us, hey? I can start the paperwork this afternoon, and you can be on your way out of here in a few days. I'll rush it right through. Whadaya say, hey? You can go to Hong Kong or Bangkok and get one of them little gals who can suck on your dick till your head caves in, hey?" Burns had his arm around Willow's shoulders, and he gave a little squeeze each time he said hey.

"You can even make Honolulu," Burns went on excitedly. "Think of it, Jack. The World! Land of the Big PX, hey? Then when you get back here you'll be all rested and ready to kick some ass, hey? Make those lousy dinks pay for this, hey?"

"Uh, yeah . . . uh, thanks, Major. Can I have some time to think about it?"

"Sure you can, Jack. But what's to think about, hey? You just let me know whenever you're ready, hey?"

Willow wormed out of the major's grip and stepped out the door. He lit a cigarette and dragged the smoke deep into his lungs. Then he walked slowly down the dirt road that led in the direction of the Chu Lai officers' club. As he walked he counted cadence to himself in an effort to empty his head. Hup, Hoop, Tadalep. Hup, Hoop . . . HreepHor. Without being aware of it, he fell into an Old Guard stride, his hips snaking, his upper body rigid except for the swinging arms, his hands stopping on the upswing at the point precisely eighteen inches to the fore. The midday sun was a violent explosion straight overhead.

When he had been on the road for ten minutes or so, a jeep full of officers, Majors Burns and Pyle among them, sped past at breakneck speed, covering Willow with a layer of fine, white dust. The jeep did not stop to offer him a lift.

21

Hazard took it as a good sign that he had not yet found his belongings piled up outside his apartment door. He kept a spare dop kit of toilet articles at Samantha's along with a portion of his meager civilian wardrobe. Despite his suggestions, Samantha had refused to move in with him—a matter of propriety, she said—and they never knew which apartment they would call home on any given evening.

Clell Hazard had lived alone for much of his adult life. It had stopped bothering him long before and, in time, he had come to prefer it that way. He could cook, do his own laundry, and clean house as well as any woman, and he rarely resented his own company. He would read or watch the ball games on television or sit at his small, cluttered desk and tie trout flies against the day when he could once again stand hip-deep in bright, moving waters. It was an acceptable way of life . . . until Samantha Huff came along.

For the past couple of weeks he had felt like a recent amputee. The itch on his missing sole—soul?—was driving him crazy. He listened for her comings and goings. If he stood at the edge of his living room window and twisted his body like a Flying Wallenda, he could see her leave the lobby and cross the parking lot to her car. He found himself living for such moments.

261

But he was careful to avoid chance meetings. In the mornings he snuck from his apartment like a cat burglar. If he saw her car in the parking lot when he pulled in, he would wait a full ten minutes to make sure she was not waiting for the elevator or in the corridor when he went up. He longed for the sight, smell, and sound of her, but he was not ready for a confrontation. He went over a thousand possible scenarios in the event of a chance encounter—he would say this, then she would say that, then he would say this—but he could not come up with a single variation that would play acceptably. He sat alone in his apartment night after night, neither reading nor watching television nor tying flies. He listened to music, anguished country ballads, mawkish and true. He politely refused all invitations from Goody and Betty Lou, touched by their efforts to tide him over a bad time but adamant in his determination to scrutinize his feelings and his predicament in private.

His reluctance to face Samantha was out of character, and all the more bedeviling for that. Hazard was a man who prided himself on meeting difficult assignments head on, the kind of man who made it a point to tackle the most unpleasant duties first, just to get them behind him and get on with the mission. But in this instance he seemed paralyzed. He was both angry and ashamed. He was angry that Samantha would let anything, *anything*, insinuate itself between them. When people found the kind of happiness that he and Sam had found, they had to defend it. They had to set up a defensive perimeter and fight shoulder to shoulder against any and all encroachment. You surrounded such joy with your strongest wire, set out your claymores, and stayed alert.

He was ashamed. He had lost control of himself. He had done just what he accused the U.S. Army of doing. He had substituted firepower for brainpower. He had overreacted and overresponded to Brubaker. It was not so much the deadliness of his attack on the man. He had been appalled by the carnage, of course, but he understood how it had happened. That had been the response of a nervous system conditioned by its experiences and training. You fought to win, and the Marquess of Queensbury could go fuck himself. What really bothered him was that he had let it come to that. Telling himself that Brubaker had goaded him into the fight just didn't wash. Was he some schoolboy to be dared and doubled-dared? Was it enough to be able to whine to the principal, *But Mr. Jones, he started it*? What would it have cost him simply to have laughed and walked away? If Brubaker had persisted and swung on him, he knew, he was quick enough to have dodged and sideslipped the overweight and out-of-shape ex-jock all night long. That would have succeeded both in making the big man look foolish and in keeping the look of revulsion out of Samantha's lovely blue gray eyes. The truth was, he had performed for his woman. He had permitted himself to be provoked so that he wouldn't be shamed in front of her and then had used that as an excuse to strut his stuff. How he had misread her . . . and himself. Such false pride and faulty judgment had grave implications. If he allowed himself to so completely lose control in a combat situation, it could prove far more disastrous than one man's broken jaw.

But angry and ashamed as Hazard was, mostly he was afraid. Afraid that his puerile behavior had cost him Samantha. The thought made him nauseous. He kept seeing the look of horror on her face as he stood over his bloody conquest like some atavistic gladiator. It would take a long time of atonement to erase that look . . . if she gave him the chance. She had to. The alternative was unthinkable.

Okey-doke, he told himself, let's do it. He stationed himself at the door and listened until he heard her come home. He put his hand on the doorknob . . . and froze. He went to the kitchen to fix himself a Wild Turkey and water. Then he brushed his teeth and gargled with mouthwash so she would not know that he'd needed bottled courage. He took a couple of deep breaths, crossed the corridor, and knocked on her door. When she opened it, he said, "Can I talk to you for a minute?"

In the past two weeks Samantha had been beaten twice on stories by the *Washington Star*. Neither involved cataclysmic zigs or zags in the march of history, but it rankled nonetheless. Her editor, a kindly man who thought highly of her, had merely left the *Star* clippings on her typewriter. Across the most recent he had scribbled, "Is anything bothering you?"

Clell Hazard was bothering her. His absence from her life was proving far more disturbing than she had thought possible. At work she was jumpy and caustic. Unlike so many women in journalism, Samantha had never been bitchy. During the past couple of weeks, her colleagues agreed, Samantha had been bitchy. She could not seem to cope with the little mishaps of everyday life: the taxi that would not stop, the official who did not promptly return her call, the coffee spilled on a freshly laundered dress. Things that she had always handled with aplomb or a wry laugh now infuriated her. She was fully aware of the personality change taking place but seemed powerless to do anything about it. She thought, this must be what it's like to withdraw from alcohol or barbituates. Samantha had the psychic D.T.'s.

Samantha's aberrant behavior did not stop there. She found herself listening for Clell's movements. Coming home from a late interview one night, she had even pressed an ear to his door thinking she heard a woman's voice inside. She tensed there, quaking with the thought that he might suddenly pull open the door and she would go tumbling in. But all she could hear besides the pounding of her own heart was some godawful country and western queen on the hi-fi. When she was safely inside her own apartment, she fixed herself a stiff drink and went to bed, but not to sleep. Instead, she masturbated for the first time in years.

Samantha realized that while she had accused Clell of thinking "my country right or wrong," she was just as guilty for thinking "my man, right or wrong." She faced the fact that she wanted to hold on to Clell Hazard. Her mental and physical well-being depended on it. But she did not know how to go about it. She did not want to give him the impression that she had forgotten or fully forgiven his crime. At the same time, she knew that if there was to be a reconciliation, Clell's stiff-necked pride would undoubtedly require her to make the first move, to take chisel in hand and chip away at the wall separating them. In her mind, that wall was not of her doing, nor even Clell's. It was the Army's. Every brick had "Government Issue" stamped on it.

Samantha believed Betty Lou's argument that it had been Clell's training that had taken over that night. She had to believe it was the Army's fault and not something mean deep inside the man himself. That made it all the more imperative that Clell leave the Army. Her determination to help him reach the same conclusion was absolute. But she knew she would have to be clever about it. Linda Hazard's open hostility to the Army had soured her life with her husband. Samantha would have to make it seem his decision. It would be difficult, but not impossible. Clell was already leaning in that direction. A gentle nudge from her might be all it took to push him over the edge of decision.

She fervently hoped so. He was in her blood, and there

was no way to get him out short of opening a vein and letting life itself spill out along with him. Compared to Clell Hazard, the men she had known before seemed pale and puny. They were all so soft, so verbose, so . . . Betty Lou had been on target there, too . . . so safe. There *was* something excitingly dangerous about him. It was a side of him that thrilled her. She knew it was a stupid reaction on her part, as ridiculous as a schoolgirl crush on the captain of the football team, but there it was nonetheless. But it was also the side of him that gave her the most misgivings. She wanted that *something* to stop well short of being sinister.

Samantha spent an inordinate amount of time trying to analyze her attraction to Clell. Inevitably it came back to comparisons with other men of her experience. The greatest discrepancy was always in the bedroom. He made the act of love a matter of primary importance to her. But there were other, less carnal things as well. His economy of speech and movement was so at odds with the voluble sloppiness of the others. There was a discipline about Clell that bespoke a strong will and great force of character. He knew who he was and what he could do. There was a surefooted competence in everything he did. With the exception of that one night in Georgetown, he always seemed in total control.

And the most glaring differences of all, she thought, were between Hazard and her former husband. Farrell Pridgen was . . . was—she had to borrow a slang word from Goody Nelson—a wimp. A wimp without moral underpinnings. Farrell was very stylish, very handsome, very popular, and totally incapable of original thought. He had never made a move, uttered a syllable, or harbored an idea that had not first been strained through the filter of how it would be received by other people, "the right people." He had all the charm of a fraternity house greeter on pledge night, a function he had actually performed at Duke. Farrell vetted everyone and everything in terms of family or money or social standing. His clothes, his car, his hair style, his thoughts were always carefully considered and painstakingly calibrated to match the ganglia of ambitions that shaped him. He would not hesitate to jettison any one of them for something more useful. It did not surprise Samantha to hear that Farrell had turned his law office in Wilmington's old section into a headquarters for an assault on New Hanover County politics. There was not a single thing about Farrell Pridgen that was set in a foundation more solid than hot tapioca, and Samantha had no doubt that he would someday parlay his empty charm into state or even national office.

Why Farrell had married her was a mystery to Samantha. Her family was respectable—achingly so, with not a single colorful reprobate hidden somewhere in the foliage of the family tree. Her family was boringly middle class. The Huffs were not Wrights or Trasks or Sprunts or Camerons or any of the other families who dominated the Cape Fear Country Club and pulled the strings that pulled southeastern North Carolina in whichever direction they chose. Samantha had not even been a debutante, an almost unpardonable crime.

Farrell's family was solidly middle middle class as well, of course, but that only made it more remarkable that he should have married her. Samantha Huff had provided no easy access to high society. The best Samantha could explain it was that Farrell had been too young, too naive, and too smitten to know that her good looks and intelligence would be of minimal help to his career. He had discovered it soon enough, however, and his constant suggestions—no, *orders*—about what she should wear, what she should say, and whom she should befriend had finally driven her to pack her bags and flee to Charlotte.

Farrell had been openly relieved to be rid of her. He wasted little time in securing a divorce and courting and marrying the plain and stupid daughter of a judge powerful in the local Democratic party. The judge's daughter had an overbite like a tiger shark.

Why Samantha had married Farrell was even more of a mystery. Had she really been so impressed with his good looks and barren style? By the aggressive ambition she first diagnosed as healthy get-up-and-go? With the fact that he knew not only the best people in tiny Wilmington, but in Charleston, that social crucible to the south, as well? Or had it simply been time for her to marry *someone*? Getting married, after all, was what southern girls did best.

She and Farrell were married immediately upon graduation. At that age she was not desperate for a husband, even on a southern timetable. She was not, as they said in the Carolinas, ''right anxious.'' She married him because she wanted to.

They had met two years earlier when she was home from Chapel Hill and he was home from Durham, at a party at a Wrightsville Beach cottage owned by one of Farrell's fraternity brothers. Samantha had been the prettiest girl there, and Farrell had made straight for her. She could not remember what they had talked about—you could never quite remember what you talked about with Farrell—but she could recall being giddy from his swarming attentions. He seemed to know absolutely everyone, and she had been impressed. He was *so* handsome and *so* charming. He even managed to con the boy who brought her into letting him take her home, ensuring he went away thinking Farrell Pridgen a swell guy. Yes indeed, Farrell Pridgen would go far in politics.

That summer had been wonderful, she had to admit. They went to the Lumina at Wrightsville Beach, to the Carolina Moon Pavilion at Carolina Beach, and danced to the music of the swing bands, fair-to-middling imitations of Miller or Goodman or Shaw. The Lumina, of course, was not the Lumina of the early 1930s, when Wilmington society threw a Depression Ball and came in expensive imitation rags to dance to Loop McGowan and his Loop Boys, but it was good fun nonetheless. It did not stop being good fun until she was married to Farrell and had to live with him.

She was engaged to Farrell Pridgen for two years. In all that time she never managed to get an intimate view of him. Chapel Hill and Durham were not very far apart, but going to different schools during the engagement still meant constant separations. Her senior year at Carolina corresponded with his final year at the Duke law school, and he was so burdened with work they were lucky to see each other on alternate weekends.

Samantha knew nothing, for instance, about his prissy fastidiousness, an obsession with privacy and personal hygiene that bordered on the phobic. After their wedding and after he had set up a Wilmington law practice funded by his partner and college roommate, he had found a house for them on Front Street, along the Cape Fear River. It had two full bathrooms: one for him and one for her. Whenever he found evidence that she had used his bathroom—a stray hair, a forgotten bobby pin, the toilet seat left down—he flew into a rage. He had also insisted on twin beds, and she often felt he would have preferred separate bedrooms altogether.

After the first few months of marriage, their sex life had trickled away to almost nothing. Even before that, it was a bizarre practice of quick and furtive couplings that invariably left her jumpy and short-tempered for days afterward. Farrell never fully undressed for these unions. He would leave on his pajama tops and on a couple of occasions even left on the bottoms, his member poking out through the fly. In seven years of marriage she had never seen her husband completely nude. And he always, always, used a condom.

To fill the various voids in her existence, Samantha had put her education to work and had gotten a job on the society page of the Sunday *Star-News*. At first Farrell had been furious. What would his friends think, her working? Then he had reconsidered. She would be in a position now to legitimately gather and disseminate gossip, and her power to insert certain names into the columns of the Wilmington paper could enhance his social clout. He reversed his stand.

Samantha proved an excellent reporter and a crisp, clean writer. When the offer came from the Charlotte paper, she accepted it and quietly informed Farrell she was leaving him. He had not put up even a show of an argument.

Getting away from Farrell Pridgen had such an exhilarating effect on Samantha that she had fallen straight into an affair with a colleague in her new paper. It was six months before she discovered the man was married. It was three years before she found herself entangled once again, this time with a city councilman. This one got her pregnant. When she told him, he treated her as if she had committed the ultimate boorish sin. His parting act had been to arrange an abortion for her, an operation performed at a Mecklenburg County farmhouse by a doctor with dirty fingernails. The carelessly performed procedure led to hemorrhaging and the removal of more than just a fetus.

The long drought between the councilman and Clell Hazard could be directly attributed to that experience . . . and the fact that most of the men she'd met in Charlotte and later in Washington all had too much of Farrell Pridgen and the councilman about them. They were all successful and glib and self-concerned and about as deep as highland topsoil.

Clell Hazard was no intellectual, but he had uncommon common sense and an instinct about what was important. He felt deeply about the few things he considered worthy of feelings, and he did not spend his time or emotions foolishly. He had a way of cutting straight to the core of things. He picked his few friends—people like Goody Nelson—for what they were, not who they were. He had picked a career without the usual concern for financial return or high status, but out of a strong and genuine desire to be of service. He had chosen unwisely, Samantha thought, but in good faith.

Thinking it through, Samantha concluded that Betty Lou had been right yet again. Clell Hazard *did* have a good heart. He *was* one of the few men of integrity she knew. There was nothing wrong with Clell Hazard that getting him out of the United States Army would not fix. But to accomplish that, to salvage Clell Hazard, she would first have to permit him to woo her back. But how was she going to go about that? Not one idea that came to her seemed likely to work.

"Can I talk to you for a minute?"

Not since that first day in the elevator had Samantha seen Clell so awkward and ill at ease. When she invited him in, he stood hesitantly just inside the door and fidgeted until she asked him to sit. She offered him a drink, and he accepted with unusual alacrity, specifying whiskey and water, as if she had forgotten or had thrown out the bottle of Wild Turkey he knew she kept for him. This was the man who was always so sure of himself, always in control? If Samantha had not been so nervous herself, she would have found it all very amusing.

She brought him his drink, sat down across from him, and looked at him expectantly. He looked back without speaking. The seconds dragged into minutes. She was beginning to think he would never say anything, that they would pass the years and grow old together just sitting there, staring at each other. She was also thinking that that might not be such a bad way to spend a lifetime when he said, "I've missed you, Sam."

Samantha's instincts told her this was not the time for tactical advantages. Clell would not tolerate such folderol in the best of circumstances, much less now. She knew that if she insisted on clearcut victory, on pressing her point of view or lecturing him or demanding an explanation, the victory would be a Pyrrhic one. So she said simply, "I've missed you, too."

Hazard leaned forward, his elbows on his knees, his long fingers wrapped around his glass. A muscle twitched along the line of his jaw. "I'm sorry for what happened," he said. "I know how you feel about it and why you feel that way. It won't ever happen again. You have my word on it." He stopped. That was it. He had nothing more to say.

"Fine," Samantha said. "Now, what shall we do tonight?"

22

Delta Company milled in place in the alley between the Delta and Honor Guard barracks. Corporal Willow carefully examined each man in his squad and sent Wildman racing back upstairs to shave again. When Wildman returned and passed muster, Willow approached Sergeant Hazard. "My squad's ready, sarge."

"Okey-doke, Jack. I'll start my inspection in a couple of minutes, so get 'em formed up." When Willow turned away, Hazard hooked a finger in the boy's belt. "Hold up a minute, Jack. I know it's awful short notice, but can you come to supper at my place tonight?"

"Sure, sarge. I'd love to."

"Fine. Twenty-hundred hours. Or better yet, come on home with me after we stand down from this parade. Or maybe you'd like to bring a date? You just got time to get to the orderly room and call somebody. Go ahead, I'll cover for you."

Willow shook his head. "I don't have a girl."

"There's a new WAC at battalion HQ who doesn't have to sneak up on a meal to get something to eat. Want Goody to fix you up?"

"I'll just come stag if it's okay with you."

"Suit yourself," Hazard said. Then for no discernible

reason, he laughed and did a clog dance, his shoe taps clicking on the macadam, his chestful of medals clinking like wind chimes. Willow grinned. Whatever it was that had cheered up his platoon sergeant lately was as welcome as rain in Kansas. After weeks of lugging around a foul disposition, Hazard was positively ebullient these days. Others had remarked on the change as well. Just this morning Willow had overheard Sergeant Louder telling Sergeant Cook that it was damn near safe to use the coffee machine in the ready room again, even when Hazard was around.

When the platoon had been formed, the men all dressed right, Hazard inspected them. Then he turned them over to the platoon leader and Lieutenant Webber walked through the ranks. When all the platoons were ready, the first sergeant addressed them. "Comp'ny . . . teeench-HUT. Pa-raaaade . . . HREST. All right, listen up. This here cluster-fuck is the last parade of the season, so the results are gonna stick for a long time. Us and them pussies at Honor Guard"—the Slasher jerked a contemptuous thumb at the Honor Guard barracks—"are dead even on the number of firsts we've took during the summer, so this is our last chance to show who's top comp'ny round here. You men take first place today, and they's gonna be beer in the mess hall tonight. You don't take first place, and your lives ain't gonna be worth what the little bird left on the pump handle." With that, the Slasher did an about face, saluted the waiting Captain Thomas, and informed the Old Man the company was all accounted for and ready for his inspection.

Thomas, checking his watch at frequent intervals, walked quickly through the company and found everything to his liking, or so they assumed. At least the company commander did not have that familiar pinched look on his face, as if he had just stepped into an enlisted three-holer after a field supper of stale beans. Thomas gave them left face and right-shoulder arms, then took his place at the head of the column with the first sergeant and Specialist Fourth Class Queen, the company driver and guidon bearer, right behind. The company marched in column the few steps across the street and into the staging area at the edge of the Fort Myer parade field. Honor Guard Company was already waiting and Bravo and Alpha could be seen coming up the street.

The companies of the Old Guard arranged themselves in order of march, four columns across with platoon sergeants in the right guide positions. In front of them the U.S. Army Band, in baggy blues, fiddled with instruments. Right behind the band the Old Guard Fife and Drum Corps, in tight-fitting colonial uniforms complete with white stockings, buckle shoes, and powdered wigs, waited with the stiff and haughty bearing of true thespians.

Willow could see that the grandstand centered along the bottom edge of the parade ground was filling rapidly. Up high on the reviewing stand sat Colonel Godwin, host for the day's parade, and a group of Pentagon officers, guests of the assistant undersecretary of the Army who was retiring today and in whose honor the parade was being held. In the spectators' bleachers were Army dependents and civilians. Coming out to watch the Third Infantry march on Sunday afternoons was one of the few free-of-charge tourist attractions of Washington, and there was always a good crowd on hand for the final parade of the season. The Old Guard on parade made a colorful snapshot, almost as good as the changing of the guard at the Tomb of the Unknown Soldier.

When the battalion was ready to go . . . it was time to wait. "At ease. Smoke 'em if you got 'em" echoed up and down the line, and the men leaned on their rifles and lit up, chatting easily and giving each other last-minute blouse tucks, the helper standing behind and pinching the blouse tight across the front, folding the excess material back at the sides while the man being helped tightened his belt. They stood there for nearly an hour, trying to stay calm and still so dark sweat stains would not ruin their uniforms. It was an unusually hot and humid day for September, almost as bad as the worst of the parade Sundays during July and August. A few of the men pulled at the windsor knots of their neckties, fighting off dizziness. Every man there prayed that the assistant undersecretary would keep his speech short. The noncoms, cursing the delay and sensing danger, wandered among the men dispensing salt tablets and advice. "Don't lock your knees out there. There ain't nuthin that'll put you on the ground quicker'n lockin' your knees. Keep a slight bend in 'em when we're at attention. Just enough to take the strain off. Ain't nobody gonna see it. . . . If a man goes down near you, for fuck's sake let him lie. We'll lose some points but not as many as we will if some asshole breaks ranks to help him. . . . When we make our approach to the reviewing stand, stay alert. Every man memorize his number in the rank. The NCO on the end of each rank will be dressing you up on the approach. If he calls out your number you better know it. . . . But don't look over at the guide. Keep them eyes locked straight ahead until you get the command 'Eyes right.' Then snap that fuckin' head so hard you think you broke your neck. . . . You people don't pay attention here, and *I'll* break your fuckin' neck."

Willow practiced standing at attention, glancing down to see how far he could bend his knees before they broke through the straight plane of his trouser crease. After he got the feel of it he tried it with his eyes straight ahead and had another man check him out.

The troops were playing this game when the signal came down from Sergeant-Major Nelson on the reviewing stand.

Everyone field-stripped their cigarettes and dressed their lines. Then orders ricocheted down the chain of command at ear-splitting volume, in decibels meant to reach the audience in the bleachers. They started with the battalion executive officer, Lieutenant Colonel Johnson, and were relayed by the company commanders and then the platoon leaders. "BATTALION. . . ." "Company. . . ." "Platoon. . . ." The men assumed the parade rest position. "TENCH . . ." "Tench . . ." "Tench . . ." ". . . HUT." The Old Guard snapped to with a clack of heel taps. Johnson bellowed: "FIX . . ." and his subordinates relayed the command: "Fix . . ." "Fix . . ." "BAY-O-NETS." Drummers from Fife and Drum started a roll, measuring out the five-count drill with sharp booms of the bass between snare rolls. On the first count—BrrrrrrrBoom—the troops brought the muzzles of their M-1's across their bodies to the left hand. On the second count, their right hands did a snap roll and grasped the hilt of the bayonet in the patent leather scabbard on the left hip. On count three, the chrome bayonets came out in a sweeping arc that caught the sunlight and were snapped immediately onto the end of the rifles. On count four, the left hand pushed the rifle back across the body to the right side. On count five, the men snapped back to the original position of attention. The drums stopped. Colonel Johnson brayed, "RIGHT . . ." and the company commanders and platoon leaders echoed, "Right . . ." "Right . . ." Johnson finished: ". . . HACE." The battalion pivoted to the right. "RIGHT SHOULDERRRR . . ." "Right shoulderrr . . ." "Right shoulderrr . . ." "HARMS." The rifles came up. "FOR'ARD . . ." "For'ard . . ." "For'ard . . ." ". . . HARCH." The band struck up "Be Kind to Your Web-Footed Friends," and the battalion marched in column to the top edge of the staging area, executed a column left on command, and strode across the top of the parade ground toward a spot directly in front of the reviewing stand. As they marched, the platoon leaders counting out cadence with help from the bass drum, Willow could see a row of Army ambulances parked along the street on the back boundary of the field, their crews lounging and laughing and enjoying the spectacle. They reminded Willow of vultures standing off from a down but not yet dead animal. The way he felt they might well be rewarded in their vigil. The parade had only just begun, and already he was exhausted.

He was tired, so very tired. What a contrast from the way he had felt eight months earlier when the plane had banked lazily over Tan Son Nhut and he had caught his first glimpse of Saigon sprawled below, the river sparkling in the bright sun, the broad tree-lined avenues, the clutter of thatch and tin-roofed houses, the grand French colonial architecture in the center of the city. His pulse had raced and he had felt an almost pure joy. He was proud of the shiny brown bar on each shoulder . . . proud of the way his uniform hung on a body hardened by the strenuous weeks of OCS and jump school . . . proud of his new skills. And so anxious to put them to use.

Now, walking along the dusty road, sweat forming wide salty rings in the armpits of his fatigue blouse and running in tickling streams from his crotch to his knees, he laughed bitterly at the memory of that young and artless lieutenant of Infantry. It all seemed like a million years ago. It was a mere thousand years since those first few days back from Daisy Mae. For days afterward he was preoccupied and moody. In the mornings he would lay on his cot with his hands beneath his head and send out lines of skirmishers on the ceiling of his hootch, searching for ways to make things come out differently. In these ruminations, his commands were always crisp and clear and there was no confusion, no numbing noise. His troops performed magnificently, and he was able to turn the fight around every time.

In the afternoon, after his sessions with the G-2 debriefers, he would join Otis Harmon and Charlie Dell, the company's other surviving platoon leaders, at the officers club and review the debacle over pizza and beer, a world away from the roiled ground of Fort Doom.

The day after they were lifted off the firebase, the three men had gathered at the club, and they had propped an extra chair at their table and had set out an extra beer in a wholly felt, half-assed tribute to the Marshal. Captain Crowder was dead, too, but no one set a place for him or for the thirty-four Bravo Company noncoms and enlisted men who had come off of Daisy Mae in body bags. The Marshal had been a platoon leader, one of them. Besides, it was a question of room.

"Boy-o-howdy, we really got the shit shot out of us," Harmon had said that first day in the club.

"We really did, didn't we?" said Charlie Dell.

"We really got our asses handed to us," said Harmon.

"Wow, we surely did," said Dell in affable agreement, his massive head bobbing up and down, a rueful smile on his wide, Irish peasant face.

"We really ran into a ten-ton shithammer," said Harmon.

"Didn't we though?" said Dell, eyeing the last piece of pizza and wondering what was the right thing to do, really wanting it now that it had gotten cold and the cheese had hardened. He'd rather eat cold pizza than pussy once that cheese hardened. It reminded him of the fried cheese sandwiches his mother used to make back in Alabama.

Willow rocked in his chair, his thumbs hooked into his web belt. He had been watching the exchange as if he were at a tennis match, swinging his head with the volley. When Harmon opened his mouth to serve again, Willow broke in. "I really must congratulate you gentlemen on your brilliant, incisive analysis of the battle of Fire Support Base Daisy Mae. Your grasp of strategy and tactics brings to mind Jackson at Manassas, or perhaps the campaigns of Von Lettow in East Africa. If we had been blessed with you gentlemen as instructors at Benning, perhaps we'd be winning this war instead of losing it.''

Dell and Harmon looked at each other and shrugged in unison. Harmon smiled, a thin hatchet slash in his angular East Texas face. Dell shrugged again and made a decision and reached for the pizza. He smiled around his cud when no objection was lodged.

Willow glared at them both for a moment, then looked out the large picture window. The club sat on a sandy rise overlooking the Chu Lai beach and the blue bay and the green and brown curve of the Battangan Peninsula beyond. Near the tip of the peninsula, white smoke rose, and Willow could see the snakes and slicks—Cobra gunships and Huey assault choppers—buzzing like angry hornets over the smoke. If they could not keep the enemy cleared off a slim finger of land surrounded by water on three sides and within shelling distance of the headquarters of the largest division in the United States Army, he thought, then what had happened on Daisy Mae was not really so remarkable after all.

Willow looked across at the meaty face of Charlie Dell, watched him wolf the food. A wave of disgust washed over him—disgust with the staff officers, the REMF's, drinking and laughing around them; disgust with Dell and with Harmon; and, yes, disgust with himself. What were three platoon leaders whose company had ceased to exist as an effective fighting force barely twenty-four hours before, doing here drinking and eating in air-conditioned comfort? ''Why aren't we on our fucking shields?'' he asked in a hoarse whisper.

Willow's companions did not reply. They just looked at

him and then at each other again with puzzled and worried glances. "Hey, take it easy, Jackie boy," *Harmon drawled softly.*

Willow shook his head. "You take it easy. We spend months, months, getting sniped and booby-trapped and walking into ambushes that last for three minutes before the gooks break contact and vanish. Then we get a go at a company, a whole fucking company, and we step on our dicks. We should have been ready. We knew they were out there. Everybody knew it except for that lame bastard Bean. How could the Army give command to a man like that?"

"Well," said Harmon, "I had me a top sergeant at Riley who used to say that any army's only as good as its ability to overcome the incompetence of its field grade officers."

"But Bean's a West Pointer, for chrissakes," said Willow. "An Academy man."

Harmon gagged on a swallow of beer. "Jackie boy, you're a good ol' boy," he laughed, "but you don't know sheep shit from winter grapes. The South Hudson Institute of Technology, affectionately known as S.H.I.T., don't give you one of them nice rings of theirs until you hand over both your brains and your balls."

Charlie Dell stole a peek at his West Point ring and frowned, the insult working its way slowly from aural canal to brain box. Harmon laughed again and patted Dell's beefy shoulder. "I didn't mean you, Charlie boy. You were a football player, not Young MacArthur. The only Woo Poo bullshit you were ever guilty of swallowing was the preposterous idea that y'all could beat Navy."

"We could've if it hadn't been for that goddamned Staubach," Dell pouted.

Harmon chuckled. "My point here is that West Point is a tad overrated as a molder of men. If you wanted your

*character built, Charlie boy, you'd a done a hell of a sight
better by taking that scholarship to Alabama and letting
Bear Bryant build it for you.''*

A muffled boom rattled the club's windows, and everyone in the room glanced disinterestedly out across the bay
to the Battangan, where a string of clouds rose like white
toadstools from the jungle canopy. Veteran headquarters
staffers murmured knowingly to newer officers, "Arclights.
B-52s. Nothing can survive under an arclight."

Harmon, Dell, and Willow had sat there all afternoon,
nursing their tepid beers and unfocused grudges, getting
stupidly drunk, coming no closer to understanding what
had happened to them up on that hilltop.

Remembering that day as he plodded toward the club,
Willow began to roll an idea, a vague plan, in his head—
one that frightened him a little but also filled him with a
mild euphoria. He stopped by Second Battalion HQ and
left a message for Major Burns: He would accept the
generous offer of a leave if the major would be so kind as
to cut the orders.

Harmon and Dell were not at the officers club. Their
usual table was occupied by a group of headquarters
officers. Everything else was the same. Out the window
and across the bay, there was fighting again on the
Battangan, the smoke and hovering gunships now such a
familiar scene that it all seemed permanently etched onto
the glass.

Willow asked the bartender, a buck sergeant, "Did a
Lieutenant Harmon or a Lieutenant Dell leave a message
for me?"

"You Lieutenant Willow?"

"Roger that."

"Yessir. They said to tell you they couldn't wait any
longer. To tell you they went to town. To Mimi's."

"Thanks." Willow went back out into the heat. He did

*not feel up to more walking, and he waited in front of the
club until he finally caught a ride to the base gate in a
three-quarter ton. Outside the gate he dickered with a
wizened cyclo driver for five full minutes in the hot sun,
misunderstood in three languages: pidgin English, pidgin
French, and pidgin Vietnamese. In the end he surrendered
and agreed to pay three hundred piasters for the hundred-'p'
ride to Mimi's. Anything to get a breeze, no matter how
weak, on his face.*

*He hopped into the cyclo, nothing more than a rickshaw-
like carriage welded to the front half of a bicycle. The
papasan who pedaled it had to be seventy-five years old.
He had a white scraggly Ho Chi Minh beard and wore a
pith helmet, a tattered U.S. Army fatigue blouse, and a
pair of torn shorts that showed the walnut color of his ass.
And flip-flops, of course. Willow often thought that the
lowly shower-clogs should be officially recognized as the
national symbol of South Vietnam and accorded a place of
honor on the country's flag.*

*Without even faking a glance in any direction but straight
ahead, the old papasan wheeled his contraption into the
rushing stream of traffic, his scrawny legs pumping furiously to get up merging speed, the muscles in his calves as
round and hard as crabapples. Tough old bird, Willow
thought, probably a retired Viet Minh fighter from the
French war. Or maybe not retired at all. After the war
they'd find out he was a general in the North Vietnamese
Army. Maybe it was General Giap himself, doing a little
recon on the Americal.*

*Willow closed his eyes and tried to relax, the air gener-
ated by General Giap's lumpy calves almost cool on his
hot face. It was no use. The street noise was deafening.
Cyclos, motorized cyclos, tin taxis, and the occasional
water buffalo all crammed the dusty thoroughfare and
raised an unholy din. After being so long out in the*

boonies, Willow was still jumpy and uncomfortable with so many people around.

Smoke from the cars, trucks, and motorcycles filled the air with a blue haze. Maybe they should put a Honda on the flag next to the flip-flop. The cyclo rolled through the acrid smell of exhaust and nuoc-mam, the stinking but surprisingly good-tasting fish sauce into which the Vietnamese dunked every morsel they ate. They rolled past countless soup stands, the customers squatting and rocking back on their heels as they relayed news and gossip and ate their bowls of fa and soup chinoise.

To take his mind off the very real danger of getting sideswiped by a rocketing truck or taxi, Willow watched for women. Vietnamese women were among the loveliest in the world, he decided, the long black hair so much like Rachel's, and the exquisite bone structure and slim, boyish bodies. The delicacy of their features sure as hell masked a tough-as-nails center, though. Vietnamese women were usually far more formidable than their menfolk. But what could you expect? It was the woman who had to run things on the home front, who had to keep the family together and rice in the rice bowl while her man was pressed into fighting VC, or ARVN, or Americans, or French, or Japs, or Chinese. It had been like that for hundreds of years, and it would be like that for Buddha knew how many more.

The peasant girls in from the countryside for a day at market or as permanent refugees wore conical hats and black or white pajamas, baggy and loose-fitting and not very revealing. Willow switched his attention to the girls in the flowing ao dais, the tight-fitting trousers and tunics that could show a lot when they rode their bicycles. What wonderful, tight little asses these girls had.

Willow knew, however, that Vietnamese women rated a split decision from American GIs. There were two distinct schools of thought. One maintained that Vietnamese girls were wonderful in the sack, and these men went so far as to marry them in support of their conviction. To them, Occidental women would forever more seem too bulky and coarse and graceless. The other group contended that Vietnamese women were the world's lousiest lays, totally devoid of inventiveness or enthusiasm in bed, without even enough gumption to fake it. The joke in this school of thought was, "Fucking a Vietnamese means you're too lazy to jack off."

Willow was still doing research into the matter.

General Giap finally puffed up to Mimi's and stopped, thus giving the small army of street urchins who had been running for blocks after the American in the cyclo, a chance to catch up. Willow found himself surrounded by ragged, dirty-faced kids, each and every one of them with eyes like a copperhead. They called in a shrill chorus:

"You, you, you. You gimme Salem, Joe?"

"You, you, you. You gimme money, Joe?"

"Hey, Joe. You want boom-boom? Fuckee-suckee?"

When Willow shook his head and moved toward Mimi's door, one hand over the pocket that held his wallet, the chorus shifted tone and intensity.

"Hey, Joe. You cheap charlie."

"Hey, Joe. You numbah ten."

"Hey, Joe. Fuck you, Joe."

The war had been kind to Mimi. The bar was large and plush with vinyl-covered booths along the walls, neat for-mica tables in the middle of the room, and a jukebox with the latest sounds from the Land of Round Doorknobs. A battery of air-conditioners pumped salvos of ice-cold air into the room, and Willow went from fear of heat stroke to worry about frostbite in a matter of seconds.

As his eyes adjusted to the gloom, he saw that the place was empty of Americans. The first person he picked out was Mimi's mother sitting on her high stool behind the *cash register, a wrinkled old crone with the eyes of a gunfighter and a dark cave of a mouth filled with nothing but gums blackened by betel nut juice. Then he saw Mimi herself coming toward him, a happy smile on her pretty round face.*

"Jackie-san, you come back to Mimi!" she cried, throwing her arms around his neck and kissing him flush on the mouth. Willow didn't let it go to his head. Mimi greeted everyone this way, especially after they had been in the bush for a couple of months and especially on a slow, early afternoon. And she had a phenomenal memory for names. She could probably tick off the entire Americal Division. Hell, she had probably laid the entire Americal Division.

He laughed and backed off, trying to get a closer look at her. Something was wrong. Something was different. Holy shit! She had round eyes!

"Mimi! Goddamn! You did it! You really did it! You went and got your eyes fixed!"

Mimi giggled happily. "I tol' you I fix 'em. You like?" She batted her lashes at him.

"No, I no like," he said truthfully. "It takes away all the mystery of the Orient. It makes you look scrutable."

She laughed and said merrily, "Fuck you, Jackie-san. Ever-body else like. Mimi make plenty money now, you bet you ass. You look more. You see more?"

Willow looked more. "Jesus! The tits, too! You've had a silicone job!"

Mimi giggled again and said, "Now Mimi just like Playboy. Numbah one titties. Make plenty money."

Willow shook his head. "Christ, what's next? A hymen restoration?"

"What is high man restation?" Mimi asked with a frown, afraid she might be missing a trick in the world of cosmetic surgery.

Willow laughed. "Hymen restoration. It's where they give you back your cherry."

"Ahhh yes, I know that high man restation," Mimi said with relief, back in familiar territory. "Maybe I get cherry when war is over and Mimi ready for husband."

"The war will never be over," said Willow. "By the way, is Otis Harmon here?"

"Oh yes," Mimi said brightly. "Otis-san and Alabama boy out back with my girls. You go get them. Tell them time is up. They no come now they pay more, you bet you ass. I go get you beer."

Mimi headed for the bar; Willow walked to the back and pushed open the door, stepping from a world of naughahyde and air-conditioning into one of stifling heat and the smell of nuoc-mam. He was in a small dirt courtyard surrounded by three wings of poured concrete painted blue, the wings cut up into tiny rooms, cribs for the whores. The rooms had no glass in the single windows and no doors in the doorways, just thin curtains. Most of Mimi's girls were in residence, resting up for the night shift, cooking over hotplates and playing their radios, sad, whining love songs that invariably told the story of a waiting girl and her soldier lover up on the DMZ. He thought of Sergeant Hazard's comment about the Vietnamese language. This sounded like ducks fucking to music.

There were two living creatures out in the courtyard itself, and both reacted to Willow's sudden appearance. One was a scruffy lame dog which rose, sniffed Willow's leg, then hobbled over to where a large block of ice was slowly melting away. The dog cocked its bad leg and pissed on the ice. The other was one of Mimi's girls, a new one, who sat in a small patch of shade with a naked baby on her lap. She called out to Willow in a bored voice, "Hey, Joe. You want boom-boom? I love you no shit." Willow shook his head with a smile. The girl's baby *began to cry and she casually and absent-mindedly reached around and jacked its tiny penis, sliding the foreskin back and forth. The baby stopped crying.*

The curtain on one of the cubicle doors parted, and Harmon stepped out, blinking in the bright sunlight. A moment later Dell emerged from the adjacent stall. They waved to him. Willow waved back and jerked a thumb toward the bar at his back. Then he turned and went back into the arctic air.

The three men sat in a booth near the unplugged jukebox. Mimi brought them bami-bas, the "33" beer that the French had foisted off on the Vietnamese. It was a foul brew with a formaldehyde preservative base. Willow thought of the lame dog and checked to make sure Mimi had not put any ice in his. He paid her, and she headed for the courtyard to make certain that if Harmon or Dell had given her girls anything extra, she got her cut.

"Well, how'd it go at the inquisition, Jackie boy?" Harmon asked.

"The object of the exercise seemed to be to establish the bravery and leadership of one Lieutenant Colonel Abner Bean," said Willow.

"Yeah, same with me," said Harmon.

"Did Pyle tell you that Bean was up for the Silver Star?" Willow asked.

"Yeah. Bean gets the Silver Star, seventy-seven boys get the Purple Heart, and thirty-eight unfortunate souls get the Royal Order of the Permanent Hurt Locker. Yessirreebob, it's Academy Awards night in ol' Veet Nam."

"Hey, wait a minute," interjected Dell, his bulldog face angry. "Colonel Bean deserves a medal. To keep gettin' up like that to fight, that's pretty great stuff in my book. He's in bad shape, and they say over at the hospital that he might not make it."

Willow and Harmon exchanged glances, and Willow

*finished off his beer and stood. "Speaking of the hospital,
I'd better get over there and see the boys—the ones who
aren't getting Silver Stars."*

*"You best tread softly, Jackie boy," said Harmon. "I
was over there this morning, and some of them were less
than overjoyed to see one of their noble leaders."*

"Gee," Willow said bitterly. "Imagine that."

". . . our enemy, despite massive assistance from the
Communist aggressor to the north, is on his last legs. The
peace-loving people of South Vietnam have rejected him
time and again. They voted against him with their feet in
1954 when they fled the North's oppressive red regime,
and they are voting against him now, using bullets for
ballots, every day and in every corner of their brave and
beleaguered country. The South Vietnamese are fighting to
live free, and it has been a privilege and an honor for me
to have played a small part in the United States' effort to
aid these little tigers in their struggle. . . ." The assistant
undersecretary of the Army droned on, reminiscing on a
career that spanned more than thirty years, apparently
determined to recall and savor each and every minute of it.

Out in front of the massed battalion stood the color
guard from Honor Guard Company, its flags and battle
streamers drooping along their shafts, not a hint of breeze
to stir the memories of past glories. Willow could feel the
sweat running from under his hatband and down his face.
His uniform was soaked through and sweat dripped from
his right wrist and onto the stock of his rifle. Within the
arc of vision allowed by the lock of head and shoulders, he
could see that at least a dozen men had already gone
down. The white-jacketed buzzards would have a feast.
Two ranks in front of him he could see Wildman anchored
steadily in the parade rest position—feet spread, left arm
tucked across the small of his back, rifle jutting forward in

the extended right hand. Willow was surprised. Given Wildman's appalling physical condition, he would have bet a pay envelope that the hapless private would have been among the first to drop.

". . . and we have transformed the topography of South Vietnam, giving that nation an infrastructure unparalleled in Southeast Asia. The airport our engineers have built at Tan Son Nhut is the busiest in the world. The deep-water ports we have constructed at Cam Ranh Bay and Danang are among Asia's largest and finest. We have put down thousands of miles of modern highways in places where before only water buffalo had trod. We have built bridges and dams and culverts and. . . ." The assistant undersecretary seemed impervious to the heat. In the bleachers, spectators fanned themselves with their programs. They looked like the card section at a college football game.

Willow blinked to clear the salty, stinging perspiration from his eyes. He was just in time to see the man in front of him begin to sway. In unconscious imitation of his platoon sergeant, Willow warned urgently, "Steadeeee." It was too late. The wobbling man issued a guttural, gargling moan and pitched forward. He twisted slightly to the left as he went down, like a diver doing a half gainer. The tip of his bayonet led the way and it caught the man in front of him, Wildman, at the spot where the bunched material of his blouse was tucked at the waist. There was a loud ripping noise. Wildman staggered, caught himself, and settled back into place. But the left side of his uniform looked like Cinderella's work dress before the fairy godmother got to it. A giggle spread through the ranks behind the pudgy private, and it grew louder when Wildman began to mutter hysterically, "Ohfuckoshit. Itain'tmyfault. They can't blame it on me. I'll kill the bastard—killim, killim." From his place in formation Sergeant Hazard could not see what the commotion was about, but he could hear it well enough. He put down the ripening anarchy with a growl. "Steady goddammit."

There was a smattering of relieved applause from the grandstand. The assistant undersecretary had sat down. Lieutenant Colonel Johnson spun on his heel and faced the troops. The sun flashed off the five-pointed star suspended from the pale blue ribbon around his neck. He surveyed the formation with a proud and haughty sweep, the look of a Roman tribune or an SS officer, and bawled, "OLD GUAAAARD. . . ." These were the opening words of the command to pass in review. Unfortunately, they were also the opening words to the Third Herd's unofficial battle cry. And almost to a man, each trooper in the formation decided spontaneously to complete that cry. Each man thought it might amuse the half dozen or so men closest to him. This collection of individual impulses was transformed by a thousand throats into an audible mass response—"SUUUUUCKS."

The men managed to shock themselves. Some were stone silent. Some began to titter. They all looked expectantly at Lieutenant Colonel Johnson. Even the men in the back rank could see the battalion XO's eyes grow wide with disbelief. His body began to quiver as if someone had shoved an electric cattle prod up his backside. His face turned livid. He finished his interrupted command with a thunderous snarl: "PASS IN REVIEW."

The four company commanders, as stunned as Johnson, somehow managed to remember their own commands: "Comp'ny . . . AAtench . . . HUT. Right . . . HACE. Right shoulder . . . HARMS. Fo-arrrd . . . HARCH." The Old Guard, in part appalled and in part enormously pleased with itself, stepped off in column behind the blaring band and the fifes and drums. They marched to the edge of the field, made a flanking movement, marched in rank to the bottom of the parade ground, and did a series of half-lefts to complete a wheeling manuever that brought them into their final approach, marching in rank along the grandstand.

The NCOs at the end of each rank closest to the bleachers were all struck by the same communal thought, much as their men had been a few moments before: If the troops made a particularly good showing, perhaps battalion's retribution for the quirky mishap of a minute ago would be muted. All along the edge of the formation, the sergeants stage-whispered instructions: "Number Six, back the fuck off." "Number Nine, suck in your fuckin' gut." "Number Seven, you cocksucker, this ain't no fuckin' horserace." "Number Seven, bring your motherfuckin' bayonet up . . . No, no, that's too far, cunthead!" "Get in step, Six, you simple shit."

The troopers of the Old Guard strutted by the reviewing stand at eyes-right, their officers frozen into perfect salutes. They marched past the stand, off the parade field, and into the staging area. On that part of the field where they had listened to the assistant undersecretary meander through his life, the bodies of their fallen comrades lay in a variety of poses. The medics, carrying stretchers, were moving among them like a graves registration detail. It looked, thought Willow, like the ground at Shiloh.

The men were marched off to their company areas and told to fall out by commanders still too distraught to reprimand them. Later, much later, even the battalion brass would concede that, on a strictly military basis, the Old Guard had never looked better than on that day.

23

Jackie Willow had not been so taken with an older woman since the day he had met Rachel Field's mother. Miss Huff and Mrs. Field even resembled one another. The difference was that Miss Huff was transparently in love. She was seldom far from Sergeant Hazard. Every time he came within range, she would reach out to touch him. She would run a hand along his arm or across his leg. Or she would sit on the arm of his chair and play with the back of his neck. To have won the heart of such a woman was quite an accomplishment. Willow now understood Hazard's recent good cheer. And not only was Miss Huff beautiful and intelligent, she was a wonderful cook. Willow told her so.

Samantha smiled at the mooning young man and shook her head. "I didn't do it," she said in that raspy voice of hers, the June Allyson voice. Willow flushed and turned an apologetic face to Betty Lou Farmer and said, "I'm sorry ma'am. This meal is really wonderful." Betty Lou laughed and said, "I didn't do it, either." Willow was too confused to be embarrassed. "Then who did?" he asked. Both women hooked thumbs toward Hazard.

"I had a little help from Goody," Hazard said with a nonchalant shrug. Willow stared, speechless. They all laughed while the young corporal digested this information. It certainly did not fit the picture he had of his platoon sergeant eating out of surplus C-rat' cans, kept from scurvy and ptomaine only by greasy-spoon restaurants and the kitchen of Miss Huff.

Sergeant-Major Nelson was speaking. "Clell, I got some good news for you, and I got some bad news. Which do you want first?"

"The bad news."

"Spoken like a true grunt," said Nelson, looking to the ladies. "Groundpounders always want the bad news first, because they know the good news ain't never all that good." He turned back to Hazard. "To start with, our leaders are incredibly pissed. When the Herd came out with their showstopper today, Godwin damn near choked to death."

Hazard smiled. "So did I. Did he say anything?"

"Well, all the generals and the assistant undersecretary kinda looked over at him with these puzzled looks. They didn't quite know what they had heard. So this two-star leans over and asks Godwin, what did they say? And the Old Man, slicker'n owl shit, says '*Rocks*, General. They said *Rocks*.' The general says, '*Rocks*?' And Godwin says, 'Yes, *Rocks*. It's an Old Guard tradition: In the sweeping tide of battle, the Third Infantry stands like a rock'."

Hazard laughed and said, "And that's why Godwin will be a general himself someday soon. No doubt about it."

"What's the colonel going to do to us?" Willow asked.

"They haven't decided yet," Nelson chuckled. "But they're sure having a lot of fun going over the options. The whole battalion is in deep yogurt. There was talk about shipping the whole outfit to the Aleutians. There was talk about wholesale castration. There was even a suggestion that we transfer the whole lot of you to the Marine Corps."

"No, no, not that," cried Hazard, recoiling in mock terror. He grinned and said, "While we wait for the axe to fall, why don't you tell me the good news."

"You might think it's good news. As far as I'm concerned, 'mere anarchy is loosed upon the world. The blood-dimmed tide is loosed. And everywhere the ceremony of innocence is drowned. . . .' "

"At ease, Sergeant Yeats. Just gimme the news."

"Oh yeah. Well, you got your druthers. Third Platoon, Delta, will be the aggressor team at A. P. Hill."

"Hot damn. Thanks, Goody. I knew you could do it."

"Don't thank me yet, doofus. In the immortal words of William Tecumseh Sherman, or somebody: you'll be sorrreeee."

"What about the umpire?" Hazard pressed. "Were you able to do anything for me on that?"

"You remember that real sharp Special Forces captain we worked with around the Seven Mountains in Chau Doc?"

"The green beanie on loan to the CIA? Uhh, Captain Race?"

"That's the one. Except he's a major now and a chairborne commando at the Pentagon. He hates his job, and he volunteers for anything that'll get him out into the fresh air. I briefed him on what you got in mind, and he arranged to be your ump. He's real excited about it. He's polishing up his strangling wire, putting black crud on his face, the whole ball of wax. You two children should have a real nice time playing soljer together."

"That's great, Goody, just great," Hazard grinned. Willow and the women were listening with puzzled smiles, happy that Hazard was happy but unsure why.

"What's this all about, Clell?" Samantha asked.

Nelson answered for Hazard. "Clell has thoughtfully

volunteered his platoon to play the enemy in our upcoming field exercises." He turned to Willow and said, "That's our little secret, of course. If Webber finds out how all this came about, Clell will find himself advisor to the Botswana army. I don't think Sam would like that very much. Botswana ain't got no newspaper. Come to think of it, Botswana ain't got no army, neither."

Hazard was staying out of it, toying with his food and grinning. Betty Lou asked Goody, "So why is this cause for celebration? Why would Clell want to be the enemy?"

"He's got this cockamamie idea that since most of our boys are gonna end up pulling Nam duty sooner or later, he should give them a taste of commie tactics."

Willow broke in. "But Webber's the platoon leader. He might have different ideas."

"Webber has no combat experience," said Nelson. "He'll let Clell run the platoon. Hell, he lets Clell run the platoon day-to-day anyhow. Besides, Webber will be with battalion CP most of the time, coordinating, fixing target locations, and finding out who the brass wants you to hit next. That sort of thing."

"I don't see what the big deal is," shrugged Willow. "Small-unit tactics are small-unit tactics."

Nelson smiled a Buddha smile. "No they ain't, son. There's *our* small-unit tactics and there's *their* small-unit tactics. Clell is gonna use theirs."

"What's the difference?" Willow asked skeptically.

"The difference between winning and losing, boy. Theirs is better."

"With all due respect, sergeant-major," Willow said stiffly, "I cannot accept the idea that they are that much better soldiers than we are."

Hazard spoke up at last. "They're not. You ever hear

Goody or me suggest that there's anything wrong with the American soldier? The kids we got today are as good as those we had in Korea or W-W Two. Hell, they are better. They're smarter and they're stronger. Once the shooting starts, there is no better killer on the planet than your average aw-shucks farm boy from North Dakota.''

"So what's your complaint?" Willow asked.

"It's not with our troops," said Hazard. "It's with our leadership, both military and civilian. And it's with our strategy, our tactics and our motives. They're all cockeyed. But my biggest gripe is with the attitude of the people of this country. The people we're fighting are totally committed to this war, in it with their every resource and willing to sacrifice everything to win. What in hell has anybody in this country given up? If it wasn't for Walter Cronkite, most Americans wouldn't even know there was a war going on.''

Samantha was biting her lip so hard she threatened to draw blood. "And just what would you have us give up, Clell?" she asked in the cool, slightly mocking tone she used when interviewing a hostile source.

Hazard recognized it and did not like it. "One thing you can give up is your profit," he snapped. "There are people making money on this war. But the first thing you can give up is your indecision. The American people have to decide whether this war is worth fighting. If so, they have to get behind it—and us—and let us do what has to be done to win it. If they decide it's not, fine. But they have to get that message to the politicians so we can pull our boys the hell out of there.''

"There are people trying to do just that, Clell," said Samantha.

"Not enough. And not the kind of people anybody listens to.''

"Thanks for the compliment," Samantha said coldly.

"Is that it? Isn't there anything else we can give up for our boys in uniform?"

"As a matter of fact, there is," said Hazard, matching her sarcastic tone. "The upper classes in this country can give up what the working class is already giving up: their sons. If half the ingenuity that's going into beating the draft were applied to Vietnam, we'd be booking tours to Hanoi by now. I didn't have one kid in my platoon over there who wasn't from a blue-collar or farm family. In 1941 whole classes left college to enlist. These days there are more American college kids in Toronto than Southeast Asia. Whatever happened to the concept of *service*? It's time for people to start paying for the tailfins on the new car and the ranch house in the suburbs."

Betty Lou, the peacemaker, suggested in a firm voice, "It's time to talk about something else. Something important. Like the Tar Heels playing Duke this Saturday. Who do you all think is going to win?"

Goody Nelson jumped in to help her. It disturbed him to see Clell and Samantha arguing so soon after patching things up. "Who cares who wins?" he thundered. "What I want to know is where a ridiculous name like *Tar Heels* comes from? I mean, don't you people wash your feet down there? What kinda dumb name is that?"

Betty Lou looked blankly at Goody. "Why, I . . . I don't really know where it came from. Samantha darlin', where *does* it come from?"

Samantha laughed a thin laugh. She was still agitated, but she was also relieved that the conversation had been moved to safer ground. "I'm not sure. Isn't that disgraceful?"

"Nobody knows for sure," announced Willow. "But there are two conflicting theories."

They looked at Willow in surprise. "How would you know?" Betty Lou asked.

"My father's family originally came from the mountains of North Carolina," Willow said. "And I've read something about this in my books on the Civil War."

"So what are the theories?" Goody Nelson asked.

"Well, one version is that during the Civil War a Confederate general praised the North Carolina troops by saying that in battle the Carolinians stuck to their positions as if they had tar on their heels."

"Why what a nice thing to say," beamed Betty Lou.

There was something about the way young Willow delivered his information that reminded Goody Nelson of how he had been set up during the command inspection. "What's the other version?" he asked Willow, his eyes twinkling with anticipation.

"The other story is that in the middle of an important battle, the Carolina troops broke and ran, taking to their heels across the Tar River."

Betty Lou sputtered, "Why, I never . . ." and Nelson hooted and gave Willow a pat on the back that promised to break the boy's spine.

Hazard did not even smile. He was silent through the remainder of the meal. The others bantered easily and paid him little mind, although Samantha threw a few pensive looks his way. He was not pouting, not even angry. Just quiet.

Willow helped Hazard clear the table and joined the others for an after-dinner drink in the living room. Then, feeling a bit like a fifth wheel, he said his thanks and departed. Samantha and Betty Lou volunteered for KP, and while they were in the kitchen doing dishes, Hazard and Nelson sat quietly in the living room with cigarettes and brandy.

"It's the saddest thing in all the world," Hazard murmured, more to himself than to Nelson.

"What's that, ol' buddy?" Nelson asked.

"A man with memories. A man remembering how it used to be."

"So tell me how it used to be, ol' timer," Goody smiled.

"Simple," said Hazard. "It used to be simple. We had a mission that everyone understood and accepted and approved, and we were pretty good at our jobs. We had us some times, Goody. Some good, a lot of them not so good, but even the not so good times were sometimes good afterward, with the remembering."

"Yeah," Nelson agreed noncommittally. "We had us some times."

"But is there anything sadder than a couple of old farts sitting around drooling over old times?"

"Not if you say there ain't," Goody said amiably, not quite sure what Hazard was talking about. Or why.

"And the saddest thing of all," Hazard went on, "is remembering ourselves—the way we used to be."

"So tell me how we used to be," Nelson said softly.

"Younger. And stronger. And so goddamned sure. Sure of who we were and what we were doing."

Nelson sighed melodramatically and asked, "Okay, numbnuts. What brings all this on?"

Hazard shrugged. "I don't know. I just find myself wishing that the last five years or so hadn't happened. Except for a few things, of course, like meeting Sam."

Nelson shook his head and laughed. "Jesus, we ain't exactly in our dotage, you know. Hell's bells, I ain't drooled in days. And I only shit my sack once or twice a week. For chrissakes, Clell, you make it sound like we're a hundred years old."

"That's what I'm trying to say. I feel like I'm a hundred years old, Goody. Don't you? Every time I'm around Willow I feel it. I can't seem to cope with his . . . his enthusiasm. It's been so goddamned long since I had any."

Nelson rubbed an itch on his shiny pate with a calloused knuckle. "Listen, pal. You can't have both enthusiasm *and* experience. They are opposite states of existence. And what we got now is experience. And as far as I'm concerned, I wouldn't trade it back for all the chapped lips in Siberia. Because I don't know whether we got any more combat coming our way—and I hope to hell we don't—but if we do, just remember: Enthusiasm gets *you* blown away. Experience lets you blow *them* away."

"Bullshit," Hazard said calmly. "Think of all the dumbfuck things we did and still we got away clean. Then think of all the experienced veterans we've seen wasted." Hazard's hand drifted to his side to trace the line of the scar under his shirt, and he amended his statement. "Well, relatively clean."

"Relatively is right," said Nelson, opening his shirt collar to show a scar of his own, a neat hole just below the collarbone.

"My point is that it's all chance, Goody. One big cosmic accident that either happens or don't happen, to either you or the next guy."

"I see. So we can just forget training altogether, seeing as how it's all chance. We can just throw the little shits into the line with no preparation at all. Chance will sort 'em out. Is that what you're saying? Is that what you really believe?"

"No, I don't reckon I do." Hazard grinned at his friend. "Ahh, I don't know, Goody. I guess I'm just feeling useless in this Mickey Mouse outfit. I'm nervous in the service."

Nelson laughed. "That's the first sensible thing you've said all evening. C'mon, let's see just how old and tired that government-issue body of yours really is. Gimme fifty.''

Hazard grinned, set down his drink, and hit the floor. He was doing push-ups when the women came in from the kitchen. Betty Lou Farmer took one look, smiled her impish smile, and drawled the old joke: ''Hey, mister. I hate to be the one to tell you, but your girl has done gone home.''

''I like Jack,'' said Samantha. ''He's a nice young man. Smart, too.'' She and Hazard sat alone in the living room with a nightcap. Goody and Betty Lou had retired to the third floor.

''Yup. I like him, too.''

''Is he anything like his father?'' Samantha asked.

''He's a lot like his dad was when I first met him in England when we were getting ready for Normandy. But Jackie's a lot more sophisticated.'' Hazard laughed. ''When I first met Shelby Willow he still had a lot of Kentucky on him. But then I had a lot of Montana on me. We sort of banded together to protect our young hick selves from the city boys. Nobody messed with us much, though. Shelby was hard and tough as a twice-used corncob. He'd been up in the northwest building roads and bridges for the CCC. That was hard work and on top of the time he'd spent in the coal mines he was in pretty good shape.''

There was a faraway quality in Clell's voice and a tenderness that nearly made Samantha jealous. She found herself pining for that vast sum of years that Clell Hazard had lived without her—and she without him. And she found herself missing Shelby Willow, a man she had never known.

''Shelby was already goin' bald, even then,'' Hazard was saying. ''He had this theory that it was the lamp, the mining hat, that took his hair away.''

"You all might just as well be as bald as Goody with those dreadful haircuts you have," said Samantha.

"First time I laid eyes on Jackie he was just as bald as his daddy," Hazard laughed. "It was this snapshot Shelby had. Shelby was proud as a racehorse about having a son. Jack had been born just before we shipped over. Shelby and me were on the same troopship, and we went onto Omaha Beach in the same wave, and I remember him asking me to check up on the boy and his ma if anything happened to him. And I asked him to make sure Linda was okay if anything happened to me. It was a scene right outta a John Garfield movie."

"So you didn't actually meet Jack until he came to Fort Myer."

"Nope. Fort Lewis, a couple years after the war." Hazard paused. When he resumed, that ten-thousand-yard stare was back in his eyes. "I remember that first Christmas at Lewis. We were living right next door to the Willows. Shelby was kinda sour on Christmas at the time. It was still too close to the Christmas of '44 and the Battle of the Bulge. We were positioned in the Ardennes in '44, about halfway between Malmedy and Monshau when the Germans hit us. I remember we were taking it easy, thinking the Nazis had shot their bolt, that it was just a matter of chasing 'em all the way to Berlin. Shelby had foraged up a handful of spuds from somewhere, and he was cookin 'em over a fire in his steel pot when we heard this low noise. It kept getting louder and louder, and the ground began to shake and big gobs of snow started falling out of the trees. We didn't know what the hell was goin' on. Then a whole bunch of Tigers came crashing out of the trees at us. You could see the Iron Crosses on 'em, they were so close. We couldn't believe it. They ran right over us. We skedaddled out of there as best we could. I remember seeing Shelby without his helmet. It was still back there on the fire with the potatoes in it, ready to eat. Our bazooka teams tried to cover our withdrawal, but they didn't do much good against those Tigers. We'd never seen tanks that big. One team was kneeling there in the snow firing point blank on this one, and it just rolled right over them. You could hear their bones breaking a hundred yards away.'' Hazard wound down and stopped. There were goosebumps on his arms from the Ardennes cold in the winter of 1944.

"Fort Lewis?'' Samantha nudged.

"Oh, yeah. Well, I remember that Jackie got a sled for Christmas that year, and he and my Mackie were out playing in the snow. We adults were inside snortin' a bit of Christmas cheer when we heard this godawful bawlin'. Seems that Jackie had run his new sled into a tree. We ran outside to see what the ruckus was all about, and there was Jackie running at us with his hands up to his face. It was just a nose bleed, nothing serious, but when Shelby saw the blood on the snow—and nothing ever looked more red than blood on clean snow—he fell apart. He just pointed at it and began screaming, 'Tigers, Tigers!' and then he began to vomit. Seeing his father like that must've scared Jackie even more, because he started screaming louder. Then Mack started bawlin', and by that time Angela and Linda had come out, and when *they* saw Shelby carry'n on, *they* started yellin'. Jesus, what pandemonium. They damn near got me goin'.''

Samantha was silent for a moment, then said, "After such an experience, I'm surprised Jack wanted to join the Army.''

Hazard shrugged. "I don't know about that, but I'm glad he did.''

"Why?''

"Because the Army needs kids like him. He's smart and

he's committed and he has a love for the history and traditions of the service. Young men like Jackie Willow are the hope and promise of the Army. He's pigheaded and awful dumb about a lot of things, but he's got the enthusiasm and dedication it's going to take to turn the Army back on the right track.''

"Could it be that he reminds you of yourself at that age?" Samantha asked with a smile.

Hazard smiled back. "Could be."

"So, you have a protégé."

Hazard shook his head. "It's not that. It's just that I . . . I sorta promised to keep an eye on him."

"To Shelby Willow?"

"Yes. To Shelby Willow."

They were quiet, each thinking his or her own thoughts. Hazard got up and poured another splash of brandy into their glasses. He said, "Look, Sam. I'm sorry I lectured at you tonight."

"I was a bit snotty, too," Samantha said.

Hazard gave no sign that he heard her. "I've said I'm sorry more times in the past few weeks than I have all the rest of my life put together," he said. "Seems every time I make a move these days I step on my dick—" He winced, looked over at her quickly, and blurted, "I'm sorry." Then he laughed. "See?"

Samantha put down her glass and came over and sat on his lap. She ran her fingers through the brushy stubble on his head that passed for hair and kissed him. "I must have been out of my mind to get mixed up with a soldier," she said lightly with a smile. "I hate soldiers."

"I know you do, Sam," Hazard said seriously.

"But I love you," she said quickly, keeping an affectionate humor in her voice.

Hazard refused to lighten up. "I'm a soldier, Sam. I

know you don't like it. Sometimes I don't like it. But it's what I am. Can you live with it?''

"I love you," Samantha repeated stubbornly.

"I know you do, Sam," Hazard said softly. "But that wasn't my question. Can you live with it?''

"I don't know."

24

"Ashes to ashes . . ."
"Dust to dust . . . ."
"Let's lower this lard-ass and get on the bus."
"Steadeeeee."

A lieutenant colonel. Closed casket all the way. The colonel's C and C chopper had been blown from the sky while he was monitoring a firefight over Happy Valley. Rumor had it there wasn't much inside the box. Willow thought about that. He did not, could not, imagine himself in such a sorry state and did not even try. Instead, he wondered how he would react to seeing someone else, a buddy perhaps, torn asunder. A soldier had to steel himself to show no emotion, no undue sorrow. Professionals knew that such an end was not only possible, but probable— knew it and accepted it. It would be hard, Willow concluded, but he could do it.

The Ninety-first Evacuation Hospital was a collection of long, low wooden buildings connected by a fully enclosed corridor through the center, forming a string of H's. All the walls and ceilings were painted the ubiquitous pale institutional green so beloved by the Army. The floors were covered with cheap linoleum kept spit shined by a

crew of bored, sloppy soldiers who would spend their
entire time in-country buffing floors and listening to grown
men cry.

Willow walked down the central corridor past enlisted
men who leaned on their polishing machines and regarded
his brown bar and his dirty boots with ill-disguised hatred.
He wanted to tell them that he had been an enlisted man
once himself, but they did not look as if they would care.
As he made his way, he could hear the buffers start up
behind him as if his passage had broken some electronic
beam that in turn, triggered the machines. Even that noise
did not mask the thrum of the air-conditioners. When he
passed by the wards reserved for wounded Arvin, the
air-conditioners were even louder, and the temperature in
the hallways bordered on freezing. Having gone centuries
without it, the South Vietnamese had embraced air-
conditioning with a passion that outstripped even their
newfound love for mentholated cigarettes. Carrier and Salem,
thought Willow, America's contribution to Indochinese
culture.

He found Bravo's wounded toward the end of the hospital in two facing wards. There were no orderlies or doctors or nurses in sight. Willow shaded his eyes and peered
through a small window in the double door of one of the
wards. He still could not see any hospital staff, but he
recognized Private Winter in the bed nearest the door. He
pushed in. Several heads swiveled his way when he entered.
A couple of the men smiled when they saw him, but most
just closed their eyes and lay back on their pillows.

Willow stopped at Winter's bed first. "How's it go,
Winter?" he asked. He wanted to use the boy's first name,
but he did not know it. Winter was one of Otis Harmon's
men. The boy had taken a burst of AK fire across both
knees.

"Okay . . . I guess . . . sir."

"*You don't seem happy to see me,*" Willow said with forced joviality.

Winter produced a weak grin. "*Sorry about that, sir. When you come in, I was kinda hoping it was the nurse coming to give me a morphine shot.*"

"*You want me to find her for you?*" Willow asked quickly.

"*Nah. Wouldn't do no good. I just had one a couple hours ago, and she wouldn't give me another one this soon nohow. They don't want us to become dope fiends.*" Winter ventured another weak smile.

"*They going to medevac you out of here?*"

This time the boy's smile was real. "*Yessir. I'm going to Japan in a day or two, and then maybe to Honolulu or maybe even Letterman's, in Frisco. Nam better take a good look at my ass, cuz it ain't never gonna see my face again.*"

Willow laughed. "*I know how you feel. By the way, Lieutenant Harmon asked me to say hello.*"

"*Yessir. He was in here this morning. He told me about Lieutenant Earp gettin' greased. Real sorry about that.*" Winter rearranged his teenager's face into a picture of sorrow, and Willow had to choke back a laugh. It was not that he doubted the sincerity of Winter's regret—after all, the Marshal had been more popular with the grunts than any of them—it was just that the boy naturally assumed all officers were family. It was like a southern black man solicitously asking one white boss about the health of another. A portrait of dissembling.

"*Yeah. Well. You take it easy. When you get to San Francisco, try to think about us poor grunts every once in a while.*"

You've got a hell of a touch with the little people, Willow told himself bitterly as he moved slowly down the line of bunks like a priest working the charity ward,

*issuing a feeble litany of hey-how-you-doings and you-take-
it-easy-nows and feeling progressively more uncomfortable.
At each station of the cross, he was met with indifference
or outright hostility. A black soldier named Carmichael
from his own platoon muttered "Fuck off" and rolled
away from him. Another man from his outfit feigned sleep
when he saw Willow coming.*

*Willow needed a friendly face. He looked around the
ward for Sergeant Robinson but could not find him. He
asked a friend of Robbie's, another lifer NCO, and was
informed that Sergeant Robinson had died in surgery that
morning.*

*With a rising sense of panic, Willow spied Private
Sanderman, and he passed by several bunks to get to him.
The Sandman had been Willow's RTO for a week when his
regular radioman, Rubberlegs, had gone off for an in-
country R and R at China Beach. Willow and the Sandman
had gotten on well together. They had spent many a dark,
wet night huddled together under a poncho whispering
about girls and places and their stateside lives, the PRC-25
lying between them like an infant in bed with new parents.*

*The Sandman had lost both legs just above the knees,
and only more operations at the hospital in Tokyo would
tell whether he would ever see out of either eye again.
Both stumps, both eyes, and half his face were covered
with heavy bandages. When Willow told him who it was,
Sanderman began to cry. Willow had to imagine tears
behind the dressings.*

*"I'm really glad you're here, Lieutenant Willow," the
boy said with a quivering mouth. "I got a few questions I
been wanting to ask. Like how did the dinks sneak up on
us like that? And where were our patrols? And what were
you fuckin' officers doing? You're supposed to take care of
us. How come you didn't take care of us?"*

Willow said nothing. He put out a hand to touch the

*sobbing boy's shoulder but let it fall. He got up slowly
from the end of the bed and moved toward the ward door.
Hearing him go, Sanderman struggled up onto his elbows
and shouted in the direction of the footsteps, "One last
question, lieutenant. How can I go home like this? Answer
me that, you cocksucker."*

*Every man in the ward who was awake and able was
now up on an elbow or had turned a head to watch, and
enjoy, Willow's rout. Just before Willow reached the door,
a black trooper from Dell's first platoon motioned him
over. The man had taken some shrapnel in the back and
buttocks. He grabbed at Willow's sleeve and babbled in a
singsong rhythm, "Hey, loo tenant. Hey, man. They sayin'
I be back on line in two weeks. Hey, man, you tell 'em I
ain't goin back on no muthafuckin' line. You tell 'em Li'l
Jimmy Weeks done gone and quit their muthafuckin' war.
Hey, man, what they gonna do to me? Send me to Veet
Nam? You tell 'em Li'l Jimmy Weeks gon go to LBJ, the
Long Binh Jail, fore he go back on muthafuckin' line. You
tell 'em."*

*In the next bed another black soldier was sitting up,
nodding his head and snapping his fingers in time with
Weeks' beat as if he were plugged in to Gladys Knight and
the Pips. The man's eyes, wild with painkillers, were like
two brown buttons sewn to black felt. He said, "Right on,
Bro," and reached his one good hand across to Weeks for
an abbreviated dap. Then he looked straight into Willow's
eyes and began to chant crazily, "Tell 'em. Tell 'em. Tell
'em. . . ." Weeks grinned and picked it up. "Tell 'em.
Tell 'em. . . ." Then every conscious man in the ward.
"TELL 'EM . . . TELL 'EM . . . TELL 'EM . . . TELL
'EM. . . ."*

The rattle of musketry echoed over the hills and dales of
the cemetery, dredging up ghosts. Willow imagined veter-

ans of a dozen campaigns struggling to sit up to salute
as the firing party ceded the stage to the bugler who blew
an acceptable, if inelegant, taps, his lips numb with the
cold.

The large party of mourners huddled close like cattle in
a Wyoming winter pasture. Between bugle notes Willow
could hear them snuffling, their frozen noses dripping as
predictably as ghetto plumbing.

A lieutenant colonel. It was rare that such a high-
ranking officer was actually killed in action. Field grade
officers who were killed or wounded must, by definition,
be excellent leaders, Willow concluded. That's the kind of
officer he would be. One who wouldn't ask his men to do
anything he was unwilling to do.

*There was another ward to visit, but Willow could not
bring himself to go in. He leaned against the wall of the
central corridor with a hand over his eyes. After a while,
he straightened and began to prowl up and down the
corridor, peering into the wards and rooms until he found
the one he was looking for.*

*It was a small, comfortable room with two beds. One
was empty. In the other, Lieutenant Colonel Abner Bean
lay on his back, his arms down along his sides, palms up
like a crucified holy man. On either side of the bed hung
I-V bottles, the tubes running like guy wires to both of
Bean's arms. Other tubes fed into the colonel's nose and
mouth. Bean's head, shoulders, and upper body were
swathed in dressings. The satchel charges had pitted his
face and neck with dozens of small, black holes, like
peppercorns implanted in a slab of meat. Restraining straps
had been tightened across his chest, arms, and legs. On
the pillow beside Bean's head, someone had pinned a
Silver Star, even though the paperwork for the award had
not had time for forwarding and approval.*

The colonel's eyes were open and clear, and they fol-lowed Willow into the room.

Willow sat in the chair beside the colonel's bed for a moment without speaking. When he did finally speak to his battalion commander, it was in a voice soft and almost tender. "You fought well, sir. No one could have fought any better."

Bean's eyes were fixed on Willow's, and already there was something heavy and resigned in them.

"But that's not enough, is it, sir? Fighting well isn't enough. I used to think it was. But it's not. One of my boys in the ward just asked me why we didn't take care of him. And he was right, wasn't he, sir? We're supposed to take care of them. It's our duty—our most sacred duty. And we failed, didn't we, colonel? We didn't take care of them."

Colonel Bean blinked once, twice, but his eyes never left Willow's.

Willow stood. Moving carefully, gently, he shut off the valve on the tube feeding the colonel's right arm. Then the left arm. Then he closed the valves on the rest of the tubes. Colonel Bean did not move. He just slowly closed his eyes and waited.

Willow sat down and lit a cigarette and calmly watched Bean's face. He smoked slowly, savoring each draw, exhal-ing the smoke through his nostrils. When the burn reached his fingers, he put the butt out on the spotless floor, grinding it thoroughly into the wax job with his boot. Without haste, he got up and turned the valves back into the open position and stood staring down at the colonel. When Bean's eyes opened and his breathing had returned to normal, Willow turned and left the room.

25

The idea was insane. He had told his platoon sergeant that it was insane. And now that they were rapidly approaching the jump-off hour, Willow told Hazard for the umpteenth time that it was insane. Hazard just smiled.

"Battalion is going to shit, sarge," Willow said.

Hazard shrugged.

"I mean they're *really* going to shit," Willow insisted.

Hazard shrugged again and said: "With any kind of luck, they won't know who to shit on."

"Does the sergeant-major know anything about this?" Willow asked, full of hope. If Goody Nelson approved, there was a chance.

"Nope."

"If we get caught, even he won't be able to save your ass."

"What are they gonna do to me? Send me to the Old Guard?"

"They can bust you," said Willow, genuinely concerned.

Hazard laughed and said, "Well, it wouldn't be the first time."

Willow was surprised. Hazard was a secretive sonofabitch. Bits and pieces of his platoon sergeant's life had a habit of popping out like this. Willow's curiosity made him forget

314

the object of his argument for a moment. "You lost a stripe before? How come?"

"We ain't got time for my life story, Willow. I got to check the troops. I suggest you check your squad like I told you." Hazard went back down the center aisle, moving among the men of the two squads he had ticketed for the night's mission.

Each man wore thermal underwear, light webbing, and soft headgear—black knit longshoreman's caps. Each man had smeared his face with black greasepaint, both to cut glare from the full moon forecast for that night and to disguise his identity. Hazard ordered everyone to empty his pockets. He passed around a roll of dark tape and instructed each man to tie a strip around thighs and calves. It minimized the rustling sound, he told them. He also told them to stick a piece of tape across their nametags, and he told them to lace one dogtag into each boot, along the tongue where it would be clearly visible yet secured by the laces. "I don't anticipate too many casualties tonight," he told them with a smile, "but you might as well get used to doing it the right way. In real combat, a man might lose one foot, but seldom both. We wouldn't want to inconvenience the graves registration detail, now would we?"

Then he checked the equipment. Hazard had cut a deal with Sergeant Beech in supply. In exchange for pulling Beech's next turn as sergeant of the guard, Hazard had gotten a twenty-four-hour loan of the following equipment: twenty M-16 rifles with extra clips taped front-to-back; four radios; twenty fragmentation grenades; and a dozen claymore mines, complete with det cords, trip wires, blasting caps, batteries, and slide-trigger mechanisms. All the ordnance was dummy.

"Okey-doke, gather round," he called. The squads—Willow's and Carey's, but with Sergeant Moreau of Fourth Platoon in command of Carey's squad—pressed around

Hazard. The men were having fun. They knew that what they were about to do would cause a major flap at battalion. They also knew that they were covered by the Army's first commandment—cover your ass—and that all the blame would fall on Hazard. They looked expectantly at Hazard, their faces a mixture of awe and affection.

Hazard spoke quietly. "Listen up, people. By now every swingin' dick in this comp'ny knows about this except for the officers. We're just gonna have to count on people to keep their mouths shut. I especially want you men to keep quiet. I don't want you braggin' about this to your buddies in other companies. Do you read me?" The heads in the circle around him bobbed.

"Okey-doke. Most of you know what we're trying to accomplish here, but I'll go through it once more for the dumbfucks. Listen up, Wildman. This platoon is going to pull aggressor duty during this year's field exercises. We don't have many opportunities to practice, so I've decided to invent one. What we're gonna work on tonight is movement and trail discipline. You've all been given a refresher course in hand and arm signals. Stay alert and obey them instantly. If any of you think this is a game or a big joke, forget it. Any man who blows our mission through carelessness or inattention will find out it's no game, because I'll hit him so hard on top of the head he'll have to unlace his boots to take a shit. Do you read me?" The heads bobbed.

"Now. We are going to launch a surprise attack on a simulated enemy field headquarters. The target tonight leaves a lot to be desired, but it's the best I could come up with." Hazard unfolded a large detail map of Arlington National Cemetery. Taped to one corner was a hand-drawn map of the Tomb of the Unknown Soldier and the Memorial Amphitheater. "Our objective is the Tomb guard ready room in the basement of the Amphitheater. That's our enemy HQ, and the Tomb guard detail is the enemy staff." The men chuckled. "You got that shit right," one man muttered.

"At ease, goddammit," Hazard growled. "Okay. We move in two squads. Second squad, under the baton of guest conductor Sergeant Moreau, goes over the cemetery wall here, two hundred meters this side of the chapel gate. Third squad, under Corporal Willow, goes over here, two hundred meters that side of the gate. I want you squad leaders to send the first man over at exactly 0300 hours. At 0310 hours we'll rendezvous here." Hazard hit the map again with his telescope pointer. "It's an old grave with a tall obelisk. You can't miss it. From the grave, we will move in column to the Amphitheater. There we split again. Sergeant Moreau's squad will take up positions in an arc right here behind the Amphitheater and wait. We'll *circumsize* our watches just before we split the column, Al." Moreau smiled, and Hazard continued. "Give us exactly five minutes to take out the Tomb guard before you move on the ready room entrance. I'll be with Corporal Willow's squad, which will advance to the line of tombstones along this line right here. We'll get the Tomb guard and then join the assault. Any questions so far?" There were none.

"I've gone over everything with your squad leaders and they know what to do. You just follow their orders and signals. I want you all to move using shadow, trees, and tombstones as natural cover. There's a full moon tonight, and I don't want you crossing terrain without some kind of mass at your back. Now, once we get into the basement, we hold everyone there at bay while the designated ambush teams set up our MA's along the sidewalks. We're pretending they're trails. After the mechanical ambushes are in place and I've inspected them, we just pronounce everyone dead or captured and dee-dee the hell out of there, using the escape routes we decided on. Any questions?'' No questions.

"Okey-doke," said Hazard. "Now Honor Guard's Tomb platoon is certainly not expecting anything like this. This would be a piece of cake—and useless as a training exercise—except for a couple of things. One: Getting away clean could be tricky. The Tomb boys won't know what the hell's going on, but you can bet your hairy balls they'll be on the horn to the military police the minute we disengage. We can cut the line in the ready room, but there may be other phones in the Amphitheater that I don't know about, so we gotta expect MPs all over the place. I almost hope there is a phone we don't know about. It would be a simulated failure of intelligence and therefore valuable as a training tool. God knows you can count on a failure of intelligence in real life.'' The men laughed.

"Our exit point is here, and your squad leaders know the route back to the company. With any luck, we'll make it. The minute you get back here, I want you to stow your gear and get into the showers and get that shit off your faces. Do it in the dark. I don't want lights drawing attention to the Delta barracks. There won't be any problem with the charge of quarters. Sergeant Moreau is CQ tonight.'' The men laughed again.

"Problem two: There's gonna be military police patrols in the cemetery. They've been having trouble with kids climbing over the wall and spray-painting dirty words on the tombstones. There's at least one, maybe two, two-man jeep patrols. And there is a two-man foot patrol . . . with a dog. That dog ain't gonna know this is a drill, and it could flat chew your ass up, so good use of available cover and absolute silence are essential. Any questions?''

"I've got one," said Willow. "Suppose the Tomb detail comes to the conclusion that Russian paratroops have just dropped into the nation's capital and decide to go down fighting for the American way of life?''

"Use force," said Hazard.

"Force?" Willow said incredulously. "What kind of force? Step on their spit shines? Muss their brass?"

"There's no way for them to know our 16s aren't loaded, the way we know those toy rifles of theirs aren't loaded. That lack of information should keep them quiet."

"What if it doesn't?" Willow insisted.

"Then crack the first guy who gets out of line across the knees with your rifle butt. That should discourage any other would-be Medal of Honor winners. If it doesn't, we run like hell. Any other questions?" Hazard looked around. "None? Okey-doke. Hit the rack. I'll roust you out at 0200 hours."

Willow's squad went over the wall at precisely 0300. Wildman sprained his ankle on the short jump and was sent back to the Delta barracks by a disgusted Sergeant Hazard. Just before he unceremoniously shoved the fat private back over the wall, Hazard hissed, "Wildman, if you get spotted in that get-up, I will personally butt-fuck you with a two-by-four."

Arlington National Cemetery's gates were closed to the public at 7 P.M. each evening. The only living things authorized on the grounds after that were Honor Guard Company's Tomb platoon and the post police. Hazard's Hellions, as the ersatz commando team promptly dubbed itself, were in violation of at least a dozen ordinances and regulations.

The two squads met at the obelisk-marked grave and, on a hand signal from Hazard, moved out in column in the direction of the Amphitheater. The men scuttled from tree to tree, grave to grave, with Moreau's squad in front. Hazard had asked Sergeant Moreau to lead one squad because of Moreau's Vietnam experience. Willow was proud that he had been allowed to retain command of his own squad, even though Hazard traveled with the squad as overall team leader and Willow's advisor.

Moreau walked point. Willow was at drag. Hazard moved up and down the length of the column monitoring trail technique. Even with the generous light from the moon, Willow could not see Hazard come and go. His platoon sergeant would pop up alongside him from behind a tree or headstone, even, it seemed, from out of the ground itself. The first time it happened, with Hazard suddenly at his side and whispering an urgent "Close it up, Jack," Willow's heart had stopped. Where in fuck had the man come from? After that, Willow carefully scanned every possible bit of cover, determined not to be caught by surprise again. The next time Hazard visited the rear of the column, announcing his presence by putting a stranglehold on Willow from behind and hissing, "I said close it up, fuckhead," Jackie Willow pissed his fatigues.

Concentrating on this losing game with his platoon sergeant, Willow nearly missed the hand signal from the man in front. He flopped to the ground and looked around wildly. It was a moment before he saw the jerky beam from the headlamps of a jeep flashing through the clump of oaks on his right. The column was perilously close to the road.

Willow's only cover was a stone marker eight feet to the fore and he crawled to it, his heart hammering in his chest, and angled himself so the headstone was between his body and the road. Although the night was bitter cold, Willow was sweating, and the crotch of his trousers felt warm and sticky where he had fouled himself. Moonlight shone spookily off the white marble stone at his nose. He raised his eyes and read, Levy, David, Capt., RA, 9th Armored Div., 1913–1945, KIA Remagen, Germany. A Star of

David was carved above the name. The jeep passed within fifteen feet.

As squad leader and drag, Willow had one of the four radios. When the jeep's taillights disappeared around a bend, he broke squelch four times but did not speak. It was the signal for all clear.

The column had not moved another twenty yards when the dog hit Willow from the side.

It came out of the darkness with a whoosh of air and a gargling sound. The impact knocked Willow down and he curled up in a ball, too stunned for anything beyond that simple reflexive response. His only salvation was that the Alsatian was programmed not to inflict serious injury, since the presumed target was a teenaged vandal. The animal loosed three piercing barks and clamped its mouth on Willow's boot. From a long way away, Willow heard the dog's handler shout and then another form came hurtling out of the shadows. He heard a sharp yelp and then another gargling sound, this one from some deeper place within the animal. The pressure on his foot eased, then fell away altogether.

Sergeant Hazard helped him to his feet and whispered, "You okay?" Willow nodded weakly. Hazard calmly and deliberately reached over and wiped the bloody blade of a sheath knife across the front of Willow's fatigue blouse. Then he picked Willow's radio off the ground and spoke into it. "Al, how close are you to objective? Over."

Moreau answered. "I can see the lights now. We heard the dog. Do we abort? Over."

"Negative. But we quick-time the rest of the way. The dog is no longer a problem, and the patrol jeep is heading away from us. Don't bother with finesse, just get 'em moving. Over and out."

"Roger that. See you at the rendezvous. Over and out."

Willow was staring dumbly at the spot where the dog

lay jerking spasmodically. Willow's trouser legs were covered with the animal's blood. "G-Goddamn, sarge. You . . . You killed him," Willow croaked.

"No shit. Let's move."

Willow could not take his eyes off the dog. It was dead, but all four legs were still moving in syncopated rhythm as if it were asleep and dreaming of chasing rabbits. Willow's trance came to an end when his platoon sergeant kicked him hard in the ass and said again, "Let's move." Hazard's face reminded Willow of a West African ceremonial mask he had seen once in a museum. Hazard's eyes glittered and his mouth was set in a skull-like grin. The young corporal moved.

The column quick-timed it the rest of the way and formed up in a shallow swale a stone's throw from the Tomb of the Unknown Soldier. Floodlights bathed the Tomb and the Amphitheater in a harsh white light, and the reflection off the marble joined with the moonlight to create a pocket of daytime in the frigid October night.

Hazard and Moreau synchronized watches, and Moreau led his squad off and around, keeping his men low and shielded by the groundswell. At the edge of the illuminated area, they stepped into darkness as suddenly as if they had fallen into a hole. When they were gone, Hazard crawled up the short rise on his elbows and peered carefully over the top, then crawled back to Willow and whispered, "I'll take out the Tomb guard. Keep me under observation and bring the rest of the squad on the double when I signal."

The soldiers of Honor Guard Company's Tomb platoon were specialists among specialists. Assignment to the platoon was considered an unparalleled honor within the Old Guard. Only those of the strictest military bearing were accepted. The platoon's members wore metal badges—a replica of the Tomb—on their blouse pockets.

Willow had often watched rookie members of the Tomb platoon drilling in the alley between the company buildings. Each new member spent weeks practicing the sliding manual of arms in front of full-length mirrors. Then they spent a matching amount of time walking the mat, striving to perfect that odd girlish stride, hips moving like precision-machined gears, an exaggeration of the already exaggerated Old Guard march. Twenty-one perfectly measured strides from one end of the mat to the other. Pause, order arms, facing movement, right-shoulder arms, pause, facing movement, pause, stride, a twenty-one-count for each phase of the routine. Then came another long training period to get down pat the military ballet that made up the changing of the guard ceremony, the platoon NCOs as theatrical as divas as they snatched the weapon away for inspection and twirled it like a baton. It was a performance that had thrilled generations of high schoolers on their senior trip to Washington.

When a man had completed his company area training, he was put on actual Tomb duty . . . at night, when only the dead could tsk-tsk at any lapses. One hour on, two off; twenty-four hours on, forty-eight off. When the platoon commander decided that a man was ready, he was transferred to weekdays, then to weekends. If the man was among the very best, he was promoted to summer weekends, when the crowds often swelled to five thousand or more.

To Willow, the men of the Tomb detail looked like interchangeable parts. Every one of them was young, square-jawed, over six feet tall, and slim as an anemic. Every one was clear-eyed and shorn almost bald. And like their counterparts at Buckingham Palace, each was impervious to the whims of weather and the taunts of mere humans. To falter or faint in 100-degree temperatures meant instant reassignment. To twitch when a tourist leaned over the restraining chain to pop a flashbulb in your face meant instant reassignment. To react when a small boy darted under the chain to tweak your buttocks—"I just wanted to see if he's real, mama"—meant instant reassignment. To try and catch a better glimpse of the girl who had just tossed her measurements and phone number onto the mat and then bent over to promise you the best blow job of your life, meant instant reassignment. The only concessions to physical comfort were sunglasses in summertime and a sentry box for hard rains. The soldiers of the Tomb guard were special. They were perfect. The majority of Old Guardsmen, including Willow, hated their guts.

Willow snaked his way to the top of the rise while Sergeant Hazard crab-walked off toward the same dark pit that had swallowed Moreau's squad. Willow was acutely alert. This was a chance to see how Hazard managed to move so silently and invisibly. He kept the Tomb guard in the periphery of his vision and scanned the approaches for Hazard. Sneaking up on the Tomb guard would be no problem, Willow saw. The man was wearing a long dress blue overcoat against the cold and had on a fur cap with the earflaps tied up. A thin, light-colored wire ran from underneath the cap and into the guard's left ear. What the hell! thought Willow. The Tomb platoon did not take the deaf. The fucker was listening to the radio! The radio was on top of the man's head, under the hat.

Even so, Willow did not see Hazard until his platoon sergeant was suddenly *there*, standing upright against the back of the sentry box at the end of the mat. Hazard waited until the guard walked back toward the box and had completed his facing movements. Willow saw Hazard slide his .45-caliber automatic from its holster. Then, in the middle of the guard's twenty-one-count, Hazard stepped out and stuck the frigid barrel against the dumb bastard's neck. The operation had been timed to catch the Tomb guard in midshift. The weather insured that the rest of the detail would be in the snug ready room in the Amphitheater basement. Except for the encounter with the dog, everything was working out exactly as planned.

Willow saw Hazard's signal and motioned up the rest of the squad. When they reached the mat, Hazard said, "Gentlemen, allow me to introduce PFC Tunnicliffe of Honor Guard Company. He will accompany us to the next installment of our adventure this evening. Please treat him kindly, as he is a mite confused." PFC Tunnicliffe's eyes were the size of golf balls.

Hazard fingered the transmit bar on his radio and told Moreau, "We're on our way, comrade." At the word *comrade*, Tunnicliffe's eyes grew even wider. Hazard grinned and handed Tunnicliffe's useless rifle to a squad member, then led the way toward the Amphitheater's basement staircase.

The two squads, Willow's and Moreau's, met at the entrance. The men could feel the heat from the ready room below, and they could hear the Rolling Stones singing "Paint It Black." Hazard made two quick hand movements, and one fire team scattered to provide a defensive perimeter while another lugged the claymores toward the paths to set up the ambushes. Pushing the bewildered Tunnicliffe in front of him, Hazard led the way down the stairs, paused for a moment to let the others bunch up behind him, and kicked open the door to the Tomb guard ready room.

26

"It was you, you sonofabitch! You did it!" Goody Nelson was screaming into the phone, and Hazard could picture the veins bulging atop the sergeant-major's shaved head.

"Did what?"

"Don't fuck with me, Clell. It was you. I know it was you!"

"What are you talking about?"

Nelson's voice softened, inviting confidence. "Jeezuz, Clell, it was slicker'n owl shit. The brass are going batshit. How'd you do it?"

"Do *what*?" Hazard asked, trying to sound exasperated.

Goody began screaming again. "You know WHAT, you fuck! And you know ME! I'm gonna get the goods on you. You know I will. Then I'm gonna pull your guts out through your asshole and feed 'em to you."

Hazard said nothing, and there was a long pause. He was glad he was not face to face with Nelson.

Nelson went back to the cajoling tone. "Sure, I would've tried to talk you out of it. But if your mind was made up, I could've helped you. No doubt you left a trail Fearless Fosdick could follow. I could've helped if you'd only come to me."

Hazard said nothing, and there was another pause. Then Goody said softly, "Didya have to kill the dog? Christ, Clell, he was a soljer, too. Just like me'n you. I could've arranged it so he was on the other side of the cemetery or something. Ya know? I mean for Chrissakes, Clell, didya have to kill the fuckin' dog?" Nelson hung up.

Hazard felt bad about the dog. But it had happened to him once again. The moment he'd dropped over the cemetery wal! it had become real. It was no longer a mere prank, ill-advised or not. It was real, all of it. The objective, the enemy, everything. The dog had threatened the mission, so he'd killed it. Just like that. In a rush of adrenaline. And what if it had been one of the MPs who had gotten hold of Willow? Would he have cut *his* throat, too?

The thing with the dog ruined everything, but it had served to sober Hazard, to bring him back to earth. And by the time they had burst into the Amphitheater ready room, it was *not* real anymore. Thank God for that—that and the good sense of Sergeant First Class Bill Laramie, the Tomb platoon's ranking NCO.

The door had come clean off the hinges from the force of Hazard's kick. It landed flat on the floor and served as a welcome mat for the black-faced men who stampeded into the room. They found the Tomb guards frozen in a variety of poses, their shocked faces turned blankly toward them. One man was in the process of shining a pair of shoes. Another had his hand on the handle of the steam press, holding it down on a pair of blue trousers that had already begun to smoke. A couple more were playing chess, one player's hand poised in midair over his knight. Nearly all the guards wore skivvies and t-shirts only, their uniforms hung neatly on hangers. Mick Jagger sang, "Paint it, paint it, paint it . . . paint it black."

The frieze was broken by an Honor Guard soldier who tossed aside the patent leather bayonet scabbard he had been polishing, picked up the bayonet, and started slowly toward Hazard as if he were in a trance. Willow jumped in front of his platoon sergeant, threw his weapon to his shoulder and bellowed, "STAND FAST OR DIE!" The soldier stopped. "Drop the bayonet," Willow ordered. The soldier hesitated. Sergeant Laramie, who had been sitting at a small metal desk when the door flew open and who had not moved a muscle since, slowly reached over to click off the radio and said quietly, "Do what he says." The man hesitated. Laramie repeated more loudly, "Do it, boy!" The blank, unfocused look on the soldier's face dissolved and he dropped the bayonet.

Sergeant Bill Laramie was a tall, rangy man from Americus, Georgia, and a twenty-five-year veteran. He had a short, snow-white crewcut and eyes that could make a snake blink. He had a reputation as the strictest noncom in the Old Guard when it came to discipline and appearance. He took his job seriously. He had been the Tomb platoon's ranking noncom for six years, and not one of the men who passed through the platoon could ever remember seeing him smile. But they saw him smile that night. The cold eyes actually crinkled and he smiled. He looked straight at Hazard and asked, "Did that fella of yours *really* say 'Stand fast or die'?"

Hazard smiled back. "I actually believe he did," Hazard said, and both men burst into laughter. The Tomb guards' sense of shock deepened. They did not know what was more amazing; the sudden appearance of these hostile-looking armed strangers or the sight of Sergeant Laramie laughing.

Laramie said, "I don't know what the hell is going on here, but I'll play along with you. I don't want anybody to get hurt."

"Nobody's going to get hurt," Hazard reassured him.

Laramie stood. He was fully dressed except for his

blouse, and even now he paused to adjust his gig line. "What do you want us to do?" he asked calmly.

"Just sit tight," said Hazard. "We'll be out of here in a minute." He turned to Willow. "I'm going out to inspect the ambush site. You cut the phone line."

Laramie interrupted. "Can I put my man back on the Tomb? It ain't right to leave it unguarded, not even for a little bit."

Hazard hesitated, then said, "Of course."

Laramie turned to Private Tunnicliffe and said, "Get back out there. Just do your job."

Hazard and Tunnicliffe left together. Hazard was back inside of five minutes. "Okey-doke, we're disengaging," he told Willow and Moreau. "Simulated hot extraction." The Delta troopers, all grinning, filed out.

"Can I speak to you for a second?" Laramie asked Hazard. Hazard nodded, and the two NCOs walked out of the room and into the stairwell.

"I'm gonna have to report this, Clell, what with the destruction of government property and all," Laramie said, motioning toward the broken door. "I just want you to know that."

Hazard flinched when Laramie used his name.

"I knew it was you the minute you broke in my god-damn door," Laramie said, smiling for the second time in ten years. "I don't know what's goin' on or what you're up to, and I don't want to know. You can tell me about it over a brew someday. But I *am* gonna report this the minute you're outta sight. I ain't gonna tell 'em it was you, but I'm gonna tell 'em everything else. Fair enough?"

"More than fair," said Hazard. "Thanks, Billy."

"Yeah. Now get the hell outta here and let my boys get back to work. It's comin' up on time to change the guard."

Willow found Hazard in the Delta NCO dining room with Sergeant-Major Nelson and Slasher Boudin. Sergeant

July was buzzing around the sergeant-major and doing his minstrel show routine. "Ummm-hmmm, it sho am a pleasure havin you wif us for chow today, sarn't-major. Ummmm-hmmm. I gots a steak yay thick a-comin for you. Ummmm-hmmmm. 'N' some nice fries. Ummmmm-hmmmmm. 'N' some nice blackeye peas. Ummmm-hmmm." The mess sergeant flashed a huge and phony smile at Willow and without breaking stride asked, "How's you today, Cop'ral Willa? You gon eat? Sit raht down, and we gon gitcha nice steak. Ummmm-hmmmm."

"No thanks, mess sergeant," Willow said, trying not to laugh. "I just want a cup of coffee. I can get it."

"Naw-suh. You jist set raht down and let Sarn't Joo-lie git one of the KPs to fetch it fo you. Ummmm-hmmm." Sergeant July waddled from the mess.

Goody Nelson shook his head. "You know, I was here when Sergeant July first arrived, three years ago. He didn't talk like Amos 'n' Andy back then. Spoke better goddamn English than Paul Robeson."

"That's show biz," Hazard laughed. He looked at the papers in Willow's hand and asked, "What you got there, Jack? Is that for me?"

Willow cast an anxious glance at the first sergeant, who sat glowering at the end of the table. "Uh, it can wait, sarge."

"Both of us are gonna be in the garden all afternoon, so what the hell is it?" said Hazard.

"Uh, just some rating and evaluation forms I'd like you to fill out for me. And as long as you're here, sergeant-major, maybe you could fill one out, too—if you want to, of course."

"Evaluation forms?" said Nelson. "What are we evaluating?"

"Me."

"What's this for, Jack?" Hazard asked. "Your OCS application?"

"Uh, yeah," said Willow, looking toward the Slasher again. Boudin snorted in disgust and stabbed his steak viciously.

Goody Nelson grinned. "I'd be glad to do it, Jack. In fact, I just might put a word in for you at battalion if you was to buy the beer this evening over at the lounge."

"You bet, sergeant-major."

"How's it coming with this thing, Jack?" Hazard asked.

"I've taken the ten- and twenty-series courses for rank from the Army General School, and I've passed the OCT. All I really need now is approval and forwarding from Captain Thomas and then from battalion."

Slasher Boudin murdered his meat again and muttered, "Fat chance, Dildo."

"I'll have a talk with the Old Man about it," Hazard told Willow, but with a grim smile aimed at the first sergeant.

Private Padelli came in with a tray holding Nelson's steak, a glass of milk, and Willow's coffee. He put the steak and milk in front of the sergeant-major, then handed Willow the coffee with a grin. "How's it goin', Jackie?" he whispered.

Before he had been made an NCO, Willow had pulled KP with Padelli on several occasions. In fact, every time Willow had drawn kitchen police, Padelli had been there. Despite Sergeant Cook's complaints to the company commander, the Slasher continued to stick the boy from Brooklyn with KP several times a week.

"How come you're not officers mess orderly?" Willow asked Padelli.

Padelli shrugged. "One of 'em complained the other day when I dumped some mashed potatoes in his lap," Padelli grinned. "It was an accident."

"Yeah," Willow grinned back.

When Padelli left, Willow turned to the Slasher. "Top,

how come you don't like Padelli? You got him on KP every other day."

"None of your fuckin' business, Dildo," Boudin snarled. "I got my reasons. That fuckin' guinea. You just be grateful somebody fucked up and gave you stripes, or you'd be pullin' it with him."

With Hazard and Nelson there to protect him, Willow opened his mouth to retaliate, then caught sight of Sergeant-Major Nelson lifting his glass of milk. "I'm not sure I'd drink that if I were you, sergeant-major," he said quickly.

The glass stopped. "Why's that?" Nelson asked.

"Aw, nuthin. It's probably alright. I'm sure he wouldn't do it to you . . . or any other NCO."

"Do what?" Nelson asked suspiciously, the milk still poised an inch away from his mouth.

"Aw, it's just something I've seen Padelli do," Willow said.

"WHAT, for fuck's sake?" boomed Nelson.

"Well, you see, Padelli hates officers," said Willow. "I don't know why, he just does. Sergeant July found out about it, so naturally he makes Padelli officers' orderly every time. He makes Padelli wait on them hand and foot. So Padelli tries to make the best of it. Every time he brings one of the officers a glass of milk, he takes it over behind the cold locker first and dunks his dick in it."

"Aaaggghhh!" Nelson dropped the glass as if he had just spotted a spider floating in it. The milk spread across the tablecloth and dripped onto the floor. Hazard was already on the floor. Willow had never seen anyone literally fall off a chair laughing before.

Nelson was holding his throat with both hands. His mind worked frantically. He could not remember whether or not he had taken a sip. He didn't think he had, but he didn't know.

"That's not all," Willow said with a laugh. "When any

officer asks for an apple or a pear or something like that, Padelli rubs it up under his balls. I once saw him drag a carrot stick through the crack of his ass. He does stuff like that to *all* their food.''

Hazard was howling and beating on the floor with both hands. Willow himself had begun to laugh so hard that his last few words came out in gasps. Goody Nelson was staring at his steak—a steak missing several bites—with unabashed horror. He did not know whether to vomit or scream. So he screamed. "PADELLIIIIIIIII!"

Padelli appeared in the doorway. "Somebody want me?" He saw Sergeant Hazard on the floor. Then he saw the blotchy face of the battalion sergeant-major. He thought Hazard had suffered a heart attack. Or that the sergeant-major was strangling on a piece of meat.

"Padelli, did you . . . did you . . ." Nelson sputtered. Then he shuddered and said, "No, no, I don't want to know. Get the fuck outta here."

Padelli, puzzled and curious but imbued with a street-bred instinct for survival, fled.

The Slasher was looking oddly at Willow. "Hey, Dildo. Are you shittin' us or is that the truth? Does Padelli really do them things to the officers?"

"It's the truth, Top. I swear."

The Slasher scratched the side of his broken nose. What passed for a thoughtful look came into his dull gray eyes. "You know, Dildo, I think I mighta been wrong about Padelli," said Boudin. "Yeah. I think he may be a pretty good guy."

Willow smiled with satisfaction. He would wager a month's pay that Padelli had just pulled his last day of KP.

Willow would have lost his bet. Slasher Boudin was busy trying to noodle up a way to get his new friend, Private Padelli, onto the KP roster and into the officers dining room on a permanent basis.

Willow found the battalion sergeant-major perched perilously atop his usual barstool in the Old Guard NCO Lounge.
The Naughahyde cushion was flat as a skillet under Nelson's
towering bulk.

"Clell coming?" Nelson asked.

"No. He went home," said Willow. "He said he wanted
to see Miss Huff before she left. She's working tonight or
something. He said he might meet us later at Zeke's."

"No Zeke's for me," said Nelson. "I'm gonna be
working tonight, too. Gonna be busier than a cat covering
up shit."

"Still planning for A. P. Hill?"

"Nah, that's mostly done. Now I'm working out SOP
for Veterans Day ceremonies in the garden. It's one of our
finest hours, you know."

Willow ordered a beer for himself and the sergeant-
major. He smiled at Nelson and said, "I talked to Padelli,
sarge. He assured me he didn't do anything to your food."

"I don't wanna talk about it," Nelson grimaced. "I
will, however, spread the word around battalion about the
great chow at Delta Company. You just keep me informed
when Padelli has KP, and I'll steer the whole fuckin' staff
his way." Nelson cackled at the thought.

Willow laughed and said, "When I get my commission,
I'm going to make it a point to always pick up my own
food. I've got a feeling there are thousands of Padellis in
the Army."

"Speaking of getting you a commission, I talked to
Colonel Godwin about you this afternoon," said Nelson.
"I lied my ass off and told him you were a crackerjack
soljer and that your IQ was bigger'n your pecker. He said
that if your scores were okay and you got your company
commander's approval, he'd put his stamp on it."

"That's great, sarge. Thanks."

"Don't mention it. Better you should become an officer than continue to give the NCO cadre a bad name."

Willow laughed and picked his change off the bar. He wandered over to the jukebox. "What do you like?" he called to Nelson.

"There ain't no Caruso, not even any Mario Lanza. So how about Merle Haggard?"

Willow made a sour face and punched some buttons. The music started playing before he reached his stool.

"What in the name of suffering Jesus is *that*?" Nelson howled.

"Pretty good, huh?" Willow laughed. "It's a new group from San Francisco. The Grateful Dead."

"If they was dead, I know I'd be damn grateful."

"It's a great name, don't you think?" Willow laughed again. "Makes me think of the garden."

"Speaking of the garden," said Nelson, "how did you enjoy your little romp among the tombstones the other night? Think you learned anything?"

"I think it was very—" Willow snapped his mouth shut. "What do you mean, sarge?" he finished lamely.

Nelson grinned. "Hazard's Hellions, my ass."

Willow blanched. He looked around worriedly and whispered, "How do you know about that?"

Nelson laughed outright. "I got my ways, Jack, I got my ways. You can't fart in this battalion without ol' Goody smellin' it."

"You pissed off?" Willow asked tentatively.

"I was, but I ain't anymore. The brass have cooled off, so I can cool off. I'm just disappointed in Clell. It was a silly thing to do. He's already in enough shit around here without taking a chance on getting caught doing something like that." Nelson sighed and took a swig of beer. "Tell me something though, Jack. Was it absolutely necessary for Clell to kill the dog?"

"Yeah, it kinda shocked me at the time, too," said Willow. "But looking back on it, I'm sure glad he did. If that dog had not been silenced, I'd be in the stockade now. My boot still has teeth marks in it."

"So, it was Clell who killed the dog."

"But you said . . ."

Nelson shook his head. "I didn't know for sure, but I suspected. Jesus, maybe it was necessary, but I'm getting worried about that man. First that fist fight, now this fuckin' dog."

"What fist fight?"

"Never mind about that. I'm just afraid he's working himself up to steppin' into some *real* shit."

Willow was quiet a moment, then asked, "Do you know anything about Sergeant Hazard getting busted before?"

Nelson looked surprised. "Hell yes, I know something about it. I was there when it happened." He took a sip of beer and asked warily, "He told you about that?"

Willow shook his head. "Not the details. Just that he'd been busted. What was it all about?"

Nelson took another pull on the bottle. He seemed to be thinking it over. Finally he said, "What the hell. I guess it's alright. But you don't go spreading it around, right?"

Willow nodded. "Right."

"It was when we were advisors in the Delta. Clell was an E-8, a master sergeant just like your daddy was. So was I at the time. It's funny, I met your dad in France in '44, but I didn't meet Clell till Korea, even though he knew your dad in France, too—was in the same outfit in fact. After our little 'police action' I stayed with the Second Infantry while Clell went off to the Screaming Eagles, the 101st Airborne. Then damn if we don't both get assigned to MAAG. That was the Military Assistance and Advisory Group, the forerunner of MACV. And damn if we don't pitch up with the same Arvin outfit. Christ, it was good to see him. We'd been pretty tight in Frozen Chosin.''

"Uh, you were going to tell me about him getting busted?''

Nelson smiled. "Do I digress? I guess I do. Hell, maybe Clell's right. Maybe I am getting old.''

Nelson finished off his beer, signaled for a couple more, and went on. "Anyway, I was advising at battalion level; Clell at company level. His Arvin counterpart was a real loser. One of them fuckin' self-styled mandarins, you know, the kind with a pinkie fingernail half a foot long.'' Nelson stuck out his little finger. "It's supposed to show he don't have to do no manual labor or something like that—that he's one of the elite. What he was was worthless. His family had connections so he got himself a commission. But I guess they weren't good enough connections to keep his sorry ass out of the field, and you can bet he didn't want to be where he was. He'd go to great lengths to avoid running into bad guys. Clell did everything he could think of to get this wimp to find, fix, and fuck the VC, but ol' Marvin the Arvin wasn't havin' none of it. Always had some damn excuse or other. I think ol' Marvin also had a hair up his ass because he was an officer and Clell was only a noncom. He thought that if he had to have an American advisor at all it should at least be a colonel.''

"Er, sarge, the bust?'' Willow prodded.

Nelson laughed again. "Goddammit, I'm gettin' there. Hold your water. It's kinda complicated, and I'm sneakin' up on it in my own way. Anyhoooo, there was this VC regiment working the AO, and it was giving our little tigers fits. We couldn't find the bastards. We didn't have all the helicopters and FACS like we got now. But one day we *do* find 'em. The way we find 'em is that one of our companies bumps smack into them, all together and ready to kick ass—yessireee, hair slicked back and ready to dance. Now, it don't take Chuck long to figger out he's got the numbers on his side and first he flanks our boys, then surrounds them altogether and proceeds to chew ass. Battalion is goin' batshit. We got some birds heading our way, but we don't have them right there, right then. You understand? The closest and quickest help just happens to be ol' Marvin the Arvin. We get on the radio and tell Marvin the situation and tell him to haul ass over there and see if he can break a hole in the VC cordon so our people can get out. But do we get an answer from Marvin? Fuck no. From what Clell told me later, it seems Marvin takes out his damn pistol and puts a hole in the radio. He don't want to hear what it's telling him. Clell goes bananas. They're only about two klicks away from the fighting— they can hear it and everything. But Marvin not only refuses to head his troops in that direction, he issues orders to saddle up and dee-dee the *other* way. So Clell slaps his face. BAM! Knocks the chickenshit motherfucker down. Big loss of face for a gook, you understand. Then Clell takes over the company and humps them to the action at gunpoint and dives in. He punches a hole in Charlie's line and blazes away while what's left of the trapped company withdraws through it. By this time our birds have arrived from Can Tho, and we come barreling in with reinforcements. I'd been monitoring the radio and knew Clell was getting the shit kicked out of him, so I went along too, just to make sure he was alright. Well, to make a long story a little shorter, our arrival convinced Chuck to bug out. But I went in on the first CA, and damn if I didn't get blown up before I could take three steps. Clell had cut out an LZ for us and was waiting. When we were comin' in I could see him down on the ground, laying down covering fire for the birds, throwing grenades, killin' dinks left and right. He was a regular Audie goddamn Murphy. When we landed, he came running toward me grinning like a fool, face all covered with dirt and blood, waving at me with one hand and firing from the hip at the tree line with the other. When BLOOEY! The same mortar round that got me, got him. We was both hurt real bad, but somehow Clell got up, got to me, and hauled me back aboard the chopper—same goddamn bird I'd come in on, and those babies don't hang around a hot Z too long, so that tells you how short a fight it was for me, Jack, I shit you not. I never got off a round."

"Damn!" said Willow, thrilled to the bone.

"A few weeks later we was both in the hospital in Tokyo when this major comes on the ward and hands Clell this official-looking envelope. Inside it were three things: a Purple Heart, a Silver Star, and notification that he'd been broke back to E-6—one stripe for each offense."

"Two offenses?"

"Yeah. Striking an officer of an allied army and leading troops in combat. You gotta remember, in them days we were only supposed to advise, not fight. You could shoot back to protect yourself, but you couldn't go looking for trouble."

"But that's not fair," Willow announced with indignation.

Nelson roared. "Nobody ever accused the Army of being fair, Jack."

Willow was not mollified. "Well, it's still not fair," he pouted.

Nelson drained his bottle and hopped off his stool. "Well, while you ponder life's little injustices, I'll mosey on back to work," he said.

"Okey-doke, sarge," said Willow. "And thanks for telling me about Sergeant Hazard and all."

Nelson smiled. *Okey-doke?* Next thing you know the kid'll be saying *yup.* Goody Nelson felt a stab of regret that he had never had children, never had a son. Ol' Clell had lost the handle on one boy, but damn if it didn't appear he might have found a surrogate in young Willow. Today he's talking that cowboy shit, tomorrow he'll be calling Clell *pop*, thought Nelson. Well, the boy could do worse. So could the man.

Nelson looked at Willow with affection and said, "You bet. And listen, Jack, the next time Clell gets a notion to go out and play war, you let me know about it ahead of time. We gotta keep him out of trouble. Next thing we know the sorry bastard will be attacking the fuckin' Pentagon."

Willow laughed and waved goodbye as the sergeant-major rumbled from the room. He ordered another beer and sat nursing it. He felt the stares of some of the other noncoms in the lounge. They're probably wondering why an unapproachable, starchy, mean-as-a-junkyard-dog man like the battalion sergeant-major would hang out with a young punk like me, Willow thought. To tell the truth, he didn't know why either, but he was glad of it. Both Nelson and Hazard were remarkable men in many ways. Of course they were superior soldiers—damn, that story the sergeant-major told had raised goosebumps on his arm—but there was something else, too. Most of the other noncoms in the Third Herd were competent enough, but none of them had worked to better themselves the way Hazard and Nelson had. Here were these two old Army buzzards with no real formal education, and he would rather spend an evening with either one of them than any professor at Arizona. He had been impressed by the books Hazard had on the shelves in his apartment. Instead of the cheap paperbacks, the westerns and adventure novels that made up the literary diet of most NCOs, there had been everything from Marcus Aurelius to J. D. Salinger. Nelson, too, gave every evidence of knowing and appreciating the finer things. Some of the sergeant-major's literary references were startling for a lifer NCO. And he had heard Nelson whistling pieces of operas when he was preoccupied or concentrating on something. Both Nelson and Hazard were careful to speak the fractured, ungrammatical English of the lifer noncom, but they had to—it was the badge of the profession. They were really remarkable men, when you thought about it. Maybe that was why they were such good friends and why neither man seemed close to anyone else on post. All Willow knew was that he was pleased, and proud, to have been included in their company. It was probably because of his father, but deep down he suspected that for some reason or other they actually liked him for himself, Shelby Willow or no Shelby Willow. And for that, someday, he would do them proud.

By the time he had finished the walk from the hospital to the officers club, darkness was falling, coming swiftly with a spray of yellow and pink, then a long slide into lavender and smoke.

The club had filled to overflowing, and it took him several minutes to push his way through the throng to the table where Harmon and Dell had said they'd be.

The room was full of the boisterousness of men intent on forgetting where they were. The game room off to the side was packed with officers who loudly cheered or hooted every stroke of the cue stick, every slam on the Ping-Pong table. The jukebox was playing the Doors' "Light My Fire" at full volume, and a few officers were trying to dance with their nurses or Doughnut Dollies, the spaces on the jammed dance floor opening and closing like the mouth of an asthma sufferer. Near the back of the club, an enlisted man on the verge of tears was trying to thread a projector for the night's film. The young EM was tight-lipped and mute with rage as drunken officers jostled his arm or kicked the plug out of the wall socket.

The decibel level in the roaring room was as dangerous

*to the ear drums as a salvo from 175-mm guns, and men in
varying stages of lost sobriety shouted in full-throated
desperation to other men less than a yard away. Willow
caught snatches of conversation as he picked his way
through them:*

*". . . so I told that sumbitch where he could stick his
goddamn requisition form. . . ."*

*". . . she had titties that'd damn near poke your eyes
out, just as round and perky as a couple of fresh-fried
eggs. . . ."*

*". . . so this dumb grunt brown bar on the ground pops
green smoke. Green fuckin smoke on an LZ hotter than
hell or Houston. And here I come boppin' in thinking
everything is copacetic, ya know? Numbah One. Routine
dust-off. And I run smack into a world of hurt. So I flare
out and dee-dee the fuck out of there, but not before losing
my left-door gunner and gettin' my plexi turned into a
colander. When I get a-holt of that shithead looey a coupla
days later, he just smiles sweeter than shit and says he
popped the green because he was afraid I wouldn't bring
the bird in if I knew the Z was hot. . . ."*

*". . . an outstanding leader, just outstanding. He was
with the First Cav in the Ia Drang and then in the highlands with the 173rd Airborne, and he was involved in all
the big ops, like Austin Six and Crazy Horse and Haw-
thorne Two. Yes, I think Burns is just the man to take over
for Bean. Of course, that means they'll have to give him
his colonelcy. . . ."*

*Harmon and Dell were there. They had a pitcher of beer
on the table and had somehow saved a chair for him.*

*"How'd it go at the hospital?" Harmon yelled over the
din.*

"Numbah Ten."

"Yeah," Harmon nodded sympathetically.

"Hey, I hear you're getting a leave," Dell shouted, his

mouth puckered in petulance. "You piss them off and get a leave, while I'm a good boy and get doodely squat. You must be living right, Willow. I heard all about it from one of my friends in division."

"That's what you get for having friends in division, Charlie boy," said Harmon.

"What's that supposed to mean?" Dell asked. Then the big man's eyes widened and he started out of his chair. A brief look of alarm flashed across Harmon's face and he straightened quickly.

But Dell did not see the look, because he had gotten up for entirely unrelated—and peaceful—reasons. "There's my friend now," he said, smiling. "I'm goin' over to see him."

Harmon slumped back in his chair as Dell left the table. "Jesus H. Kee-rist," he laughed. "I thought that dumb ox had finally cottoned on to the fact he was being made sport of and was on his way to drop-kicking me into Laos. I was gonna try to hit him in the head with this here pitcher, then run like hell while he was pickin' glass outta his nose."

"You wouldn't have gotten very far in this crowd, Otis," Willow laughed.

"Yeah. Well, tell me, Jackie boy, where you going for your leave?"

"Honolulu, officially. But I'm going to try to get over to the mainland."

"No shit? The World? You lucky dawg. Maybe I shoulda given Pyle a hard time, too. Well, them that's got gets. You go and have a good time. I'll keep Veet Nam safe for you so's you won't find the land you love changed any when you get back."

"I don't know if I'm coming back, Otis."

Harmon chuckled. "You get the brass so pissed off they're transferring you altogether?"

"No. No transfer. I'm just not sure I'm coming back."

Harmon's bantering tone vanished as suddenly as if Willow had pulled a knife on him. He looked around quickly as if to gauge the precise depth of their privacy, then leaned forward and looked at Willow closely. "What do you mean by that, Jackie boy?" he asked.

Willow looked around the noisy room and said, "Not here. Let's get out of here."

They pushed their way through the crowd and out into the night air, heavy and humid but still refreshing after the smoke and smell of stale beer and stale bodies. Willow led the way around the building until they were facing the bay and the Battangan. They sat on a dune, the club's picture window to their backs, the light from inside throwing a yellow rectangle on the darkened sand.

"Okay, now what did you mean by that, Jackie boy?"

"I'm not real sure yet, Otis. I haven't thought it out fully. But I'm thinking about Canada maybe. Or Sweden. Someplace like that."

Harmon closed his eyes, shook his head, and whistled softly. When he opened his eyes again, there was a gentleness in them that seemed totally out of place in the Texan's hard face. "You serious?" he asked quietly.

"Yes."

"It's stupid, Jack. Look, you just go on and take your leave and have a good time, and then when you get on back here, you'll only have three months to go. You can do eighty-nine days and a wakeup standing on your head."

"No. I can't."

"You're asking for a world of hurt, pardner. It ain't worth it," Harmon said.

Willow shrugged.

"Look," said Harmon, desperation creeping into his voice. "You were the most gung-ho dipshit I ever saw when you first came in-country. You really believed, man! Okay, so you've learned a little about the real world. So

take what you know, the knowledge you earned the hard way, and use it to survive ninety goddamn days, and then you can walk away from it all like it was a bad dream. But you go off to Canada or Sweden, and this slant-eyed monkey of ours is gonna ride your back the rest of your life. It just ain't worth it, boy.''

Willow said nothing.

"Just tell me why, for chrissakes!" Harmon said with exasperation.

Willow snorted. "You have to ask? Jesus, Otis, you're on your second tour. You've seen more of it than I have. The United States Army, in case you hadn't noticed, has lost its mind.''

"It ain't the Army that's lost its mind, Jackie boy. It's you.''

Willow ran a hand across his face. "You know something, Otis? You may be right. Did you know that I've been a soldier all my life? I mean it, all my life—even when I was a kid. I used to see myself in these famous battles. I had these dreams . . . except they were more than dreams; they were like visions or something. The detail in them was fantastic, Otis. I'd know things about those battles that I really didn't, couldn't know. You get what I'm saying? I'd find a book later on that would tell how it really was, and it would have things in it that I already knew, things that I had already seen. I wasn't just dreaming about those battles, Otis. I was living them. I was there! In the Crimea, in the Argonne, at Rorke's Drift, at Thermopylae with the Spartans, routing out the Huks in the Philippines. I was there. And now I'm here because I had to fulfill the destiny of those dreams. I had to be a warrior. But now that I'm here, something is terribly wrong, Otis. It wasn't supposed to be like this. There was supposed to be blood, sure. And death. And sacrifice. But not stupidity; not moral cowardice; not drugs and fraggings and . . . ah hell, Otis. I'm scared.

This place scares me. It scares the shit out of me. Maybe I am crazy.''

"Hell, Jack, we're all scared," said Harmon. "The only thing dumber than being in this place at all is being in this place and not being scared. It don't mean nuthin'. I've seen you perform, and you're good. You're real good. You can make it."

Willow shook his head sadly. "You don't understand, Otis. I'm not talking about that kind of scared. I'm not so much afraid of losing my life as I am of losing my soul. It's not my ass I'm worried about. It's theirs." Willow made a sweeping motion with his arm in the general direction of the Ninety-first Evacuation Hospital. "There's no way people like you and me can protect them from the Beans and the Pyles and the Burnses. Hell, Otis, there's no way I can protect them from us. And if I can't do that, then I don't want to be here to see them get hurt. I don't want any part of it."

Harmon was getting angry. "Bullshit," he snapped. "You can't help anybody by going to Canada. You give such a hot shit about them boys, then you stay right here and do what you can to keep the Beans from drinking their blood. So you can't guarantee them anything. So you can't promise they won't get hurt. But you can be a buffer for them. You can still make a difference."

"How can you make a difference the way the Army is running this cluster-fuck?" Willow yelled back. "Jesus, back at Myer I had this platoon sergeant—the one I told you about, Sergeant Hazard. He saw it all happening. He tried to tell me, but I was too stupid to hear it. And even he didn't know how bad it was going to get. All this new horseshit about Vietnamization. Christ, Otis, how many troops have we got over here right now? More than half a million. And how many are grunts, in the line? Less than fifty thousand. So what are the rest of them doing? They're *running bowling alleys or selling candy bars in the PX or running R and R centers or fixing drinks at the officers club. Okay, you need support troops. But half a million to back up fifty thousand? I'm surprised that right in the middle of getting our ass kicked on Daisy Mae a chopper didn't bring us fresh ice cream. It's happened before. I'm surprised we don't have air-conditioners in our bunkers. That's next. Then when a Bean fucks up our men can die in seventy-two-degree comfort.''*

''C'mon now, Jack.''

''Dammit, Otis, you know I'm right. We don't need more creature comforts or more helicopters or more planes. We need some goddamn leaders. To think I spent the better part of my life dreaming about becoming an officer, a leader of men. To me it was like being named a knight of the Round Table. But just look at these assholes. How many battalion commanders have you seen in your two tours? Bean's just the latest in a long line of career boosters. They change every six months—generals and colonels and majors, all getting their tickets punched so they'll have a combat record and can go on to the Command and General Staff College at Leavenworth. They should be at Leavenworth alright, but not in no fucking college. When they're here they spend their 'combat time' flying around in C and C ships, counting up the dead pigs and water boo so they can report a good body count. Half of 'em aren't around long enough to learn the names of their officers, let alone their men. You think Bean knew who the fuck Lieutenant Richard Earp was? It was a long dry spell between Korea and Nam and, by God, they're gonna make the most of it, because who knows when the next one will come around? It ain't much of a war, but it's the only war they got. Hazard tried to tell me, but I wouldn't listen. It was the only war I had, too.''

''You finished?'' asked Harmon.

"Yeah, I'm finished."

"Ninety days, Jackie boy," Harmon repeated stubbornly.

"You ain't heard a word I've said," Willow said, shaking his head. "Christ, Otis, people like me and you, we're just as bad as Bean. We tell these kids they're well trained and ready for this place. What shit. How do you get a kid ready for some slope who can zip right through five strands of concertina wire and carry a bag of satchel charges in the bargain? Do you wanna know what I saw a couple days ago? Right here at Chu Lai?"

Harmon shrugged. "No. But I'm sure you're gonna tell me anyway. Your mouth seems to be stuck on full automatic."

Willow ignored him. "Division put on this demonstration down at the ball field for all the clerks and cooks and the other REMFs. They had this captured sapper, prob'ly from the same outfit that fucked us over. Anyway, they had a whole mess of wire laid out—mines, tin cans full of gravel, the whole schmere. Some guy blew a whistle, and the sapper flops over on his back and starts workin' through the wire. I mean, shit . . . he's like he's on a Sunday stroll. He's tying off strands with these little strips of cloth, just easy as shit. He's humming the latest hit from the Hanoi Top Forty, cool as ice and never rattling a can or nuthin'. And when he's through, our guys jumped up and gave him a standing ovation, a standing fucking ovation. The poor dumb bastards were clapping for their own funerals."

"Ninety days, Jack."

"No. Not if I'm going to do more harm than good. Those guys out there deserve a grown-up for a leader, not some jerk off with visions who's looking for ways to get them blown away so he can realize his fucking destiny."

"I don't know what the fuck you're talking about," Harmon said with disgust. "Losing your goddamn soul, visions, routin' out the fuckin' Huks. What kind of shit is that? The only way you're gonna lose your soul is by doing some dumbshit thing like runnin' off to Canada.''

Willow picked up a handful of sand, then opened his fingers one by one and let it trickle away. "I just don't know, Otis. First thing I'm going to do when I get back to the World is go see Sergeant Hazard. I'll talk to him. Then I'll decide.''

Harmon let out a lungful of air and looked at Willow. "Then all I can say is good luck to you, Jackie boy,'' he said softly.

Behind them, inside the club, the lights went out and a beam from the projector hit the wall and began to dance jerkily toward the screen set up near the door. It was a war picture—The Green Berets with John Wayne—and a lusty cheer and raucous laughter went up. They had all seen it before—a fun film, unadulterated horseshit.

Through the picture window and across the bay, obsidian in the night, an illumination flare hung like a star over the tip of the now invisible peninsula. Red and white tracer rounds winked like passing cronies on their way up from the NVA ground batteries and on their way down from the Spooky gunships overhead.

No one turned away from the movie to watch the show.

27

Hazard watched Samantha struggle into her heavy, fake fur coat. He made no move to help her, his way of registering his complaint. "How late do you think you'll be?" he asked, undisguised hope catching in his throat like a chicken bone.

Samantha laughed. "Very late, I'm afraid. Don't even think about waiting up for me. I'll sleep in my own bed tonight so I don't wake you when I come in."

Hazard rolled his shoulders. "No need for that. I'll still be up. I'm thinking about meeting Goody and Jackie at Zeke's for a few beers anyhow."

Samantha ran the back of her hand on his cheek and said in a motherly tone, "Absolutely not. You look tired, darling. Go to bed early and catch up on your sleep."

Hazard shrugged again. "We'll see." He tried one more time. "You sure you can't do this story in the morning?"

"I'm sure."

"Okey-doke. I reckon that's that."

He began missing her before she had time to reach the elevator. The evening stretched out in front of him like a jail term. He could not for the life of him remember what he used to do with his evenings before he met Samantha— grew old in tiny increments, he guessed. He had been dead without even realizing he'd been sick. He splashed some Wild Turkey into a tumbler and wandered toward the living room window thinking he could hold back the night, for a moment anyway, just by watching her cross the parking lot.

He took up the old, familiar position at the edge of the window and did his best Harry Houdini imitation. He could see her car in the corner of the lot, but no Sam as yet. He craned his neck a little farther so he could watch the street and sidewalk in front of the lobby. He saw her emerge, but instead of moving toward the parking lot, she stopped next to a new black Porsche parked there with the engine running, the exhaust pipe belching white cumulus into the dusk's chill. The door on the driver's side opened; a man got out and walked around the back of the car and through the smoke to open the passenger door for her. The man was big, big as a football player. And he had a Prince Valiant haircut.

Clell Hazard was aware only of a hissing white noise that rushed between his ears and filled his cranium. When the noise went away, he found himself sitting on the couch, the glass empty in his hand, and the level in the Wild Turkey bottle down two inches from where it had been—not down far enough to stop the nasty pictures from forming in his head. He saw Brubaker touching her. He saw them laughing together. He saw them naked. He saw the big, beefy body moving above her. Steadeeeee. This wasn't fair to Samantha. But she had lied about having to work. Steady now. There must be some explanation. But he could not think what it could be.

While he sat there unmoving, his questions chasing their own tails, the phone rang. He did not answer it. He did not hear it.

Willow put down the telephone and thought. He must be at Zeke's waiting for me. He paid his tab and pulled on his field jacket and left the lounge. He passed through the gate and crossed U.S. 50, chilled by the time he reached the saloon.

The place was full, and it took several minutes to determine that Hazard was not there. He turned down several invitations to join friends and found Zeke at the draft tap. "Hey, Zeke. Sergeant Hazard been in here tonight?"

"I ain't seen him, Jack," Zeke laughed. "Clell don't come in as often as he used to. Not since he fell in love."

Maybe he had been in the shower. "Yeah. Well, if he comes in tell him I've gone over to his place and wait. I'll be back."

By the time Willow reached the apartment building, he could no longer feel his feet. He spied his platoon sergeant's Pontiac in the lot and went on up. It took several knocks before the door finally opened. Hazard looked ill.

"Oh, hello, Jack," he said listlessly.

"Hi, sarge. Just wondered if you were up to going to Zeke's. I'm buying."

"I . . . I don't think so, Jack, not tonight." He showed no inclination to ask Willow in.

"You alright, sarge?" Willow asked with concern. "You don't look too good."

"To tell you the truth, Jackie, I don't feel too good. I think I'll turn in early. Hope you don't mind."

"No sweat. I just wanted to let you know, chop-chop, that the sergeant-major seems to know it was us who pulled the Tomb raid."

Hazard nodded. "Yes, I know."

"You do?"

"He knew from day one. Goody always knows from day one. Don't worry about it."

"If you're not worried, I'm not worried. I hope you feel better, sarge."

"Thanks," Hazard said distractedly. "And thanks for coming by."

"Right. Well, g'nite, sarge."

"Yeah, g'nite."

He was waiting for her when she came home, and there was something in his face that told her he knew. His eyes seemed set back in their hollows even deeper than usual, and there was a pain in them that made her want to kiss them shut. She could see the nerve that jumped along the line of his jaw when he was agitated. His apartment door was open, and he sagged in a chair directly in line with it, a bead drawn on her door. Samantha felt her face flush. "Oh, you're still up."

"Yup. I'm still up. Want a drink?"

"Sure." She closed the door, took off her coat, and hung it in the hall closet. He got up slowly and moved toward the kitchen. Perhaps he didn't know, she thought with a surge of hope. No. He knew. There was something missing from his face, his eyes. It was like the first time he had taken her trout fishing. When she had reeled in her first fish, the first fish she had ever caught, she had thought that she'd never seen anything so alive and beautiful. The thin rainbow colors danced down the trout's silver sides. She had called to Clell to come take out the hook. He had laughed and splashed over to her. He complimented her on her prowess, then announced they would have the fish for supper, in celebration. He had taken a small, wooden club—he called it a *priest*—and rapped the trout sharply on top of the head. She remembered vividly how the life went out of the fish. Something happened in the eyes, and the wonderful colors seemed to fade, to lose their glow and then die. That's the way Clell looked. Oh yes, he knew.

Hazard came into the living room with the drinks. "Did you get your story?" he asked dully.

"Yes. Yes, I did."

"What's it about?"

"There's going to be an antiwar protest at the Pentagon next week," Samantha said. "I had dinner with one of the organizers." That much, at least, was the truth, she thought.

"Who was it? Anybody I might have heard of?" he asked, watching her with those flat, Indian eyes.

Samantha had to decide. If he did not know and she told him, she would needlessly cause a row. But if she did not tell him and he did know, the damage would be irreparable.

"Larry Brubaker." There. It was out. She felt herself relax, almost melt, and became aware for the first time that she had been holding every muscle in her body in isometric tension.

The nerve was jumping in his cheek again. "Why him?" he asked.

"As I said, he's one of the organizers. You do remember that he is president of Attorneys Against the War? AAW. Awwwww." She ventured a weak smile. He did not smile back.

"Why didn't you tell me earlier?"

"Because I thought it would upset you—needlessly. And it looks as if I was right. I'm sorry, Clell. I know you don't like it, but I had to do the interview. It's my job." Samantha had decided not to tell him about her visit to the hospital or the bargain she had made with Brubaker. Besides, it was true that they had discussed the march at length and that she would be writing a story, a curtain raiser.

"Couldn't you have seen him at his office?"

"I suggested that," Samantha fibbed. "He insisted we do it over dinner. When it's the paper that wants the interview instead of the other way around, our policy is to let the source set the time and place. That's how it's done, Clell."

"Did you have a nice time?"

"No, I did not have a nice time," Samantha said testily. She was getting angry. A righteousness welled inside her in reaction to the baseless guilt she was feeling. Just what did he think he was doing, interrogating one of his prisoners of war?

"Did he make a pass at you?"

"N-no, of course not. H-he was a perfect gentleman."

"Bullshit," snapped Hazard, some animation coming back into his voice. "The Brubakers of this world are *never* perfect gentlemen. They all think they're God's gift to women. It's something that comes over them the first time a cheerleader spreads her legs for them. I *know* he tried to get into your knickers, Sam. His kind always does."

Samantha said nothing. Brubaker had, in fact, made a succinctly suggestive suggestion at the end of the dinner, and she had taken a taxi home. She blushed.

Clell laughed, and some of the color came back into his own face. "Don't worry," he said. "I'm not going to act the enraged bull elephant and go hunt him down and finish him off. I promised you I wouldn't do anything like that again and I won't. That *is* what you were afraid of, isn't it?"

"Yes."

"Well, don't be," he smiled. "And now that you've seen how confession can be good for the soul, are there any other sins you'd like to get off that wonderful chest of yours?"

She did not want to check the return of his usual good nature, but it was now or never. "Yes, there is." She hesitated. "You were right, Clell. Brubaker is a pig. But we talked a lot about the war tonight, and I found myself agreeing with much of what he said. I'm going to that protest at the Pentagon."

"Sure," he said, puzzled. "To report on it."

"No," she said defiantly. "To participate in it."

He just stared at her for a moment, then said, "I see. I would think your newspaper would frown on that sort of thing."

"It's none of their business. The protest just happens to be on my day off. I can spend that day any way I damn well please."

Hazard regarded her solemnly. Finally he sighed. "Sam, I find Mr. Brubaker so distasteful that I'd almost rather you two had a meeting of the bodies than a meeting of the minds."

"Clell Hazard, you are as much against the war as I am or he is. You know that's true."

"If Brubaker's agin it, maybe I should be for it."

"Don't be childish."

Hazard was quiet again, then said, "Don't you think taking part in this protest is kinda like putting a knife in my back?"

"No, I do not," Samantha bridled. "It's got nothing to do with you."

"The hell it doesn't," he said quietly. "Tell me something, why the Pentagon?"

"What do you mean?"

"Just what I said. Why the Pentagon? Why don't you go march in front of the house where that jug-eared fella from Texas lives? He's the one who started this ball rolling, and he's the one who can stop it."

"Oh, Clell. Really!"

"I'm serious. What are all those young kids over in Vietnam going to think when they hear about this?"

"They'll think what they must already think—what I think, what you think—that this war is a mistake."

Hazard said quietly, "Sam, every war is a mistake. And nobody knows it better than the people who do the fighting.

But you don't have to rub it in. You don't have to tell some boy who's just seen his best buddy cut in half, 'Hey, kid, no sweat, it's a mistake.' He knows it's a mistake. I know it's a mistake.''

"Then we have nothing to argue about." She cocked her head. "Oh, Clell, please let's not argue. I hate arguing with you. It's like self-flagellation. I just feel like this is something I have to do."

Hazard shrugged. "Okey-doke, do what you gotta do."

Samantha laughed. "Is that some more of your Gary Cooper talk?" She playfully tucked in her chin and growled, "A man's gotta do what a man's gotta do."

Hazard did not smile. "Just answer one question," he said softly. "Does this protest of yours mean you'll be seeing Brubaker again?"

"No."

"Good."

Samantha put a hand on the back of his neck and kissed him lightly on the nose. She brought her other hand up between his legs and squeezed gently. "Come take me to bed," she said. "I promise there will be no protests tonight."

The coffin was made of glass. He could see clearly through the lid, but no one seemed able to see him. He screamed and kicked, but there was not much room for leverage and the glass was strong, much too strong. He could hear everything. The bulldozers, the volleys of the firing party, the clear and heartbreaking notes of taps. Why couldn't they hear him? Why couldn't they see him? I'M ALIVE! A casket bearer leaned over the box, and he saw the man had no eyes. He could see deep into the man's sockets, the veins glistening with blood and criss-crossing like wires in an electrical box. None of them had eyes.

He saw Samantha, dressed in black and crying, her tears dripping from empty sockets. He saw Brubaker at her side grinning sightlessly, his arm around her back, a big hand on her breast. SAM! Samantha wept, dabbing at the gaping holes in her face with a black lace handkerchief. He saw Nelson, standing fierce and tall in dress blues, and beside him Willow. GOODY! JACKIE! HELP ME! They, too, wept. Behind them stood the honor platoon. None of them had eyes. Their mouths were open in a Gregorian chant: Ashes to ashes . . . dust to dust. . . . SOMEBODY, for God's sake! JACKIE!

As he called out to Willow, the boy's face began to melt. The face dripped onto the uniform. Willow's hair caught on fire, and his hands began to melt. Behind Willow the faces of the honor platoon began to dissolve. Their skulls were achingly white, the bone shiny and wet like new enamel. Goody was okay . . . and Samantha—even Brubaker. They had no eyes, but they had faces. Only the young men had no faces. They were skeletons in uniform. Their bony fingers held the rifles at present arms. Their neckties and collars hung loose around their spinal stalks. Their flesh dripped hotly onto spit shined shoes. PLEASE! Can't anyone hear me? Shut off the bulldozers so you can hear me. Please. Sam. SAMANTHAAAAA!

"Shhhh. I'm here, Clell. I'm right here, darling. Shhh. It's alright now. Go back to sleep. Shhhh. Shhhhh."

28

Delta Company was awake and moving well before the dawn broke over Veterans Day. The troops scrambled into fatigues and field jackets and, hounded by their NCOs, double-timed to formation without stopping for shaves, showers, or breakfast. The noncoms counted them off and fed them into the line of buses waiting to take them to the cemetery. The men were packed in until leaf springs flattened and axles threatened to snap. They were used to standing up on buses. They leaned against one another and dozed in place.

A short ride later, the buses dumped them in the dark on a road cutting through the Fields of the Dead. The men were herded out, formed up once again, and counted off. The noncoms circulated with clipboards in their hands. Each man was assigned a row of graves, then loaded down like an Army mule with as many bundles as he could carry of small American flags stapled to sticks with sharpened points at one end. Order of the day: one miniature Stars and Stripes to be planted precisely one foot in front of each marker. The NCOs would sight the lines to make certain the flags dressed up properly in a straight line of red, white, and blue. As far as the eye could see, troopers from the other Old Guard companies stooped and planted like migrant field hands.

As soon as one section was completed, Delta's Darlings were loaded back aboard the buses and hauled to another. By the time the sun peeped up over the horizon, bathing the Washington Monument in the smoky distance with amber light, they were finished . . . for the moment. They had two hours to return to barracks; shit, shower, and shave; eat breakfast; and be back in the garden, standing tall in blues.

Willow was polishing his brass when Hazard approached, clicking down the center aisle, taps leaving scratches in the floor wax like bird tracks on a beach. "Jack, your squad will be pulling public assistance for the first three hours or so," Hazard said. "We'll have charts waiting for you at the main parking area. With the name and year of death, you'll be able to direct people to the grave they're looking for with no sweat."

"Right, sarge."

"Then I'm gonna turn your people over to somebody else and switch you to NCOIC on the Kennedy gravesite. It always gets a lot of people on Veterans Day. You know the drill—just keep folks moving as best you can if it crowds up, and answer their questions."

"Right, sarge."

"Any questions?"

"Yeah. We wearing overcoats today?"

"Hell yes. It's freezing out there."

"Does that mean I don't have to finish this brass?"

Hazard laughed. "Why, Corporal Willow, I'm surprised at you. I thought you were gung-ho, STRAC."

"Not at this hour of the morning," Willow said. "Besides, if we have our overcoats on, who's to know?"

Hazard smiled and patted him on the shoulder. *"You'll*

know, Jack. *You'll* know." Hazard clickety-clicked away, and Willow went back to the Brasso.

"Sergeant, could you help me, please."

"I'm just a corporal, ma'am."

"Oh . . ."

"Can I help you find someone, ma'am," Willow said with a smile. The woman was bundled up in a bright red woolen coat, and she clutched two bunches of bright red flowers. Her eyes teared from the cold.

"My husband . . . and my son," she said. "Everything looks so different from before . . . from the funeral. I can't seem to get my bearings. Every place looks so much like the next place." Her voice trailed off.

"Yes, ma'am, it does," Willow said politely.

"I've come down from Rhode Island, you see," the woman said by way of explanation.

"Uh, yes, ma'am. If you could give me their names and dates of death?"

"Oh, yes. Sergeant William H. Renner, 1944, and Sergeant William H. Renner, Junior, 1965."

"Yes, ma'am." Willow stood behind the foldout table near the gate and leafed through the computer printout sheets, checking under year, then surname. He found them. He picked a mimeographed map of the cemetery from the stack, flipped it over, and made some jottings. "Ma'am, here is a map of the cemetery. On the back here, I've marked the section, row, and marker number of the ones you want. If you require transportation, you can board one of the buses parked over there. For your husband, you should take the bus marked Blue Route. Your son is on the Red Route. You'll have to come back here to change from one route to the other. Okay?"

"Yes, thank you, young man."

"Yes, ma'am."

The woman started for the buses then stopped, turned, and said, "I wanted my son to be buried next to his father, but they wouldn't let me."

"Yes, ma'am."

"They wouldn't let me," she said again, with both apology and accusation in her voice. Then she walked slowly toward the buses.

Willow stamped his feet, trying to get some circulation in his toes. He didn't mind this duty on Memorial Day. The crowds were larger then, but at least it was May. The thin, white cotton gloves were useless. The tailored blue overcoat had nice deep pockets, but it was against regulations to put your hands in them. He wondered if anyone was watching from up the hill and compromised by tucking a hand under each armpit. He watched an elderly man slowly approach his post. The man was lame and wore only a light blue windbreaker. He seemed impervious to the cold.

"Mornin', sonny," the old man called out.

"Good morning, sir," Willow snapped briskly, throwing the old man a salute. He had seen a VFW button pinned to the windbreaker. "Do you need assistance in finding a friend or loved one, sir?"

"Hell no," the old man snorted. "I know where my own damn brother is. Right up the side of that damn hill." He pointed. "What I need, sonny, is a damn crutch to get me up there."

"I think we can help you, sir," Willow said with a smile. "WILDMAN, FRONT AND CENTER." Wildman trotted toward them clumsily, blowing steam with each step. Willow told the elderly gentleman, "This is Private Wildman, sir. He'd be happy to assist you up the hill. Won't you, private?"

"Sure thing," Wildman said to the old man.

The man looked doubtful. "You don't look in too gooda shape to me, sonny."

"No problem, sir," Wildman said, taking the old man by an elbow and leading him away.

A few minutes later Willow saw Sergeant Hazard step off a bus that was returning for another load and walk toward him.

"How's it go, Jack."

"Fine, sarge."

"Good," said Hazard. 'Sergeant Carey will be relieving you in a few minutes, and you can relieve the NCO in charge at JFK. That bus I just got off will take you to the Amphitheater, and you can hoof it over from there."

"What's happening up at the Amphitheater?" Willow asked.

"Nothing much. A few people are starting to gather. The ceremony don't start 'til 1000."

"Is the President coming?"

"Jeezus, Willow, don't you ever read a newspaper? LBJ is in Nam, touring bases and trying to drum up some support for the cause. He wasn't too pleased with that march on the Pentagon last month. Hell's bells, boy, you should've known that. Second platoon Delta was at the airport to see him off."

Willow shrugged. "I must've missed it, sarge. The only reading I'm doing these days are training manuals. I want to be ready for OCS."

Hazard looked around. "Where's Wildman? If that sad sack is ghosting again, I'll have his butt on a biscuit for breakfast."

Willow laughed. "It's okay, sarge. He's assisting the public." Willow pointed to a spot halfway up the hill where two figures could be seen struggling up the steep, grassy slope. One figure, a man in a light blue windbreaker, was helping the other, a soldier, to his feet.

The buses for the public had seats. Willow stood anyway, perched in the doorstep. His body swayed with the turns and he shifted his weight with unconscious expertise.

Two middle-aged civilians in the front seat nearest the door were arguing quietly over something, and one man finally said in a louder voice, "Let's just ask this soldier here. He might know."

"Can I help you, sir," Willow said dutifully.

"I hope so, corporal. My friend and I are in disagreement about the inscription on the Tomb of the Unknown Soldier. Can you tell us the exact wording?"

Willow smiled. "Yes, sir, I can. It says: 'Here rests in honored glory an American soldier, known but to God.' "

"You see!" The man who had asked the question laughed and punched his friend playfully on the arm. He turned back to Willow. "And there are three bodies inside the Tomb, right? One from World War One, one from World War Two, and one from Korea."

"Uh, nosir, I'm sorry. The Tomb itself holds only the remains of a World War One veteran. If you look closely, you'll see that there are two flat markers in the area slightly in front of and to the sides of the Tomb. One is inscribed 1941–1945 and the other 1950–1953. The unknowns for those wars are buried there."

"Ha!" said the other man, punching the first man back. The first man studiously ignored his friend. "Is there going to be a place for Vietnam, corporal?" he asked Willow.

"I'm sure there will be if the war produces an unknown soldier, sir. But there may be a problem in that our Army bureaucracy is getting better. So far as I know, all the deceased from Vietnam are present or accounted for."

"Well, I guess that's good," the man said.

"Yessir, I guess so."

The man checked Willow over carefully, then asked, "You been over there yet, corporal? To Vietnam?"

"Nosir, not yet. But I will be going," Willow said emphatically.

"Can't wait, eh?" the man asked with a smile.

"No, sir. I can't wait."

Traffic at the Kennedy gravesite was sparse. Business would not pick up until after the ceremony at the Amphitheater and the autumn tourists had heard the speeches, watched the changing of the guard at the Tomb, and then wandered over to the Custis-Lee Mansion and the Kennedy grave just below it.

JFK duty was far less formal and rigorous than Tomb duty. The troopers and NCO who made up the detail were allowed to move around and talk with the public. Willow made certain that each of his men knew to stick to the general vicinity of his assigned corner of the site and then circulated among them.

The detail was from Bravo Company. Willow did not know any of them. He introduced himself around and lingered to talk with a spec four named Younger, a seemingly articulate young man about Willow's own age.

"You should have seen the crowds this place got during the first few months after the assassination," Younger was saying. "We musta had ten thousand people a day coming through."

"Jesus, Younger, have you been in the Herd that long?" Willow asked, making it sound like hard time on a Georgia chain gang.

Younger nodded. "Four years this month. I reported in two days after the funeral. I was real sorry to have missed something historical like that, you know? Everybody was still talking about it. It must have been something. The Old Guard hadn't pulled a state funeral in God knows how long, and people were up seventy-two hours straight, studying the SOP and drilling and all.''

"Sergeant-Major Nelson was here then, wasn't he?" Willow asked.

"You bet. The word was that he did all the real work of planning the thing. They said he was a real terror. After it was over, he took the entire Irish honor guard out on the town. They hit the Hayloft and Benny's and the Rocket Room and a bunch of other joints. The micks had never seen anything like it. At one place they got into a fight with the Special Forces contingent that was up for the funeral. Nelson and them Irish left a trail of bodies that kept the D.C. police and the hospitals busy for a week."

"The Irish honor guard?"

"Yeah. They were invited because of Kennedy's Irish heritage, you know? The Old Guard put them up in the barracks. They were real sharp, I was told. They did everything on silent commands and . . . uh, corporal, don't look now, but there's this really good-looking girl who's been watching you. Or maybe it's me."

"Oh yeah?" Willow said without interest.

"I mean she's *really* good-looking."

Willow sighed. "Okay, where is she?"

"Behind you and to the left."

Willow nonchalantly adjusted his body. He caught a glimpse of coal black hair and sloe eyes, and then his chest seemed to implode. He shut his eyes, waited a heartbeat, and opened them. She was still there, smiling a small smile, the large, dark eyes amused.

Without a word to Younger, Willow walked slowly toward her, confused and frightened and happy and incapable of planning.

"Hello, Rachel," he croaked.

"Hello, Jackie."

"W-What are you doing here?"

"Visiting President Kennedy's grave. I'd never been here before."

Willow's brain refused to function. He simply stood there looking at her while muddled signals raced around his nervous system.

She seemed content to stare back. Finally she smiled the small smile again. "You look very handsome in your uniform."

"Uh, yeah, thanks. I mean, what are you doing here, in Washington?"

"My parents live here now. My father is at the Pentagon."

"That's . . . nice. You, too?"

She shook her head and made the raven hair dance around her face. "No, just visiting. I'm still living in Europe. Germany now. I transferred to the American university of Heidelberg."

"Oh. How long will you be here?"

"I've got to go back tomorrow, Jack. I've been playing hookey."

"Oh." Reason was beginning to return, but Willow still teetered on the edge of panic, afraid she might disappear. He said quickly, "Rache, can you have dinner with me tonight?"

Her face clouded with regret. "I'm sorry, Jackie. I have a date tonight."

"Aw for God's sake, Rachel, *please*," he blurted in anguish.

Rachel did not answer for a moment, then she said, "I'm not sure it's a very good idea, Jack."

"Please?" he whispered hoarsely.

After another pause she gave a slight, reluctant nod. "Alright, then. Arlington Towers, apartment ten-C. Eight o'clock?"

Willow exhaled heavily and nodded. His sense of relief

was absurd in its force. He had been ready to grovel, whine, cry, anything at all. He didn't know what to say now. He just stood and looked at her. Then he heard a clicking of heel taps and saw Hazard coming.

"You are allowed to assist the public, Corporal Willow, but you are *not* allowed to kidnap anyone," Hazard said sternly. He looked at the girl, smiled, and added, "No matter how great the temptation may be."

Willow said stiffly, "Sergeant Hazard, I'd like you to meet Rachel Field. Rachel is . . . ah . . . an old friend."

Rachel held out a gloved hand, and Hazard took it in his own gloved hand. "Pleased to meet you, Miss Field."

"Thank you, sergeant," Rachel said with a smile. "I'm sorry I detained your sentry. I won't keep him any longer. It was nice meeting you."

"There's no need to rush off. I'll make an exception in your case," Hazard said.

The girl shook her head and the hair danced again. "No, I really must be going." She looked at Willow. "I'll see you tonight then, Jack," she said, then turned and walked away.

Hazard watched her go. He turned to Willow. "Wow!"

"Yes. Wow."

"Is that someone special, Jack?"

"Yes."

"Look, I'm sorry. I didn't mean to scare her off."

Willow was not listening. He watched Rachel getting smaller and smaller as she climbed the slope toward the Lee mansion. Even bundled up in a heavy coat, her walk was distinctive to Willow, recognizable at a thousand yards. He could see her walking to class in the corridor at Buena High, her books clutched to her cashmere-covered breasts, a pleated skirt swishing around her hips. He thought he would faint from longing.

He turned to Hazard. "Sarge, can I borrow fifty dollars. I'll pay you back payday."

"Jesus Christ, Jack. Aw, hell. Yeah, you can have it."

"I'll need to borrow your car, too."

General Field answered the door dressed in an expensive smoking jacket. It was the first smoking jacket Willow had ever seen outside of the scotch whiskey ads in the magazines.

"Why hello, Jack. Come in, come in."

"Thank you, sir."

The apartment was large and had a nice view of the Potomac. The boy recognized much of the furniture, including the candelabra, now set on the mantle over the fireplace in the living room. He saw the silk Persian carpets and could remember the feel of them on his bare back. On a small, rolling cart in the corner, he saw the silver decanter and wondered if it still contained cognac. General Field walked over to it. "Care for a cognac, Jack? Rachel will be a few minutes, I'm afraid."

"Uh, yessir. Thank you."

"I'm sorry Mrs. Field isn't here to see you," the general was saying as he poured, his back to the boy. "She's been feeling a little under the weather lately. She's at Walter Reed for a few days for some tests. That's why Rachel is home, actually." He turned and handed Willow a snifter and motioned the young man to a chair.

"I'm sorry to hear that, sir," said Willow. "Nothing serious, I hope."

"No, nothing serious. Some sort of liver trouble, we think." The general took a chair. "So, tell me, how are you, Jack?"

"Fine, sir."

"Rachel told me it was quite a shock seeing you this morning."

"Yessir. For me, too."

"Yes," General Field smiled. "I can imagine. It's been quite a long time, hasn't it."

"Yessir, it has."

General Field watched him over the top of his glass. His lips were pursed and there was something of a smirk in his eyes. "Rachel tells me you're a . . . ah, corporal, and that you're with the honor guard up at Myer. That's a fine outfit . . . for the Infantry."

Willow le. the dig pass. "Yessir. Are you still working in electronics, sir?"

"Oh my, yes," the general laughed. "I'm heading up a major research and development project. Tell me, Jack, have you ever heard of the McNamara Line?"

"I think I've read something about it, sir. It has to do with electronic surveillance along the Ho Chi Minh Trail, doesn't it?"

"Yes, something like that," the general said with a smug smile. "It's still somewhat hush-hush at this point. We're doing some wonderful things, Jack. I *can* tell you about the SLAR we're putting into some of our twin-engine Mohawks. It's a sideways-looking radar that can pick up a man who is moving at a running pace of three to five kilometers an hour. It can locate bicycles, carts, trucks—anything that's moving. SLAR gives the operator a readout within fifteen to twenty seconds so he can immediately radio in his find and bring artillery to bear." The general was now talking with animated enthusiasm. "We have other Mohawks fitted out with *red haze*, an infrared device that can pick out any spot on the ground that's warmer than those around it. It can catch the most well-concealed cooking fire or a still-warm truck engine. All it needs is a three-to five-degree difference in temperature to make a reading. I tell you, Jack, this war is a boon to R and D, a veritable boon. It is directly responsible for some very significant technological breakthroughs."

"Yessir, I'm sure it is." Willow wondered if science had yet developed a decent lightweight and effective body armor . . . or a way to reduce to manageable portions the seventy-pound load the typical infantryman had to hump, and still provide the grunt with field essentials . . . or a steel pot that didn't bounce around or slip down and cut the bridge of the nose or turn into ancillary shrapnel when holed by a shell. He didn't ask. He doubted very much that General Field worried about easing the burden of the lowly boonie rat.

Rachel walked into the room, and Willow stopped thinking about things military. She was gorgeous. She wore knee-high boots, a tweed skirt and jacket and a white, ruffled blouse that set off her olive complexion and dark eyes and hair. Willow felt his heart bump. It already knew what his head was just coming to realize: He loved Rachel Field as much now as he had then—maybe more. He knew he would not trade her for West Point now. His eyes filled up with her and threatened to spill over.

General Field deftly managed to break Willow's spell. "I thought you had a date with young Peterson tonight, dear?" he said to Rachel. "How did you ever shake him? I find him to be a very persistent young man."

"I managed," Rachel answered tersely. She turned to Willow. "Shall we go?"

Willow nodded and stood to shake hands with her father. General Field smiled without friendliness. "Goodbye, Corporal." He put emphasis on both words.

They did not speak until they were in Sergeant Hazard's limping Pontiac, rattling toward the expensive French restaurant on Embassy Row that Willow had chosen. "Who's young Peterson?" Willow asked.

Rachel shrugged her shoulders. "A civilian scientist who works in my father's department."

"Is he important to you?"

"He's important to my father."

They rolled in silence up Massachusetts Avenue.

They reached the restaurant. Willow turned the Pontiac over to a valet parking attendant, who slid behind the wheel with a wrinkled nose and obvious reluctance. It looked as if he expected to get some ineradicable stain on the seat of his striped trousers. He gunned the machine toward the Chrysler New Yorkers and Lincoln Continentals that filled the lot.

Inside, they were hastily seated by a maitre d' whose eyes widened with consternation at Willow's GI haircut and ill-fitting suit and who spent an inordinately long time scrutinizing the reservations book, openly hoping there was some mistake.

They ordered cocktails and Willow probed to get conversation started. "I'm sorry to hear about your mother," he said.

"She's much better now. She'll be home in a few days."

After more silence, he tried again. "I see your father hasn't changed much."

"No, he's still the same S.O.B. he always was," Rachel said coolly. Then, with warmth in her voice, she asked, "How's your father?"

"He died of a heart attack last winter."

"Oh no." Rachel's hands flew to her face. "Oh, I'm sorry, Jackie. I liked your father. I liked him very much." There was honest pain in her eyes.

"I know you did, Rache. He liked you very much, too."

A waiter arrived with the drinks at the same time another came to take their dinner order. Willow, feeling rushed, asked for more time to decide. He lifted his Wild Turkey and water, a drink he had adopted ever since the dinner at Sergeant Hazard's, and said: "To old times."

Rachel touched glasses and countered: "No. To today."

Willow nodded and said, "Today's good, too. In fact, today's kinda wonderful."

Rachel did not comment on that. Instead, she asked, "Is the Army everything you hoped it would be, Jack?"

Willow shrugged. "Yes and no. Mostly yes. I'm still waiting for OCS and Vietnam. But I'll get them. I'll get 'em both."

"You *want* to go to Vietnam?" Rachel asked with arched eyebrows.

"Of course," said Willow, surprised she would ask such a question.

Rachel smiled a wry smile. "Oh yes, I should have known. I guess at Fort Myer you don't get too many opportunities to change the world. It's hardly 'the right place at the right time.' "

Willow grinned sheepishly. "You remember."

"Like it was yesterday," Rachel said without a smile.

"Well, I still believe it's true that a soldier in the right place at the right time can change the world," Willow said defensively.

"That's too bad. I had rather hoped you had outgrown that."

"Dammit, Rache—"

Rachel shook her head quickly. "I'm sorry I said that. Please, let's not pick at old scabs. Let's just make small talk. There's a lot to catch up on."

Willow looked at her solemnly for a moment, then said softly, "No. Let's *not* make small talk. I don't care how you like school. I don't care how you like living in Europe. I don't care if you've read any good books lately."

"It's safe talk, Jack," Rachel warned, a look of alarm spreading across her lovely face.

"To hell with safe," Willow said angrily. "I love you,

Rachel. I never stopped. Do you still feel anything for me?''

"Jackie, don't. . . ."

"Do you still feel anything for me?" Willow insisted.

Rachel flared. "Ask me that when you're a civilian again."

"I'm asking you now, Rachel."

"Well, I'm not going to answer you."

"You have to."

"I don't have to do anything of the sort!" she said, mad as he. "God-DAMN you, Jackie Willow! How dare you ask me that! You had your choice and you made it. You poor gullible boy. There was never any appointment to West Point. NEVER! My father was afraid I was about to marry beneath myself, that it would hurt his career, and he wanted you out of the way. It was so easy for him. You made it so easy."

"Rache—"

"I loved you so much, Jack. So much. And you shit on me." She started to cry softly.

Willow took her hand and kneaded it. "I've paid for it, Rachel. Every day. I swear I have. I've been hollow inside all this time. I haven't even touched another person since that day with you in the canyon."

"Well I have," Rachel said bitterly.

Willow flinched but said, "I don't care." The moment the words were out of his mouth he knew they were true. He didn't care.

Rachel shook her head tragically. "Too much has happened, Jack. Too much time has gone by. We're not kids anymore."

Willow was about to argue when he became aware of their waiter and the maitre d' standing nearby, staring. Diners at the surrounding tables were staring, too.

"Rachel, are you very hungry?" he asked.

"N-Not anymore," she said, wiping her eyes.

Willow took a ten-dollar bill from his wallet and tossed it onto the table, then stood and helped Rachel with her chair. He turned to the maitre d', smiled pleasantly, and said, "That's for the drinks, Frenchy. Fuck you very much."

They ransomed their coats and went outside. The parking attendant was slumped against the building. He did not jump to attention. "The keys are in the ignition," he said in a bored voice. "It's over there between the white El Dorado and the Lincoln. You can't possibly miss it."

"We've got to talk some more," Willow said when they were underway, moving back down Massachusetts.

"I don't feel like going to another place like that," Rachel said listlessly. She was slumped against the door, her head resting against the cold glass.

"Do you want to go home?"

Pause. "No."

"I know a place where we could be alone," Willow said carefully. "We . . . we could stay all night . . . if we wanted to."

Rachel did not answer. Her eyes were closed, and Willow could not read her face in the sparse light. They rode along in silence. Up ahead he saw a service station with a phone booth. He pulled in and said, "Let me make a quick phone call. I'll just be a minute."

Rachel gave no sign that she heard him.

Willow got out. He fumbled in his pocket for a dime and dialed.

"Yo."

"Sarge, it's Willow."

"Jesus, what now?" Hazard sighed. "You got all my money. You got my car. I suppose now you want to borrow my dick so you can get laid."

Willow laughed. "Sarge, you gotta stop bumming around

with the sergeant-major. Your language has deteriorated something awful.''

"The hook, boy. Just gimme the hook,'' Hazard grumbled.

"Well, uh, actually . . .'' Willow's embarrassment oozed along the wire. "I was . . . uh, wondering if I could borrow your, uh . . . apartment? Or maybe Miss Huff's. Uh . . . if one or the other is free.''

There was a pause, then Hazard said, "Okey-doke. You can have my place. There's a little tear in the hall carpet right in front of my door. I'll leave the key in there.''

"Thanks, sarge. I really appreciate this.''

"Yeah, yeah. Just don't call me again tonight, huh? I'm *wearing* my only clean pair of skivvies.''

They chugged across the bridge into Virginia, the Pontiac huffing with the effort. Rachel finally spoke up, "I'm not going to sleep with you, Jack.''

"Of course not,'' Willow said quickly. "I just want to talk.''

"It would create too many complications.''

"I just want to talk. Honest, Rache.''

She smiled thinly in the gloom. "Sure you do, hotshot.''

He smiled back. She had changed. Matured. She was a woman now. More a woman, he suspected, than he was a man. Willow was fully aware that he had not put all childish things behind him. He didn't care. If what he had had with Rachel was childish, a bad case of puppy love, then he never wanted to grow up. He would make love to her tonight, somehow. He would show her in word and deed, whatever it took, that he loved her, that he would not give her up again.

"Where are we going?'' she asked.

"Sergeant Hazard is giving us his apartment. He's the one you met this morning, remember?''

"Oh, yes. He was nice."

"Yes, he is."

"He reminded me a bit of your father. Don't you think so?"

"Yeah, kinda."

"What is he going to do while we occupy his house?"

"His lady friend lives across the hall. He's in love, too."

"That makes two of you," said Rachel.

"You don't mean that, Rachel. I know you don't."

Rachel said nothing.

Willow parked the car in Hazard's lot and led her into the building, his arm around her shoulders. She did not resist.

He found the rip in the rug and was on his knees groping around for the key when the door swung open. Hazard stood looking down on him. Hazard was dressed in fatigues, and he had his webbing on. Miss Huff stood in the doorway behind him.

"Oh," said Willow. "You're still here."

"Afraid so, Jack," Hazard said. "The call came two minutes ago. Full alert."

"Alert?" Willow, confused, scrambled to his feet.

Hazard nodded. "My guess would be that this is it. A. P. Hill." He looked at Rachel and said, "I'm sorry, Miss Field."

"But it can't be," Willow protested. "Not now. Not tonight. We were up at 0300 this morning to put in those dumb flags. We busted our butts all day long in the garden. We're tired."

"You can tell it to the chaplain in a couple of weeks," Hazard said with a smile. "I'd bet my bottom dollar this was Goody Nelson's idea."

"What's going on, Jack?" Rachel asked quietly.

"Field exercises," Willow wailed.

Hazard said, "Uh, Miss Field, this is Samantha Huff. She'll drive you home. Jack and I have to move, chop-chop."

"Sarge," Willow pleaded. "I've got to talk to Rachel."

Hazard regarded him with sympathy. "Five minutes, Jack. Sam's apartment is open. You can go in there." He closed his door, opened it again to hold up a spread hand and mouth "Five," and closed it again.

Willow hustled Rachel into Samantha Huff's apartment. He took her by both shoulders and said earnestly and desperately, "Rachel, I love you. I was going to spend all night telling you that, over and over again until it got through. But there isn't any time. I'm sorry for what I did. I don't want to lose you again. I couldn't take it. I hoped you believed me when I told you I wanted to marry you and that I was willing to give up the Army."

"You never told me that," Rachel said.

"Honey, I did. In all those letters I sent to Switzerland."

Rachel dropped her eyes. "I didn't open them. I . . . I was so angry and so hurt. I didn't trust myself to open them. I just wanted to forget you."

"Did you, Rache? Did you forget me?"

She did not answer.

"Look," he said. "I'll do anything you want. Anything. If you want me out of the service, I'll get out. I've got two years to go on my hitch, and I want to make the best of those two years, but if that's what you want when it's done, then that's the way it will be."

She did not answer.

"You've got to tell me if there's any hope for me, Rache. I've got to know."

"Do you mean it?" she asked uncertainly. "Everything you just said?"

"Oh God, yes."

"I-I've got to have time to think, Jack. I'm very confused. The last thing I expected was to see you this morning."

She closed her eyes and wondered aloud, "God, was it only this morning?"

Willow clutched at straws. "I can live with that. As long as you don't shut the door on me."

"I'm not shutting any doors," Rachel said. "Or opening any. Y-You can write to me."

"Yes. Leave your address with Miss Huff. I'll be in the field for the next two weeks, but I'll mail off a long letter soon as I get back."

There was a pounding on the door and Hazard's muffled voice. "Jack, let's go, boy. Saddle up."

Willow kissed her. A lingering kiss full of passion and despair, tenderness and frustration. Breathless, he said, "Remember, I love you."

"I . . ." She did not finish.

29

The company area looked like a town in the path of an advancing enemy army. Delta was in chaos. Jeeps, three-quarter tons, and deuce-and-a-halfs filled the alley, the quad, and the road at the rear of the barracks. A half dozen work parties, dressed in fatigue trousers and t-shirts despite the cold, labored mightily to pack them.

Sergeant July, his dialect forgotten for the moment, tongue-lashed his KPs as they loaded the field kitchen. A detail from Fourth Platoon, the weapons platoon, filled a truck with mortar tubes and baseplates, machine guns, and blank ammo. Sergeant Beech's supply detail loaded the supply truck with everything from extra poncho liners to gas masks. And everywhere, men ran in seemingly aimless circles, dressed in full field gear, steel pots flouncing. Off to one side stood an amused noncom from battalion HQ, one of Goody Nelson's henchmen, taking notes and checking his watch with disgusted shakes of the head.

In the Third Platoon troop bay, Hazard and Willow found even greater confusion. Men yelled and cursed and struggled into horseshoe packs. Sergeant Carey was bellowing at this man or that, trying to restore some modicum of order. The men ignored him. Willow rushed to his own locker to get his gear on. Hazard spent a few seconds surveying the scene and then yelled, "AT EASE, GOD-DAMMIT!"

The uproar slackened, then died away completely. Men in the throes of a dozen different activities froze and turned sheepish faces toward their platoon sergeant.

Hazard said nothing for a moment, just looked at them with loathing. Finally, in a voice that was not a shout but carried like one, he said, "Listen up, assholes. This is not difficult. It is simple. Simple-minded people should have no trouble understanding." He spoke slowly and distinctly, like a teacher talking to a room full of kindergarteners. "You wear fatigues, field jackets, and full packs. You wear helmets and helmet liners. You wear field gloves and field glove liners. Into your packs you put your toilet articles, mess kits, extra socks, and skivvies and longjohns if you have them. If you have a roll of asswipe, put that in, too. When everyone is ready, I want you to line up in squads, facing the door. Then we will walk, not run, to the arms room. Step up to the window, draw a weapon, and give the armorer the serial number. We are getting M-14s, for this here cotillion. Then you walk, not run, to trucks number eleven, twelve, and thirteen, all of which are parked in a neat row at the rear of the building. Line up by squads once again. Sergeant Carey will be there with a platoon roster. Give him your name and get into the truck. There will be no talking, no smoking, and no grab-ass. DO YOU READ ME?"

The troopers nodded or mumbled, "Yes, sergeant."

Hazard turned to Carey. "How many we got not present or accounted for, Frank?"

"I . . . I don't know, sarge," Carey stammered.

Hazard looked at him coldly. "You are supposed to know, Frank. You may be only an E-5 buck sergeant, one of the lowest forms of NCO life, but you are still supposed to know. Now listen up. Washington, Perinowski, and Bullard are on leave. Jones, Robert N., is in the hospital. Tallon is on TDY. Jones, James E., is in the stockade at Meade. Everyone else should be here. Undoubtedly we have a few people under barstools in D.C. at this very moment. Army Regulation Number One-A: There's always ten percent who don't get the word. They will be left behind. Don't worry about them. They'll be trucked out to us tomorrow. You got all that?''

"Roger, sarge," Carey mumbled, looking at the floor.

"Okey-doke, then," Hazard said in a kinder tone. He looked back to the troops. "WHAT THE FUCK ARE YOU WAITING FOR? MOVE!''

The truck, rigged with full canvas, crawled through Arlington, then Fairfax, picking up speed only when the convoy had left the more densely populated areas behind.

Most of Willow's squad dozed, the long day, begun before dawn in the garden, finally taking its toll. They sat facing one another on the hard, fold-down benches, their new rifles, still stinking of cosmoline, stuck between their knees and serving as crutches that kept them from pitching face-first onto the floor of the truck bed. A few men smoked, passing the butts down the row to be flicked out the back flap, scattering sparks on the highway.

Willow sat on the end of the bench next to the tailgate. As the ranking enlisted man aboard, he was in charge of the truck. Sergeant Hazard was in the truck just ahead. Far up at the head of the convoy, riding in the battalion commander's jeep, was Sergeant-Major Nelson. Willow was not looking forward to facing the sergeant-major when they got to A. P. Hill. Delta had not shown well. It had taken the company two hours and forty minutes to get ready to roll, and a full fifth of the company roster had been left behind. The last Willow had seen of Captain Thomas, just before they had moved out, the Old Man was sitting in his jeep, stiff as a parson's collar, his arms folded and his face furious, refusing to speak to anyone.

Even so, it was impossible for Willow to feel low. What a day it had been. He had found Rachel again. He went back over it in his mind, rehashing the good moments, minimizing the bad. She still loved him. He was sure of it. It would just take some time and some careful handling. If he could cobble up the money somewhere, he would spend his next leave with her in Europe. He would take her to that romantic old hotel built into the wall at Rothenburg ob der Tauber, the place he and his family had once stayed on holiday. Then Paris. Even after all these years, he bet he still knew every nook and cranny of the city he had prowled as a teenager—places she could not know about. Give him a month with her and he would carry the day. Maybe he could even talk her into getting married in Europe. Then, if he got into OCS like he planned, he could go to work on changing her mind about his staying in the Army.

Wildman, sitting across from him, broke into his reverie. "Hey, Corporal Willow. How high is this A. P. Hill we're goin' to? Are we gonna have to climb it?"

Willow was annoyed with the interruption, but he was even more annoyed with the gross stupidity of the man. "Wildman, you are one simple shit, you know that?" he said with a sigh.

"How come? I dint do nuthin'. Just asked a question."

"*Camp* A. P. Hill is not a hill, Wildman. It is a place named after Lieutenant General Ambrose Powell Hill of the army of the Confederate States of America."

Wildman, grievously wronged, pouted. "I never heard of 'im."

Willow sighed again and parted the back flap to peek out.

"Where are we?" Wildman asked, anxious to get back on the good side of his squad leader. With some arduous field work coming up in the days ahead, he did not want his share of it to be any larger than necessary.

"We're passing the Manassas battlefield. You ever heard of that? Manassas?"

"Oh sure," Wildman said breezily. "It was a big battle in the Revolutionary War."

Willow shook his head. "Close, Wildman, real close. You're only off by about ninety years. It was the Civil War." He lit a cigarette, then said, "This is pretty historic country we're in. Just to the east is Old Tavern and the Plains. Farther to the south is Fredericksburg and Spotsylvania." Wildman's face was obscured by the dark, but Willow could almost feel the dumb, bovine eyes staring back at him. He might as well be naming craters on the moon.

He forgot about Wildman and tried to get his mind back to Rachel. No, he'd save that for when he was alone tonight, wrapped in his poncho. Instead, he thought about First Manassas and how McDowell's army had made this very same trip: Arlington to Fairfax to Centreville and finally to Manassas Junction, where the rebel army was massed and waiting. McDowell had put 1,450 officers and 30,000 men on the road. Fifty regiments of infantry, ten batteries of field artillery, and a battalion of cavalry. But McDowell had no trucks and no paved highway. That army had moved along a dust-choked track in a maddening stop-and-go column that moved like an accordion, with some men standing stock still while others behind them, in full gear, trotted to catch up under a blistering sun. It had taken them the better part of a week, only to be soundly whipped for their effort by Stonewall Jackson.

Willow leaned back and closed his eyes and dreamed of great armies on the move.

"Jack. Jackie boy. Wake up."
Willow's eyes opened instantly. Harmon was leaning

over him in the dark. Willow sat up and swung his feet to the floor. "What is it?"

"Get your gear. We're moving out."

"I'm going to leave tomorrow," Willow said, confused and shaking his head to clear the cobwebs from his brain.

"It's gonna have to wait, Jackie boy. Li'l Abner's gettin' hit—hit hard. They need help, and what's left of Bravo has been ordered up—including you. Let's go."

"Shit," Willow said.

He dressed hurriedly. He grabbed a weapon and followed Otis to a jeep waiting to take them to the chopper pad. The sky was clear and full of stars, and the rush of the wind past the open jeep felt cool on his face in the clammy dank of the night.

Charlie Dell was already there. They found him briefing the noncoms, the remnants of Bravo Company pressing close around to hear what they could hear. The men looked gaunt and frightened. The glowing end of cigarette butts briefly illuminated tense faces. Around them, the officers and NCOs from other outfits were noisily forming up their own men on the perimeter of the pad. Generators hummed and bathed the pad with an unnatural white light.

When he spied Willow and Harmon, Dell broke away from the pack and trotted to meet them. Even in the strange light, his flat, Irish peasant face was flushed with excitement.

"It looks real bad," Dell told them. "One of the pilots just told me they've already had three birds shot down trying to get in reinforcements. They think it's a whole goddamn regiment of NVA main force."

"Jesus," said Willow, a sense of foreboding washing through him. "It's way too soon for our people to go back out there. They're not ready for this."

Dell laughed a strained laugh. "That's just what Otis tried to tell Major Burns. Burns said they weren't taking no fuckin' vote on it."

"*Shit,*" *said Willow.* "*Alright. Let's get these slicks loaded.*"

Camp A. P. Hill encompassed several thousand acres of dense woods, swamp, and rolling hills and was bounded on the south by the Rappahannock River. It was not triple canopy jungle like the Mekong Delta or rugged mountain like the Central Highlands or Eye Corps up by the Rockpile and the DMZ. But it shared many things in common with those hard grounds. This land, too, had absorbed its share of American blood.

And while it was ground more suited for training for its own war, the Civil War, than Vietnam, it was all the Third Herd had to work with. In deference to the conflict of the hour, A. P. Hill had been redesigned to approximate the types of terrain and structures found in Indochina. An engineer battalion from nearby Fort Belvoir had constructed a half dozen or so mock-ups of Vietnamese villages, complete with flimsy thatch-roofed hootches, spider holes, tunnels, and underground cache chambers. They had built some well-camouflaged bunker complexes. They had thrown up some scaled-down compounds typical of allied base camps. And they had gone into the thickest of the thickets to cut out a network of narrow, winding footpaths. In this they were helped by the local deer population. The genuine animal paths appeared on no map of the AO and were much more authentic than the engineers' handiwork. The training ground at A. P. Hill was neither as elaborate nor as detailed as the one at the Infantry center at Fort Benning, Georgia, but veteran cadre at Benning did not think all that much of their model either.

It was 0300 hours when the Delta Company trucks pulled up in front of a string of twelve-man tents facing one another across a deeply rutted dirt road. It had been exactly twenty-four hours since they had been roused out

of their sacks for Veterans Day festivities. Willow un-
loaded his people, arranged them in ragged formation, and
waited for *the word*.

Headquarters platoon and the other line platoons were
checked off and assigned tents. Third Platoon was told to
stand fast. Sergeant Hazard, carrying a clipboard and a
flashlight, walked over and told Willow's squad, "We're
gonna be here awhile. Smoke 'em if you got 'em."

He pulled Willow to the side and told him in a low
voice, "The aggressors are being segregated from the rest
of the company, Jack. Nobody's supposed to know where
we are right from the start. We'll be moved out when the
rest of the outfit gets settled down. But there's no reason
we can't put dead time to good use. I want you to take my
flashlight and do a little recon. If this is gonna be Delta's
CP, we just might want to shoot it up in a day or two. Get
a good fix. Note all trails leading into the area, the location of the latrines, the generator, where they're likely to
set up the kitchen, shit like that. Okey-doke?"

"Right, sarge," Willow said, excitement starting to
build in him.

Willow sauntered into one of the troop tents on the
pretext of bumming a smoke. The tent had a concrete floor
and electric lights strung from the vertical poles. There
were twelve cots, six on a side, and a converted oil-drum
stove in the center. He wandered out the back flap and
crossed fifty paces of cleared ground before he hit the
latrine trench. On the way, about twenty-five paces out, he
passed several piss tubes, sections of six-inch pipe jutting
from the ground and connected to buried fifty-gallon drums.
The bush began just behind the latrine trench, thick and
impenetrable-looking in the dark. He marked the location
of the HQ tent and generator and circled the perimeter
checking for paths.

By the time he had scouted the entire perimeter and

returned to the trucks, Third Platoon was remounting. Willow caught Hazard's eye and gave him a thumbs-up, then scrambled aboard. The drivers hung slit canvas covers over the headlamps, making instant blackout lights, and eased their machines into the woods.

They rode for almost an hour at a worm's pace. Willow could see very little in the dark, but the motion of the truck told him they were constantly switching back and often leaving the track. When the trucks finally stopped and the engines were turned off, Third Platoon dismounted and walked another 300 yards through dense bush. Sergeant Hazard instructed each man to hold on to the handle of the entrenching tool strapped to the pack of the man in front of him. Hazard himself took point, and Willow walked slack. Even holding on to one another like elephants trunk-to-tail in a circus parade, men stumbled and fell, filling the inky black night with their curses.

It was nearly 0500 hours before they reached their accommodations: a dank, smelly bunker complex overgrown with grass and clumps of thorn, with only the firing slits showing above ground.

Hazard called Willow, Carey, and the two other squad leaders to him and said, "Don't worry about anything tonight. Let the men get a few hours' sleep. Lieutenant Webber's spending the night back at the company CP. He'll wait for our stragglers to be trucked up from Myer and bring them out here about 0900. We'll brief everyone then." He turned to Sergeant Carey. "Well, Frank, you think you can give me an accurate TO and E report this time?"

"Roger, sarge," Carey said, flashing Hazard an obsequious grin. He flipped a sheet on his clipboard and clicked on his light. "Table of Organization and Equipment is as follows. Personnel authorized: one officer and forty-three enlisted. Personnel assigned: one officer and forty-two enlisted, broken down into three rifle squads of ten men each, one heavy weapons squad of eleven men, and one platoon sergeant with no known function or talent.'' Carey paused to make sure Hazard knew he was joking, then continued. ''Present disposition: one officer and six enlisted not present but accounted for. Four enlisted neither present nor accounted for—assumed whereabouts: facedown in the gutters of D.C. Weapons authorized: six light machine guns, twenty-eight rifles, M-14 in type, ten pistols, US 1911A1, forty-five-cal. automatic in type; and six grenade launchers. Weapons assigned: as per authorization, with the exception of one rifle, M-14 in type. Additional ordnance on hand: ten grenades, nonlethal in type, per man; six hundred rounds of ammunition, 7.62 NATO, nonlethal in type, per man; and two dozen claymore mines, nonlethal in type. That nonlethal in type shit means they're blanks, sarge.''

Carey grinned with pride. Hazard smiled, then stopped smiling when the sound of music drifted over from the bunker. ''And one radio, civilian in type, possibly lethal, and definitely unauthorized,'' Hazard said.

''I'll go confiscate it,'' Willow said, heading toward the bunker.

''Bring the man to me,'' Hazard called after him.

Willow returned a few seconds later holding Wildman by the scruff of the neck. Wildman started to whine even before he was in speaking range. ''I'm sorry, sarge. I dint know it was against regs. I won't—'' Hazard held a finger to his lips, and Wildman shut off as if someone had turned a faucet handle.

''It's okay,'' Hazard said.

''It *is*?'' Wildman and Willow asked together.

''Yup. But I only want it turned on when I say so. You got that?''

''You betcha, sarge,'' Wildman said with relief.

"You happen to catch any news on that thing today?" Hazard asked.

"Yeah," grumbled Wildman. "They break into the music every hour with that garbage."

"Anything on Dak To?"

Wildman knit his brow. "Yeah, there was somethin' about that. Lemme see . . . ahhh, oh yeah, U.S. forces engaged a large concentration of North Vietnamese regulars which had massed on Dak To." Wildman beamed. "That's almost word for word, sarge."

Hazard sighed. "That was a week ago, Wildman. They made contact a week ago. Was there anything more recent?"

Wildman frowned and concentrated some more. Then he beamed again. "Oh yeah, the guy on the news said that heavy fighting was still taking place. Official spokesmen ain't giving out many details, but it's believed that casualties are running heavy on both sides."

Hazard nodded. "Good boy. Go ahead and hit the rack now. And don't turn on that fuckin' radio unless you clear it with me first." He watched as Wildman scooted back to the bunker, then shook his head and said quietly, "I hope to hell it's Marines and not Army that's gettin' lit up at Dak To, or else Honor Guard Company is gonna be up to its ass in drop jobs while we're gone."

The men were cooking C-rations over heat tabs the next morning when seven men emerged from the tree line. Four of the men were Third Platoon members who had missed the move from Myer the night before. They were greeted with laughter and catcalls. With them were Lieutenant Webber, Sergeant-Major Nelson, and a tall, muscular major dressed in tiger-striped cammies and a green beret adorned with the patch of the Fifth Special Forces Group.

Webber made the introductions. "Sergeant Hazard, this is Major Race from Military District of Washington. He's been assigned to be an umpire and will be traveling with your aggressor team.''

Hazard stifled a smile and said with a straight face, ''Good to meet you, sir.'' Race, his blue eyes twinkling, nodded curtly and said, ''Sergeant Hazard.''

Webber said primly. ''Sergeant, please call your squad leaders over.'' When they were gathered, Webber said officiously, ''Men, this is the poop from battalion. For the next four days Alpha, Bravo, and Delta companies—minus this platoon, of course—will be engaged in both classroom and simulated combat training. There will be lectures in the mornings. In the afternoons they will be conducting sweeps through hostile villages, practicing fire and movement assault tactics against enemy fortifications, and brushing up on both artillery and air support procedure. Throughout these exercises, the Old Guard will have at its disposal four Huey UH-1 helicopters, which will depict both our troop ferrying capability and tactical air support. At the end of the refresher courses, the battalion will begin conducting search and destroy operations against enemy elements in the AO. That's you, men. Until that time, you enemy elements will reconnoiter the battlefield and work up some suggestions for simulated enemy activity.''

''But won't you be with us in direct command, lieutenant?'' Hazard asked innocently.

''No, sergeant, I won't,'' Webber said, trying to work some disappointment into his voice. ''Unfortunately, my presence is required at battalion CP for purposes of coordination. I protested, but I was overruled.''

''That's a damn shame, sir,'' Hazard said, choking back a smile. ''I was looking forward to working with you in the field.''

''Yes, well, we'll be in constant touch by radio, of course. Now I believe the sergeant-major has some poop to dispense.'' Webber turned to Nelson. ''I'll wait for you back at the jeep.'' He turned back to Hazard and said, "Good hunting, Hazard.''

They waited for Webber to make the tree line before breaking up. "Holy shit, what a tight ass,'' whooped Major Race. "I know he's a leg and that you can't expect much from legs, but Jeeeesus!''

Like many paratroopers, Race had only contempt for *legs*, the walking infantry. "Why, major,'' Hazard said with mock censoriousness. "It's not becoming for an officer to denigrate a fellow officer in the presence of unwashed enlisted personnel.''

"Fuck you,'' Race laughed, hugging Hazard. "Damn, Clell! How they hanging, man?''

"Loose,'' Hazard laughed back. "They're hanging loose, sir.''

Race kept an arm around Hazard's shoulder and put the other arm around Goody Nelson's shoulder. "Damn, it's good to see you assholes. It's been a while, huh?''

"How did they manage to get you behind a desk, major?'' Hazard grinned. "Was that the price you had to pay for those gold leaves?''

"Aw, hell, Clell. I've been trying to get back over, but they said four tours in Nam would ruin my Army career. I told 'em it might ruin my Army career, but I wasn't in the fuckin' Army, I was in Special Forces. They wouldn't listen. I've been writing to my old boss, Colonel Rheault, in Nha Trang, asking him to help spring me, but he hasn't been able to do anything yet.''

Goody Nelson was eyeing the two of them dubiously. "Listen, you two mavericks. You better keep this little outing within bounds. Individually you're both crazy enough, but together you scare the shit out of me.''

"You best say sir when you address an officer and magnificent hunk of American manhood, sergeant-major,''

Race said gruffly. "Besides, we don't know what the fuck you're talking about, do we, Clell?"

"I'm talking about that little escapade you two pulled at Chau Doc when you snuck into Cambodia and greased a few innocent Khmer."

"Oh that," shrugged the major. "Innocent, my ass. But don't worry, Goody. We'll be a couple of regular boy scouts."

"Right," Nelson said skeptically. "Listen, I'd love to stay and trip down memory lane, but Webber's probably shittin' his pants being so far away from an officers club." He turned to Hazard. "Clell, I'm gonna need a detail to come back to the jeep and haul up some stuff I brought you."

Hazard called over to Willow. "Hey, Jack. Round up one of your fire teams and head 'em over to the sergeant-major's jeep. Tell them to wait for him there." Willow bounded away, and Hazard asked Nelson, "What did you bring me?"

"All sorts of good shit. There's a box of red armbands for your boys to wear at all times. Red for the Reds. And there's a map case with maps of the entire AO. All the villes, base camps, and trails are marked. You'll also find coordinates for the supply caches we've set out for you. Once the war starts, you'll have to get all your rats and ammo from the caches cuz you gooks don't have no air resupply. If the good guys—the Blue team—finds them, you starve to death. And I got you six radios, Prick twenty-fives. Taped to each one is a list of the frequencies you'll be using on battalion net. Blue Team don't know your freq's, so they shouldn't be eavesdropping. That's about it. You got any questions?"

"Not at the moment," Hazard said.

"Okay. Keep in touch. And behave yourself. See you later, major." Nelson strode off to rescue Lieutenant Webber.

Willow was back, standing discreetly off to the side, trying to catch snatches of what was being said and trying to figure out the easy, bordering-on-insubordinate relationship between the two senior NCOs and this Green Beret major. The major was the finest-looking soldier Willow had ever seen—a recruiting poster come to life. He had short blond hair, azure eyes, and clean, square features. He stood at least six-foot-two and had wide shoulders and a waist that looked to be about a size 32. He reminded Willow of Elroy "Crazylegs" Hirsch.

Hazard noticed Willow's obvious interest and motioned him over.

"Major Race, I'd like you to meet my best squad leader, Corporal Jack Willow."

"Howdy, Jack," Race smiled, extending a hand. "Always happy to meet the best. Of anything."

"Jack, round everybody up and sit 'em down in front of the bunkers," Hazard said. "I'll be over to give you a short briefing."

Willow sped off and Hazard turned to Major Race. "Sir, how tight a leash is battalion going to put on me?" he asked.

"Tight as Little Orphan Annie's pussy," said Race. "They're going to tell you which patrols to ambush, which facilities to hit, so on and so forth. They're going to set the time and the place and the mode."

"And how many of these planned activities take place during daylight hours?"

"Every single one of them."

"Shit," Hazard spat. "The VC and NVA hardly ever initiate daylight contact if they can possibly avoid it. It makes them too vulnerable to air. It's stupid."

"I know that and you know that. I even mentioned it and was told to butt out. They want to practice calling in arty and tac air."

Hazard was silent for a moment, then asked, "Would you go to bat for me on this, sir?"

"What you got in mind, Clell?"

"Could you talk to Colonel Godwin and make a case for some unstructured aggressor activity? Tell him that we can pull the scheduled stuff as planned but to let us put out one squad, ten lousy men, on their own to look for targets of opportunity. It would give battalion a chance to see how well they themselves react."

Race shook his head. "I dunno, Clell. I don't think he'd buy it."

"You could suggest that we try it for twenty-four hours, and if he doesn't think it's working out, he can call us off."

Race grinned. "Except, of course, your radio will be malfunctioning, and you won't get the order to cease and desist."

Hazard grinned back. "Just a little trick I picked up from an Arvin counterpart. What do you say? Ten lousy men, one squad. Where's the harm? They'd still get to play with their radios and their arty and tac air."

Race thought about it for a moment. Then he shrugged and said, "Oh, what the hell. What can they do to me? Put me behind a desk in the Pentagon and arm me with a stapler? I still don't think it'll work, but I'll talk to him."

Hazard grabbed the major's hand and pumped it. "Sir, you have no idea how good it is to be working with a real professional again. Of course, if you do pull it off, it means you won't be getting much sleep."

Race shrugged again. "I get all the sleep I need in that fucking office of mine." He clapped Hazard on the back. "I'll go test one of those unreliable radios of yours and see if I can call myself a cab. I'll be back out with the word as soon as I know something. You just keep your fingers crossed."

"He bought it?"

"He bought it."

"Yaaaahoooo!"

"Don't get your balls in an uproar," Race cautioned. "He's giving it forty-eight hours, then he re-evaluates. And I'm having second thoughts about your malfunctioning radio."

"Sir, it's the old cliché, but it's true. This is as close to the real thing as these kids are going to get. We may only have a few days, but something we teach them in those few days might save their ass one day."

"Well, we'll see about it if and when the time comes. Maybe Godwin will let it run."

"When does the forty-eight hours start?" Hazard asked.

"Right off the top, first day," said Race. "There's something else. I've been detached to move with your renegade team exclusively."

"Hot damn! That's great."

Race smiled a rueful smile. "Not necessarily," he said. "What Godwin said was that he wants someone to keep hold of the reins and that someone is me. That's why I'm not as thrilled with this radio business as I once was. It's my cock that's sticking out there, Clell."

Hazard laughed. "We won't let anybody chop it off, sir." Then he frowned. "Oh-oh. I got a problem. I don't know who to put in charge of the other three squads. Carey's sloppy and I want Willow with me."

"Problem solved," said Race. "The Old Man told Webber to take over. Said he was just cluttering up the place at battalion. He's on his way out here now. And he's not too happy about it."

Hazard grinned. "Well, as a philosopher friend of mine by the name of Nelson says, some days you eat the bear, some days the bear eats you."

Hazard finished briefing Willow's squad. "So that's the story. You people won't be getting much sleep in the next few days. Between now and the time the war starts, we'll be spending our days mapping fixed positions and selecting potential ambush sites along the trails. We'll be digging pits and setting out booby traps, just like real gooks. And at night we'll be out in the boonies."

"Doing what, sarge?" one of the men asked.

"Developing some night legs and some night eyes," Hazard said. "I know I can't teach you how to operate smoothly in the jungle at night in just a few days, but it's important that we get in as much night work as we can. Once the shooting starts, we're going to hole up and sleep during the day and operate only at night."

"How come?" another man asked uneasily, obviously not relishing the idea.

Hazard smiled. "Because the night is the enemy's most effective weapon. American soldiers don't like to work at night. They're uncomfortable with the dark and avoid it when they can. It's one of our biggest failings in Vietnam. We give half of every day to the other side. The Communist soldier uses the night and uses it well. Hell, he loves it! And why shouldn't he? It cancels out our control of the air. It allows him to manuever as he pleases. He knows we don't love it and that we won't have many patrols out. Look, the Vietnamese is born superstitious. He's afraid of the dark just like we are. The Arvin aren't any better at night operations than us—much worse, in fact. The VC and NVA weren't born loving the night. They trained themselves to love it. And that's what we've got to do. So we're gonna creep through the night just the way Luke the Gook does."

"Doing what, sarge?" the same voice asked, not fully convinced.

"Blue Team will be sending out *some* night ambushes. We're gonna ambush their ambush."

Willow's squad averaged three hours of sleep a night over the next three days. By sunrise each morning they were on the move. They practiced working with map and compass. They worked on trail discipline. They visited several base camps and villages, making detailed drawings of the structures, noting fields of fire and marking the approaches. They hunted for and found deer trails and carefully penciled them onto their maps so they could avoid using the same communications network Blue Team would be using. They strung mines and laid out trip wires. They mined depressions along the roads and the engineer-built trails and selected nearby ambush sites to complement their work. They dug pits on and to the sides of the trails and camouflaged them with leaves, grass, and fallen branches. At the bottom of these pitfalls they left crude, hand-lettered signs that read: *The bottom of this pit is planted with bamboo spikes covered with human excrement. Any personnel who have fallen into this pit are hereby declared combat ineffective. Signed: Hubert P. Race, Maj., Inf., USA.* Willow read one of these signs and stared wonderingly at the magnificent Major Race and thought, Hubert?

At night it was a different story. On their first after-dark outing, they blundered into trees, fell down embankments, tripped over one another, got lost, and made enough noise to raise Ambrose Powell Hill himself. Their pratfalls reminded Sergeant Hazard of circus clowns. He remembered his South Vietnamese troops with new fondness—they had been merely inept. "NO, NO, NO!" he yelled. "You *glide* through this shit. You don't clomp through it. *Feel* the terrain. Feel it, don't fight it. Open your senses to it—all of them, including your sixth sense. This ground is *not* an obstacle. It's your *friend*. Use it! Let it help you. *Love* it. Love it and it will love you back.''

Hazard demonstrated. He sent them out singly, up to 100 paces, to find a place to hide from him. They scattered through the dense bush, half afraid that Hazard would find them, half afraid he wouldn't. One by one Hazard snuck up on them, and the woods was filled with strange sounds: "Aaarghh!" "Eiiiiii!" ". . . .HOLy shit, sarge!" "GODdamn you gave me a fuckin' heart attack, sarge!" Hazard got Wildman in the middle of a giant yawn. Wildman was sitting with his back against a tree with clumps of brush all around to protect him. He closed his eyes and yawned. When he closed his mouth, his teeth clamped down on the barrel of Hazard's .45. The hammer was back and Hazard pulled the trigger with a click that seemed to thunder through the forest. Hazard said softly, "This tree is wearing your brains, shithead, and frankly they look better on it.''

Each successive night they got a little better. It took Hazard longer to track and finish them. And on the third and final night, Willow killed Sergeant Hazard. Once again he had sent them out to hide from him. Once again he had gotten them all—all except Willow. Hazard was pleased—with everyone, because it had taken him far longer than usual to find them. With Willow because he was still out there. It took him almost an hour to find Willow, but find him he did. His squad leader was in a clump of bushes in the middle of a small clearing. Hazard was happy. Willow had given himself a clear field to spot any encroaching danger. Hazard grinned and began circling, closing slowly and silently. It took nearly another hour for the stalk. Then he sprang out, sheath knife in hand, malevolent grin on his face . . . and there was no one there.

From behind him in the tree line at the edge of the small clearing, Hazard heard the snap of an M-14 firing pin and

Willow's laughing voice. "Bang, bang, you're dead, sarge. You have been vanquished by the forces of Yankee imperialism."

On the day the combat exercises began, Willow's squad stayed in their bunker sleeping, playing cards, or hanging around Hazard's radio, listening to battalion net for news of the exercise. They could monitor all the action on frequencies gleaned through Major Race's ability to read upside down during his trip to battalion CP.

It was going well or badly, depending on point of view. In the early afternoon of the first day Lieutenant Webber's aggressor team ambushed third platoon Bravo and was cut to pieces. The Bravo platoon leader had counterattacked immediately with heavy return fire, charging Webber's ambush just the way he had been taught at the Basic Infantry Officer's Course at Fort Benning. Webber pulled back and tried to regroup, but the Bravo officer called in artillery to finish the job.

At first, Sergeant Hazard and Major Race took turns listening to the three-way radio traffic between the Bravo platoon leader, the fire direction control center, and the umpire. Then they grinned and broke out another radio so both could listen to the Bravo officer call up his fire mission . . .

Bravo: 44/15 fire mission, over. Grid 217/96, direction 0400, shell WP, enemy visible prox 700 meters, over.

FDC: 15/44 grid 217/96, 0400, out.

Bravo: 44/15 shoot, over.

FDC: 15/44 shoot, out.

Umpire: Let's call that one long and a little to the left, shall we, gentlemen?

Bravo: 44/15, R 50, drop 75, shell H and E, request

zone fire, three quadrant, three mills, battery 2, over.

FDC: 15/44, R 50, drop 75, shell H and E, three quad, three mills, out.

Bravo: 44/15 shoot, over.

FDC: 15/44 shoot, out.

Umpire: Bingo. Someone please notify Lieutenant Webber's next of kin.

. . . and howled with laughter, much to the bewilderment of Willow and his squad.

Later that same afternoon, Webber's team was jumped by a patrol from second platoon Alpha and suffered heavy casualties. Hazard and Race played endless games of gin rummy and smiled a lot for no apparent reason.

When the sun began to sink behind the trees, the squad that had nicknamed itself Willow's Warriors began to stir. They painted their faces, laced dogtags along boot tongues, and taped down loose gear. They pinned on red armbands. They cleaned weapons and taped extra clips back-to-back for quick reloading. A few of them watched the land grow darker and actually nodded with approval.

Hazard appointed one two-man team to hump the machine gun and another to pack the mortar, one man carrying the tube, the other the base plate. None of these men were proficient in the use of those weapons; they were "simulated experts." Two more men were harnessed with PRC-25s, and the remainder had mines and mortar bombs strapped to their packs. When they were ready to move, Hazard's pep talk was brief: "Remember, complete silence, obey signals, and keep contact with the man in front of you. I'll take point; Willow's at slack; Carey is at drag. Let's go."

Their first objective was a supply cache buried at the foot of a small hill three kilometers from their starting

point. Each man picked up two cans of meat rations and a
two-and-a-half-pound ration of rice packed in a clear plastic tube that coupled like a garden hose and was worn like
a bandoleer. It was enough food for five days. Each man
carried four canteens and filled them from a camouflaged
lister bag hidden in the trees.

They moved slowly, taking an hour or more to travel
one hundred yards where the bush was especially heavy,
but Hazard was surprised and pleased with the trail
discipline. There was only one real lapse. It was Wildman,
of course. He fell heavily; compounding his error by
yelling, "SHIT!" Hazard halted the file, made his way
back to Wildman, put his knife against the private's throat,
and said calmly and with utter believability, "One more
sound out of you and I'll kill you." Willow remembered
the dog in the cemetery.

That first night they walked for three hours before stopping for ten minutes to eat a dinner of cold, tasteless
canned meat and a gob of sticky, precooked rice. Then
they humped another hour before Hazard halted them and
signaled them up to him. They were sprawled in a tree line
outside an Alpha Company laager. They were less than
fifty meters from an OP, and they could see the glow from
the man's cigarette.

They lay quiet until just before midnight, when they saw
an Alpha night ambush team pass through the perimeter
line and start down the only trail. Hazard got his people up
and led them back through the trees to interdict the road
ahead of Alpha's patrol. They hastily manned the L-shaped
ambush they had prepared at a spot along the track where
they had mined a deep adjacent ditch. When Willow's
Warriors sprang the ambush, the Alpha squad predictably
jumped into the ditch to take cover. Willow triggered the
command-detonated mines. Major Race, wearing a white
umpire's armband, leaped into the ditch, tagged everyone

in it KIA, and took their names. Willow's Warriors silently withdrew.

The next night they snuck up on a Bravo Company night defensive position and began lobbing mortar shells and raking the wire with machine-gun fire, faking a major probe. As Hazard had predicted, the Bravo platoon under attack panicked and radioed for reinforcements from the Bravo Company HQ camp a kilometer away.

Willow's Warriors set up and waited for their real target, the relief column. They used an X-shaped ambush this time, remembering Sergeant Hazard's lecture: "You get caught in an X ambush and you're fucked. They got you coming and going. There's no way out. You can't charge it, and you can't run from it. All you can do is curl up in a ball, stick your head between your legs, and kiss your ass goodbye." It worked like a charm. Bravo's reinforcement column kissed its ass goodbye. Willow's Warriors killed nine, wounded fifteen, and withdrew.

On the third evening, just at dusk, as they were preparing to leave the bunkers for the night's mission, one of Willow's lookouts broke squelch on the radio—three followed by a pause, then three more, the signal that Blue Team forces were entering the area. Hazard quickly moved everyone into the bunkers. He had the machine gun set up at one firing slit and filled the others with riflemen. He left Willow and Wildman out to act as bait. Willow and Wildman allowed themselves to be surprised by the Blue patrol. They fired one quick burst each and sprinted in apparent panic for the hidden bunkers. The Blue team, its bloodlust up, came after them at dead run, firing from the hip and screaming. The lead elements of the Blue patrol were only steps away from the firing slits when the leader, a second lieutenant, saw the snout of the M-60 poking out of what he had thought was an innocent mound of earth. The machine gun team could see the young man's eyes

widen in shock and his mouth form a perfect "O" just
before they cut him down. Major Race marked seven men
in the Blue patrol KIA and the other three WIA.

Later that night they caught two separate Alpha Company patrols in V-shaped and minuet ambushes. Hazard
was showing his boys all the variations.

Tired and happy, they were making their way back
when Spec Four Ladd, Hazard's RTO, broke silence.
"Sarge," he whispered urgently, "battalion's calling Red
Man Four. Should I acknowledge?"

"Not yet. I'll be with you in a minute," Hazard said.
He found Major Race halfway back in the file. "Looks
like this is it, sir," he said. "Battalion's on the horn, and I
got a feeling they're gonna call us in. What do you want to
do?"

Race grimaced, then sighed. "I'm surprised they let us
go this long. Shit, Clell, I don't want to quit. I'm having a
ball."

"I know, sir. Me too. But I've been thinking on it, and
it does sound mighty suspicious if two radios go down."

Race said nothing for a few seconds. Then he grinned,
only his teeth and eyes showing in his blackened face.
"What the fuck, Clell. Why can't two radios go down?
War is hell on equipment. Everybody knows that."

"You mean you want to go on?"

"Hell yes."

A slow grin spread on Hazard's face, and he shook his
head with admiration. He called over the two RTOs and
told them to lay their radios on the ground. He scouted
around and found a rock the size of a small watermelon.
He lifted it high over his head and smashed one radio, then
the other. He looked at the wide-eyed radio operators and
said, "These radios were damaged on submerged rocks
when you both slipped and fell while crossing the blue
line, the river. Right?"

"R-Right, sarge," they mumbled in unison.

"Okey-doke. Let's move out."

They did not go back to the bunker complex. They slept that night in shallow fighting holes dug back against an outcropping of rock fronted by heavy brush.

Before they turned in, Major Race invited Hazard and Willow behind a large boulder and produced a thin, leather-covered, silver flask. He passed it to Hazard, who took a long pull and passed it on to Willow. They kept their voices to a whisper.

"The way I figure it, Clell, we can only pull one more operation," Race said. "Whoever we hit next is going to insist on giving us the word from battalion."

"Yup, that's what I was thinking, too."

"So, what's it going to be?"

"I dunno," said Hazard. "Maybe we should make use of that good recon Willow here did back at Delta CP. Besides, we ain't hit Delta yet, and it don't seem fair to discriminate against your own outfit."

"You want to do the CP itself?" Race asked.

"Why not?"

The major chuckled softly in the dark. "Well, for one thing, it won't endear you to your commanding officer."

Hazard shrugged and smiled. "Some days you eat the bear. . . ."

Both Race and Willow smiled. "How do you figure to do it?" Race asked.

"We just keep it simple. Me and Jack will get past the perimeter guards somehow, then sneak into the Old Man's tent and capture him. Then the rest of the squad lights up the place, and we slip our captured enemy commander into the bush during the ensuing ruckus."

"Simple, huh?" Race laughed, pulling at the flask.

"Yup."

"Clell, you sure you were never in Special Forces?"

"No way, sir. I only got one of the five things you got to have to be a green beanie-weenie."

"Oh yeah?" Race said warily, knowing he was being set up but curious nonetheless. "What five things?"

Hazard grinned and ticked them off on his fingers: "A Montagnard bracelet; a tiger-eye or star sapphire ring from Thailand; a stainless steel Rolex wristwatch; a sports car; and a divorce. The sixth thing, the earring, is optional."

Major Race choked on the effort to keep his laughter to a whisper. "Goddamn you, Hazard," he sputtered. "They made me take off the earring when I got back to the World."

It worked out just the way Hazard said it would.

They lay low the next day, disturbed only by a passing helicopter fitted with a PsyOps loudspeaker that blared, "Red Man Four, Red Man Four, this is Silver Fox One. Your mission has been canceled. Repeat. Your mission has been canceled. Return to battalion CP at once."

At 2000 hours they emerged from the trees and began the long hump to the Delta Company command post.

Getting past the perimeter guards was no problem. There were none. Not one. Hazard knew it was only an exercise, but the lack of a defensive perimeter upset him. Thomas had been a competent, if uninspired field commander in Vietnam, and it wasn't like him to be so lax. Undoubtedly Thomas knew there was no scheduled aggressor activity at night and that Hazard's team had been called in by battalion headquarters. But that was no excuse. Bad habits died hard.

The discovery prompted Major Race to join Hazard and Willow on their infiltration. They left the rest of the squad in the trees behind the latrines and one by one—first Hazard, then Willow, then Race—casually strolled across the open ground, nothing more than GIs returning to their cots after a midnight shit.

Nor was there a problem getting into the company commander's tent. Hazard simply put an ear to the canvas, heard the heavy, regular breathing, and stepped through the rear flap. Willow and Race waited a beat and followed.

They stood around the cot looking down on the sleeping officer and shaking their heads sadly like doctors over a dying patient. Hazard pulled an olive drab washcloth from his pocket and handed it to Willow. He opened his mouth wide and pointed to it, then pointed to the washcloth. Hazard leaned over Captain Thomas, waited for the man to exhale, then reached down and gently pinched the man's nostrils shut. Without missing a beat, the captain began breathing through his mouth. Hazard drew his sheath knife, laid the blade against Thomas's throat, and nodded to Willow. Willow jammed the washcloth down his company commander's throat.

Thomas's eyes snapped open in terror. He knew instinctively not to move, that a knife was lodged against his windpipe. There was no real danger, since Hazard was using the flat of the blade, but Captain Thomas did not know that. All he felt was the cold burn of the steel.

Major Race leaned over and said pleasantly, "Evening, captain. You have been taken prisoner by the aggressor forces. Please do not resist, or I'll have to mark you deader'n a deacon's dick."

Thomas was trying to tell them something, but with the rag in his mouth all they could hear was, "Mmmmmmmmm."

Hazard used a tent rope to tie Thomas's hands behind his back, and he stuck Willow's rifle through the openings at the elbows. He decided not to call up the remainder of the squad. There was no need. Delta Company slept like hibernating bears.

They checked the clearing behind the row of tents, saw

no one, and herded their prize to the tree line. The rest of the squad guffawed when they saw their company commander trussed like a pig on the way to market.

They could have ended it there, but didn't. Instead, they marched Thomas three klicks through the woods, and did not remove his gag until they had dug in and set up a perimeter for the night.

When Hazard finally pulled Thomas's plug, the words came out in a torrent. "Goddamn you, Hazard, you'll pay for this you sonofabitch! You were supposed to come in two days ago. Battalion has been trying to reach you. Why haven't you answered your goddamn radio. I'll get you for this. Untie me this instant." Flecks of spittle danced around his mouth.

"Excuse me, sir," Hazard said calmly and politely. "Are you saying we've been called in? We're not supposed to be doing this anymore?"

"No. I mean yes, that's exactly what I'm saying. Battalion has been trying to raise you since night before last," Thomas seethed.

"Damn! I'm awful sorry, sir. Here, let me get you out of that rig." He cut the captain's bonds. "We didn't get the word, sir. We lost both our radios two days ago."

"Don't give me that shit, Hazard," Thomas spewed.

"It's true, captain," Major Race said with authority. "We had a bad time crossing the blue line, and both our radios were damaged."

Thomas was somewhat mollified by this verification from a superior officer. He lowered his voice an octave, but it was still angry. "You *saw* it happen, major? With your own eyes?"

"Certainly. One of the RTOs nearly drowned," said Race. Willow had to walk away to hide his face.

"Well," said Thomas. "If *you* say so . . . but what about the chopper?"

"Chopper?" Hazard asked innocently. "What chopper?"

"Battalion's been trying to raise you by loudspeaker. That bird flew over every inch of the AO."

Hazard shook his head in remorse. "I'm afraid we didn't hear it, sir. We were holed up in a deep cave during the day. I do remember hearing a chopper for a moment yesterday, but it was off to the east of us, and we laid low thinking it was just part of your sweep."

Thomas was not entirely satisfied, but he could not say so without contradicting Major Race, who, after all, did work at the Pentagon. "Well," he said again, "you'll have to square all this with Colonel Godwin. He is extremely perturbed. You people have played hell with the exercise."

"We were just doing our job, captain," Hazard said firmly, going over to the offensive.

"And doing it damn well," Race added, throwing in reinforcements.

"Perhaps too well," sniffed Thomas. "You've gotten everyone so paranoid about night attacks they've had to stay on alert all night. The quality of the daytime operations has suffered. Everyone's been asleep on their feet."

"Sorry, sir," Hazard said with a straight face.

"Yes, well. Let's get back to the CP, shall we?"

"Now, sir? It's pretty late. Maybe we should get a couple hours' shut-eye and report in at first light."

Thomas sighed heavily. "I guess you're right."

"Here, sir. You can have my hole," Hazard said solicitously.

Hazard and Race went through the story again for Colonel Godwin. The battalion commander listened impassively, tapping the ebony swagger stick topped with German silver softly against a palm. Behind him stood the battalion, XO, Colonel Johnson, and the battalion sergeant-major.

Nelson watched with a pursed mouth and an indefinable look in his eyes. He obviously did not believe a word of it. When Major Race began his backup tale, the sergeant-major yawned conspicuously.

When the two men were finished, Colonel Godwin said, "I see. It seems we have been victims of an unfortunate combination of accident and misunderstanding. That is regrettable, but there is nothing to be done about it now. I was remiss in approving your suggestion in the first place. You, both of you, were remiss in not calling your operations to a halt when your radios were rendered inoperable. But to be perfectly honest, Sergeant Hazard, I am not nearly so displeased with you as I am with our company officers." Godwin looked at the squirming Captain Thomas before continuing. "Your squad gave them a far more exacting test than they were expecting, I'm afraid, and more than they could handle. The observers from Military District of Washington are not happy. Nor am I."

Hazard said nothing. He just stood at attention and stared at a spot three inches above the battalion commander's eyes.

Godwin smiled a tight smile. "You did a remarkable job, Sergeant Hazard. I'm glad you are on our side . . . or at least on our side most of the time."

Hazard smiled. "Yessir. Thank you, sir."

Behind the colonels, Goody Nelson looked like he wanted to throw up.

30

Dearest Rachel,

Your last letter, like those before it, gave me a bad case of eye strain. I kept reading between the lines trying to find, among all the chitchat about your school work and your weekend trips, some indication that I'm getting through to you. I know you're leery about committing yourself, but it HAS been five months since we saw each other and you've had plenty of time to think about it. Can't you take pity on a tortured soul and give me some small sign that you love me? Because you do. I know you do. And you know you do. So why not put it in a letter? It's easy. Just write like this: I . . . Love . . . You . . . Jack. See how simple it is?

Yes, I know I never made myself clear about how my squad could have had a successful field exercise last fall and still be in dutch with our company officers, but it's just something I'll have to tell you about in person. I'm still working on my plan to spend my leave with you in Europe. It's just a matter of money and I'm making a little headway.

Have you been reading your Paris *Trib* regularly?

The news has been all gloom and doom in recent
weeks. First it was the *Pueblo* seizure then, of course,
the Tet Offensive. I think the pictures from Hue made
the situation look more desperate than it really was, but
Sergeant Hazard disagrees with me on that. We disagree on just about everything connected with Vietnam.
I say General Westmoreland is right and that we broke
the Communists' backs in the Tet fighting. It was a
disaster for them. It's just a matter of time now before
we finish them off. Sergeant Hazard says the offensive
was just one more sign that we'll never finish them off.
He's wrong. No army can suffer those kinds of losses
and continue to fight effectively. Sergeant Hazard also
says that the siege at Khe Sanh was just a Communist
ruse to tie up our marines while the VC and NVA ran
amok in the rest of the country (those are his words). I
don't agree. I think General Giap fully intended to
storm the place and turn it into another Dien Bien Phu,
and the only thing that stopped him was our build-up.
Sergeant-Major Nelson (I told you about him) agrees
with Sergeant Hazard. They are both wonderful soldiers,
but I'm afraid they tend to see the negative side of
everything.

   The problem is that their kind of doomsaying is
gaining ground in this country. All the big liberal
newspapers are taking the negative approach to Tet and
just last night Walter Cronkite called the war a stale-
mate and said negotiation is the only out. There are
other signs, too, Rache. Senator McCarthy is running
against LBJ on an antiwar platform and there are ru-
mors that RFK is going to go for the nomination on a
similar campaign. What bothers me most, though, is
I've even heard veteran NCOs and officers here in The
Old Guard expressing doubts lately. It used to be that
Hazard and Nelson were kind of outcasts because of

their views, but lately others are beginning to talk the same way. Christ, Rache, can't these people see they're playing right into Hanoi's hands?

Even Miss Huff is on the bandwagon (by the way, I understand you two got to be friends on that fateful night after Sergeant Hazard and I left!). Anyway, she's joined this antiwar group made up of professional women (lawyers and journalists and congressional aides and the like). She even got arrested for a few hours during a march on the Pentagon last October. Maybe she told you. She's got a right, of course, but it's giving Sergeant Hazard fits. He doesn't like the war very much but he likes the war protesters even less. I think he and Miss Huff fight about it. Well, you and I certainly understand that the course of true love is not always smooth—don't we?

While I am convinced that the Tet fighting was a great military victory for us, casualties were high on our side, too. The week ending Feb. 17 we had 543 KIA and 2,547 wounded. That's nothing compared to the VC and NVA, of course, who have lost close to 30,000 people. But the result was that last week was one of the worst in my life. You can't imagine how hard we worked. It was utter chaos in the garden (that's what we call the cemetery, ha ha). Delta pulled 20 drop jobs a day (that's what we call funerals, ha ha) for three days running. Sergeant Hazard, who was in as foul a mood as I've ever seen, contended that our work load proved his argument. I told him he should be grateful he's not in North Vietnam's honor guard. I wasn't trying to be flip or anything, just reminding him that their losses were far bigger than ours.

All this depressing news just goes to show that I really do need a little something from you to help me through the days. A simple "I love you and of course

I'll marry you" should do the trick. Write to me, Rache, and tell me. Remember, it's as easy as one, two, three: I . . . Love . . . You.

Jack

The turnover in Delta Company began in March and snowballed. The first to go was Wildman. He was stopped in the mess hall by a grinning Slasher Boudin and told to report to the orderly room before the afternoon's drop jobs got underway. Waiting there for him were orders reassigning him to the Ninth Infantry Division and calling for his immediate shipment to Vietnam.

During the next few days, while Wildman went through processing, the jokes caromed around the Third Platoon bay.

"Hey, Wildman, Luke the Gook may be a shitty marksman, but even he ain't gonna be able to miss your fat ass."

"Oh, hell. There goes the war. And just when we had it in the bag."

"Hey, Wildman. Kill a Commie for Christ, man."

Willow did not take part in the good-natured ribbing. It was not that he resented losing Wildman—the man was a disgrace and the squad would be better off without him. Willow was jealous. It was beyond him why the Army would send an incompetent fuck-up who didn't want to go, rather than a STRAC trooper like himself, who wanted it more than he wanted anything.

Sergeant Hazard eschewed the hilarity as well. On several occasions Willow caught Hazard watching Wildman pensively, a worried look on his face. On Wildman's last day, Hazard helped him pack and then took him out onto the veranda for a long talk. Watching them through the bay windows, Willow saw that Hazard did all the talking and that Wildman looked serious and nodded a lot.

A week after Wildman's departure, two men from Second Platoon got orders for Vietnam. The following week it was a man in First Platoon. Then it was Third Platoon's turn again. Top of the roster this time, Lieutenant Webber.

"I don't know why it's happening now," shrugged Goody Nelson when people asked. "I guess it's just our turn. But it must be bad over there if they're scraping the bottom of this raunchy barrel."

In late March, the company lost Slasher Boudin, but not to Vietnam. Pete DeVeber, the company clerk, told Willow what had happened.

When Lieutenant Carlson, Webber's replacement as Third Platoon leader, arrived at Fort Myer, he went directly to Delta Company to report in to Captain Thomas. When he entered the orderly room, he found DeVeber at one desk typing letters and Boudin at the other, working on his tainted duty rosters. Carlson put his orders, other papers, and cunt cap on the edge of the Slasher's desk and said breezily, "Hi, Top. Is the Old Man in?"

Barely looking up from his duty rosters, the Slasher reached out a massive arm and swept Lieutenant Carlson's belongings to the floor.

At first, Carlson looked stunned. Then he smiled wanly, thinking it must be a gag, some kind of company ritual for new people. Not funny, but what the hell, when in Rome. . . .

"Uh, Top. You want to pick that stuff up?" Carlson said uncertainly.

Still concentrating on his rosters, the Slasher grumbled, "Pick it up yourself, asshole."

Carlson grew angry, game or no game. "Now look here, first sergeant. I'm your new platoon leader."

"I don't give a flying fuck who you are," Boudin replied, turning his baleful gray eyes on the officer for the first time. "Nobody puts his shit on my desk unless I say so, especially no faggot officer."

When Carlson opened his mouth to retort, the Slasher, with a quickness that belied his bulk, bounded from his chair, grabbed the lieutenant's collar with both hands and lifted him off the floor. He began to pound the officer against the wall. The thumping on his office's outer wall brought Captain Thomas to the door to see what was going on.

The rest, as DeVeber said, was history. Thomas eventually managed to quiet Boudin down. Military police were summoned, and the Slasher was led away in handcuffs. Because of his rank and superlative combat record, Slasher Boudin was not court-martialed and sent to the federal penitentiary at Fort Leavenworth. Instead, he was sent to Walter Reed Army Hospital for a few days of psychiatric tests; then he was busted a stripe and transferred to the Second Infantry Division in Korea. The first sergeant never returned to the company, but his little red notebook, the one that chronicled officer cowardice in combat, was never found. DeVeber looked for it everywhere.

That was how DeVeber, a changed man, told the story. The clerk was so happy to be out from under "the ragin' cajun's" heavy thumb that he issued himself a seventy-two-hour pass, forging the Slasher's tortured signature, and went home to Boston to celebrate. "It was the Slasher's final administrative act and a wonderful gesture on his part, don't you think?" DeVeber said to Willow, a crocodile tear in his eye. "I'll never forget the man."

The reassignments went on, sprinkled throughout all the companies of the Old Guard. The EM, NCO, and officers clubs did a booming business, as did the nearby civilian watering holes. There was at least one going-away party every night at Zeke's but, for their own reasons, neither Willow nor Hazard attended any of them.

Third platoon Delta lost a dozen more men in mid-April, then that many again in late April, including Sergeant Carey. It was a busy time for Willow and Hazard. They had the growing funeral load to contend with as well as the added burden of breaking in the flood of replacements. The days passed quickly, and except for missing Rachel and having to bear grim witness as so many others got Vietnam assignments, they were good days for Jackie Willow.

The good days had begun as soon as they had gotten back from A. P. Hill. It was as if the reappearance of Rachel in his life brought Willow a bright, new dawn. He began to spend more and more time with Sergeant Hazard and Miss Huff, becoming something of a fixture at Hazard's apartment. He would play chess or listen to records or browse through Hazard's books or just talk. He took many of his meals there, and when the talk ran late he would stay over, sleeping in Hazard's bed or Miss Huff's, whichever was free. At first he worried about intruding, but Miss Huff was always as gracious as a queen and seemed to enjoy his company. On those evenings when Sergeant Hazard had to work late and he did not, Miss Huff would even call and invite him for dinner. She would feed him and he would help her with the dishes and they would play Scrabble, Miss Huff's favorite game, until Sergeant Hazard got home. Hazard would find them laughing and arguing over her sneaky attempts to use newspaper jargon that appeared in no dictionary Willow had ever seen.

Willow spent Christmas with them, and New Year's Eve, too, joined by Sergeant-Major Nelson and Miss Farmer. On Christmas they all exchanged gifts.

The five of them often ate together, at home or out, and took in movies on the post. When they all ate at home the two senior NCOs did the cooking. Willow picked up a few culinary tricks. One evening they let him prepare the entire meal and were kind enough to eat it afterward.

Willow had no friends his own age; he did not want any. He was content. He never brought a girl to any of these gatherings and Hazard and Nelson stopped trying to fix him up. They understood about Rachel and never made him feel that his solitary presence upset the balance. Miss Huff became an ally in his letter campaign to win back Rachel Field. She had a long talk with Rachel the night he'd been shanghaied to A. P. Hill, and while she would not reveal the details of that talk, Miss Huff did offer some quiet suggestions as to how he should proceed.

The prospect of having Rachel back in his life thawed Willow's sexual reserve, and energies long suppressed and dormant threatened to leak when he thought of her. He burned them off on the basketball court. Sergeant Hazard and Miss Huff and Sergeant-Major Nelson and Miss Farmer came to the games to cheer on Delta Company and Jackie Willow, Miss Huff screaming, "YEAAA, JACKIE," her voice piercing the crowd noise. Every once in a while Willow spotted Hazard and Nelson slumped down in their seats, pretending to hide.

Jackie Willow's good times continued unabated. In March, he was promoted to buck sergeant, E-5. Goody Nelson took them all out to a fancy restaurant to celebrate, and afterwards Miss Huff insisted on sewing the three shiny yellow chevrons onto each of Willow's uniforms.

From Pete DeVeber, the clerk, Willow heard that Sergeant Hazard had pushed his promotion, and it seemed to bring him even closer to Hazard. Whenever there was a spare moment in the work day, Hazard would take him to the parade ground and instruct him in the use of the fly rod. On weekends he went fishing with his platoon sergeant and Miss Huff. Miss Huff would pack a picnic basket, and they would enjoy a long, leisurely lunch along the Patuxent. There was only one ground rule on these outings: Talk of the war was off limits.

The engine noise made talking impractical. No one felt much like talking anyway. Night flying was a dangerous business even when the LZ was cold, and every man aboard knew that this LZ would not be cold.

The door gunners hunched over their weapons, flexing their fingers like pianists before a concert and staring without seeing into the imperceptible jungle below. Off to the side and a few hundred feet below their position, Willow could see the running lights of another troop-laden Huey and, beyond that, a Cobra gunship flying shotgun. It was cold at that altitude, and the chill from the steel-plate floor seeped up into Willow's haunches and spread through his body. He looked across at Otis Harmon. The reedy Texan flashed him a tight grin and reached over and patted his knee.

They saw Li'l Abner from a long way out. Just an odd speck of light at first, then more specks of light, and then all the neon dazzle of a used-car lot. Illumination flares hung over the land and tracer rounds winked lasciviously in the night. They would not need a strobe to mark the LZ on this mission.

Willow struggled to a crouch. "LOCK AND LOAD. WE'RE GOING IN." The men around him rapped sharply on the heels of their clips to seat them and flipped safety tangs over to full auto.

The helicopter banked precipitously and fell like a gut-shot duck toward the treetops, then cut again, maneuvering like an airplane, to skim along the roof of the jungle. Holding tight to a D-ring bolted to the floor, Willow shoved his head into the rush of wind. Now he could hear the fight as well as see it. His mind seemed to be simultaneously standing stock still and racing wildly as he regis-

*tered quick impressions. Most of the fire from inside the
base was going out, toward the bush line. The perimeter
was still intact, but the volume of fire coming from the
trees told him that a massive concentration of enemy soldiers was kicking on Li'l Abner's doors.*

*There was no time for more than a fleeting look. The
noise grew to a crescendo. The pilots yelled into their
headphones. The door gunners opened up the big .60s,
working the tree line with tracers, swinging the guns on
their mounts in sweeping arcs. The trees shot back. Green-
ish blue flashes of light whipped past the open door of the
helicopter, so close, Willow thought, that he could reach
out and catch them. A sharp snapping sound accompanied
the flashes of light.*

*The noise grew even louder. Mortar rounds slammed
into the center of the compound. On their flank, Willow
could see the Cobras standing on their noses, hanging in
the air like mating dragonflies, and firing their rockets into
the jungle. A haze hung over the camp, the thicker pockets
of white smoke shimmering like ghosts in the light of the
flares.*

*And then they were in the vortex. The ship flared
abruptly, rearing on its hind legs for a heart-stopping
moment, then, the skids and nose dropping, banging to the
ground with a jar. The last thing Willow heard was Otis
Harmon, his mouth wide in a madman's face, scream,
"GET SOME, MOTHERFUCKER!" and then he was out
the door and sprinting.*

In May, a week before Memorial Day, Willow got his
orders.

He was on the drill field, working with the new men in
his squad, when Sergeant-Major Nelson pulled up in a jeep
and told him he was wanted in the Delta orderly room,
chop-chop.

"What's it all about, sarge?" Willow asked.

"I ain't sayin'," Nelson answered. There was an odd look on the sergeant-major's face and Willow's stomach began to churn. The last time . . .

"Is there anything wrong in my family?" he asked quickly.

"Nah, it's nuthin' like that," Nelson said reassuringly. "Of course, if you was to haul your sorry ass aboard this fuckin' jeep, you'd prob'ly find out a little quicker, wouldn't you?"

Willow grinned with relief. He appointed a newmeat to be in charge and told the men to carry on, then climbed aboard. They rode to the barracks in silence. A sense of excitement began to build in Willow. If it wasn't anything bad, then it must be something good. Orders! It had to be orders. Hot damn, I'm goin' to Nam!

Sergeant Hazard and the new top, First Sergeant Richards, were waiting in the orderly room. Back behind his typewriter, DeVeber was grinning.

"What's up, sarge?" Willow asked Hazard.

Hazard nodded to the company commander's door. "Old Man wants to see you." Willow could read nothing in Hazard's face.

Willow knocked, heard an acknowledgment, and went in. "Sergeant Willow reporting as ordered, sir."

Captain Thomas wore a broad smile. "Ah, Sergeant Willow. Outstanding. You're here for your orders, I imagine."

Willow's heart leaped. "Yessir! Vietnam, sir?"

Thomas laughed and shook his head. "That'll be coming soon enough, I'm sure, sergeant. But no, not Vietnam. Fort Benning."

Willow's heart crash landed. "But, sir . . ."

"Officer's Candidate School to be precise. Congratulations, Willow."

Willow's heart took off again. "Sir, that's . . . that's great! That's just great!"

Thomas nodded happily.

"I . . . I didn't expect word so soon," Willow went on, babbling with excitement. "They haven't had the application all that long, and I thought it would take a lot longer than this, being the Army and all, and—"

Captain Thomas held up a hand to stem the flow. "Well, it doesn't surprise me at all," he said. "From what I hear, the Infantry is hurting for platoon leaders, and they've speeded up the whole cycle at Benning. In fact, I read somewhere recently that the average life expectancy of an Infantry platoon leader in his first engagement is something like thirty-seven seconds." Thomas threw out the grisly statistic with a jovial laugh, and Willow laughed along with him.

"Well, again my congratulations, sergeant," said Thomas. "I think you'll make an outstanding officer. The next class begins in less than two weeks, so you'll have to begin processing out of the Old Guard immediately. No time for a leave, I'm afraid. So good luck and stop back in to say goodbye before you leave."

"Yessir. Thank you, sir." Willow saluted, pirouetted, and practically danced out the door.

Sergeant Hazard and Sergeant-Major Nelson pumped his hand and promised a celebration party. First Sergeant Richards, already sucking up to a future officer, lamented that he would not get a chance to get to know a fine soldier like Willow. Pete DeVeber merely slapped Willow heartily on the back and mused, "You know, Dildo, it's a real shame the Slasher couldn't be here to see this. He would've really enjoyed it."

Sergeant-Major Nelson expedited his processing, making sure he got front-of-the-line treatment. Sergeant Hazard took over his squad until a new squad leader could be decided upon. But his platoon sergeant seemed strangely withdrawn and spent an increasing amount of time sitting in the NCO ready room listening to the war news.

The two senior noncoms did give him the celebration they had promised. It was just the five of them, and everyone got cheerfully drunk, even the ladies. Miss Huff and Miss Farmer even cried and kissed him on the cheek when they said goodbye.

The sergeant-major had work to do; the Memorial Day flag planting would begin before dawn the next day. So he said his goodbyes in the Delta Company parking lot.

"Give 'em hell, kid," Nelson said gruffly. "Because 'somebody's got to do it.' " He gave Willow a handshake and a playful cuff to the jaw and walked away quickly, a bald, shambling leviathan that lesser creatures gave plenty of room.

Like the last time, Sergeant Hazard drove him to the airport in the rickety Pontiac. Conversation was doled out like chocolate cake in an orphanage, one small piece at a time.

"You got plenty of money?"

"I'm fine, sarge."

"You sure now?"

"I'm sure."

Silence.

"Your flight goes to Atlanta?"

"Yes. I change there for Columbus."

Silence.

"Think you'll be going to jump school before you ship over?"

"I think so."

"Try to get Sergeant Tune . . . Woody Tune. He's tough, but he's the best man in the cadre."

"I'll do that."

Silence.

"I told Rachel to give you a call if she happens to be in town visiting her folks. Is that alright?"

"Sure. We'd be delighted to see her."

"She doesn't have many friends here."

"She does now."

Silence.

"When you get over there, get yourself a good platoon sergeant."

"I will."

"It's important."

"I know."

Silence.

They parked and went into the terminal. Willow checked in and they went straight to the gate; the plane was boarding. Hazard gave him a quick, awkward hug and said, "Write and let us know how you are."

"I will. I promise. Thanks, sarge. Thanks for everything."

"No sweat . . . sir."

"I'll try to make you proud."

"You already have. Keep your powder dry . . . son."

Something knocked him down. He lay on the ground trying to get his wind back. There was a tingling sensation in his ears. The noise, the dreadful noise, had stopped. He could still see men shooting and running and falling, but there was no sound.

He crawled toward the bunker, the same bunker he had been running toward when something knocked him down. There was no thought of trying to stand. He did not know where he had been hit—somewhere behind him, down low in the back—but he knew he could not stand. He could feel the ground trembling beneath him as if the earth were a giant dish of jello, and it made even crawling difficult.

There was a man sitting on the ground ahead of him.

The man yelled to him, but he could not hear it. He saw that it was Harmon. Harmon's mouth was working and he was holding out an arm, the fingers pointing at him. Harmon's other arm was gone from just below the shoulder; a jumble of bone and sinew and strings of shredded muscle dripped blood the color of molasses.

Oh God, Otis, hang on. Please hang on. He crawled.

Willow saw Otis pitch over onto his face. Harmon was dead by the time Willow got to him. Willow wanted to stay with him, but he knew that if he did not get to the bunker he, too, would die. He crawled.

It was a small bunker, above ground, the dirt floor flush with the sandbagged entrance. It was crowded with men, but Willow kept crawling, through the entrance and toward the back, going over prone men when there was no space to go around, like a determined ant making its way through a woods. For some reason it was important he get to the back.

When he had it, he used his hands and arms to pivot his body and dead legs around and put his back to the wall. He sat there panting, unhearing.

Most of the men in the bunker were dead or wounded, dragged inside by their buddies. Willow could see the mouths of the wounded opening and closing with their pain, but he could not hear their cries. He imagined that they were screaming at him for leaving Otis outside. A few able-bodied soldiers kept up a desultory fire from the portal. Willow could see them firing, could see the faint wisps of smoke curling up from the flash suppressors, but he could not hear the shots.

Then the shooters broke away from the entrance, and Willow saw a grenade bounce into the bunker. It exploded. It knocked down two of the men and clouded the deep room with swirling dust. Willow could feel the shock of it. The men who were still standing threw down their weap-

ons and hoisted their hands high into the air. The North Vietnamese soldiers came through the entrance with fixed bayonets, their mouths open in silent screams. They soundlessly shot the Americans still on their feet and then began to bayonet the wounded on the floor. They moved methodically and without a sound toward the rear, where Willow still slumped, unmoving, against the bunker wall.

Behind them, through the doorway and the dust and smoke in the compound outside, Willow could see the first blush of rose-colored light from the rising sun begin to creep up the sandbag revetment around the base of Li'l Abner's observation tower. He closed his eyes and out in front of him spread a broad valley with trees and running water, ringed by mountains all around. Rachel was there, watching him with gleaming eyes and smiling, the sun catching the smoky highlights in her long black hair as it danced around her face. His father was there, sitting under a wide shade tree, laughing silently and telling stories and drinking beer with Sergeant Hazard and Sergeant-Major Nelson. It was a peaceful place. A wonderful place. There was no noise there and no dreams of battles long ago.

EPILOGUE

The Anger of
the Legions

For Clell Hazard and Thurgood Nelson it was as though they had walked into an X-shaped ambush. The world was coming apart, and there did not seem to be anything they could do about it. They could not attack it head on; they could not even mount a fighting withdrawal.

It was the little things, for the most part, that got to Hazard. The blatant inflation of the body counts. The increasing reports of fraggings. The stories about drug addiction. The combat refusals.

Each evening he watched the news on television, paying particular attention whenever there was an interview with a grunt, a man in the line. And when it was over, he sat back, perplexed and uneasy. It was not the long hair . . . or the peace symbol stenciled on the helmet . . . or even the strange new language of 'there it is' and 'sorry about that' and 'it don't mean nuthin',' although that was part of it.

It was something in their eyes, in the sag of their faces, that was alien and worrisome—some inability to track, an inability or unwillingness to look the camera in the eye.

Hazard knew he was not your average lifer NCO who dismissed the whole lot of them as a spaced-out, spoiled generation. He liked these boys. He believed in them—in their good brains and their strong bodies and their astounding ability to endure. But something was terribly wrong. They had the haunted look of abandoned children.

Goody Nelson had taken it all pretty much in stride . . . until the news of the Army club scandals. That Sergeant-Major Wooldridge, the sergeant-major of the Army and the nation's top ranking NCO, could be involved in payoffs and kick-backs and Swiss bank accounts was like discovering his mother was a whore. As the investigation dug deeper, turning up more and more evidence against Wooldridge, a man Goody had known and admired, Nelson seemed to shrink in size. His shoulders slumped, his Paul Bunyan stride shortened, the mischievous light in his eye dimmed. He sat, morose and ten years older than the year before, and asked, "Where's the honor anymore, Clell? Where did the fuckin' honor go?"

A week before they had sat in trucks parked in the company street, dressed in full battle gear, live ammo in their clips, awaiting orders to attack Americans. There were 250,000 people marching on Washington to protest the war, Samantha Huff among them, and the Old Guard stood ready to act as shock troops in the event of trouble. As it turned out, they had not been needed, but Clell Hazard had sat there for hours, wondering if he really would shoot tear gas, or worse, at the woman he loved if ordered to do so.

And now this.

They sat in Nelson's office at HQ, drinking cup after cup of thick, foul coffee, newspapers scattered across the sergeant-major's desk.

"The way the women are carryin' on, you'd think you

and me personally killed those people," sighed Thurgood Nelson. "What's the damn world comin' to, Clell?"

Hazard shook his head. "I don't know, Goody. But as far as Sam is concerned, I did do it. It wasn't you. It wasn't even Calley. It was *me*, all by myself. She wouldn't even sleep in the same bed with me last night."

Nelson nodded and said with sarcasm, "Yeah. I'm really gettin' worried about Betty Lou, too. She should see a doctor about all them headaches she's been gettin'."

Hazard said, "I'm surprised it's hitting Betty Lou like this. She's always taken things more in stride than Sam."

"Some guy on Kennedy's staff asked her if she was still going out with 'that baby killer,'" Nelson said. "She says that for the first time she's ashamed of me."

Hazard got up, went to the hotplate, and brought back the pot to pour them more rancid coffee. "My fight with Sam last night probably wouldn't have been so bad if I hadn't defended Calley."

"You did?" Nelson asked with surprise. "Just how the hell did you manage to do that?"

Hazard shrugged. "I asked her what the hell she expected. You take a kid like Calley, your basic loser to start with, and run him through an accelerated shake-'n-bake OCS course. Then you stick him out in the boonies where he soon learns that you can't always tell our gooks from their gooks. Then you make him watch his men get blown away by *mamasans* and *babysans*. And bingo! His superiors, all the way to COMUSMACV, are hollering for bigger body counts. His platoon is getting pecked to death by ducks in a hairy AO, and a lot of it seems to be coming from this ville My Lai. He's half crazy with fear. He can't tell the good guys from the bad guys. So POOF! He kills 'em all and lets God sort 'em out."

"You said that?" Nelson asked, a look of admiration on his craggy face.

430   *Nicholas Proffitt*

"Yup. I told her that while I don't condone what happened, I sure as hell could understand how it happened. Then, as the youth of today say, I blew her mind."

"How?" Nelson asked with anticipation.

"I told her that while Calley was the one who got caught, this kind of shit happens all the time. I told her there were a hundred Calleys out there, a hundred My Lais, a hundred bloody ditches."

"Oooooo shit. What did she say to that?"

"She looked at me like I'd just confessed to being personally responsible for bubonic plague, the Spanish Inquisition, *and* nailing that hippie from Nazareth to the cross. I just couldn't take anymore, Goody. Her smug righteousness, her accusatory tone . . . her heartbreaking innocence. So I topped it off by saying that if it was left up to me, Calley wouldn't be prosecuted at all."

"Oh Jesus, Clell," Nelson cackled. "Whadshesay, whadshesay?"

"Just that. She said, *'What did you say?'* "

"And what did you say?"

"Well, then I tried to make a point, but I don't think she got it. I said that the way it was shaping up, they were going to nail Calley and Medina and maybe Henderson. I said it was gonna be a whitewash. I said they were starting at the wrong end of the chain of command. They should start with the generals, Koster and Young, and work down from there. I said that all Calley and his noncoms were guilty of doing was what they had been led to believe was expected of them in that place and under those conditions."

Nelson shook his head sadly. "Clell, I think you've just had your last piece of ass. Did she buy any of it?"

"Nope."

"I'm not sure I do either. Not about that whitewash business. The Army can't cover this one up. General Peers will get 'em all. He's a good man. He's not a member of the West Point Protective Association. He'll get the big brass.''

Hazard laughed bitterly. "Don't count on it, Goody."

Nelson asked, "Was that how it ended with Sam?"

"Nope. She got a bit hysterical. We were both drinking while all this arguing was going on, and I don't know how much of it was the booze and how much was something else, but she got this crazy idea that Jackie was involved in all this somehow—in My Lai. That *he* had done it. Not only that, but he did it because of something *I* taught him. I don't know how she knew, because she never pays attention to things like unit numbers, but she knew that Calley had been in Jackie's outfit. I had to calm her down. I reminded her that the incident happened last year, even though it's only coming out now, and that Jack was still in the States when it happened. I'm not sure she was convinced. She seemed to *want* to hold onto the idea that I had corrupted this wonderful boy and that he was mowing down women and children in an effort to win my approval. I suspect Dr. Freud could write a fuckin' book about that one.''

Nelson was quiet a moment, then asked, "How is Jackie? You heard from him lately?"

"I got a letter just the other day. He's not good. Seems his company got hammered and took pretty heavy casualties. He said it was a matter of gross negligence on the part of the battalion commander. He sounded pretty bitter—about a lot of things.''

"Welcome to the wonderful world of war, Jack," Nelson said.

They sat in silence for a while, sipping their coffee, thinking their own thoughts. Finally Hazard said, "Sam's after me to get out."

Nelson shrugged a so-what shrug. "She's been after you to get out damn near since you met her."

"It's really serious this time," Hazard said softly. "She's given me an ultimatum. Get out of the Army or get out of her life."

"Jesus. You think she means it?"

Hazard nodded.

"Your current hitch is about up, ain't it?" Nelson asked.

"This month. I've been putting off visiting the re-up office."

"Hell's bells, Clell, one short-shot hitch and you got your thirty. It makes a difference on your pension. Didn't you tell Sam you'll be out in a couple of years anyway?"

Hazard nodded again. "Yup, I told her. She says that ain't good enough. She says if I quit now, it'll be making a statement; it'll *mean* something. If I go ahead and make my thirty, it won't."

"How the hell did she know it was re-up time for you?"

"I asked her that. She said Betty Lou told her."

Nelson looked skeptical. "How the fuck would Betty Lou know?"

Hazard gave his friend a wry smile. "I asked her that, too. She said Betty Lou got the information for her . . . from you."

Goody Nelson jumped to his feet to protest his innocence. Just as abruptly, he sat back down and put his shiny head in his hands. "I remember," he groaned. "I thought it was just small talk. Oh, that sneaky bitch."

Hazard laughed a pained laugh. "If there's a sneaky bitch in the woodpile, it's Sam, not Betty Lou."

"So what are you gonna do?"

Hazard jiggled his shoulders. "Hell, Goody, I don't know. Maybe Sam's right. Maybe I should pack it in. I've been moping around here for months bitching and moaning about everything and not doing a goddamn thing about it. I've been a laughingstock. People avoid me like I have halitosis. Maybe it is time to make some kind of statement, some kind of personal protest. There's sure as shit enough to protest about. The way things have been goin' lately . . ." His voice trailed away.

Nelson's face suddenly lit up. He began to chuckle. "Don't be so sure about that," he said. "The news ain't all bad. In fact, every once in a while something comes along that suggests maybe, just maybe, we may be doing something right."

"Oh yeah?" said Hazard with a doubtful smile. "What's that?"

"You seen the latest *Army Times*?"

"No. Why?"

"Guess who just got awarded the Congressional Medal of Honor for actions against the enemy in Veet Nam?"

"Who?"

"Guess who saved his buddies' asses?"

"Who?"

"Guess who took out a whole army of bad guys single-handedly?"

"For chrissake, Goody, WHO?"

Nelson grinned a sublime, shit-eating grin. "Wildman."

Goody Nelson continued to chortle long after Hazard had gone. It was still a world full of wonder. Wildman, for chrissake! Had he or Clell—or even Jack, who had been the man's squad leader, after all—been remiss in not spotting seeds of greatness in the fat little fuck? No. There was never any way to tell beforehand. Courage under fire came from all sorts, the smart as well as the smart-ass, the steadfast as well as the moral coward. Winners and losers. The Army had actually commissioned studies of Medal of Honor winners, their behavior before the act, trying to find patterns or tendencies. It had been a waste of taxpayers' money. Great physical bravery was often nothing more than a nervous response to a desperate situation, the unthinking, impulsive act of a man who thought he had nothing to lose. On the face of it, you'd expect somebody like Willow to be a candidate for heroism, but you'd be wrong. Willow would do fine, he guessed, but Jack was cursed with the worst disease a man could carry into combat: a good imagination. Fear came easiest to those who could clearly imagine all the horrible possibilities. Most heroes were dull clods. People like Clell were the real heroes, scared shitless but still able to function with professionalism, still doing whatever had to be done. Men like Clell, and him, too, had earned their medals the hard way, shaking every step of the way.

Nelson was still thinking about it when his clerk, a mousey Spec 5, entered his office and dropped off the detail sheets for the next day's burials. The sergeant-major idly leafed through the stapled papers. Perhaps it was because he was still thinking of Wildman that he turned first to the names beginning with W.

"Captain Thomas? Sergeant-Major Nelson here."

Delta's commander cradled the telephone in his neck and picked a piece of lint from his sleeve. He rolled it up into a little ball and arced it toward the ashtray. Army was trailing Navy 64–65 with two seconds left on the clock. Thomas jumps, he pumps, TWO! ARMY WINS! The Corps of Cadets goes wild. "Yes, sergeant-major. What can I do you for?"

"Sir, I've just sent the detail sheet for tomorrow's drops over to you."

Nelson's voice sounded strained and under tight control. Something about it made Thomas take his feet off his desk and sit up straight. "You usually send it over about this time of day, sergeant-major. Is anything wrong?"

There was a slight pause and then Nelson said, "Lieutenant Jack Willow is on it."

"Willow? On what? On the *list*?"

"Yes."

"Oh shit. That's a shame."

"Sir, I was wondering if you would break the news to Sergeant Hazard. He and Willow were very close."

"Of course," Thomas said. "I'll do that right away."

There was another pause. "I should probably do it myself," Nelson said slowly. "But I can't. I should, but I . . . just can't. I hope you understand, sir."

"Yes, of course," said Thomas.

"And, sir, perhaps you'd like to assign this one to Third Platoon?"

"I guess I could do that easily enough," Thomas said. "Sergeant Hazard is the only one left in the platoon who would remember Willow. Do you think he would want to do it?"

"Yessir. I think he would."

"Alright, consider it done. I'm truly sorry about this, sergeant-major. Willow was a good man."

"Yessir. He was." Nelson hung up.

Captain Thomas punched the button on his intercom. "Top, do you know if Sergeant Hazard is in the building?"

"Yessir," Richards' voice came back. "He was just in here a second ago picking up tomorrow's detail sheet. It just came in. I think he took it to the ready room."

"Oh Christ." Thomas came from the behind the desk with a lunge. When he opened his office door, he could hear loud crashing noises coming from somewhere down the hall. There was the sound of breaking glass and wood splintering.

Sergeant Cook came flying into the orderly room. "Hazard's goin' nuts," Cook panted. "He's tearing the shit outta the NCO room. What should I do, Cap'n?"

The first sergeant popped out of his chair and started for

the door. Thomas stopped him. "Hold up, Top. Just leave it alone."

"Leave it alone? But sir! It sound's like he's destroying the place."

"Trust me, Top. Just leave it. What you can do is take the Chapultepec Baton out of the case and put it someplace safe. Then when Sergeant Hazard is, ah, finished, ask him to come see me. And Top, ask him politely." Thomas walked slowly back into his office. He left the door open. The noise from the NCO ready room went on for five minutes.

After another few minutes, Richards stuck his head through the CO's doorway and said, "Uh, sir. Sergeant Hazard's here, sir."

"Ask him to come in. And please close the door."

Hazard stood at attention in front of Thomas's desk, his face white and drawn. His eyes were sunk deep in their hollows. A nerve jumped along the line of his jaw. "Yessir?" he said in a strained voice.

"Uh, sit down, Clell. Please."

Hazard did not move.

"It's . . . uh . . . it's a shame about young Willow. I know how you must feel. I, uh . . . I'll arrange for Third Platoon to provide the honor escort."

Hazard shook his head slowly. "No, sir. I won't bury this boy for you. I won't bury any more of them. Not one more."

Thomas waited for Hazard to continue, but nothing more was coming. He exhaled heavily. "I do understand how you feel, Clell, believe me. This job gets to a man after a while. Perhaps it is time for you to leave the Old Guard. Maybe I was wrong to keep you here against your will. I'm sorry. Tell me where you'd like to go, and I'll try my best to get it for you. If you still want Benning, I'll see that you get it. I owe you that much. Just submit another request for transfer, and I'll sign it with a strong recommendation for approval.''

"May I be dismissed now, sir?"

Thomas sighed again. "Yes, Clell. You can go."

Hazard saluted stiffly, turned about, and went through the door. He went out the Delta front door and turned up the street toward battalion headquarters.

He found Goody Nelson sitting in his office. Nelson was leaning back in his chair with his eyes closed. The sergeant-major opened his eyes when he heard his office door bang shut. "Oh . . . Hello, Clell."

Hazard skipped the salutations. "What kind of forms do I fill out to retire?" he asked without preamble. "You got 'em?"

"Yes, I guess I got some around here somewhere," Nelson said slowly. "But do you think it's wise to make that kind of decision now, when you're upset?"

"Get the forms, Goody."

Nelson spread his big hands. "Clell, I know it hurts. I'm hurtin', too. Why don't you go home and sleep on this?"

"Get . . . the . . . fucking . . . forms . . . Goody."

Nelson looked at him. "Alright," he finally nodded. "Sit down. I'll be back in a minute." Goody walked over to the S-5 section, stopped at a water cooler for a drink, and returned with a sheaf of papers in his hand. Hazard was sitting on the edge of a wood folding chair, his body straight as a plumb line from noggin to navel.

"Here they are, Clell. You can take 'em home and—"

"I'll do it here," Hazard said brusquely. He filched a ballpoint pen from Nelson's pencil mug and went to work on the forms.

Goody Nelson leaned back in his chair and studied his friend. After a while, he said, "Hey, Clell, you remember that time you and me and Shelby got in that fight with the jarheads in Seoul? It was all because of that little double-jointed Korean girl, wasn't it?" Goody smiled and shook his head. "I can't even remember now which one of us it was that wanted her favors. All I remember is that there was no way she was about to go home with no marine. We really cleaned those gyrenes' clocks, didn't we?" He chuckled softly.

Without looking up, Hazard asked, "What are you supposed to put where it says reason for request for separation from service?"

Nelson stopped chuckling. He chewed on the inside of his lip for a second, then said gently: "Why don't you just put down *Grief*?"

Hazard glanced up with a murderous look, then bent back to his scribbling.

"Or how 'bout *No guts*?" Nelson suggested.

Hazard stopped scribbling. He glared at Nelson with cold eyes. "How 'bout you shutting your mouth before I rip out your fucking windpipe?"

Nelson stared back calmly. "I loved him, too, Clell. You got to bury your dead and go on. That's what the Army's got to do and that's what you got to do."

The two men stared at each other until finally Hazard blinked a few times and broke eye contact. He scrawled his signature in a few places and shoved the papers across the desk to Nelson. "Push 'em through for me, will you, Goody?" he said in a defeated voice. Then he stood and walked out the door.

Thurgood Nelson waited until Hazard had time to clear the building before he picked up the papers, aligned them by tapping them on the desk, and ripped them into halves, then quarters. Then he picked up the telephone and dialed Samantha Huff.

"Hello, Sam. It's Goody."

"Hi, Goody," Samantha said brightly. "What's up?"

"Sam, Clell is heading your way."

"Not armed, I trust," she laughed. "It's okay, Goody, really. You don't have to warn me. Clell and I have more or less made up. I know it sounds like we have more ups and downs than a couple going steady in high school, but we'll work things out."

"No, Sam, it's not that. Clell was just in my office filling out the papers to quit."

"Quit? Quit the Army?"

"Yes."

There was a pause. "I know how you must feel, Goody," she said, "but I'd be a liar if I didn't say that that is wonderful news to me."

There was another pause. "I tore 'em up, Sam."

"Tore what up?"

"The papers."

"You WHAT? You . . . you had no right! You listen to me, Thurgood Nelson, I've worked long and hard to get Clell to take this step and—"

"Sam, honey, it doesn't have anything to do with that. We . . . We got word today that Jack Willow has been killed in action."

"Oh . . . oh," she said in a little girl's voice. There was silence on the line. Nelson thought he could hear her crying inside the silence.

Goody spoke slowly and urgently. "Sam, I wish I could talk to you face to face, but there's no time. So listen to me carefully. The only thing that could hit Clell any harder than losing Jack would be to lose you. But there's one thing that would be worse, and that's for him to lose his profession. Clell is no quitter. He's never run from anything in his life, and if he does now, it'll fester inside him and kill him. Believe me, Sam, it will. You didn't quit your country because it made mistakes. You went out and tried to do something about it. Let Clell do that, too. Not to finish his career out would be spitting on twenty-five years of work. It would be saying his life was a waste. And Shelby Willow's life. And Jack's life. Soldiering means everything to Clell. It's what he *does*. It's what he *is*. I'm begging you, Sam. Don't kick him when he's down like this. He wouldn't feel the way he does right now if he didn't care so goddamn much. If he quits, he'll regret it, and so will you. Out of the Army he won't be the man you love. He really won't, Sam. If you let him quit, you'll lose him. Let him stay, Sam. Not for my sake or the Army's sake, or even his sake. Do it for your sake. Will you, Sam?''

Samantha said nothing.

''Will you at least think about it? There ain't much time.''

''Thank you for calling, Goody. Goodbye.''

Samantha Huff sat alone in her apartment and thought about Jackie Willow. She thought about how he had always called her ''Miss Huff,'' his manners more truly southern than her own. She thought about the shy awe and respect he had shown her—partly, she suspected, because of a young man's crush on an older woman, but mostly because she was Clell Hazard's woman. She remembered his intelligence and his good humor and his puppy-dog desire to please Clell. And she wept.

She thought about the evening she had spent with Rachel Field. They had spent the night sipping wine and talking and had discovered that they liked each other and that they shared a common goal: to pry their men away from this hideous mistress of theirs, this slattern in olive drab. Rachel had told her of her past with Jack, of her Army brat life, of her father's career maneuverings, of her mother's loneliness and the drinking problem that had finally landed her in the hospital. Samantha thought about

Rachel and wondered if she knew . . . and wept some more.

Samantha dried her eyes and looked up the Fields in the directory. She dialed and a woman's voice answered. "Oh, Mrs. Field. My name is Samantha Huff. I'm a friend of Rachel's."

"Oh, yes. Rachel has told me about you, Miss Huff." Mrs. Field had a throaty voice, a voice much like Samantha's own.

"Mrs. Field, I . . . I was calling to find out if Rachel has heard the news . . . heard about . . . about Jack Willow."

After a pause, Mrs. Field said, "Yes, she has. I had to tell her the day before yesterday. Jack left instructions with his mother to inform Rachel and an Army sergeant friend of his at Fort Myer if anything happened to him. Mrs. Willow called me instead of Rachel."

"I'm a friend of that Army sergeant," Samantha said. "He was not informed until today."

"That doesn't surprise me, Miss Huff. Mrs. Willow apparently shares our feelings about the Army, if what Rachel told me about your own feelings is so. It was a strange conversation. Mrs. Willow seemed very detached. She said she would not attend any Army funeral. She said she had no son named Jack, that he died when he joined the service. Rachel has told me that Mrs. Willow has had some, ah, mental problems in the past."

"Oh, I see."

"Perhaps we Army women should form a club of those who despise it," Mrs. Field said in a wistful voice. "It would be a large organization."

"Is Rachel alright?" Samantha asked.

"No, she is not."

"I'm sorry. It was a stupid question."

"I'm the one who is sorry, Miss Huff. I had forgotten

you were so close by. I should have informed you. But now that you've called . . . I wonder, would it be too great a burden if Rachel stayed with you for a night or two? She's flying in tonight for the funeral. She and her father have been feuding, and she was planning to stay in a hotel. I'm not feeling as . . . as strong as I might, and I don't think she should be by herself in the evenings.''

"That's a very good idea, Mrs. Field. Please bring her by any time.''

"Thank you, Miss Huff. I'll be picking her up at the airport at eleven.'' There was a pause, then Mrs. Field's voice quavered slightly. "Rachel had such hopes—as we all did . . . once upon a time. It's so . . . so sad.''

"Yes,'' said Samantha. "It is.''

She heard the sound she had been dreading. Clell's key in her lock. She sat back in her chair and held her breath.

She had set out a bottle of whiskey, ice, and two glasses. He went straight for it, poured out two drinks, handed her one, and sat across from her and looked at her out of eyes that made her want to cry again.

He cleared a frog from his throat and said, "Sam, Jack Willow . . .'' He cleared another frog and started over. "Sam, Jack Willow . . .''

Samantha closed her eyes and held up a hand. "I know. Goody called.''

"He wanted a CIB, a combat infantryman's badge,'' he said after a moment. "He wanted it more than anything else.''

"Clell . . .''

"Most kids his age want a promotion to assistant vice president of sales, or a bachelor pad with a hi-fi built into the wall, or a fucking sports car, for crissakes. But not him. He wanted a CIB.''

"Clell, I . . .''

"I keep thinking that if I'd done my job it wouldn't have happened. That there was some technique, some little trick I could have taught him. Something that would pop into his head at just the right time. Something that could have saved him."

"Oh, Clell, please . . ."

"If I could just have slowed him down some, made him a little less in a lather to get over there. If I could have weaned him away from this idea that he wouldn't be, *couldn't* be, a good soldier until he . . . I tried to tell him. Goody tried. We weren't very convincing."

His face looked like something lifted from one of the lack Goyas, contorted and frightening.

"Don't, Clell, please."

"I thought I could do it from here, Sam," he said with a twisted laugh. "If the bastards wouldn't let me have Benning, I'd teach them right here. I was going to help them survive combat by running their asses through the trees playing silly games. No sweat. Can do. I'm Sergeant Hazard, the boot-tough old vet. Listen to me, boys. I'll pull you through—"

"Stop it, Clell!"

"What a sorry excuse for a man I am. I can't do it here. And I can't do it at Fort Benning. I can't help them, Sam. I guess I've known it all along. But I thought that if I can't help them all, how about just one? What if I put all my energies into just one? Just one boy. Just Jackie . . ."

Hazard began to cry. He put his face in his hands and wept, without restraint and without bottom. There was no happy past and no hopeful future, only this harrowing moment, and the pain would never stop.

Samantha went to him and cradled him. She stroked him and said the things women say at such times, while the strongest man she knew cried with his face buried in her lap.

After a while he quieted and then stopped, only the occasional ghost of a sob shaking him, a shuddering hiccup of grief. Finally he lay completely still with his face on her thigh, his eyes open. He lay like that for a long time and then sat up and said, "I'm sorry."

Samantha did not answer. She had a lost look in her eyes and her face was bunched as tight as his was loose now that he had cleared some of his pain.

"Where *can* you do it, Clell?" she asked.

"Do what?"

"Help your boys. Teach them. If you can't do it here or at this Benning place, where can you do it?"

Hazard shook his head and looked at the floor.

"Could you do it . . . there?" she asked in a hollow voice.

"Where?"

"You know damn well where," she said with a flare. "Don't make me say it. I don't want that place in my mouth."

He shrugged. "I guess there is as good a place as there is. It's where it counts, anyway."

Samantha took a deep breath. "Then go," she said quietly.

He looked at her in stark amazement. "You want me to go back to Nam?" he blurted.

"I don't *want* you to go anywhere. But it would seem that you *have* to. Maybe you *can* help someone . . . someone like Jack . . . come home to the people who love him."

He gaped at her in wonder. Then his eyes narrowed. "And what happens to us? What do you do while I'm off on my mission of mercy? Ride off into the sunset with Larry Brubaker?"

Samantha gave him a pitying look and shook her head. "No, Clell. I don't ride off into the sunset with anyone. I wait. I sit here, in this apartment, alone and scared to death. And I wait.''

He looked away, ashamed. He poured himself a drink with a shaky hand and paced the room with it. Samantha sat primly, ankles together, hands folded in her lap, and watched him wander.

He sat back down and asked; "How long, Sam? How long do you wait?''

"Two years," she said in a firm voice. "You'll have your precious thirty years then. That's enough.''

He nodded and said, "Yes. That's enough." He sipped on the whiskey for a few minutes, and neither one of them said anything. Then he spoke. "It doesn't square. What about your feelings about this war?''

"My feelings have not changed a bit," she said. "I will continue to do everything I can to stop the war. I will march and carry signs and pester congressmen. If you consider that a 'knife in the back,' so be it. You have your job to do, I have mine.''

Hazard nodded slowly. "Okey-doke. I have just one more question. If I was to do this . . . would you marry me before I shipped over?''

"Yes." She had been expecting the question and she did not hesitate.

Hazard closed his eyes—just for a second. But when he opened them again Samantha could see life there again. And when he stood and moved toward the telephone, there was a spring in his step that had not been there earlier.

"I've got to call Goody about something," he said as he dialed. "Then I have to talk to my company commander. I'll just be a minute. I . . . I love you, Sam.''

Samantha watched without hearing as he spoke into the telephone. He was smiling and gesturing with his free hand as he talked. There was an animation about him she had not seen for months . . . not since Jackie Willow left.

He did not notice her stand up and slowly walk to the bathroom. She locked the door and sat on the edge of the tub, hugged her stomach, and rocked from side to side weeping.

Somewhere deep inside the cemetery a bulldozer worked, its drone rising and falling, riding the air like an eagle aboard a thermal. From the brick chapel by the gate, an organ gathered up its hymn, signaling an ending. The soldiers waiting outside in the broad, cobblestoned street field-stripped cigarettes and fidgeted into straight ranks.

From his place at the end of the front rank, Sergeant First Class Clell Hazard could hear the shuffling gait of the casket bearers coming through the chapel doorway, carrying Jackie Willow to the waiting caisson. Lieutenant Carlson called the platoon to attention and there was a clatter of heel taps and rifle buttplates.

The mourning party came behind the casket team. There were two older women and one young woman with long black hair, and a bald bear of a man dressed in a blue uniform with the insignia of a sergeant-major—three yellow stripes above, three rockers below, and a star in the middle.

From the back rank of the honor platoon came a low, anonymous voice. "Ashes to ashes . . ."

It was picked up by another man farther down the line. "Dust to dust . . ."

Hazard let it go. These boys had no memories of the boy in the box. And no fears for the future. They were so young and had so very much to learn.

The refrain came from a trooper at the far end of the front rank: "Let's bury this bastard and get on the bus."

Then, with a weary growl, Sergeant Hazard said: "Steadeeeee."

END

POUL ANDERSON
Winner of 7 Hugos and 3 Nebulas